David Milsted lives in Islay with his wife, writer Jan Holt, and four children. He claims that at 6′ 3″, he is probably the tallest living writer of humorous prose fiction in Scotland. Born in Sussex in 1954, he trained as a schoolteacher in Newcastle, and has lived in Carlisle and Orkney. At present he is completing a Craigfieth sequel.

DAVID MILSTED

The Chronicles of
Craigfieth

GRAFTON BOOKS

A Division of the Collins Publishing Group

LONDON GLASGOW
TORONTO SYDNEY AUCKLAND

Grafton Books
A Division of the Collins Publishing Group
8 Grafton Street, London W1X 3LA

Published by Grafton Books 1989

First published in Great Britain by
Mainstream Publishing Company (Edinburgh) Ltd 1988

Copyright © David Milsted 1988

ISBN 0-586-20412-1

Printed and bound in Great Britain by
Collins, Glasgow

Set in Baskerville

For Jan

THE AUTHOR'S EXCULPATION

Craigfieth is a fictional town, as are all the other communities of Mid Lummock, that mythical district of the imaginary Eastern Region. Thus the affairs of Central Perthshire, whose inhabitants are creatures of the mind, have as much to do with those of any real Scottish county as the concerns of Middle Earth have to do with the daily round of our own dear planet. It follows, therefore, that the occasional intrusion of apparently real-life persons and institutions in these fantasies cannot for one moment be taken seriously; nor, indeed, are they intended to be.

1

The Domino Theory

The small town of Craigfieth in Perthshire is not the sort of place which you would expect to hear of being embroiled in controversy or rocked by scandal. Indeed, if you are aware of the town at all, it is likely to be as 'that rather twee place on the A9, with the pretty gardens'. Although it cannot be said of Craigfieth that if you blink, you miss it (the 30 mph limit sees to that, or should do) it is certainly not likely to remain imprinted on the memory, and despite the artfully placed notices at either end of the town, Welcoming Careful Drivers and exhorting them to Haste Ye Back, it is unlikely that many people do, unless they be hastening somewhere· else. Craigfieth does a modest summer trade in golfing holidays for mature gentlefolk who pass a placid fortnight in one of its clean guest houses or in the one unexceptional hotel, and take moderate exercise on the well-maintained though undemanding links.

The passing motorist may feel, if his adherence to the speed limit affords him the time to reflect, that this is a community whose citizens have made a decorous bargain with birth, love and death, and have those three disturbing creatures of unruly Nature firmly under control. As for the sins of the flesh . . . surely, you think, here is a place which copes with such threats to its gentility in much the same way as Queen Victoria is said to have dealt with lesbians: by denying, calmly but firmly, that they exist. Further acquaintance with the town is unlikely to alter this view; Craigfieth is a place that keeps the promise of its first impressions, its morality, like the badge of its High School, an open book.

Only the most dogged investigation could hope to find the uncut pages; whether the story they contain is written by malicious fate or by blind justice is a matter of opinion. The protagonists of this tale hold differing views on the subject, and I do not feel qualified to judge. As the storytellers of the nineteenth century were wont to say, it is you, gentle reader, who must decide for yourself.

It was in January of last year that the calm waters of Craigfieth's public life were first ruffled. Mrs Dalghety, proprietrix of Brown's Newsagents and General Stores in the High Street, died, peacefully in her sleep. Mr Dalghety had long predeceased her, and there were no children, so the executors, mindful of the town's need for daily papers, advertised the premises for sale.

Within two weeks, the shop was bought by a Mr Haq, from Glasgow, who caused (as you might expect) much talk by opening, under his trading name of Haq's Universal Emporium, on a Sunday. Craigfiethans who were brave enough, or brazen enough, to enter the shop that day (having previously been accustomed to collecting their Sunday papers, circumspectly, at the back door) reported great changes: a variety of exotic and unheard-of foodstuffs was on display; where the pet food and tinned vegetables used to be there was a pungent, some said almost Popish, smell in the shop, and they were served not by Mr Haq himself, whom few had yet seen, but by a slim, sloe-eyed girl in her early teens, who wore much jewellery and a vivid mauve sari. There was also a new till, an electronic one that told the time in decimals, which the girl handled with considerably more efficiency than Mrs Dalghety had ever shown. Instead of the old thump, thump, rattle, ping, this machine bleeped, and the change slid, unhandled, down a chute at the side.

But before the townsfolk had time for considered reaction to these disturbing developments, there came a second, much more profound shock, and of all people it was Mrs Burgess who acted as the town's seismometer. Being of the strongminded among the community, she went to Haq's on Monday morning to collect her *Sunday Post* and to purchase her weekly supply of J Cloths. There was quite a queue at the till (undoubtedly word had got round and many people were anxious not to be left behind in the quest for outrage) and, as she waited, her eyes strayed over the magazine rack that now ran the full length of the wall opposite the counter. There, on the top layer, she saw a number of titles previously unpurchaseable between the boundaries of 'Craigfieth Welcomes Careful Drivers' and 'Haste Ye Back'; titles whose glossy covers portrayed scantily clad women, with the unashamed promise of unclad delights within. If her astonished eye rested longer on one title out of the half-dozen on display, no one noticed, but few forbore to comment afterwards on the state of agitation which this contemplation produced in her as, with lowered eyes and stumbling speech, she gabbled out her requirements to the proprietor (for the sloe-eyed girl had joined the Second Year at the High School) and left without collecting her change. Deaf she was to the importuning of Mr Haq, who (some thought ostentatiously) put it in an empty sweetie jar behind the counter.

What Mrs Burgess had seen was *porn*, and where her eyes had rested, others alighted. Yes, there it was, unabashed and unconcealed, names which the eyes of Craigfiethans had previously glimpsed only on station bookstalls or in unhomely newsagents in other places; images which properly belonged in the privacy of one's own bathroom. Before noon, word had got round, and there were few people, it seemed, who did not test this opportunity for moral upset for themselves; by closing time, Mr Haq's stock of salacious periodicals was all but exhausted. But, by then, Mrs Burgess had acted: to her fell the initiative, and, quite to the surprise of her fellow-citizens, she seized it. They thought they knew her, but they were to stand corrected in their assumptions in the days to come.

She was an incomer, which is to say that she had resided in Craigfieth for only eight years. A widow, she had taken up residence in the house of her mother-in-law on the sudden death of her husband, a son of Craigfieth who had sought his fortune with an Edinburgh manufacturer of sanitary fixtures. A sudden heart attack struck him down, between sales drives, and his relict quite properly sought the respectable comfort of his mother's home in Dundas Crescent after her bereavement. The following winter the old lady, too, passed on, and Mrs Burgess remained. To be a widow, living alone, is a testing experience; in Craigfieth, it is to lay oneself open to critical examination, particularly when one is a widow in one's still attractive thirties. Yet she passed the test; passed, indeed, with the highest accolade. She dressed soberly, attended church, and had no callers. She kept her house well; she did not excite comment. When, at the end of her first year of widowhood, she took in a lodger — a temporary teacher at the High School — no one who knew her felt cause for censure, and in the years that followed, during which she lodged some half-dozen teachers in the early years of their vocation, there was not a whiff of scandal. Indeed, when pressed, all her boarders attested to the propriety of the house.

For, if she had any peculiarity it was one dear to the hearts of Craigfiethans, that of cleanliness. The town, as must be obvious to the most casual observer, is nothing if not neat: its windows reflect the stream of summer traffic, its herbaceous borders and annual beds are a blaze of weed-free colour, its domestic interiors are models of order. No householder was more diligent in this respect than Mrs Burgess who, in rubber gloves and nylon housecoat, kept number twenty-three Dundas Crescent in a state of permanent perfection, from its geometrically paved front garden to its crimson-tiled roof. Six days a week (Sundays, of course, were excepted) her washing line proclaimed, weather permitting, her industry, and the more discerning would comment on the absence of what some called 'foundation garments', others 'personal clothing' and a few, boldly, 'underwear'. And if people commented on her habit, in dry weather, of sluicing her roof clean of bird droppings, it was in the knowledge that there, but for an unconquerable laxity of purpose, sluiced they. She was, in short, the personification of the domestic life of the town.

Now, after her shocking experience at Haq's Universal Emporium that Monday morning last January, she sought out Mr Maxwell, the Headmaster of Craigfieth High School, and there was an unerring rightness in her choice. Mr Maxwell had progressed from Craigfieth High School to Edinburgh University, where he read History, and back to Craigfieth High School as an Assistant Master. There he remained. After eighteen years he entered, as proprietor, the Headmaster's Office, and there, fifteen years on, Mrs Burgess found him, grey and solid behind his big square desk. He was not merely a Headmaster, of course; few among Craigfieth's professional class content themselves with one occupation, one connexion to the town's life. Mr Maxwell had several. He was the Treasurer of the Golf Club, he was an Elder of the Kirk and, by virtue of his family's drapery business, a Rotarian;

above all, perhaps, given his professional interest in the younger generation, he was a leading light in the town's Boys' Brigade. Nowhere in Scotland, perhaps, was the Brigade's faith in the Protestant virtues of hard work, honest gain, clean minds and unpolluted bodies so keenly exercised as it was, under his authority, in Craigfieth. He had been in his youth a lad o' pairts; now he was a man of authority. On the subject of immoral magazines in Mr Haq's shop, he was the choice of Mrs Burgess when she sought a cleanser of this Augean gutter. She could not have chosen a better man.

He did not so much formulate a campaign as give birth to it, fully formed and fully armed, from his greying head, after Mrs Burgess had told her tale. She was surprised herself at the alacrity — almost, she could have sworn, the alarm — with which he responded to her plea. No sooner had she mentioned the offending material, and the name of one well-known magazine in particular, than his eyes seemed to harden, his cheeks to flush and his knuckles to whiten as he gripped the arms of his leather swivel chair. Within days, his mission was accomplished. Leading members of the Chamber of Commerce had occasion to speak to Mr Haq; he was invited, conditionally, to join the Rotary Club; stern hints were issued at school assemblies. When these pressures failed, and the interior of Mr Haq's shop became unendurable during the school's morning interval from the sheer pressure of scholars at the counter, Mr Maxwell went public. Events followed swiftly on his appearance on the 'Scottish TV News', and the report in the *Daily Record*.

"I am not," Mr Maxwell maintained, "a racialist, nor am I a killjoy: I am merely concerned, as are we all in this town, with the moral welfare of our young citizens."

A petition was organised.

Mr Haq crumbled after that. Although the shop remained open on Sundays, it sold nothing more erotic than *Slimmers' Weekly*. Even *Health and Efficiency*, permitted in the days of Mrs Dalghety, perished in the reforms. Decorum reigned, more supremely than before; Mrs Burgess, who had been strenuous in her campaigning efforts, retired to her exemplary household duties (the temporary teacher who left her house shortly afterwards to live in a caravan on a farm outside the town bore witness to the unimpeachable spotlessness of number twenty-three) and Mr Maxwell was elevated in respect, if that is possible for one who was already firmly seated on its pinnacle.

Then, some six months later, his wife sued him for divorce on the grounds of adultery, citing Mrs Burgess as co-respondent. This was indeed a moral bomb that threatened to blow the town apart, and it was to me that she handed it.

I had been working for nearly a year with a Solicitors' practice in Pitlochry, as the most junior member of the firm. The daily bread of Crawford, Crawford and Potts was not the stuff of which legal drama is made; Scottish Law on property conveyance does not permit the sort of skulduggery and excitement enjoyed by our colleagues south of the border. We are, for the homeowner, a haven of sanity and rectitude. My work was largely confined to undertaking the formalities after the buyer and seller had struck their irrevocable bargain; that, and my occasional appearance in the Sheriff Court on behalf of an unspectacularly erring motorist, was at that time the limit of my vocation.

Mrs Maxwell had driven the fifteen miles or so from Craigfieth and arrived at eleven o'clock one Monday morning, without an appointment. Two of the partners,

Potts and the younger Crawford, were closeted with clients and Crawford Senior was wont not to appear in the office before luncheon, so it fell to me to interview the lady.

Her appearance, as a serious litigant, was not promising. Ample, kind, and woolly were the epithets that sprang to mind. Hers was a style of life that had no need of serious thoughts on her part, so she had long since ceased to have any. Meeting her at some function — a school prizegiving, say, or a Rotarians' Dinner Dance — one might sum her up, albeit unkindly, as the epitome of comfortable female Scottish provincial middle age, a sort of bodied vacuum. But the shock of adversity can bring about strange and terrible transformations in a person, and what confronted me now, across the formica desk in my poky apology for an office, turned out to be a steely, efficient, litigious machine under a camouflage of tweed and fawn cardigan.

It transpired that this sea-change had been wrought in Mrs Maxwell exactly forty-eight hours previously. Her husband had left the house at ten o'clock for a committee meeting at the Golf Club, followed by a pre-prandial round with the Convener of the District Council. About an hour after his departure, the telephone had rung; it was a parent calling to say that her Murdo had lost his end-of-term letter home, and please could Mrs Maxwell tell her when the new term began? If Mrs Maxwell felt put out that a Headmaster's privacy should be breached by so trivial a request, she did not show it. She gracefully asked the caller to hold on, while she checked. She knew her husband kept material pertaining to the daily round of the school in the left-hand desk drawer of the office he had made out of the box-room next to the bathroom. Pleased, in a quiet way, with her initiative in the matter, she went upstairs to look. What she found there, in addition to the master copy of the lost circular, now lay between us. She did not know what had possessed her, having located the sought-for letter, to look inside the plain brown envelope that rested on it, but she had looked, and there it was.

That she had calmly returned to the phone and given the dates of the coming session, had afterwards prepared six meals and eaten them in the company of her spouse, had even been to church with him on Sunday morning, was a tribute to her fast hardening *sang-froid*. It was a blessing, she admitted, that they slept in separate beds. A thorough search later on, in the potting shed and the garage, had revealed two more damning packages. They were in her handbag, should I wish to see them.

Mrs Maxwell had evidently got over the embarrassment of their contents and her coolness left me unprepared for what I should find. I opened the packet she had placed in front of me. It contained, in order of discovery, a pair of ladies' pants, somewhat used, a letter, written on two sides of a sheet of cheap lined paper, and a set of photographs. The letter, penned in mauve ink, was addressed to 'Master' and signed 'Your Slave'. It fell into three sections: the first described what the writer would like to do to the reader, the second outlined the things the writer would like the reader to do to her, and the third was a sort of running commentary on what the contemplation of the first two activities had prompted the writer to do to herself. The photographs were by way of being an illustration of the third section. They were numbered, one to ten, on the back. The first two showed a woman dressed in an open nylon housecoat, and the aforementioned pants (which were apricot in colour) regarding herself in a mirror. In photograph number three, the underwear was removed and the subsequent pictures revealed the lady, still wearing the coat which by now covered only her arms, cavorting in a clinical sort of way with various household appliances: a floor mop, a feather duster and a window cleaner's squeegee, among others. Although she was clearly engaged in what is known among the practitioners of such behaviour as 'pleasuring', the expression on her face (not that her face was intended to be the most prominent feature of the photographs) hardly denoted pleasure: it was a mask of concentration. Only in the last picture, in which the lady achieved quietus with an upright Hoover, did the facial expression alter. It became that compromise between a snarl and a rictus which is intended to denote orgasmic bliss. If so much was left to be inferred by the imagination, nothing else was.

Neither was the identity of the lady: although appearing somewhat younger than in workaday life, it was, unmistakably, that of Mrs Burgess, of Dundas Crescent.

My client spared me the awkwardness of breaking the silence.

"I checked the writing," she said. "It's the same as her writing on the petition against that Haq man."

She passed across a folded sheet of paper, on which was written, in a loopy, rounded hand, and in mauve ink, the first draft of Craigfieth's petition against depravity and corruption. You did not have to be any sort of expert to see that it matched exactly the writing of Your Slave's letter.

"And you may as well see these, too."

She passed me two more brown envelopes. Their letters and photographs represented none-too-subtle variations on the theme of the first. Only the colour of the pants — one pair blue, another red — was radically different.

"So I would be obliged to you, Mr MacIain, if you would put the matter in hand. I shall be staying with my sister, in Dunkeld; here is the address."

She rose to go. I tried to make my voice as calm and businesslike as possible. It is always the hardest part of any consultation when one has to explain that the legal process is not as simple and straightforward as one's client imagines.

"If you feel up to it, Mrs Maxwell," I said, "there are one or two preliminary formalities we need to undertake at this stage."

I must have achieved the right blend of blandness and import. She resumed her seat. I continued.

"I should feel happier, as your legal representative, if we had some tangible proof that an adulterous relationship has in fact existed between your husband and this, er, lady."

"Tangible proof, Mr MacIain? What more tangible — or more disgusting — proof do you need?"

"Well —" I tried to sound competent and reasonable, not an easy feat in such circumstances. "It is true that we have the photographs, but they only show the lady — Mrs Burgess — on her own. The underwear by itself does not prove anything, and the letters — well, you will have noticed that the pertinent passages are written in the future subjunctive?"

I had lost her.

"That is to say, the sections which have a bearing on your husband's conduct express, ah, activities which are taking place in her mind, in the future. They have not, in a material sense, happened. She is thinking about them happening."

Silence.

"They have not, on the evidence of the letters, actually happened."

I wondered if at this point I should give the famous Solicitors' Health Warning, the bit about having to play Devil's Advocate with one's client. I decided it was perhaps better not to mention Satan, in the circumstances. Her eyes narrowed to hard, piercing points.

"Mr MacIain," she hissed, "I do not know what sort of circles you move in, in your private life, but I can assure you that, so far as Mr Maxwell is concerned, such sentiments, such . . . such *intimacy* as is expressed in this . . . these . . . *filthy* things, could only be uttered after a liaison had taken place. I think perhaps I should take my business elsewhere."

"No!" I cried. "I'm sorry, Mrs Maxwell, I have expressed myself badly. What I'm trying to say is: your husband is a respected man. Could it not be that this material has been sent quite out of the blue? By Mrs Burgess? Might she not be suffering some sort of derangement? It will be said in court that there is, as yet, no proof of any liaison between them. She does not address him by name, for instance."

She replied with simple logic, "And who do you suppose held the camera?"

I retreated into professionalism again.

"The point is, Mrs Maxwell, that I am worried lest we do not have sufficient concrete evidence to establish a case. The Legal Aid people require substantial evidence before they will agree to fund a civil action that is likely to be defended, and I feel that, as yet —"

She stiffened; for the first time, her cheeks coloured.

"Had I been in need of Legal Aid, Mr MacIain, I would have said so. I have savings. I have no need of charity."

I sighed, I hope not audibly.

"In that case, if you wish to proceed, we will proceed. I will cause a writ to be served on your husband and on Mrs Burgess as co-respondent, and I will brief an Advocate when the time comes to represent us in the Court of Session."

Suddenly, I thought I saw a gleam of light, a flicker of hope.

"Have you spoken to your husband about this? If we could negotiate a legal separation first — it has no force of law, but any arrangement that is mutually agreed could be helpful — if you spoke to him along these lines —?"

"I have left him a note. I have not spared him the details. He will have found it by now."

There was only one line of defence left. There is one question which all people in Mrs Maxwell's position — and I speak from experience of both sides, as it were, of the solicitor's desk — dread to hear. Consciously or unconsciously, they go to superhuman efforts to put it out of mind. I asked it now.

"Mrs Maxwell, are you absolutely sure you wish your marriage to end?"

She preceded her reply with a long, basilisk stare.

"It is out of my hands, Mr MacIain. It is not within my will to alter. It has ended."

She left.

I opened her account with Crawford, Crawford and Potts, Solicitors and N.P. The writs were served, and Mrs Maxwell informed.

In the weeks that followed, she called at the office promptly at eleven every Monday. She never made an appointment. Although I dreaded her visits — there is a limit to the number of ways in which even the most honey-tongued lawyer can vary the message 'nothing happening' — I kept the time free every week, and grew edgy if by five past I had not heard the determined clomp of her square, brown, low-heeled shoes on the worn linoleum of the stair. When there was news to report, it was not encouraging. Mr Maxwell replied through a firm of solicitors in Perth that he intended to 'vigorously contest' the action. He denied adultery, with Mrs Burgess or anyone else, and pointed out — or rather, his agents, quick to spot the enormous, gaping hole in our case, pointed out on his behalf — the lack of evidence to suggest that any act of adultery had taken place. Mrs Burgess intimated that, if called into the witness box, she would aver she had met the defender on only two occasions, once in his office at Craigfieth High School for ten minutes, the second time in a meeting attended by some fifty persons in the upstairs lounge of the Ben Almond Hotel. Clearly, if the Lords of Council and Session were going to pronounce the marriage dead, they would want more to go on before they did so on the pursuer's terms.

Intelligence slowly seeped in. Fictional lawyers engaged in such matters are frequently to be found hiring sleuths to ferret out the dirt on their clients' loved ones; for all I know, this may happen in the moral stews of Edinburgh's Morningside or the respectable environs of Glasgow's Pollokshaws. Fortunately, there is no need of such recourse in the Scottish market town. It is not, of course, that small-town folk are particularly nosey or peculiarly fond of salacious gossip — ask any Craigfiethan and you may detect the note of polite shock in the denial — but they cannot help noticing things and, after all, what is the life of a community if not a caring concern for one's fellow mortals? To put it bluntly, any tryst between the Headmaster of Craigfieth High and the widow of Dundas Crescent would have stood out like an abandoned mattress on a bowling green. The eyes and tongues of Craigfieth reported none.

Five weeks after her first visit, I put the case as simply as I could to Mrs Maxwell. Though it was past high summer, the weather was still warm, and she wore a well-cut blouse of some discreetly lacy material, and a light, full skirt. Separation seemed to be doing her good.

I pointed out our lack of crucial evidence. I tried to indicate the terrible damage such a contested case could wreak, not only to the couple's finances and reputations, but to their emotional lives as well. I explained how contested cases are seldom heard quickly: it could be a year before hers came to court. I warned of the unlikelihood of the court's finding in her favour; I returned again to the weakness of our case. Keeping photographs of a lady in solitary sexual ferment might possibly be evidence of Unreasonable Behaviour on a man's part, though even in Edinburgh such things were not unknown to the judicial mind: evidence of a physical relationship they were not. The letters, even if we could prove the handwriting to be Mrs Burgess', were, for all practical purposes, anonymously addressed. Disembodied underwear proved nothing. Here she interjected, "No doubt there are *tests* that can be made."

I blanched inwardly, muttering, "Let us hope it does not come to that."

There was a heavy silence. A late bluebottle buzzed fitfully behind the yellowing lace curtains at the window. I said: "As your legal adviser, Mrs Maxwell, it is not for me to pronounce upon your marriage. You say it is finished, and I accept that: as a lawyer I undertake to do what is necessary to have it so declared. But you have your life to lead, and Mr Maxwell his career — surely it would be better to divorce in a way that is least disruptive to you both? There is no need nowadays to go to the trouble and expense of an action in the Court of Session. The Sheriff Court may decree a divorce, quickly and simply, by mutual consent after two years' separation. Do you not think this would be the wisest course — for you both?"

Her reply came with easy, devastating assurance.

"Mr MacIain, you do not seem to understand. I did not will the ending of this marriage; it was forced on me. Mutual consent, you say? I will not have it said that I consented to the wanton breaking of that which God has joined. I have my conscience to consider. No, Mr MacIain, let others say what they will: I know what I know."

Then, without a trace of bitterness, "They can have each other, and welcome."

There is really no reply to that sort of talk — not, at any rate, in Courts of Man. The weeks wore on. Summer gave way, reluctantly, to sullen autumn. Mrs Maxwell went for a little holiday to Bournemouth, with her sister; Mr Maxwell learned how to brush his own Masonic apron; Mrs Burgess planted the borders of her garden with *Cupressocyparis*. Craigfieth won the 'Scotland in Bloom' contest for the fourth year running.

Then Fate, or her nearest modern equivalent, intervened; Fate's messenger, not winged Mercury but Mrs Maxwell, triumphant, almost breathless, broke the news to me on a wet Wednesday morning in October.

She had been visited by a reporter. Now, it is not for me to cast stones at my professional colleagues, but Mr Maxwell had engaged solicitors in Perth, and they do things differently there. They employ secretaries: temporary secretaries, sometimes, girls whose loyalties are not firmly nailed to the mast of discretion and reticence. They talk, out of office hours, in saloon bars and discotheques, and the walls of these places have ears. It was always possible that a case as bizarre as that of Maxwell vs Maxwell could attract the attention of the tabloid press, and now it had happened. The newly launched, technologically white-hot journal, *Scotland Now!* had put a man on the case and, like a shark in an aquarium, it had not taken him long to catch his prey. There was nothing revolutionary about his methods: so long as there are people who bear the promise of a good story, their movements and their dustbins are in danger of investigation. Mrs Burgess had been watched; had been tracked, indeed, one Tuesday morning, from her front door in Craigfieth to a rented office room in Perth, from there to the main Post Office, and back home. Subsequent siftings had yielded an address in the Home Counties, and the workings of her inner life lay, at a stroke, exposed to the journalist's eager gaze. By way of putting the cherry on the cake, he had then presented himself at Mrs Maxwell's sister's house, had wrapped up the story over two glasses of sweet sherry in the morning room, and had supplied my client with the vital missing link.

She passed it to me now, in the form of a copy of *Ambassador* magazine, folded back to the first page of classified advertisements. Here was Nemesis, then, in semi-display:

> SEXY HOUSEWIFE WAITS TO HEAR FROM YOU!
> Letter, panties, photographs, Hot! Hot! Hot!
> £5 under plain cover, Cash Only, inc pp.
> BOX A3486.

The box number had been traced, without much difficulty, to a small office in Perth; five pounds, a small addition to the newshound's expenses, had in the fullness of time produce a brown envelope.

"He showed it to me," Mrs Maxwell concluded. "They were green this time. Dark green."

I began to think, apprehensively, of the grotesque twists this knowledge might put into the tale of the pending divorce hearing. Likely as not, Mrs Maxwell would regard this onanistic postal adultery with greater contumely than the imagined physical act. At least that might have had some touch of human tenderness to it.

"So I'm sure you will understand, Mr MacIain, that I do not wish to proceed with our action. I went to see my husband last night, and he has accepted my offer to return. If you would be so good as to render your account in due course, I shall of course pay all reasonable expenses."

I suspect that I was forced, unconsciously, into the role of the grasping Man of Law. The truth is, I thought I knew my client inside out by now, and I could not understand her train of reasoning. I said, "Are you sure this is how you wish to proceed? You do not condemn your husband's conduct?"

She smiled.

"I regard him as vindicated, Mr MacIain, as will, I know, the majority of people with good sense. Consider the strain he has been under because of the stand he took. Oh, have no doubt, I know there were those who mocked him when he undertook to drive out this — this filthy rubbish from our town. I saw the look on that television interviewer's face. But he was right, wasn't he? He said those magazines could do nothing but deprave and corrupt, not just the young people but everybody. Nobody is immune, and he said so. And see how right he was! Once let in the worm, Mr MacIain, and the rose is blighted. Yes! And even he, steadfast and upright, was tempted, and fell. But I said to him last night, I said I saw how great was his care for the community. His was no blind faith, Mr MacIain. He had only once to test his convictions, and they have been borne out — proved, utterly."

I did not say, "Well, three times actually." I was tempted, but I did not fall.

She continued, "He admitted it of course, the poor misunderstood man that he is. It is a poor general who will lead his men where he fears to tread himself. But he feared my reaction, Mr MacIain — can you credit it? He thought I might not understand. But I told him I understood, all too well, and I am thankful that he has agreed to my return on condition that we will live in the light of that understanding. He asked me to forgive him, poor soul and I told him there is nothing to forgive. I made sure he understood that I — understand."

A chill seemed to fall on the room, a reminder that it was now autumn, season of decay and the long sleep of quickness.

I had become grimly reconciled — tholed is the Scottish word for it — to the task of securing Mrs Maxwell's divorce, and my occupation was gone, I congratulated my client, but felt — sympathetically, perhaps, with her restored husband — unmanned.

Apologetically, I said, "I'm afraid I don't think there's anything we can do about this newspaper business. We have a free press, heaven help us, and it's bound to make life uncomfortable for you, for a while."

She smiled again — a serene, blameless smile.

"Oh, Mr MacIain, you underestimate us both. I shall be proud — yes, proud! — to read the report. It will show my husband to the world as he truly is. He has hidden himself too long. I told him so myself. I think he begins to understand."

And so, at last, did I. She departed, sublime and thankful.

Fortune did not, in the event, treat Mr Maxwell as unkindly as she might have done or, some might think, as harshly as he deserved. That night the news broke, in Pittenweem, of the arrest of the androgynous pop idol Jeanette, on drug charges, and his bail, on a surety sworn by Lady Moncrieff, of a hundred thousand pounds. It is not often the Scottish press gets it teeth into a home-grown story linking sex, drugs, fame, money and the Old Aristocracy, and they made the very most of it. The tale of the Headmaster's Naughty Knickers was squeezed out.

Scotland Now! was off the streets for a fortnight after that, as the result of industrial action over 'wet money', the bonus paid to those whose task it is to load newspapers on to lorries in inclement weather. Scandal quickly perishes: the story did not surface after the dispute had been settled.

Mr Maxwell took early retirement at Christmas. At a presentation held in the packed school hall, he exchanged the cares of headmastering for a set of inscribed golf clubs and the unremitting understanding of his wife. There was a very nice photo in that week's *Perthshire Gazette*. In the New Year he was pleased to welcome Mr Haq as a member of Craigfieth Rotarians; there followed, so it was reported, an interesting and lively talk from the new member on the subject of 'Moral Restraint in a Free Society'.

Mrs Burgess left the town. She departed hastily, though not before settling all her debts to local tradespeople. No one knows where she went, though it is to be hoped that she too found understanding somewhere. I sold the house for her, as a matter of fact. Winter can be a dead season for property, and it stayed on the books for some time. Eventually, though, I got her a decent price from a local trader, just starting up in the leisurewear business.

Mrs Maxwell paid my bill promptly, with a cheque drawn on their current joint account.

2

The Day of the Beast

We all know (writes 'Country Wife' in a recent edition of the Women's Section of the *Perthshire Gazette*) the names of the days of the week and the months of the year, and we are all familiar with the handy rhyme that enables us to recall how many days there are in each month. (Despite our familiarity, she goes on to quote it anyway.) But, she continues, now well stuck into paragraph three of her popular weekly column, 'From My Kitchen Window', there are times when something special occurs in the family circle, so that instead of memorialising an event as having taken place 'last Wednesday', we enshrine it as an anniversary and, for a time, build our calendar round it. For instance (she parenthesises) for some weeks her own dear ones had dated events as occurring before or after The Day Nana Lost Her Teeth. She then goes on, under the cross-heading 'Gay Harbingers', to immortalise for another two hundred words or so her sighting that week of the first crocus, giving full play to such tried and tested metaphors as would be familiar to her readers and consequently fit to print.

While the main thrust of 'Country Wife's' argument is no doubt tenable insofar as it applies to families — even, perhaps, to nations, as in The Day War Was Declared — it can scarcely if ever have applied to those communities, such as towns, that lie in between these two social groupings. The explanation for this is surely clear enough: any event significant enough to stamp itself on the collective consciousness of a whole town could hardly fail, in this

27

age of mass communication and social homogeneity, to declare itself in similar terms to a wider audience, while any occurrence too trivial to find itself thus celebrated could scarcely happen, so to speak, outwith the kinship group. Thus far, it must be admitted, 'Country Wife' is not mistaken in her exegesis.

There is, however, always the exception to every rule, however solid its basis in logic and sociological practice: is it not true, after all, that every law carries within its very framing the seeds of its own breach? And that the offence against it does not even exist until thus proscribed by statute? Any 'prentice philosopher will tell you that it is.

Thus it was that the diurnal period known to others (in their total and terrible ignorance) only as Monday, February 9th will for long remain etched on the Craigfiethan mind as The Day Of The Beast. Never before (nor, it is fair to speculate, ever since) has the town been so tyrannised, nor fear stalked its streets with such paralysing effect as it did that day. A thousand years — at least — of social order vanished, one might say, like dew in the morn.

It was a normal day, that fateful Monday, until precisely 8.12 a.m.: that is to say, until the arrival at the Post Office of the mail van from Tirrivee. For Alistair Penicuik, the driver, normality had ceased some twenty minutes earlier as, breasting the last summit of the Lummocks before beginning the long descent to the waking town below, he was stopped by the Police and questioned as to his movements that morning.

"Mercy!" exclaimed Mrs Henderson, Craigfieth's postmistress. "Imagine them not knowing that! What did you tell them?"

"Och, the lot!" replied Penicuik, allowing Mrs Henderson to pour him a second cup of fortifying tea before continuing his tale. "In no uncertain terms, I can

tell you! I told them I met the mail train at five past seven
— it was five minutes late, nothing byordinair about that
— an' I picked up the sacks as usual, an' just made the
one stop at Dalglumph PO before I met them. Then
—" he paused dramatically to swallow another mouthful
of tea — *"they showed me the photeygraph!"*

Mrs Henderson moaned piteously. Angus Monzie, the
postman, paused in his sorting to cluck appreciatively.

"My, my!" he said. "What like was yon?"

"Oh, terrible man, terrible! A great brute of a fellow
with great starin' eyes an' bushy eyebrows, an' hair like a
craw's neist! An' the mooth — oh, cruel, man, cruel!"

"Oh, merciful goodness! I hope he doesna come here!"
exclaimed Mrs Henderson.

"Likely he will," said Penicuik, "more than likely.
Where else is there?"

"Aye," agreed Angus Monzie. "That's right. He'll need
clothes, likely, and food foreby. I doubt he's here already!"

"You mean —" squeaked Mrs Henderson. "He's a —
a . . ."

"Aye, most likely, wouldn't you say, Alistair?"

"Oh, by all means, aye. Ye can tell from the face — yon
mooth o' his, an' the eyes, all slitty-like they were."

"I — I thought you said 'staring'," said Mrs Henderson.

"Oh aye, starin' they were right enough, starin' an'
slitty, ye ken my meaning? Sort of like this."

Penicuik pulled the corners of his eyes down with
his fingers and goggled psychopathically at the trembling
postmistress.

"Oh my goodness!" she breathed. "I've just minded on
. . . wait now till I find it . . .". She rummaged through a
pile of leaflets and obsolete posters under the counter.

"Is yon like him at all?"

She displayed the likeness of a man aged between 25
and 35, wearing a dark blue anorak and wanted for the

violent robbery of two sub-post offices in Renfrewshire.

"We-ell, aye, it could be him, right enough," confirmed Penicuik. "Wi'out the moustache an' the scar. Mind, that's just a photey-kit picture. The one I saw was a photeygraph."

"Maybeez they got him, an' he escaped," suggested Angus. "You'd best take care today, Mrs Henderson!"

"An' I'll lock my doors goin' back, don't you worry!" said Penicuik.

"Oh mercy!" said Mrs Henderson. "Whatever would I do if he — if I . . ."

"Aye," grunted the two men. They drank up their tea and left.

At the Police House, Sergeant Donald MacEachran spooned up the last damp fibres of his Nutri-Husks, pulled a face and, patting his jacket pocket to ensure he had his Rennies with him, bent to kiss his wife Catriona, who was poring over a pile of paint colour charts.

"I'll be away then," said MacEachran.

"Mmmm? Oh, yes, right then. Which would you like for the stairs, Quiche or Lasagne?"

"Eh?"

"Here." She pointed to a chart. "Lasagne looks warmer, but Quiche is a bit less muddy. What do you think?"

"Oh, I don't mind, whatever you prefer. Remember it's a Police House though: they're aye fond of blue and white. Look, I must be off."

"Any idea when you'll be back, dear?"

"None at all. Depends how long Simison and I spend ploutering about on the hills on this manhunt. Mind, don't tell anyone, will you? If the Mafia knew we were out of town they might just move in."

"Righto, dear." Catriona returned to her charts. "Don't forget your sandwiches."

"Oh, aye. What's in them?"

"Vita-Veg."

"Oh."

"There's a molasses bar for afters, and a Whole Earth yogurt."

Next door, MacEachran found Constable Simison picking his teeth with a match in front of the rest room mirror.

"Sorry, sarge," he said, catching the reflection of MacEachran's disapproving eye. "It's the bacon, you see. Sticks."

"Haud yer wheesht and get yer wellies," said Mac-Eachran. "It's walkies time."

Simison drove off with panache, though at some cost in tyre rubber to the ratepayers of Eastern Region. Across the street, in the grey gloom that passed for this February morning in Craigfieth, Angus Monzie stared long and meaningly, noting the details of their departure to add to that day's fearful tidings. He sucked in his cadaverous cheeks, smiled grimly to himself and, hunching his bony shoulders against unseen assault, stalked on to deliver post and panic through the town. Behind him, as he went, washing was urgently brought in from yards and drying greens.

The man stirred slowly, painfully, limbs grown stiff and sore from hours of stillness on the hard ground. He yawned, blinked and ran a grubby hand across his unshaven face. Then, gathering his few things together, he made his way cautiously down to the river Fieth and contrived to wash in the icy water. Two startled moorhens paddled tumultuously upstream and the man looked up quickly before returning, warily, to his uncomfortable ablutions. Regaining high ground he looked about him as if uncertain what to do next, his eyes half-closed against the keen air, alert, watchful. At last he shouldered his rucksack and, picking his way through the bare tangle of heather and bog myrtle, set off along the east bank of the river, taking care to keep himself well screened from human view. On the still air came the receding roar of a police car leaving Craigfieth at high speed.

At the Post Office, Mrs Henderson pinned up the poster of the wanted man and retired hastily behind her grille. Down the street, early shoppers began to congregate at Mr Haq's. Like spores on the breeze, the salient points of Angus Monzie's morning bulletin had already begun to produce strange and wonderful narrative fungi.

". . . out all night they were, and still no sign of him, even though they had reinforcements from Dunbroath."

"I hadn't heard that!"

"Oh, yes. And armed, of course."

"And there's the new Sergeant —"

"Off like a rocket, first thing, so Mrs Baxter said. She saw him herself."

"So did Mrs Biggar, so Miss Naughtie said. Looking gey grey, poor man."

"Aye! It fair makes you think, doesn't it?"

"But why for would they be armed?"

"Haven't you heard? He's got a gun, a sawn-off revolver I think, so the Hydro man said."

"I heard an axe."

"And a hood."

"A hood? I was told a stocking mask."

"Oh no, definitely a hood, Mrs Farquhar told me, and she wouldn't be mistaken about a thing like that!"

"That's right, it would be a hood, on account of the scar!"

"Scar?"

"Oh, yes, Mrs Henderson's got a poster up, I saw it myself not five minutes ago. Terrible cruel eyes!"

"Oh well, there you are! He'd have to wear a hood, wouldn't he!"

"Wouldn't *they*, don't you mean?"

"*They*?"

"Why yes, there's two of them. At least. So I heard. A whole gang, on the run."

"With axes . . ."

" . . . guns . . ."

". . . flick-knives . . ."

". . . coshes . . ."

"And all desperate!"

"My Fergus'll just have to do without his clean shirt tonight, and that's a fact!"

"Quite right, Mrs Fingal! You can't be too careful."

"You can't, and that's a fact! They could be anywhere."

"You mean . . . ?"

"In the town . . ."

"Now! This minute! Oh, these are terrible times, right enough!"

"Perhaps it's those Hell's Angels."

" Don't they have scooters, though, Miss Phemister?"

". . . or hippies. A whole convoy of hippies, on the pot!"

"Disgusting!"

"Drug-crazed fiends!"

"With no underwear!"

Behind the counter, Benazir Haq smiled deliciously and squirmed in her sari.

"My father," she murmured, "says he's a rapist."

"Which one, dear?" asked Miss Phemister.

Sergeant MacEachran hunched miserably in the passenger seat of the Eastern Constabulary Ford as it tore dangerously along the narrow Lummock roads, its near side frequently scraping the gaunt immaculacy of Europe's longest continuous beech hedge. His morning roughage churned coldly in his stomach and beads of sweat collected on his uniform moustache. Beside him, Constable Simison whistled a continuo loosely based on the theme from *Hill Street Blues*.

It may fairly be said that Donald MacEachran, 32, was not a happy man, even leaving aside his present circumstances, for he had suffered a fate familiar to many in this sad age: to the successful parish priest, for instance, suddenly transferred to a team ministry in Portobello; to the popular classroom teacher rapidly promoted to Depute Headship and the hateful intractability of the timetable, or the genial back-bench MP newly translated into a Junior Minister for something necessary in the national interest. It was not, of course, that the maintenance of law and order on his native island of Oriskay had been without its own peculiar demands: it was just that having, so to speak, been weaned on them, he had been able to establish and maintain a *régime* of policing which ensured that a certain benevolent lassitude with regard to bald tyres, Hogmanay and poaching for the pot was rewarded with a near unanimity of community co-operation when it came to dealing with the more blatant excesses of Glasgow Fair Fortnight and the Glorious Twelfth. While his urban contemporaries might strive to fulfil some imagined quota of charges per week, he had been content, when the time came to pen his periodical reports, to record nothing more threatening to the common weal of Oriskay than an occasional malicious urination in the manse garden of the Wee Free.

Craigfieth had been his reward: a town, equal in population to two Oriskays, where poaching was something you did to a Golden Lummock battery egg, and not a friendly soul in sight to offer you a dram; a constable who thought a ceilidh was something you watched on television; a job which, as today, might take him hare-arsing halfway across Perthshire instead of allowing him to get to know his patch, not that he was even sure he wanted to, anyway.

Worst of all there was Catriona — as fine a lass as ever stacked a peat — who had always shared his belief that a good meal meant a large plateful of something hot and filling, with seconds, but had now discovered Health Food and dished him up the sort of mash you'd be ashamed to offer a clocking hen.

Sergeant MacEachran sighed bitterly, then flinched as Simison flung the car round another right-hand bend.

"How much further?" he growled.

The constable pressed a button on his digital watch.

"ETA in nine minutes, sarge," he said.

"*A bhobh, bhobh,*" muttered the sergeant, and fell to chewing his moustache.

The man halted as the town came in sight a mile distant, and ran a thin tongue over his dry lips. His stomach rumbled and his clothes, wet with dew and sweat, clung to his spare frame. He braced his shoulders and made for the road: the time for concealment was over. His eyes bore the glint of unsated appetite. His rucksack, heavy with its concealed burden, bumped against his back. A low watery sun broke through the cloud base and then, as if appalled at what it saw, hastily withdrew.

Angus Monzie paused, as was his custom, halfway through his morning round, rested his haunches against the damp buttress of the war memorial and lit a fly fag, reflecting on the day's affairs so far. Though accustomed to being the bearer of tidings, both oral and postal, he was Craigfiethan enough to appreciate not only that news sometimes travels faster than the bearer but also that there is assuredly no smoke without fire. He was not unduly disconcerted, therefore, to discover his serving of intelligence already overlaid with informed sauces of speculation and hypothesis, any or all of which might be true. After all, he reasoned, in this day and age you never can tell, and it never rained but it poured; if it was true that there was a lot of it about (which there certainly was, as any right-minded person knew) then it might just as well happen in Craigfieth as in Perth or London and, since it was better to be safe than sorry, he might as well be hanged for a sheep as for a lamb. He dropped his dog-end through the storm grating between his feet — he hadn't missed since October 18th, 1968 — and, fortified in his mission to inform, set off on the second half of his round, which included the Primary School, the High School and the Eventide Home.

Whatever he was — or they were — whether armed robber, homicidal maniac, rapist, pervert or terrorist, or the whole lot rolled into one (or more) he, Angus Monzie, Government employee, bearer of the Queen's Mail, had a duty to let folk, particularly those less fortunate than himself, know. Thus assured he went on his way. Had the sun been shining his cap badge could be said to have flashed in its mercurial rays; as it wasn't, the martial ring of his steel-capped boots on the pavement must attest to his civic resolution. His hour had come at last: he would not be found wanting. He strode up to the door of Jerusalem House, home of Evangelist Bullock, and chapped upon it.

Constable Simison drew to a racing halt beside a second police car and gunned the engine before switching it off. Pausing only to scratch his left armpit, he leapt out. Beside him Sergeant MacEachran uncoiled, slowly and biliously, and followed suit to hail his colleagues, Sergeant Leuchars and Constable Coultrane from Dalglumph.

They tossed for area of search. MacEachran lost, and set off with Constable Simison across the anciently glaciated, drably corrugated plateau of eastern Scotland's most notable lateral moraine. Leuchars and Coultrane departed in the opposite direction, by car, to begin a leisurely toothcombing of barns and outbuildings.

"It's times like this, Simison," observed the Sergeant, "that I wish I'd gone into banking."

A fine rain began to bedew the shoulders of his serge jacket. Ten paces into their mission the Sergeant's right foot sank into an unsuspected incidence of upland blanket bog.

"Mind where you go, sarge," said Simison.

MacEachran's reply, which may fully be appreciated only by those whose first language is that of Eden, hinted strongly that the constable would fare ill in any society predisposed towards tact, celibacy, fidelity, natal legitimacy and due respect for the tenets anent the folly of Oedipus. A pair of Gaelic-speaking grouse flew off in alarm; Simison, however, merely grinned. The Sergeant retrieved his boot from the sucking mire and groaned in Anglo-Scots.

"What's up?" asked Simison.

"Ah think Ah've burst ma yogurt."

In the kitchen of the Bide-a-Wee Tearooms Mrs Spurtle was supervising the manufacture by her co-partner and slave, Miss Phemister, of a batch of home-baked delicacies from a catering-size packet of Mither McGoody's Instant Castle of Mey Scone Mix (No Egg Needed).

"For goodness' sake, Phemister!" barked the amazonian widow. "Stop trembling, damn you! Anyone'd think you were being outraged already."

"Ay'm sorry, Joan," the wretched Phemister replied. "Ay just can't help worrying. What if —"

"Don't be silly, woman! As if anyone would. I mean —
look at you!" She guffawed heartily.

"It's all right for you, dear," the spinster persisted. "Ay
mean you're . . . well, strong, and you have experience of
. . . things. Ay mean, you've been married and, oh you
know what Ay mean."

At least two pounds' worth (at retail prices) of Mither
McGoody's Mix flew out of the bowl. Mrs Spurtle scraped
it off the floor and put it back.

"You should get one of these, Phemmy," she said,
fishing with her clean hand in the pocket of her tweed
jacket. "Stanley knife, retractable blade. Like this!"

She thrust and carved in the air between them.

"Then you can pickle it as a trophy. That's what I'd do!
It's the only language they understand, you know."

"Oh! But Ay couldn't . . . Ay mean, he might not be
going to, you know, going to . . ."

"Ha! There speaks the voice of ignorance! What d'ye
reckon he *would* be going to do with it then, you silly
woman."

"Really Joan, Ay think you're being rather coarse. Ay
mean, he might be doing anything."

"Such as what?"

"Oh well, Ay . . . Ay don't know."

"Too damn right you don't! Believe me they're all
the same, Phemmy, I know. Besides, as I said, no
one's going to, so stop twittering like that old woman
of a postman and mind what you're doing with the
stuff."

Above the noise of the mixer the two ladies heard the
tearoom door announce its opening. Miss Phemister
started, the whirring instrument still in her trembling
hand.

"Look out!" bawled Mrs Spurtle, seizing it and switching
it off. "There, now look what you've done! Covered me in

the revolting stuff! Well, don't just stand there, woman! Go and see to it."

"B-but Joan, what if it's . . . if it's *him*?"

"Take this," replied the widow, handing over the knife. "You'll know where to sever when you see it. Well, go on! I can't go like this, can I?"

"Oh! Ay . . . Ay . . . couldn't!" breathed Miss Phemister.

"Don't then. Lie back and think of Scotland, if that's what you fancy. Oh, for God's sake Phemmy, it's probably just the Murchison chit from the Bank for their morning rolls. Go on!"

Trembling, Miss Phemister entered the tearoom, the knife concealed in the pocket of her apron.

It was not the Murchison chit.

Mrs Spurtle was nothing if not resolute. Stationed behind the hatch that separated kitchen from tearoom, she strained to hear what was being said. Failing in this, she forebore to interfere when she heard her partner's gasp. She stuck to her post when the screaming came, a chilling animal noise that would have prompted many a weaker spirit to panic-stricken action: not so Joan Spurtle, for she was made of sterner stuff. Only when she heard the unmistakable sound of crashing furniture did she allow her business sense to override her better judgment. She opened the hatch a crack and peeped through, her glistening, gristly blue orb belying the apparent flaccidity of the surrounding flesh.

She saw a rear view of Miss Phemister, still upright, thank God, but in a state of clearly recognisable catatonia, and emitting cries that might just as well have betokened ecstasy as agony, and were very probably a compound of both. Through the street door a lean male figure was fast vanishing, or attempting to vanish: his rucksack had jammed and his wrestlings and strugglings were causing

the bells above the door to tingle and jangle cacopho-
nously, like the incidental music to some surreal filmic
masterpiece.

He was the one, she noted, who was doing the screaming.

At once — and with too much synchronicity to be
cynically anatomised as cause and effect — the man
at last burst through the gap and was gone, and the
widow surged into the tearoom and was at the quivering
spinster's side.

"Did you get him?" she demanded.

"Oh! Ah! Bwbwbwwwthth!"

"What? Stinking hell, you don't mean to say he got you,
do you?"

"Mmmmmo! Ay, oh, he, ah, auugh!"

"Well, what then?"

"Ay, he, Ay . . . kn-n-n-nife, huhuhuhu —"

"Good gel! Where! In the balls? Come on, Phemister!"

"Sssssss . . ."

"What?"

"Sssstu — stu — stu . . ."

"Stuck? Stuck? Stuck what?"

"S-s-stuck it — out!"

"Ha! You mean he stuck it — and you — with the
knife? Oh, Phemmy! Where is it then? I don't see any
blood."

"Aaaaaagh!" replied Miss Phemister and then,
with sudden clarity and unprecedented outspokenness,
added:

"Oh, you are such a *stupid* woman sometimes, Joan!"
and fainted.

The man fled down the street, overtaking Mr Bullock.
The Evangelist continued on his way to the Gospel Hall
in the wake of the stranger who, careering wildly across

the junction of School Road, saw a sign saying YOU MAY TELEPHONE FROM HERE, wheeled abruptly outside the Post Office, and staggered in, clutching the waistband of his jeans.

Mrs Spurtle had laid the inert body of the frail Phemister on the tearoom counter and at length, by dint of a few brisk slaps to the face and a slosh of Jeyes' from the bottle under the sink in lieu of smelling salts, brought her partner to a semblance of coherent consciousness. Eyes streaming, shallow chest heaving, the heroine recounted her tale. She had entered the tearoom to find this . . . this man, this Beast ("You were quayte rayte, Joan, of course") standing before her, his terrible eyes boring into hers and his — his — his . . . you know, Joan, *body* heaving, and he had made an, oh, Joan, an . . . an Improper Suggestion!

"Ah!" bellowed Mrs Spurtle triumphantly. "I know: '*Time for your deep breathing*'!"

"N-no," sniffed Miss Phemister. "No, dear, that's not what he said, why should you think he said that?"

"It's what Spurtle used to say, in the early days," grunted the widow. "Never mind, go on. What *did* he say?"

"He said . . . he said — oh, Joan, it was so *awful*!"

"Come *on*, woman, spit it out!"

"Well, Ay can't remember the *exact* words, Ay'm afraid —"

Mrs Spurtle groaned.

"It's all very well for you, Joan! You didn't have to stand there, defenceless. Besides, he spoke in such an *odd* way, very . . . very husky and low, but Ay caught the gist of it: he said he wanted something fresh and hot in may oven!"

"*Ha!*"

"Well, quayte! Ay mean, Ay knew what he meant of course, because you've often told me the sort of things They say when They want to be . . . disgusting. So then

Ay pulled the knife out."

"Attagel! And then what happened?"

"Well, Ay'm not quayte sure really, it all happened so quickly . . . I know something happened because it sort of stuck — the knife Ay mean — and he stepped backwards and shouted something, Ay couldn't understand what, and then . . . and then —"

"And then I came in, and not a moment too soon! Well done, Phemmy! Now we must take action: you go and make us a nice cup of tea, while I phone the Police!"

There was a queue at the Post Office counter, Monday being a busy day for Child Allowances. Constitutionally respectful of bureaucratic authority, the man took his place in line, despite his mounting sense of panic, behind four of Craigfieth's active breeding stock, patiently waiting and clutching their order books as they themselves were clutched by their whingeing progeny. One of these, a fat blonde infant with knees that were not so much dimpled as quilted, ceased her fretful fidgeting below the vast mainsail of her mother's skirts to fix the man with that gaze of intense indifference that is the hallmark of native Craigfiethans the world over. Flinching as if from another blow, the man cast his eyes around for something to divert them, among the official notices, from the little basilisk; finding nothing, he let them warily return. He was still being stared at. He essayed a smile, with startling effect: the little girl burst at once into a paroxysm of blubbery sobbing and buried her face in the nylon immensities of her mother's legs.

"What is it now, Mandy?" she asked in a tone that suggested no sanguine hopes of an entertaining reply.

"Man!" squealed the child, stamping its little hooves as if to garnish the utterance.

"What man?" sighed the mother, turning to the child at last with vaguely maternal intentions and, in so doing, beholding the answer to her question.

The woman's face and expression was, in every hideous respect, the magnified image of the infant's. The man grinned foolishly back and then, realising that the stare had now alighted on his midriff, where one hand still performed the task of the lately severed fabric, attempted an explanation.

"Is, er, knife," he said. "So I 'ave to 'old up!"

The woman made a little choking noise.

"*Pardon? Excusez-moi madame*, I 'ave, er, said zer wrong thing, per'aps?"

Evidently he had, for the woman at once screamed in a flat, emotionless way, as if she had learned the noise from an instruction manual, and, dragging the still blubbering Mandy behind her, crashed and waded her way out to the street where she was heard to scream again, a little more feelingly this time.

Her action brought the man face to face with Mrs Henderson behind her grille: but not for long. Forgetful, in her moment of crisis, of the grille's existence and pausing only to exclaim, "*It's him!*" she seized her heavy Post Office issue sellotape dispenser and hurled it at him. It rebounded off the wire mesh and, striking the Postmistress squarely on the perm, knocked her instantly senseless. Now was the time for those not involved in the drama at first hand to do their bit by jointly and severally shouting, screaming, and throwing things.

It was not until someone realised that the fugitive had left the Post Office that the Police were called, at the number given on Mrs Henderson's poster.

The telephone rang as Catriona MacEachran was attempting, for the third time that morning, to achieve

the Lotus Position. She unravelled herself painfully
and, one hand clasped to her coccyx, hobbled across the
darkened living-room to answer it.

"Craigfieth Police Station, can I help you? . . . oh, Mrs
Spurtle, it's you . . . no, I'm afraid he's out, Mrs Spurtle,
can I — what? Good gracious! . . . And he . . . yes, yes of
course, and he . . . yes well naturally she would, wouldn't
she, have you got a d- . . . yes, quite so, Mrs Spurtle, but
have you got a descr- . . . aha, uhu, ye-es, like a what was
that? Oh, animal, yes, well I'll telephone headquarters,
Mrs Spurtle, and they'll radio through . . . oh, no time
at all, Mrs Spurtle — what? Oh yes, lock up, well I think
that's quite right indeed . . . yes, I will too. Righto then,
Mrs Spurtle."

As she dialled the number for Eastern Constabulary
HQ she hoped Donald would have time to eat at least
some of his lunch.

Out on the barren wastes of Lummock Moss a mist had
descended: thinly, but enough, in the upland flatness, to
obscure the few distant landmarks. Through this bleak,
chill country trudged Constable Simison and Sergeant
MacEachran, the latter accompanied at irregular inter-
vals by a wet, flatulent noise as his flooded right boot
descended on the cold and sticky ground. At length they
halted, midway between one nothingness and another,
like Gloucester and Poor Tom above Dover beach.

"I'm cold," said Simison, heightening the analogy.

"Bugger that," replied MacEachran, destroying it.
"The point is, where are we?"

Simison produced an Ordnance Survey map from his
inside pocket and unfolded it in the sluggish breeze.

"About here, I reckon," he said, indicating with a
perfectly manicured forefinger a substantial blank area
between Ben Gunn and Ben Waverley.

"Thanks a million, pal," growled the sergeant, reaching for his radio. "Mobile one-niner to Green Control, do you read me, over?"

He repeated the phrase twice more, then scowled at the crackling instrument.

"*Dit thu gu peanas!*" he hissed.

"Pardon?" said Simison.

The Sergeant shook his radio violently and held it up for his colleague's inspection.

"The fucking fucker's fucking fucked!" he explained. "Try yours."

Simison did so, with the same result.

"Must be a bad reception area," he suggested, adding hastily: "We'd best go back, eh, sarge?"

"Aye, laddie," MacEachran agreed.

They looked round them.

"If we can work out which way back is."

The mist began to thicken.

Meanwhile, the Duty Officer at Eastern Constabulary HQ in Dunbroath logged his call from Paisley Crime Squad and sent out another car to assist Leuchars and Coultrane who had been diverted from their search five minutes previously to attend an incident of alleged sexual assault in Craigfieth, observing to himself as he did so that the town seemed to be having quite a time of it, that morning.

Angus Monzie completed his round, alerting the lieges to the probability of impending holocaust. The Primary School doubled playground duty; the High School postponed the inter-house rugby tournament scheduled for that afternoon; at the Eventide Home, Matron wisely took all available precautions by cancelling all visits, closing all windows, locking all doors and giving each inmate an extra after-breakfast sedative. All three institutions telephoned the Police Station to request assistance: Catriona MacEachran passed their messages on to HQ. HQ, in the shape of Detective Chief Superintendent Josh 'Fancy' Menzies, called off the planned drugs swoop on Dunbroath Polytechnic and transferred all available manpower to the town. Pausing only to request a D-notice (that great standby so beloved of all right-thinking proponents of the British democratic tradition) he summoned a driver and sped westwards to supervise the excitement.

Angus Monzie passed along Lummock View on his way back to the Post Office, whistling one of the more dolorously uplifting airs of the Scottish Metrical Psalter. He paused to light a cigarette, tossing the spent match nonchalantly away into the laurel hedge bordering the golf course. It landed two feet from the dilated nostrils of the fugitive, who was cowering timorously in the sour undergrowth.

Arriving at the Post Office, Angus experienced the scaremonger's ultimate satisfaction: that of resting secure in the knowledge that, for once, he had not exaggerated.

On Lummock Moss the Sergeant and the constable trudged wordlessly on. The former had forgotten about his lunch. The latter did not have any.

The mist beaded their tunics, transforming them, from the waist up, into wraithly gossamers, silent emissaries from the commonwealth of fairies. From the waist down, they were wet policemen.

Mr Cyril Bullock (Evangelist, Colporteur and Burgh Registrar) had not, as he originally intended, gone straight to the Gospel Hall. He went home first instead. Safely inside the firm fastness of Jerusalem House it took him little time to connect the postman's intelligence with the fleeing figure he had seen in the High Street. It was clear that he had been Spared: Spared by the Almighty to take up the shining sword of Righteousness and with it to defend the Lord's flock from the wolves of Satan.

He hunted through his stock of wayside pulpit texts until he came on one he could use: " 'For thou hast been a shelter for me, and a strong tower from the enemy' — Ps 61:3." He took a felt tip pen, wrote: 'Sanctuary — Gospel Hall open all day — New Members Welcome' in his best elementary copperplate on the bottom, and placed it in the front bow window. Then he slipped a poker down his trouser leg and strode stiffly out of the house and down the road, a deceptively angelic smile playing like infernal lightning round his bland features.

A cold, fitful breeze rattled the leaves of the laurel hedge. The man shivered. Slowly, cautiously, he crawled backwards until he had room to stand up, still clutching his soiled and drooping trousers, and looked around him. On one hand lay the golf course, its deserted links stretching indistinctly away in the distant mist: thither lay escape, of a sort. On the other hand was the town: thither lay the solution to his problems, though it bristled with danger. He pondered his plight until sheer corporeal need forced a decision. He found a gap in the hedge and slunk through, dragging the rucksack behind him. He hurried past the stern villas of Lummock View, trying to look as inconspicuous as possible, and made the junction without being stopped, screamed at, knifed or bombarded. Perhaps he had simply been unlucky before, he thought. Probably they were not used to strangers here: he must smile, and not appear threatening. Above all, he must not exhibit any sign of fear or tension: like animals, the people here could obviously sense it, could smell it like a sweat. He must stay calm. He began to hum a soothing air.

The High Street was unaccountably deserted. He forced himself to pause by the Post Office on the junction with School Street while he scanned the shops for one which might alleviate the first of his pressing needs. His eye fell on Madame's Family Outfitters, prop. the Misses A & S Urquhart, with its drab display of hats and shapeless tweedy garments: a *mercerie* as well, perhaps. He would feel a lot calmer with both hands free. He steeled himself to walk the thirty paces to the door, and went in.

A curious tableau presented itself. Two elderly and identical ladies, each with her left hand across her bosom, stood together behind the counter. He smiled at them. They shrank back against the shelving, but at least they did not assault him. Encouraged, he advanced.

"Please," he said, very gently, "have you somezing of mending for my, er, oh, *pantalons*, 'ow you say, pants, no?"

The Misses Urquhart shuffled closer together, and made a little noise in their joint throat.

"*Pardon*?" He stepped right up to the counter. They gulped, and made the noise again. On the counter was a small carousel of haberdashery requisites, one of whose hooks bore several packets of safety pins.

"Ah!" he exclaimed, taking one. "I 'ave the luck! 'ow much for zis, please?"

The proprietrices emitted a series of gobbling sounds, and shook their heads violently.

"You do not sell zese to me? But for why, I 'ave money, *regardez-vous ici*!"

He brought a small fistful of change out of his pocket to demonstrate his ability to trade. A two pence piece fell on the counter: a Miss Urquhart fell on it while the other opened the till for its safe receipt, then slammed it shut.

They fled through a door marked Staff Only Strictly Private, and he heard a bolt being slid home. He shrugged: so much for his applied psychology. Still, he had gained support for his trousers and come through the transaction uninjured. It would be something to talk about when he got home. Now, he must eat. Outside, his sharpened senses were assailed by baking smells and he followed them through the portals of Glencairn's Licensed Baker.

He was the only customer. Standing with her back to him was a girl in her late teens, Mr Glencairn Junior's eldest. She wore an apron and was swaying listlessly to the tinny buzz of a personal stereo. The man coughed, once, with no effect. He repeated the cough a little louder. At the fourth attempt the girl turned round. She was evidently masticating in time to the music.

"Yeah?" she said, between syncopated chews. Then she stopped chewing, switched her machine off, and removed her headphones.

"Who are you?" she demanded.

"Me?" he asked

"Yeah," she said.

"Well — I am called Pierre de la Roche, and I am very 'ungry!"

"Why?" she said.

"Why? Well, I, er, I 'ave been out, all night, and I 'ave nuzzing to eat, you know, and so —"

"What for?"

"*Mon Dieu!* Do I 'ave to say before you will sell me somezing?"

"What for?" she said again.

"*Bon.* Zen I am ornithologist, you comprehend?"

She thought for a moment.

"Na."

"*Oh, la!* I look at ze birds, yes?"

"In the night?"

"*Oui*, in zer night, I look at birds in zer night, yes, zat is what I do, and all night I kip out of zer way of *Monsieur le garde-chasse*, because 'e like to shoot me per'aps, and now is morning, and I am 'ungry, and so — where are you going?"

The girl had gone to a door at the back of the shop and was now calling through it, loudly but without inflexion.

"Dad, it's him."

Pierre de la Roche had not spent an entire fraught morning in Craigfieth without learning something of the mores of the place. He banged a two pence piece on the counter, took two cold scotch pies and ran back to the comparatively civilised safety of his laurel hedge, meeting no living soul on the way.

Catriona MacEachran abandoned all attempts at yoga for the day. The phone simply would not stop ringing.

"Ah!" cried Constable Simison triumphantly.

"What?"

"Look!"

"Footprints," replied the Sergeant heavily.

"Not just footprints, sarge. *Our* footprints!"

"You don't say."

"Oh yes, sarge — look, there's my little ones, see, with the sort of zig-zag, and there's yours there, see. Bigger."

"Oh, aye. Right enough, constable. My, you're the clever one."

"Thanks, sarge! Well, we know what that means, eh!"

"Oh, aye. It means we're walking about in circles, in the fog. *Glé math*!"

"Oh — but . . . not necessarily, though, sarge. It *could* mean we're close to where we started. Couldn't it?"

"Maybe it could."

"Which do you think?"

Sergeant MacEachran looked long and pensively at Constable Simison.

"I don't mind," he said at last. "You choose yourself."

The Dunbroath police established their Incident Room in the Balmoral Suite of the Ben Almond Hotel, the small police station being unsuitable for the number of officers involved and the Community Centre being found to lack appropriate catering facilities.

Two Detective Sergeants were sent out, accompanied by WPCs Boyle and Proops, to interview Miss Phemister (who was still inclined to be jittery despite having made and consumed several pots of tea) and Mrs Henderson, who — forby the yards of bandaging around her head — had been seen by the good Dr Ghouleagh and pronounced whole, pending the long-term effects of the large dose of Factor's Delight he had prescribed her from his hip-flask.

Within ten minutes of leaving the Ben Almond, the two sleuths had been commanded by radio to pursue further enquiries with a Miss Floreen Glencairn at the bakery and with the Misses Urquhart at Madame's. Meanwhile, an Inspector with four discreetly armed constables combed the streets. It was after two o'clock before they all returned to report to DCS 'Fancy' Menzies, by which time the lunch-hour lull in the town's commercial thoroughfare was over, though not spectacularly so: many shopkeepers had decided to err on the side of caution, and not reopen their premises (dreich Monday afternoons in February being unconducive to good business, anyway). Only isolated groups of two or three, hurrying to the Gospel Hall, broke the dismal stillness of the High Street. The fog was steadily closing down from the Lummocks.

DCS Menzies began his briefing at 1419 hrs by his diver's-style strap-on chronograph. A thoughtful minion had provided him with a six-inch-scale map of the town, obtained with some difficulty (lunch-hours being lunch-hours, after all) from the District Office of the Regional Sewage Facility, formerly the Town House. He stood before it now, hunched over a lectern normally used only annually by the retiring President at Rotary Club Dinner-Dances. With bony hands clasped below his greyish monkey features, his pale eyes darting across the assembled constabulary, he looked very much like a man who, but for a few accidents of birth and nurture, could have made a very competent bookie's runner.

"Right then," he grated. "We've all been out looking for chummy — no go. Let's see what we've got."

He made as if to consult some non-existent notes, then continued.

"We've got a tall, swarthy man in his early twenties attempting to rape a spinster lady at the Bide-a-Wee Tearooms. He flees the scene of the attempted crime holding his trousers, the intended victim having defended herself with a sharp knife. We've got a man, late twenties or early thirties, medium build, unshaven, trying to hold up the Post Office at knifepoint, suspected of being the same man responsible for two armed raids on post offices in Renfrewshire. We have threatening behaviour at Madame's, Family Outfitters, on the part of a young, foreign-looking chap with greasy hair, who seems to be having trouble with his trousers. Soon afterwards an 'oldish-looking guy' makes lewd and improper suggestions at Glencairn's Bakery two doors down, and steals two scotch pies. In the last half hour we've been getting reports of suspicious persons seen in the vicinity of the High School, the Primary School and the McWhirter playing fields. A male resident at the Eventide Home dials 999 to say he's seen four armed men lurking in the grounds. All these sightings, all these incidents, but we've drawn a blank. Any suggestions?"

One of the armed constables stirred uneasily, and coughed.

"Yes, MacDiarmid?"

"Erm, I think the last one must've been us, sir," he muttered.

"What d'ye mean, laddie, 'you'?"

"Well sir, we were conducting a Discreet Reconnaissance of the old folk's home when this old barmp—, this senior citizen, sir, opens a window and tells us to f—, to go away, sir."

"I see, constable. And did you?"

"What, sir? Oh, yes sir, right away. He . . . he threw something at us, sir."

"Oh ho! And what was that, laddie, may I ask?"

"I'd . . . rather not say, sir."

"I see. Thank you very much, Constable MacDiarmid. All right, then, I'll ask again: apart from these four officers wallying around like pork pies at a barmitzvah, what've we got?"

This time, after what had happened to the wretched MacDiarmid, no one felt inclined to answer.

"OK. I'll tell ye what *I* think we've got: I think we've got a highly organised gang at work here: professionals!"

Somewhere in the room he detected the twitching of a sceptical eyebrow.

"Ho, yes! Aim: to pull off the big one; object: to create panic and clear the streets; strategy: mount a series of diversions while the real crime is going on; tactics: frighten the ladies with lewd suggestions; payoff: the Eastern Constabulary is made to look like a lot of dick—, sorry, WPC Rayner, thingie-heids. But we're not going to let them do that, are we? No. So here's what we do: four sectors."

He quartered the map with a large felt-tip cross whose apex was the vegetable garden at the back of Mr Meiklejohn's shop.

"Sergeants Moore and Russell, you take the lower two, DI Whitehead and I will take the upper ones which include the most sensitive areas. We'll each have an armed constable — unfortunately we're not allowed to take the arms *without* the constables — and keep in constant radio contact . Understood?"

A single hand wavered up.

"Yes, Constable . . . McCaig, is it?"

"Sir. So we're not bothered about the diversion — the guy with the loose breeks I mean — we're to ignore him?"

"Good question, McCaig! No, you're completely wrong: you're to grab him. It's my considered opinion he's the ringleader — the mastermind behind the whole operation!"

WPC Kurtz affected an air of bubble-eyed astonishment.

"You mean . . . Mr Big, sir?"

"Don't be silly, lassie. That stuff's for weans' comics. Now then, any questions, no? Then let's go!"

Before they could leap to his command, however, the door to the Balmoral Suite opened to reveal the trim figure of Catriona MacEachran.

"Excuse me, Chief Superintendent, but will you be after setting up your own phone here, because if so I need to do the shopping."

"Eh? Oh, aye, right enough, away ye go then — mind, you'd be better off the streets for an hour or two, lassie."

"I shan't be on them," replied Catriona. "I'm driving to MegaMessages. I do it every Monday. I'll tell them to patch the calls through here, then."

They trooped out into the thickening fog.

***

While Catriona MacEachran strapped herself into the driver's seat of her hatchback, her husband's attention was being drawn by Constable Simison to the curious incident of the footprints in the bog.

He studied them awhile.

"And what do you notice about them, constable?" he enquired.

"Erm, well, there's . . . there's two lots, sarge. Of each, I mean."

"Precisely so, constable. Precisely so. Now then, I'm going to sit down on this lump of rock here, and dream of the Isle of the Blessed. You may join me, or not, as you please."

"You mean . . . we're lost, sarge?"

"Not at all, not at all! We just haven't been found yet, that's all."

As DCS Menzies was dropping what the Scottish media, had it been at liberty to do so, would undoubtedly have described as his bombshell, Pierre de la Roche emerged once more from his laurel'd sanctum, a sorry figure ephemerally clothed in rags of mist. For some time, his rugged individualism had wrestled with his bourgeois upbringing: it had finally lost. Whatever was to befall him in this perfidious *pissoir* of a town, it might as well descend through the proper channels. There was nothing to be done but to seek out whatever might pass for Authority, and throw himself on its mercy. Again he found himself at the Post Office corner: which way now? *A droit, à gauche* . . . the street sloped down on his right, and he lacked the energy to climb hills. He plodded down the High Street, crossing when the shops on his side gave way to private houses. Somewhere, surely, there must be some office, some outpost of stolid *bureaucratie* in this town of lunatics? His attention was caught by a garish poster in the window of a large and hideous house at the bottom of the street, and quickly held by the one word, SANCTUARY, and the bold black arrow.

At once, his inner sight was filled with a beautiful vision: the kindly *pasteur* . . . explanations, guidance . . . hot food and drink . . . sanctuary. He forced his sore feet on in the direction indicated and very soon, at the name of Jesus, his spirit soared.

He was standing in front of a strange building, its curved corrugated iron roof suggestive of the Nissen hut it had once been, though layers of cement harling and a crow-stepped gable lent it an air of permanence and respectability. From within came a tinny resonance of loud worship. He entered the building and, finding himself in a lobby rank with the odour of damp coat, knocked three times upon the door beyond which, surely, lay the redeeming warmth of Christian charity.

The singing from within stopped abruptly with a brief dying tinkle on a tambourine. There was a long pause, then the sound of sonorous footsteps on a boarded floor. The door opened a fraction; enough to admit the extrusion of a balding head and a pair of anxious eyes which belied their owner's proselytising smile.

"Yes, young man, and what can the Lord Jesus do for you in your sin?" asked Mr Cyril Bullock.

"Sanctuary," breathed Pierre. "Sanctuary! *Sanctuary!!*" and without waiting to be invited, he pulled the door open and stepped past the Evangelist into the body of the hall.

A hundred eyes, on fifty swivelled necks, stared unwelcomingly back. It was sheer bad fortune that the one pair singled out by cruel Fate to have their stare returned should belong to a fat matron with a small blonde child who, clutching her mother's cardigan, again bawled "Man!" in piercing, echoing tones.

There followed the inevitable screaming, and a fusillade of *Songs Of Joy* (hard cover edition) reinforced from the rear by a woefully aimed kick from Mr Bullock's right brogue. Only then did the unfortunate ornithologist remember where he had last seen the man whose foot it fitted. Reeling under a hail of mawkish lyrics, he fumbled blindly for the door, and escaped.

He left the town by the Dunbroath road and ran on until the dreadful place was at last hidden by the fog. As he, and it, disappeared, the first of Menzies' bloodhounds began their manhunt, drawn by the uproar to the hysterical scenes still going on in the Gospel Hall.

"SRA!" exclaimed Simison, breaking the clammy silence.

"What?" grunted Sergeant MacEachran.

"SRA cards! You know, we had to do them at school."

"Nope," said the Sergeant.

"Oh. Well, they were sort of cards, see, with a bit of writing in — a bit story, sometimes, or an article on something — and then questions you had to answer on it. Some good, they were. We got them in English."

"Oh, aye? Fascinating."

"Yes, and I've just remembered what it is this reminds me of. There was this SRA card, see, all about someone who got lost in a fog — or was it the dark? —anyway, he walked miles and miles, right, but he found himself back where he'd started. He'd gone in a circle!"

"Wonderful," said MacEachran.

"No, that's not the point: you see, he was a scientist . . . or the other one was, that wrote it . . . I think . . . anyway, it told you the reason why he'd gone in a circle. Go on, guess!"

MacEachran regarded him balefully. "Did he have one leg longer than the other?"

"Awww! You knew it all along!"

"Don't try to be funny, Simison."

"I'm not! It's true! This man said, we've all got one leg slightly longer than the other, that's why we go in circles when we can't see. Makes you think, doesn't it?"

"No," said MacEachran.

"Oh, but it does — I mean, suppose we were to measure our legs, we could sort of make up for it, if we —"

"Simison."

"Yes, sarge?"

"Shut up."

"Excuse me," said a voice from the fog. "Hae either o' you twa gentlemen seen a red heifer aboot these perts?"

They turned to behold the grizzled countenance of an elderly man looming towards them on all fours.

"She's aye wanderin'" explained the man. "The wee teuchter!"

MacEachran growled ominously, but the man went ignorantly on: "I bocht her fae Fort Wulliam sales, y'see, oh, a pratty wee theng she is! Only she's a bugger for wanderin'."

The Sergeant crawled nearer the man, the better to address him.

"Would you be Mr Willy John Carnackit?" he asked.

The man beamed cariously. "Ah wud!" he replied.

"Fine that, then, Mr Carnackit," said MacEachran. "You just show us the way now, and we'll take you home."

"Ma heifer?"

"Safely back in the pen, Mr Carnackit. Your sister sent us up to tell you."

"Thomasina sent ye?"

"Aye, the same."

"Weel, she'd knaw!" Carnackit cackled. He leaned closer to MacEachran, breathing bellygas and mintoes into the Sergeant's face. "She's nocht but a heifer hersel'!"

"Aye, fine, now come you on, it's time to go home. Simison! Away out o' your dwam, boy, and we'll get this gentleman home."

As Mr Carnackit led the policemen away he told them how difficult it was to manage stock nowadays, what with the shortage of materials, and the blackout, and the Land Army making a right fankle of things. They listened sympathetically.

Pierre de la Roche stumbled blindly along, reluctant to rest although he reckoned he must now be a good two kilometres clear of the town. As the exertions and privations of the last twenty hours had taken their toll on his body, so the strains of this dreadful day began at last to upset his mental equilibrium. He saw faces in the hedges, shapes bulking and dissolving in the mist, and heard threatening sounds on the road behind. He forced himself to ignore these horrors, keeping his eyes firmly on the visible road ahead and concentrating his hearing on the slap of his trainers on its wet surface. Thus it happened that the car was nearly on him before he knew it and, with nowhere to hide, he was obliged to flatten himself against the hedge, close his eyes, and wait for nemesis.

He heard the car stop, and a door open. He heard a female voice call, "In you get!"

Like Fate's puppet, the wretched youth stumbled towards the open passenger door.

"Hi!" said Catriona MacEachran. "Want a lift?"

Pierre smiled weakly, allowed the woman to toss his rucksack in the back, and climbed in.

"Clunk, click!" said Catriona breezily.

"*Quoi?*" he squeaked.

"Your seat belt," Catriona smiled. "French?"

"*Oui, vraiment!*"

The car pulled slowly away, Catriona peering—though not in any disconcerting way — over the wheel.

"This shouldn't last long," she said. "It's usually just this bit of the glen that's bad."

"Ah," murmured Pierre.

There followed a considerable silence which the travellers felt simultaneously obliged to break.

"To where are you g—"

"What brings you h—"

They laughed. "You first," said Catriona.

Pierre decided his command of English was not equal to the task of narrating his recent past.

"'oliday," he said. "I am ornithologist. Yesterday I stay at Duncruddie Youth 'ostel. *Et vous?*"

Catriona decided her companion would not be able to understand the complexities of the out-of-town hypermarket; besides, another couple of miles wouldn't matter.

"Dunbroath," she replied, "shopping. Is that any use to you?"

"*Bien sûr!* I will stay in 'otel and eat much food!"

He relaxed into his seat, assured of his companion's normality as she smiled warmly across to him. She, for her part, felt confident that she had not inadvertently picked up one of those sex fiends that were supposed to be all over the mainland these days. The fog soon cleared as they drove south, and they had a most agreeable journey.

Detective Chief Superintendent Josh 'Fancy' Menzies' four Task Force Units searched Craigfieth fruitlessly for two hours, at the end of which a message from Paisley CID to the effect that the Renfrewshire Post Office gang had been apprehended after being severely beaten by a sub-postmistress in Linwood convinced the veteran crimefighter that the time had come to return to the more reliable lawbreakers of Dunbroath. Cursing the town and all its people in terms which would have won warm approval from Pierre de la Roche, now booked in for the night at the Station Hotel and with a single ticket for London (Euston) safely in his pocket, the pride of the Eastern Constabulary folded its tents and departed, leaving not a wrack behind, save a quantity of cigarette ends trodden into the Balmoral Suite's best tartan carpet and a mutilated map of Craigfieth. Slowly, wonderingly, the citizens emerged on the streets to begin the long and exciting business of exchanging experiences and theories. The Bide-a-Wee Tearooms was doing a roaring trade by five o'clock, and all sorts of unlikely people found themselves obliged to visit Madame's for packets of pins.

Willy John Carnackit stood at his byre door, peering in.

"There y'are noo, ye wee rascal!" he wheezed. "You jist bide there noo, an' nae mair mischievousness. I'm awa tae get yer mammy tae mak the polis here a bit tea an' biscuits."

The old man hirpled away to the house. The two policemen looked past the shattered hinges of the byre door to the dusty cobwebbed emptiness within.

"He's completely bloody crackers!" hissed Simison.

"He knows his way in a fog," replied MacEachran. "Come on."

Carnackit stopped them in the porch.

"Wheesht now," he whispered, a choppy finger at his lips. "Thomasina disna' approve, so we'll hae oor wee dram here, an' bugger Churchill!"

He removed a loose board from the panelling and extracted a whisky bottle from the cavity.

"Mind," he muttered when they finished. "Be like dad!"

"Wha'?" whispered Simison as the old man put the bottle back.

"Keep mum," MacEachran whispered back.

Thomasina Carnackit — a large, competent-looking lady who wore her flowered apron well — was thankful and apologetic.

"He gets these turns," she explained while her brother was out of the room. "It's ages since he had his last one. I'm aafu sorry, boys."

"Not at all, ma'am," the Sergeant replied solidly. "It's part of the job. He certainly knows his way about the hills."

"Oh aye, but he never comes back, you see, till he's fetched, and I'm too old now to go off efter him. Forty-four years he's been doing it, ever since his best heifer went missing. It fairly turned his mind, like."

"What happened to it?" asked Simison. "The heifer, I mean."

"Rationing," said Miss Carnackit. Simison looked puzzled. "Oh, aye, young man, there was a few beasts went missing then, never doot it. Gangs fae Glasgow, so they said, though it's my suspicion it was often a bit closer to hame than that. Still, what's done's done. Noo then, Willy John, is that you in for the nicht?"

"It is so, Thomasina," Carnackit replied. "Ah doot the Bosch'll no come tonight, not in yon fog."

It took the policemen some time, afterwards, to walk back to their car, and it was past seven o'clock before Sergeant MacEachran was able to shut his blue front door behind him for the night. Catriona, in sudden gallic mood, cooked them a MegaMessages special offer *coq au vin* which, though frozen, was very tasty, extremely filling when you took the chips into account, and several notches up from the wholemeal quiche he had been dreading.

By the following morning word had gone round the town (Alistair Penicuik having brought the news from the busy world outside) that for all the fuss and bother of the day before, the Beast had been apprehended by their own Sergeant, and single-handedly at that, more or less.

MacEachran found his stock had risen overnight and, not being inclined to spoil good relations with his fellow-townsfolk for the sake of a few tedious and unimportant facts, he wisely did nothing to disabuse them. When, three days later, she received a postcard from Pierre, Catriona took the same sensible attitude.

"I see he says he's keeping his safety pin as a souvenir," observed the Sergeant when he had read it. "I don't suppose that's got anything to do with all the fuss old Fancy was after making, has it?"

"No dear, neither do I," Catriona replied. "Do you want one slice of fried bread, or two?"

3

En Fête

It is eight o'clock on the morning of the last Monday in July. From the tamed waters of the River Fieth a vapour rises, golden and ectoplasmic in the rays of the young sun. It wreathes sensuously round the arches of General Wade's bridge and, borne by the gentlest of northerly breezes, spreads across the Kirk green before settling like a grey inland sea around the damp ground-floor apartments of the Manse.

Away to the north, across the tenanted acres of Lord Margoyle's estate, the mist that rises from the picture-book lushness of the home pastures performs the same office for the immaculately gaunt lower storey of Lunie Castle, that triumph of the late Edwardian massive style. All over the Laird's demesne there is activity: pheasant pens are being inspected, vermin traps emptied, drives raked, deer hand-fed for next month's sporting slaughter.

The town of Craigfieth is, by contrast, preternaturally still. The winding length of the High Street smokes gently in the first vigorous heat of the day. Blank windows betray no hint of life within. In streets, roads, wynds, loans, drives, avenues and closes, not a foot falls. Gardens bloom unregarded, as if some offended deity were daring their bijou perfection to cease existing. For these few spellbinding moments it appears that here, on a July morning in Central Perthshire, the art of deterrence has been brought to its pinnacle and demonstrated by the silent detonation of the philosopher's stone of the military

64

mind, the ultimate weapon which leaves the works of Man unviolated while their authors are, with sudden stealth, removed from the scene . . .

. . . except that the air seems to thrill with a sort of static energy whose origin must surely lie in communal humanity: it trembles, as the Arab poet puts it, like a bird whose throat is about to be cut; as if, very soon, the turning of one tiny cog in the illimitable vastness of the universal mechanism must release some huge kinetic frenzy to consummate the day . . .

. . . as indeed it now does. A man emerges from the Greenkeeper's Cottage and traverses the links on his way to the first green. His name is Auld Murdo. Forty golfing seasons have pickled his features into a mask whose expression is half amusement, half despair. He is wearing stout brogues, and is now to be seen stamping down the worm-casts around the pin. As if by prearranged signal, the town stirs into urgent, yeasty life.

For today is the day that Homo Craigfiethans acknowledges an ancient debt to his vital origins; today's events reach back beyond Bacchanalian ritual to the seminal savagery of our common ancestors whose brief spark of carnal ceremonial lit for all time the puissant torch of human civilisation. Today is Craigfieth Shopping Gala Day.

In the breakfast room of Lunie Castle, beneath the Burne-Jonesian ceiling and enclosed by light oak panelling, from a design of the William Morris school faithfully copied by long-dead craftsmen in the Lunie workshops, sit Charles, Lord Margoyle and his daughter, the Honourable Miss Davinia Moither, known on the Estate (in a perfect simulacrum of respectful affection) as Lady Davie. She is home for a spell between liaisons.

The Laird is reading the *Daily Telegraph*, the only organ to combine to any satisfactory degree his Lordship's desire to be informed of the doings of his class with his equally strong need to be confirmed in his opinions. Indeed, this journal's use goes beyond even these accolades, for he has it secured on a stand especially designed for perusal of a large newspaper at the leisured breakfast table, and purchasable exclusively through a special offer promoted in its pages. He has a napkin tucked under his chin and is eating kidneys. His moustache bristles and twitches, though whether in harmony with his mastication or as a reaction to the intelligence he is reading, is impossible to tell: the kidneys are excellent, prepared to exactly the right degree of rubbery pungency, while the paper carries an opinion poll showing the Socialists ahead. He turns to the leader page for comfort. He is wont to wheeze and grunt when engaged, as now, in physical effort — a habit which lends his speech a certain Neanderthal quality — and these sounds, for want of competition, fill the room. His daughter eats silently, though with evident appetite. She casts a sardonic eye at the latest *Harpers and Queen*, which she has propped against the coffee pot.

Against the far wall of the room, barely visible in the opaque light that filters through the diamond-paned window, hangs (so it seems) the butler, Caskitt. In his many years of service to the family, Caskitt has acquired the servant's skill of moving without appearing to walk and this, combined with a cadaverous frame and a preference for wearing the shoulders high, has given him in advancing age the look of one permanently suspended three inches above the floor. This physical peculiarity combines now with his position at the shadowy end of the room to make him look like a trophy; the tanned hide, perhaps, of some lugubrious anthropophagus.

His Lordship swallows a last mouthful of kidney and rises, with much grunting and blowing. He is not much taller now than when sitting. The Hon Davinia flicks a page over and raises one quizzing eyebrow.

"Hrra'd better phone that damn fool secretary, get him to come over, hrrugh, damn him," says her father.

Another eyebrow is raised; the forehead, belying the years that lie upon it, is barely creased. She takes her eyes away from Lord Rodney Scroope-Harrington And Friend, Weekending At Juan Les Pins, to regard him.

"Hrrruaargh. Tradesmen's thing in the town," he says. "Hrryewknow. Gala, or whatever they call the bally thing. Asked me months ago. Meant to get Snotter to ring, hrruaargh, forgot."

Davinia understands: the eyebrows are lowered, the brow smooths again, with perfect elasticity. Taking another look at Lord Rodney (who seems to have lost weight since the divorce) she commiserates.

"Too bad about Snotter being away. Never mind, Daddy, I'll be with you."

Something in Lord Margoyle's grunt as he shuffles away seems to indicate that he would prefer the company of his factor to that of his daughter. But he is in Perth, prosecuting a tenant for taking game on his rented barley field, and cannot be with his Principal today. Someone, Lord Margoyle supposes as he descends heavily on the telephone chair, has to do the blessed talking. Damn it, though. Scrymgeour has a new fly for him to try out. Been tying it all yesterday. Perfect day wasted. Blasted tradesmen. He dials the operator.

Auld Murdo has stamped his way to the fourth green, nicknamed Simmie's Prank by the last Minister but three. Sweat is beginning to trickle down the wadis of his wryly mournful face. In guest-house dining-rooms on Lummock View, those fortunate enough to be seated by a window can see him now, performing his miniature clockwise ritual on the still bejewelled baize. Most guests have planned their holidays round the Gala. It is featured in the Scottish Tourist Board brochure.

A telephone warbles in a bungalow, its outer walls hurtfully white in the strengthening sunlight, on the executive estate off School Road. The builders have all departed, and the development still has a lunar quality about it, like the picture on a child's construction kit. In the bungalow's designer-modulated lounge area, the telephone falls silent and an answering device clicks into action as its red warning light comes on, but there is no one there to warn. For about a minute it records heavy breathing: some pre-linguistic attempt, perhaps, at appeal or threat, then switches off. There is a brief whirr, then silence. Two Tretchikoffs and a David Hockney, testaments to the reprographers' art, regard each other emptily across the living space.

A council vehicle moves fitfully along the High Street, beginning at the top. The driver stops at each street light and raises the hydraulic apparatus that bears his colleague aloft. He ties a string of flags to the lamp, whistles, is lowered and conveyed across the street to the Rod And Gun shop wall.

Inside, Mr Fingal, red-eyed, gaunt, unshaven and stupid with tiredness, does not notice the bunting-men. His fingers ache from the effort of tying, in the chloral hours, whole swarms of Auld Sneakies, Craigfieth Blues, Up-and-Unders, Lummock Supremes, Lunie Bogles and Margoyle Magnificats, all of his own invention, for the delectation of today's honoured guest. His dream of dealing direct with Nobility has spurred his slothful sinews on to dawn's first tentative blush behind the sleeping hills, visible from his back room above the shop. Now, his will striving to override the insubordinate flesh, he arranges with careful precision the centrepiece of his display, a stuffed pine-marten shot in 1915 by Lord Margoyle's acquisitive progenitor, Sir Tarquin Moither, the jute baron of Dundee. His fate hinges, he is sure, on this snarling reminder of the Laird's inheritance. He affixes the label that proves its provenance.

The bunting men move on, trailing clouds of festivity across the commercial artery of the town.

All over Craigfieth, from the private residences in the West to the council houses in the East, in living-room and parlour, kitchen and bedroom, couturiers and costumiers are at work. Nervous, clock-beating fingers thread and sew. Garys and Sheenas are tetchily commanded to breathe in, straighten up, and stop twitching. It is nine o'clock. The parade starts in one and a half hours' time.

In one of the few private houses on Lummock View, Ms Maureen O'Rourke, founder, director and choreographer of the Maureen O'Rourke Dancers, sits in the lounge of her imposing Victorian villa, a glass of Templeton's White Vin Ordinaire in one hand, a menthol cigarette in the other. In the kitchen, just within earshot should the doyenne of today's performance have any last-minute inspiration, her husband, Bruce Waddell the accountant, irons her tracksuit. She is watching her video of the Commonwealth Games opening display. She is excited, apprehensive, tense: yet underlying her nerves is a deep well of confident contentment. These days, the Youth business is a seller's market, her marriage a partnership poised to make a killing. She thinks fondly of her Bruce, out there in the kitchen with his iron, and of his supportive cleverness in clinching the Lummock Leisurewear portfolio when that nice Mr Ratsey moved into Dundas Crescent last year. Dear Brucie . . . She rewinds the tape and treats herself to another viewing.

In Madame's, Family Outfitters, the Misses Urquhart totter to and fro on their four elderly feet, putting the finishing touches to 'The World of J. M. Barrie' in the

big bay window. What a rush! Even for twenty fingers,
the sewing has been exhausting, but worth it. Together
they adjust the chiffon wings of their Mary Rose, who
displays the new O'Rourke troupe colours of pink, lime
and mauve and is attired like them in tights, leotard and
legwarmers. It is the least they can do for dear Maureen
and the nice Mr Ratsey. They have booked into Harrogate
for September on the strength of it. They twitter and sniff
in busy harmony.

The flag dispensers move on. They have reached the
light outside Sounds Good (formerly the Bonaventure
Wireless Shop) where young Hamish Ganglion is in the
storeroom preparing his equipment for dear Maureen's
girls. He is wearing a pair of reflective sunglasses bought
last week from Mr Meiklejohn. He trips on a cable and
falls over. Thank goodness he is not wearing his best
stonewashed denims.

Up the street, Miss Pitt-Holyoake at the Craft Corner regards the montage she has made, of prints of the
tasteful views of Craigfieth and District that she drew for
the Gala programme. Opposite her shop, Mr Kirkpatrick
at the DIY Centre wonders if he has got it right, wonders
whether Craigfieth is ready for his display of bidet co-
ordinates and home saunas. He wants very much to get
it right. So much is at stake: the commercial philosophy
that secured him the top diploma at business school, his
position after only six months in the town as Secretary of
Craigfieth Chamber of Commerce Gala Committee, the
mortgage on his executive bungalow . . . he wishes Mrs
Gloagie would stop shuffling about behind the till module.
For her part, his assistant wishes she was still employed to
weigh nails, wishes the shop was still Mawhinney's Ironmongers, wishes she did not have to wear a pink pastel
jacket with a badge displaying her Christian name on the
lapel and hopes her neighbours will not associate her with

her employer's unsavoury window. The telephone, one of the few remaining uncontemporary features, rings in the back. Glad of something to do, she goes to answer it, grits her dentures, forces herself to say:

"Hello! This is Eulalia of Craigfieth DIY, can I please you?"

She wonders if she should join a union, whether they would put a stop to this embarrassing nonsense. The telephone says something to her that she does not properly catch.

"Was it ordered?" she snaps, feeling quite like old times again. The instrument in her hand rudely demands to know what the hell she is talking about.

"This oil you were wanting, I don't think we have it in. Not if it's for cooking, we don't. We only do lubricants. Is it for a deep-fat fryer?"

There is a volley of tinny abuse.

"I'll fetch the proprietor," she says, and does so. "You'll have to speak to him yourself, Mr Kirkpatrick, I can't make sense of it. Something to do with some oil you've arranged for today or something, I don't know."

Mr Kirkpatrick smiles. Customer relationships was his dissertation topic.

"Thank you, Mrs Gloagie, I'll deal with the matter. Good morning sir, what seems to be your prob— Oh. No, she . . . no. Of course, yes, I . . . what? Oh. Yes. Yes, of course, right away Lord Marg— Hello? Oh."

He seems to have shrunk inside his suit; his face looks pale, flabby, featureless. A dozen remorselessly accurate quartz clocks inform him that it is well past nine o'clock. He grasps an avocado bathroom suite for support.

"Oh, Mrs Gloagie, we have a problem! That was Lord Margoyle, phoning from the Castle! He expects to be collected seemingly, and driven here for the opening."

He regards his assistant for some shocked seconds. She is too concerned with feeling grateful for not having to wish the horrible man a nice day to be of any help.

"I'll have to take the van, I suppose," he says.

Mr Kirkpatrick steps outside into blinding brightness beneath the pitiless sun and the mocking gaiety of the flags. He hears the faint strains of the Young Adventurers Kazoo Band in final rehearsal. He starts to sweat. Please God, let the van start. Let it behave itself and I promise I'll get a new one, next month when the new registration letter comes out, promise. Amen.

It is parked round the corner in the undeveloped part of his premises. Its rear doors lopsidedly promise that Rintool Scaffolding Erections will give Estimates Free and do a Quick Job. He presumes they did, since they were only in business long enough to hammer the stuffing out of the firm's transport. It has a horribly permanent look about it, as if it has squatted there for the last time on its fatigued rubber and exhausted springs. The interior smells of autumn in the woods. The key is in, daring thieves to do their worst. He turns it, foot hard down on the slack accelerator, choke yanked out. There is a wheezing noise, a flatulent roar, the sound of rust protesting against itself, and a cloud of noxious blue-black smoke. Thank you, thank you God, breathes Mr Kirkpatrick. Keep it going.

He is over the Fieth Bridge and approaching 'Haste Ye Back' before it occurs to him that someone else could be doing this, some committee member with a proper car. But he knows, as the thistle-bordered sign slips by, that this burden is his to bear alone. It is his test, his knight's vigil. He must see it through.

Behind him, in a slowly clearing haze of unburnt fuel, events are taking their course. The line of flags has reached the Greengrocer's, where Mr Smellie is adding the last parsley trimmings to his model of the Wallace Memorial.

The Maureen O'Rourke Dancers are beginning to assemble in the Community Centre on Logie Baird Avenue.

Safe in the privacy of his dispensary, Mr Mieklejohn sits before a mirror brought from home that morning. He has trimmed and combed his beard and brought its ravaged hairs, torn and plucked over the weeks by the anxieties of office, into a neat, groomed point. The glass reflects the matt, porous finish of a face closely razored (forby the chin) and a head of tinted grey hair. He files his nails carefully with an emery board abstracted from the carousel in his shop while Miss Reekie wasn't looking. Her basilisk eye had been resting instead on a German tourist couple in search of prophylaxis. He is professionally obliged to sell them, as he is always telling Mr Bullock, though goodness knows (he sometimes thinks) one look from Miss Reekie and the customer's need would surely evaporate upon the instant. Still, he reflects, it has been a great month for tourists, and perhaps German campers at the Glenlummock Visitor Centre do not comprehend the Reekie Look. Whatever the reason, it has been a great season for Planned Parenthood Requisites, too. And to crown it he, Aeneas Mieklejohn, as Chairman of the Gala Committee, will present Lord Margoyle — a name synonymous with Central Perthshire — to his fellow citizens in — he checks the time — an hour and twenty-five minutes' time.

He adjusts his bow tie again, noting, not for the first time, the happy felicity with which its design, white polka dots on a green field, tones with the restrained pink of his best dress shirt. Today will be a triumph.

Deep in the heart of the Wallace Memorial, a courgette stirs. The edifice collapses.

Mrs Gloagie does not think to telephone anyone with her employer's alarming news. Instead she brews coffee in the demonstrator appliance on the central merchandising console, and daydreams of bygone days, of fork handles, and sugar soap by the quarter stone, when screws came from Messrs Guest, Keen and Nettlefold and the long, brown, wooden counter was grimed mellow by a century of retail hardware. She sighs as she waits for the coffee to belch its way to percolated climax in its secret cave of steelette and tinted perspex.

Mr Kirkpatrick drives on, grim and sleek in the Morris van, past the long, straight beech hedges that line the road to Lunie. A thin trail of powdered metal marks the final dissolution of the silencer. He roars and farts between twin rows of outraged topiary, the embarrassed centre of a universe of offended propriety. He feels Nemesis close at hand. Thou fool, thy soul, he thinks, but cannot complete the quotation. One rear door swings open. He does not notice it.

Mr Haq has escaped from a house full of female relatives to the calm of his Emporium, where he stands behind the counter smoking a small cheroot. The fuss these women make! But he is a proud man. For Benazir, fruit of his loins, is to be crowned Gala Queen and — if the donkey cart comes as promised from Glenlummock — will parade in state through the streets of his adopted town. Nor is this a chance honour, for she was elected to sovereignty by an overwhelming majority of her fellow High School pupils, as is the ancient custom. To Allah then be praise, for a dutiful family and for raising him in the estimation of the Unbelievers. Tonight he will write to his cousins in Paisley and scald their hearts with envy. He allows himself a second cheroot on the strength of this happy thought.

At the Community Centre Maureen O'Rourke arrives in her new Sierra, with dear Brucie at the wheel, to give her girls a final work-out. She has the master tape, and a cassette recorder; the Ganglion boy will have the p.a. equipment set up by now in the Project minibus, provided by the MSC. She reflects, not for the last time, that it is an ill wind . . . Some three hundred yards away, in the Drill Hall on John Knox Avenue, the Boys' Brigade is polishing its drill. Boy soldiers of the Reformed God they stamp and wheel under the stern, approving gaze of Earl Haig in daguerrotype and the more benign though no less satisfied eyes of Mr Maxwell, ex-Headmaster, Commander-in-Chief and trusty seneschal of the virile morality of Craigfieth.

Auld Murdo tramples out the eighteenth green. It is done. The Gala Tournament, ladies versus gentlemen, may commence. He stumps back to the clubhouse, darkly sweating beneath the sun's oppressive gong.

From the window of his upstairs study, known to his wife as the Heights of Abraham, the Rev Gilleasbuig MacAndrew looks out at the sweltering Lummocks beyond the town. Their outline is thickened, distorted; some summer's brew of dark heat is being stirred in the westward air. He bends his head again to the composition of a Gala Blessing.

Mr Kirkpatrick's face is hot and thundery. Sweat oozes down below the collar of his silk polyester shirt to collect in volcanic pools in armpits and navel. His crotch burns wetly. The driver's window is jammed shut; the fresh air vents belch foetid gas into his lap. Only the open nearside back door, unknown to him, saves him from heatstroke. Just in time he spies the East Lodge of Lunie, finds second somewhere in the hopeless porridge of the gearbox, and turns in with a noise like the damned in torment.

In the stable yard at the rear of Lunie Castle, Lord Margoyle improves the shining hour by breaking in his new rod, manufactured exclusively for him to a design by Commander Mudie, of Chilbolton. It sings and hisses in the cool air of the shaded yard, placing Scrymgeour's new fly with perfect precision, cast after cast. Despite the shade, his Lordship is sweating inside his tweeds. His choleric features are flushed carmine; beads of moisture quiver in his moustache. One more cast, and he had better see if Davinia is fit to go out . . . then, as the casting arm is poised at the moment of inertia before the forward flick, his attention is distracted by what sounds like a controlled explosion to the east. Too late, he tries to halt the process. His cast winds itself once, twice, three times round the telephone cable that runs from the gamekeeper's office to the Castle wall, leaving its small feathered barb hanging an inch above the noble head. Scrymgeour, who has been watching from behind a stable arch, is suddenly afflicted with a violent coughing fit.

Lord Margoyle wheezes into articulacy.

"Ughaaarghn't stand there, damn you! Do something man, see to it!"

The ghillie composes his sardonic monkey features in a pretence of deferential scrutiny.

"Ah doot wu'll hauf tae cut it, Lordship."

The chill stable yard becomes, suddenly, a furnace.

"Cut it? Gaarughron'tchew realise what that is? Hr-rantsmy best Hardy's tapered line, hrrrontchewdare go cuttin' it, hear? Ghrrroangetsome menan get it down! Hrruddyfools, all of 'em."

His Lordship's last remark is addressed to the rear windows of the Castle. Must be ten o'clock, at least: time for a stiffener. The Laird of Lunie thunders off to find Caskitt. Scrymgeour makes his way, without undue haste, to the workshops. He clicks his long yellow teeth, a habit he has acquired for such occasions as these, when thoughts must die unspoken.

Half a mile away, Mr Kirkpatrick wonders if he has taken a wrong turning.

It is ten o'clock in Craigfieth. Police notices direct traffic away from the High Street, through Lunie Road, Fleming Way and Logie Baird Avenue, and back on to the main highway. Sergeant MacEachran has supervised the setting-out of bollards. Opposite the Manse, on the spot where the Mercat Cross used to be before the Improvement Scheme, there is a stand. It has been erected by the Lions and the Round Table, with floral trimmings by the WRI and overall supervision by the Rotarians on behalf of the Gala Committee. Craigfiethans have always prided themselves on their community spirit.

At the other end of the town, opposite the abattoir, the Gala Queen's transport waits miserably in the congealing heat. Mr Cyril Bullock leaves his choirs of redemption in the Gospel Hall to make his traditional self-appointed tour of inspection round the shop displays. He finds them satisfactory, on the whole, though Mr Smellie seems to be having trouble with his, and Mr Haq's is vulgar, a raucous cacophony of Empire wares. He appears to have crammed his windows with one example each of his vast stock. Girls' tights drape tastelessly round a pocket TV of Near Eastern origin. Still, Mr Bullock charitably supposes, these people cannot be expected to know better. He decides, after a while, that Mr Kirkpatrick's display is hygienic in its intent and therefore worthy of approval. Mr Bullock is brimming over with the milk of magnanimity this festal morning.

Inside the shop he sees what appears to be an agitated conference between Mrs Gloagie, Mr Meiklejohn and Mr Glencairn, the baker. But it is ten-fifteen: no time to investigate now. He hurries back to his tin tabernacle. Little knots of licentious and Jezebel-shorted tourists drift aimlessly along the street, wondering why the shops are not open.

For the third time in five minutes, Mrs Gloagie tells Mr Meiklejohn of her employer's mission. The pharmacist tugs and knots his beard into fibrous hanks. Mr Glencairn's septuagenarian features register detached, divine comprehension. He is the Father of the Gala, as Craigfieth has come to know and cherish it. He is ready, as always, to serve and to save.

Mr Meiklejohn is distraught and plaintive.

"But we've never — never — been expected to provide transport — isn't that right, Mr Glencairn? — why, even Sir Alec drove himself, busy as he was at the time with being Prime Minister. This is quite unheard of, quite . . . unprecedented — you'll agree with me there, Mr Glencairn? Yes — quite. And he took that old van, you say? Let's hope and pray he parks it out of sight. But whatever can have happened to them? The parade starts in — good gracious! — fifteen minutes. What are we going to do, Mrs Gloagie? Mr Glencairn?"

The patriarch's moment has arrived, the time to bestow his quota of lofty patronage. He lays a blotchy hand on Mr Meiklejohn's thin shoulder.

"Dinna fouter, man. Leave it to me."

Mr Kirkpatrick stands in the stable yard by the open rear door of the van, his three-piece suit rumpled and dark with perspiration, in an agony of indecisive urgency. There seems to be no one around, and no obvious place to seek out his quarry. He feels transfixed, uncomfortable. Someone, somewhere, he is sure, is laughing at him.

A hand-made boot scrapes on the cobbles. Lord Margoyle, his rheumy eyes adjusting to the gloom, sees the awkward figure of Mr Kirkpatrick and registers the word 'scaffolding' on the van door. He draws the obvious conclusion.

"Hrrraaah! Hrryew the chap I sent for?"

Mr Kirkpatrick has never met aristocracy before, but he knows it when he sees it.

"Good day, Your Lordship," he says, bowing slightly. "I came as quickly as I could. I hope," he adds, feeling some sort of conversational pleasantry is required of him, "I find you well?"

"Wha'? Hrrruaaargh! Whasa'? Get on with what you came for, blast you! Simple enough job, dammit, but don't damage the wire, y'hear?"

The driving force behind Central Perthshire's first Homeware Superstore steps back in alarm and turns to seek support, moral or physical, where there is none. His sensation of nightmare is heightened when he feels himself tugged peremptorily, invisibly, by the lapel as his bellowing tormentor demands to know what the hell he thinks he's playing at. A voice behind him, horribly close, turns his blood to liquid ice. It is seductive, menacing, lethally languid, caressing his manly parts with silken claws unsheathed.

"Tool erections, free quick job," it slithers. "My God, what a way to advertise. Are you Mister Tool himself?"

"Hruddyfool should have got it up by now, should be on the job," says Lord Margoyle.

"Please Daddy, give poor Mister Tool a chance," pleads the Honourable Davinia. "I've only just got here.

Oh look, he's hooked!" she giggles, and tweaks his jacket from behind, like a kitten playfully teasing a dying shrew.

Mr Kirkpatrick — trapped, terrified and suspended — begins to moan, very softly. He hears himself say, "Gala Committee. Craigfieth. You rang, my Lord, take you, opening."

Then he sees the owner of the siren voice.

She is tall, blonde, elegant. She appears to be wearing a sort of belted nightdress, and is smoking a very long panatella. As she bends to attend to the hook in his lapel, cruel Fate conspires to fix his captive gaze on the space below her throat . . . in an instant, he is a child again: it is nearly Christmas, there is a sharp oily smell and high on the wonderful tree, out of reach, fragile and forbidden, are two glass globes, magically, invisibly pendant. . . .

"I'm coming with you, Mister Tool," she whispers, and burns through the Hardy's tapered line with the glowing end of her cigar. Mr Kirkpatrick is, in one sense, free.

"Aaah," he says.

The Honourable Davinia tittups away, laughing skittishly: she is thirty-five but thinks she can get away with it. She is right.

"What time is Daddy's Do?" she asks.

Mr Kirkpatrick strives to reassemble the fragments of his shattered sense of responsibilty.

"Eleven o'clock — well, that's the opening, but there's the parade first, at ten-thirty. We're supposed to be there for that."

It is twenty-five past ten.

"Then put your foot down, and thank God Daddy never wears anything but tweeds. Come on. I'll sit on the handbrake."

And she does. Lord Margoyle, speechless and apoplectic, is installed somehow in the mouldy passenger seat. Releasing the brake, Mr Kirkpatrick's hand is forced to encounter thigh, and the curve of one firm and splendid buttock. He shudders in tune with the dissonant engine.

They depart, watched only by the dyspeptic Scrymgeour, lurking in the shadow of his archway. He manages, after reflection, a venomous smile. At least, he thinks, that'll be his lads safe for a week or two. He smells rain in the offing, and the distinct possibility of trading his news for a dram in Caskitt's pantry.

The order of events in Craigfieth's Gala ceremony is one of life's immutabilities. Whatever the innovations from year to year, it is always: Parade — Speeches — Blessing — Opening — Crowning — Display — Shops. Mr Glencairn knows this, because he instituted it, forty years ago, in a bleak spring of rationing, shortages, slack trade and cruel weather. The Misses Urquhart came to him one afternoon — it was early closing day — as he and Mrs Glencairn were pinning nappies on the line. They took it in turns to be tearful, and to tell him that all they had sold that week was a yard and a half of corduroy, for patching, and a packet of pins and what did he, as Chairman of the Chamber of Commerce, think was to be done? When they left, sniffing in syncopation, the nappies had frozen. He sat up half the night thinking about what was to be done: thus was born the Craigfieth Shopping Gala.

Now he sits, at half past ten on this steamy July morning, on the VIPs' podium. On his left are Mr Meiklejohn, Mr McMurtry from the Scottish Amiable and Providential Bank, Maureen O'Rourke and the Rev MacAndrew; on his right are two empty chairs, Mr Maxwell and Miss Pollack, president of the Lummock Area WRI. The two empty chairs are for Lord Margoyle and Mr Kirkpatrick.

A message to wait for further instructions has been sent to the other end of town, where the Gospel Choir, the Young Adventurers Kazoo Band, the Kipplerigg Distillery Pipers and Miss Benazir Haq, resplendent and bridal in a tartan sari, all wonder what is going on.

Mr Glencairn's hour is at hand. He rises, blows on the microphone like they do at British Legion concerts, and begins:

"Fellow Craigfiethans and Visitors, welcome to our fortieth Gala. As I was saying to my wife this morning, it don't seem a day too long." (Knowing laughter.) "You will all know why we are here today — we are here to enjoy ourselves." (Restrained cheers.) "But, while we are waiting for our honoured guest to arrive and open the proceedings —" (Here he glances round the faces tilted up to him, at the O'Rourke Dancers and the Boys' Brigade who line the street on either side. He is looking for signs of alarm, hostility, outrage at the flaunting of tradition: he sees none. There is some puzzlement, a few blank faces, but the general expression is one of expectant complacency. He continues.) "As I say, while we are waiting, let us cast our minds back across the years to our beloved town's first Gala. It was the spring of 1947, though you could hardly call it a spring . . ."

The Honourable Davinia has her arm behind Mr Kirkpatrick's neck, her right buttock nestled firmly against his left thigh, and her legs spread wantonly on either side of the gear shift. A nagging presence in the corner of his vision, which he is attempting to clamp stoically on the highway, those twin breathtaking miracles of female nature are quivering fleshily . . . She is fiddling with his right ear and pouring the most appalling confidences into his left:

". . . anyway, Daddy was footing the bill, so I went along with it. Well, it was all very soul-baring and breast-beating and naturally I enjoyed it enormously and, at the end of it all, what Dr Schockemohle said I had was a lycophobic sexual Weltanschauung, not nymphomania at all like Rodney said. I just can't screw fat men, that's all. Well, that explained everything, I mean with Rodney it was too utterly *hopeless*, that great heavy belly squashing down all the time, even riding on the top deck wasn't much better, you still saw it all wobbling about. So we divorced after that, of course. I think he understands. Since then I've — well," she sighs, "I've done what I could, but honestly it's been pretty awful for me you know, I mean the men round here think a clitoris is something a caterpillar turns into for the winter. Daddy doesn't mind, of course, he thinks it's all part of being the great feudal aristo, doing what you like with who you like, when you like. Pathetic really, but it keeps him happy, kicking the tenants around, being beastly to Snotter, and shoving his hand up Mrs Axelrod's skirt when he comes into the kitchen with something he's shot. Little did I know" — here she nibbles his earlobe and inhales with alarming pneumatic effect — "my Fairy Godmother was sending me nice, tall, *thin* Mr Tool. I knew the moment I saw you we would get on darling, and you've got to get on to get off, as Nanny used to say . . ."

On her left, the Laird is blowing stertorously, his fingers in his large, fungoid ears. Of the remaining two functioning pairs, only Mr Kirkpatrick's, through lickings and ticklings, registers uncomprehendingly the harshly altered note of the engine.

". . . so I said to them, ladies and gentlemen, fellow Craigfiethans, I said, 'What's good for trade, is good for the town.' Now you mind that one, you young ones, mony a mickle maks a muckle, and that's what made Craigfieth what it is today . . . And someone said, 'What do you mean, Mr Glencairn?' — of course I was just a strippit youngster then, just turned thirty, and I wasn't expected to speak up — and I said — and I remember the words I used as clearly as it were yesterday sennicht — I said . . . "

The Rev MacAndrew risks a surreptitious glance at his pocket watch: ten forty-five . . . The sky over the golf course has turned a sullen cobalt.

". . . and that's as true today as it was then, Now the parade that year, this is 1948 I'm on to now, of course, I mind it well, my, what a bonny sight it was . . ."

The van roars on, an outrageous blot on all that agrestic prettiness. Inside, conditions are becoming quite uncomfortable. Davinia squirms deliciously on her vibrating perch.

"A lady could lose her honour in your van, Mr Tool," she giggles. "Do you know, when I was an innocent little girl I thought a maidenhead was something they gave you when you got married, like a silver cup. It was grandfather who put me right on that, he came to tuck me in one night and I was —"

There is an appalling noise of mechanical apocalypse: the van slews wildly across the road and back again, to the sound of grinding, and wrenching metal. It comes to rest abruptly in the middle of the road.

The Honourable Davinia has contrived to be flung across Mr Kirkpatrick, with her head in his lap. For a while he thinks he hears the vehicle still self-destructing, then realises it is only Lord Margoyle. Something is happening to Mr Kirkpatrick that causes his reaction to the catastrophe to be rather less than serious . . . the source of this unruliness disengages her face from his trousers, smoothes her hair and observes that they had better have a look under the bonnet. Mr Kirkpatrick finds himself ejected from the van as his lordship is hauled across, without verbal protest, to sit behind the wheel. The shopkeeper reflects that Lord Margoyle's daughter is obviously used to putting her men where she wants them.

The bonnet opens to reveal an engineer's hell. Swift vapours rise to defame the summer air; thicker, oily emanations coil and fawn round hot metal and melted rubber. Somewhere there is hissing, and the sound of terminal collapse. Mr Kirkpatrick reaches out a speculative hand, but it is arrested.

"Don't get dirty," she whispers, still holding it. "Not there, anyway."

He notices, too late to do anything about it even if by now he still wanted to, that her dress is open to the waist. She places his hand inside it. Slowly, inexorably, his other hand rises to join its mate. It is better than Christmas. Such firm unyielding wholeness, such . . . such *buoyancy* . . .

He gives himself over to lickerish thoughts and Babylonian imagery. He does not take his hands away until he hears the police siren.

"And that brings me to 1958. The BBs, under the able command of one Captain Maxwell" (widespread if somewhat weary applause; it hurts, after a while, to clap with sweaty palms) "paraded a likeness of the Russian Sputnik and although some of the aerials came off when it started to rain — just outside Brown's newsagents, if I remember rightly, where Mr Haq's shop is now — it was a most commendable effort. The Gala that year was opened by our MP, Sir Ashley Foutret, who unfortunately is unable to be with us today owing to pressing commitments in the Turks and Caicos Islands. I well remember his speech that day . . ."

Not everybody enjoys Mr Glencairn's robust constitution, or the benefit of the striped canopy on the podium. Among the tons of sweltering teenage flesh that line the

High Street, some of Craigfieth's youth begins to wilt. The Rev MacAndrew is fast asleep.

There are two policemen. The tall dark one unbends from his inspection of what is left of the engine.

"Next time you go out for a wee spin, sir, I suggest you put some oil in first," he says. "They go better for a wee drop of oil."

Then he starts to look at the tyres.

His colleague, the short red-haired one, is attempting to offer to Lord Margoyle (who still has his fingers in his ears) the business end of an intoximeter. Its liquid crystal display leaps gaily up and down the alcoholic scale as if in eager anticipation of the Laird's malted breath.

Mr Kirkpatrick wonders, irreverently, how they will get a urine sample out of him. His Davinia stands close behind him, making it difficult to think straight-faced thoughts.

Lord Margoyle adjusts himself at last to his circumstances. He unplugs his ears, examines the fingertips for secretions, and fixes the constable with a glare of fishy malevolence.

"Hrrurraaargh. Shouldn't think your Chief Constable wants to hear about this bally nonsense next time he shoots at Lunie."

His daughter steps forward, smiling sweetly.

"I don't think we've been introduced: Constable, this is my father, Lord Margoyle of Lunie Castle; Daddy, this is Constable — I'm sorry, I don't think I caught your name."

"Aren't the Scottish police wonderful," she observes, five minutes later.

The van has been manoeuvred on to the grass verge. The Regional Road Squad Landrover, having room only for one passenger, has departed with its noble load in the direction of Craigfieth.

She shimmers to the rear of the van and opens the back doors.

"What a naughty, thoughtful Tool!" she croons, loosening her belt. "A mattress, all ready."

Mr Kirkpatrick stumbles round to look. "It's awful dirty," he mumbles. "You'll spoil your dress."

"To hell with the dress," she says, and shows him what she means before flowing, like sinuous honey, into the van. Something brushes Mr Kirkpatrick's fly. The rest of him follows.

Miss Pollack, at the end of the platform, is the first to spot the Landrover as, headlamps ablaze and blue light flashing, it breasts the hump of Fieth Bridge. She nudges Mr Maxwell, whose thoughts are elsewhere. He leans across her, sees the vehicle pull up at the bollards and disgorge a round, volcanic personage in a tweed jacket and plus fours. He leans the other way, across the vacant chairs, waits for a pause between 1963 (Sir Alec Douglas-Home) and 1964 (Moira Anderson) and hisses a message to the Honorary Life President of the Craigfieth Chamber of Commerce.

The sudden silence startles the Minister awake. It is precisely eleven o'clock.

In the moments that follow, two fateful things occur. First, Mr Meiklejohn nods across the heads of the throng to young Darren Mawhinney, this year's High School athletics champion, who is standing on the edge of the crowd. He sprints off to relay the message that the parade is to begin. Secondly, Maureen O'Rourke's digital watch (which, though accurate to a quarter of a second per century, is precisely half a minute slow) bleeps twice. Her reaction is Pavlovian. She has imagined the sound too many times for her brain to change its prearranged reaction now. Hamish Ganglion, instructed to watch her

every move from the back of the minibus, has been
obeying orders for the last half hour. She mimes the
pressing of a key, he disappears, and a moment later the
Maureen O'Rourke Dancers are lumbering into action to
the strains of 'Modern Girl', relayed through four loudspeakers. 'Shape Up '87 — A Synchronised Work-Out'
has begun.

Unseen except by the platform party, the Gala Queen
appears at the bend in the street, followed by the Gospel
Choir giving an ambulatory rendering of 'Amazing
Grace' to bagpipe and kazoo accompaniment. Seeing the
energetic rears of the Maureen O'Rourke Dancers, some
of the pipers, kazoo players and choristers are inclined to
fall silent and halt. But they do not. The ass, veteran of
ten Galas, knows his business. He plods remorselessly on,
drawing the Queen's tumbril behind him and, perforce,
the entire parade, bags tumescent, kazoos fortissimo and
lungs swollen with loud hosannas.

The donkey, encouraged, breaks into a trot.

Benazir Haq, suddenly and terribly alone, looks wildly
round. Her eyes are wide with mute appeal.

The parade quickens its pace to keep up. The Boys'
Brigade forms ranks to greet it.

The eyes of the donkey gleam fanatically, with the
obsession of a true zealot.

Things start to get noticeably compressed. Screams
issue from some of the younger and more impressionable
Dancers. The donkey becomes excited. The crowd of
townsfolk and sightseers, for want of anywhere else to
go, is forced against the podium. Above them, only Mr
Glencairn, Mr McMurtry and Maureen O'Rourke witness
the impending mayhem; Mr Maxwell, Mr Meiklejohn,
the Rev MacAndrew and Miss Pollack are otherwise
engaged, trying to haul the prickly bulk of Lord Margoyle
up the rear steps.

At last, the honoured guest is installed in his chair, staring emptily at the scene of confusion below. Over the loudspeakers, 'Modern Girl' has given way to 'The Birdie Song'; the kazoos, pipes and choristers have moved on to the twenty-third psalm. This has an unsettling effect upon the dancers, impeded as they are by the Boys' Brigade, which is attempting to form an honour guard for the Gala Queen. Only the donkey, with a race memory of indignities far worse than these, plods correctly on, carving a straight swathe through the performers and forcing the spectators into a still smaller space. The podium lurches alarmingly.

Overhead, the sky turns the colour of a bruised avocado.

The long plateau of silence is broken at last.

"What's your name, Mister Tool?"

The young entrepreneur swallows and shuts his eyes. This is it.

"Wayne," he mutters. He opens his eyes to gauge the effect this has had. "Mam was fond of the pictures."

She turns him over.

"Guess a man's gotta do," she coos.

Open warfare has broken out at the top end of the High Street. Secure in the knowledge that each is discharging his or her appointed duty, the artistes carry on performing while fighting for space to do it in. Only the Boys' Brigade has broken ranks; its members simply fight amongst themselves. The donkey quietly chews some gladioli from the WRI display. The Gala Queen looks tearfully round.

Miss Pollack stares ahead, her hands in her lap tearing a little lace handkerchief into halves, quarters, eighths ... Mr Maxwell and Maureen O'Rourke have covered their eyes but are peeping through, nonetheless. Mr Glencairn is addressing himself on the subject of

1969, and the Girl Guides' lunar module. Lord Margoyle appears to be in some sort of coma.

The Rev MacAndrew, refreshed perhaps after his little nap, decides the time has come to put an end to this horrible travesty. He rises to his feet and spreads his arms wide, black beneath the bruised heavens, signalling silence. It descends immediately, like a blessed golden rain: the pipes moan away to nothing, the kazoos fall quiet, the Gospel Choir gives up and the tape is stopped.

The crisis is past.

"O God in Heaven pour forth we beseech Thee Thy blessings on this our Gala day and send us forth to dwell in prosperous content according to Thy Will in the Name of Thy Son our Lord and Master Jesus Christ Amen," booms the Minister. At 'Amen' he kicks Maureen O'Rourke on the ankle; she nudges Mr McMurtry, who performs a frantic mime for the benefit of Mr Meiklejohn. The pharmacist understands: he grovels under his chair and reappears with the Gala Crown, its billon magnificence burnished to a dazzling intensity. He passes it with a whispered message to Lord Margoyle, while making expressive eye signals to Miss Haq. She is assisted from her cart by two muscular Germans, who are glad to make some connexion with sane behaviour at last, and ascends in oriental tartan splendour the steps that lead her to the platform. Still under hissed instruction, Charles Stuart Bonar Moither, Lord Margoyle the Laird of Lunie, raises the crown. His perception of the scene is suddenly acute.

"Bugger me!" he roars. "It's a damn darkie!"

The Queen and her Peer are at once hideously lit in electric blue and the fabric of the sky is torn asunder; a moment later water falls and, in an instant levelling wind, the striped canopy is blown back. The platform party is exposed to the full force of the pathetic fallacy in action.

Down the street, Mr Smellie stands, unbelieving, in his shop window, ankles awash with vegetable ruin.

"Darling!"
"Mmm."
"Everything moved!"
"Mmm."
"Did everything move for you?"
"Mmm. I think we're being towed away."

Mr Kirkpatrick raises himself, as far as he is able, to peer through the strip of windscreen visible above the van's plywood divider. He sees the back of a lorry whose cab bears a board with the words 'Duff Rescue'. He groans, subsides, and feels himself slipping backwards. His feet hit cold metal which resists for a second, then yields to his pressure. He has a wild glimpse of blurred tarmac before he is caught and hauled back inside.

"Darling Tooly!" she breathes. "What will you think of next?"

He groans again. Ecstasy is one thing, but he left his shoes and socks outside.

The rain pours solidly down on the deserted street. Already it has sluiced away the puddles of lime, pink and purple dye that mark the exodus, like a stampede of rotting carcases, of the Maureen O'Rourke Dancers. There is trouble ahead for Lummock Leisurewear.

In the cramped interior of the Rod And Gun shop huddle Lord Margoyle, Mr Meiklejohn, the Rev MacAndrew and Mr McMurtry. The Laird's sodden tweeds steam continuously, reminding the banker of a compost heap. Behind the counter, Mr Fingal gathers little perspex boxes and spreads them out. In time, even his Lordship's attention is attracted by this activity. No one hears the shop door open.

"Your Lordship," says Mr Fingal, his voice quavering a little, "permit me to show you these."

His blue eyes blaze out from their augered sockets as the Laird submits his craftsmanship to breathy examination.

Lord Margoyle looks up at last, one eye glaring at the shopkeeper.

"What the hell are you doing with Scrymgeour's flies?" he demands.

"Making them for him to palm off on you of course, didn't you know?" asks a female voice, cool and immaculate.

The Honourable Davinia Moither stands inside the door. Her cheeks are a little flushed beneath the eyes but otherwise she is elegant, crisp and pure in a spotless white dress done demurely up to her slim throat.

Her father stamps towards the door, then turns to address Mr Fingal.

"Hruaaargh. Send to the Castle from now on, hear? See Snotter."

Then to Mr Meiklejohn: "Where's y'car? Eh? Hrrayre-syer*caaargh*, damn you?"

The pharmacist scuttles out after them. Mr Fingal gazes up at the plaster trout on the wall, his lips moving in a silent *Nunc Dimittis*.

Somewhere in Perthshire, Mr Kirkpatrick stops to inspect his feet, finds them puffed and purple, and does not care. He leans into a hedge, face tilted to the wan sun, and relaxes. Nothing matters. Mrs Gloagie can run the shop. Mrs Gloagie can have the shop, for all he cares. He can always sell it, or give it away, and be wanted for himself alone. Oh, Davinia, Davinia . . . they will open a boutique, a nouvelle cuisine restaurant . . . or sail away to an island somewhere and make love under the naked foreign sun . . . he could run Lunie as a Health Hydro. He can do anything now. Pastel fogs of sex and enterprise coax his brain to willing reverie.

Bathed, refreshed and energised, Lady Davie stands at her high turret window looking out at the lands of Lunie, cleansed and glazed in pale sunlight. They complement her mood exactly. She feels restored; she has laid again the ghost of Rodney. She smiles. Such an apt word.

Havers, the under-gamekeeper, walks towards the covers carrying a string of poisoned bait for the vermin. She shudders: what exciting hips the boy has!

Her lover floats on, keeping the Lummocks to his right, vaguely Craigfiethwards, where his bungalow kingdom and the new *Management Today* await him.

His answering machine is waiting too, with its message of breathy obscenity.

Composure settles on the town. The bollards are re-moved, the soggy pagoda dismantled and its floral detritus tidied away. The reassuring hiss of traffic returns to the High Street. In the shops, tills ring, bleep and rattle. Craigfieth has not forgotten the true Gala spirit. Raffle tickets are given free with every purchase over £5; Mr Smellie's greens are down in price. In the battle of the sexes on the links, the ladies are two holes up: Auld Murdo's labour has not been in vain. His morning heelmarks glisten on every green.

The doyenne of the Maureen O'Rourke Dancers has gone to bed with a headache and a stiff gin. Downstairs, dear Brucie and the nice Mr Ratsey discuss business over the remainder of the bottle.

Only in the office of the Duff Garage is there serious disquiet. There, Mr Duff and Mr Meiklejohn stare perplexedly at the footwear of the Gala Secretary, and wonder what has happened to the rest of him.

4

The Judgment

The Parish Kirk of Craigfieth dates, as the *Tourist Guide to the Lummocks** will tell you, from the mid-nineteenth century. A curt footnote adds that "a tower was built in 1887", a bald statement of mean pedantic fact that goes no way to giving the merest hint of its exciting genesis.

In fact, this addition to the House of God was planned as far back as 1843 as a balm to salve the wounds of Craigfieth's Disruption, when the then Minister, the Rev Dr Claymore Biggar, departed with the greater half of his flock to defend the faith in nearby Dalglumph. The three Kirk Elders who remained resolved upon the spot to build a tower, not (as Apothecary Meiklejohn, great-granduncle of the present pharmacist, remarked when launching the Appeal at a Rutting Dinner of the Ancient Order of Stags) as a monument to the unhappy schism, but as "a soul-inspiring bodying forth of the beliefs and affections of the True Lichts o' Lummock Vale".

Apothecary Meiklejohn's address was received with fervid approbation; a Fund was instantly set up, Trustees appointed and the first £89 17s ½d pledged by the end of the week.

The balance, however, took somewhat longer to accumulate and it was not until 1879 that the edifice was

---

* Pub. Craigfieth, Duncruddie Mains and District Tourist Assoc., 1964; reprinted twice.

accomplished, by which time the moving spirit behind the scheme had been seven years dead, of a seizure brought on by arguing the vices of State Connexion with a traveller in nostrums for the liver, from Dunfermline.

The Trustees engaged Messrs Bouche and Grothe, the celebrated engineers of their age, and the dedication ceremony was performed by the Rev Proctor on a bright July Saturday, before a crowd of several hundred townsfolk and visitors. Among the strangers at this gathering was the Poet and Tragedian Mr Wm. McGonagall, then but two years into his vocation. The first stanza of his celebratory Ode —

> Beautiful Presbyterian Kirk Tower by the wat'ry Fieth!
> To sing in your praises I vouchsafe I would lief,
> For thou art foremost among the pleasant erections of the present day,
> And this asseveration there's few can gainsay.

— is but one of many.

The tower fell down in 1887.

Once again, the true feelings of many were aptly expressed by Mr McGonagall:

> Beautiful Presbyterian Kirk Tower by the wat'ry Fieth!
> Alas! I must confess that it fills me with grief
> To report that this fine structure has completely crumbled away
> Though no lives were lost, I am glad to say.

The tragedy occurred late one Friday night, which accounts for the lack of casualties. Its cause was never fully established: some asserted that the clockworks (a late addition to the scheme by generous benefaction of A Lady, widely suspected to be the late Lady Portia Campbell of Lunie) had proved too massive for the structure to bear, forby its buttresses, while others pointed to the fact of a brisk north-west wind that night, scything down from the Lummocks on to the unprotected Kirk. A third faction, much given at that time to shows of theological orthodoxy such as the eschewing of hats on the Sabbath Day, reminded as many of their townsfellows as would listen that they had always said that no good could come of such a thing.

Messrs Bouche and Grothe, unfortunately, could not be found to make good the damage (it was for them a double blow: they had suffered a setback in Dundee two years previously) so the replacement was ordered to a design of Messrs Barlow and Arrol. Happily, the Session had taken the precaution of insuring the old tower with a reputable firm of ecclesiastical underwriters (unlike Pastor Manders they did not presume to take God's protective grace for granted) and the new one proceeded apace, clock not excluded — although because it did not form part of the original policy it had to be paid for out of the public pocket, a feat quickly accomplished thanks, once again, to a distaff of the great Clan Campbell, who always have been great ones for monuments.

McGonagall completed his triptych with the dedication of the New Tower in August 1887:

> Beautiful New Presbyterian Kirk Tower by the wat'ry Fieth!
> My heart fills with gladness to report that on the 15th
> Day of August, a bonny Summer's day*
> You were declared open, which made many folk gay,
> And I think nobody need have the least dismay.

* In fact it rained steadily all day (see Col. Mudie's Weather Reports 1876-1891) but the Poet used his Licence.

All three of the Poet's Addresses were set in type by Mr Ariel Chisholm of the Craigfieth Printing Works, though never formally published owing to an unfortunate misunderstanding regarding monies. A rare copy resides to this day in the Reading Room of Craigfieth Museum.

If anybody did have the least dismay, it was proved misplaced. The tower withstood the Great Storm of 1892, the Great Frost of 1893 and the Great Flood of 1894, when the waters of the Fieth blasphemed the Kirk Green and lapped the very foundations of the church itself. After that, no one doubted that the tower was a permanent feature of the town as well as the tallest one, being some ten feet higher even than the fire station's practice tower. which was built in 1967 on the site of the Farmers' Supply Stores after it burned down and its proprietor retired to the Canaries.

The clock was the only disappointment; it stopped at 2.50 on the 3rd July 1928 and resisted all attempts to get it going again. Estimates for its repair and renovation were sought on three occasions but proved most discouraging. The townsfolk got used to it after a while. Only successive Ministers felt a twinge of discontent at flippant remarks in the Kirk Visitors' Book anent honey and tea.

To mark the 100th Anniversary of the Craigfieth Tower, the Rev Gilleasbuig MacAndrew was planning something special. To be a little more accurate: it had been impressed on the Minister by various local organisations, including the WRI, the Boys' Brigade, the Stags, the Chamber of Commerce and the Maureen O'Rourke Dancers, that such a momentous occasion should not pass unremarked. A chance remark of his own at the General Assembly of the Church of Scotland some months before had fallen on the ear of the Rev Gus Pennyfather, the Kirk's national media liaison officer. The Rev Pennyfather was not one, as he put it, to pass up a chance to rap with the Tubies: the Rev MacAndrew was given to understand that this meant his colleague in orders would have a word with some television people. This Gus duly did.

Shortly after he returned home, the Rev MacAndrew received a communication from a Ms Baz Tinto, production assistant to Mr Dixie Docherty, presenter of Caledonian Television's popular weekly devotional programme, *Heavens Above*, inviting the Minister to share his church's anniversary celebrations with a viewing audience now estimated at over 750,000, Caledonian having secured the franchise for the nationwide worshipping slot.

The Rev MacAndrew was not happy.

A placid man, comfortably settled in his beliefs, he was fond of Order. Order, for him, consisted in the maintenance both of his own agreeable relationship with the Redeemer and of the arrangements he had made, over the years, for the salving of Craigfiethan souls. This outlook — a happy blend of Nature (he was born to a long line of divines in Duncruddie) and Nurture (he had been many years in Craigfieth and was unlikely now to try his Faith elsewhere) — disposed him to find incomprehensible the outward manifestations of the larger world, and left him with no great desire so to educate himself as to find it otherwise. His father had been a great reader of Mr Steele and Mr Addison and had brought the young Gilleasbuig up in their reassuring ambience, sending him out at last into the world of knaves and fools with Dryden's dictum ringing in his youthful ears: "My son," he had said, "you must cultivate in yourself 'Fineness of Expression and a Delicateness of Thought, the Easiness of a Gentleman, the Exactness of a Scholar, and the Good Sense of a man of Business'. And God grant that you may encourage the same in others."

This, with due provision for the honest plainness of the common soul, is precisely what MacAndrew strove to do. While Craigfieth Kirk Session could not, of course, be compared with the Spectator Club (being, as it were, long on merchants and short on kindly squires, captains of invincible modesty and sociable men-about-town) MacAndrew played his part, the philosophic clergyman of general learning, to the full, and knew he was respected for it.

He was thus inclined to view Television — particularly, as it was in this case, Commercial Television — rather as an Extravagance, born of Depraved Sentiment, and in need of Correction than (to use Pennyfather's horrible phrase) "box populi, box Dei"; besides which, he strongly suspected the Rev Gus of Enthusiasm. Nonetheless, he knew his place. God's vizier in matters of revelation he might be, but in its patterns of observance he was the servant, not the master, of his congregation; at the Session called to discuss Caledonian's invitation he tactfully abstained, allowing the Clerk to record a unanimous vote in favour of acceptance.

Ms Tinto's letter had indicated that the devotional interface component of the telecast should not normally exceed one third of the whole, and helpfully added the information that the entire transmission was scheduled to last forty-five minutes, excluding breaks. Fifteen minutes being his normal upper limit, he at least foresaw no problems there. He retired next morning to the Heights of Abraham to consult his well-thumbed Concordance, an exercise in second-hand bibliomancy which soon vouchsafed him Proverbs 18:x, "The name of the Lord is a strong tower: the righteous runneth into it, and is safe." This seemed an excellent omen: the text was topical, yet lent itself to his own inimitable brand of civilised commentary on such matters as safety and righteousness. His pen flowed smoothly across the pages, while downstairs his dear Jessie attended to her worldly tasks.

All the same, he was not happy.

On the other side of town Mr Cyril Bullock, God's second opinion, was not happy either. The town's preoccupation with the church tower smacked to him of vainglorious ungodliness — of idolatry, indeed, if not worse — while its willingness to embrace the procurers and purveyors of Satan's Peepshow was irrefutable evidence of sensuality and licentious Babylonism. A plain man himself, the immodesty of others never failed to enkindle in him an ecstasy of corrective fervour. He needed no Concordance to light his way: let the name of it, he thought grimly, be called Babel.

He offered a brisk prayer for guidance then reached for his newly acquired copy of the *Praise The Lord* Handbook*. There was no need, in this day and age, for Satan to have all the best shows.

The Maureen O'Rourke Dancers, the Stags, the WRI Glee Singers, the Boys' Brigade, the Chamber of Commerce and the High School Wind Band were, on the other hand, little short of delirious with happy expectation. The embarrassments of the Gala were forgotten as they turned their thoughts to preparations for the Centennial celebration, just two busy months away.

The headquarters of Caledonian TV comprise a sort of hyperborean Wapping at the heart of what the ungrateful local populace obstinately refuses to call by its proper given name of the Greater Glasgow Enterprise Zone. Part of this grey complex — a small part, three floors up and

* TM

facing north — is occupied by the Religious Affairs Suite. It is a large office, as minority interest facilities go, and it owes its inelegant proportions to the fact of its conversion, with the aid of a chipboard divider, from half the premises previously occupied by the disgraced former producer and presenter of *Weekend in Troon*, the popular family quiz show, whose history, though irrelevant, is worthy of brief digression:

Weekend in Troon had invited married persons to compete for various desirable prizes by identifying, from a star-studded panel, the personality with whom their partners would most like to conduct a short-term relationship, and subsequently having that choice confirmed by their putatively adulterous spouses, who had been ensconced the while in a sound-proof booth. The show had rapidly progressed from being Caledonian's sole contribution to the network to become the most popular show of its genre in every single region save one, the exception being TV nan Eilean. Nemesis overtook the enterprise on the very crest of its popularity when one septuagenarian contestant, a Mr Standfast of Golspie, put his wife's correct choice into practice and disappeared in a blaze of publicity with Miss Ulva St Kilda, the well-known chanteuse. The blackly affronted Mrs Standfast sued the station for Procuring In A Public Place, and won: in a notable judgment, the Lords of Court and Session ruled that the programme's makers had "permitted the Act yt doth Engendre Lustfulness and Affrunteth Dacencie" and imposed a heavy burden of damages. Everyone associated with *Weekend in Troon* became instant victims of what is known in media circles as Edmonds' Disease: few were heard of again.

The other half of the office houses the production team responsible for dubbing *Neighbours* into Gaelic, for schools and colleges.

The Religious Affairs Suite was occupied this June morning by its permanent staff of three. Ms Baz Tinto stirred a cup of decaffeinated Nicaraguan coffee with one hand while with the other she put the finishing touches to her script of *Joan the Baptist*, a freelance project for the Dyke Bible Workshop, Hamilton. Ex-Fr Ogilvy Todd, the unit's Spiritual Consultant, decided to plump for Antipope II in the 3.30 at Thirsk. Dixie Docherty, once known to millions as TV's Mr Soccer before his emotional rebirth at a soirée organised by the Hamilton branch of Strikers For Christ following a televised 0-0 draw between the Accies and a team from the Highland League in the second round of the Irn Bru Trophy, paced the office and read for the umpteenth time that morning a circular from the Head of Programme Planning.

"Yon's bluidy monstrous!" he exclaimed and, undeterred by the silence that greeted this remark, continued: "Whit diz he thenk thus ootfit diz, mak home movies or whit? It's focking ridiculous, pardon me, Faither."

"Granted, insofar as I am able," sighed ex-Fr Todd, marking Ark of the Covenant at Kempton Park for a double. "I sympathise with your frustration, Dixie."

"Well, ah mean tae say! Twa days maximum. Twa days *maximum*! Has yon guy no heert o' oot-takes? Christ, at this rate we'll pute Denis Norden ootae a job, It'll Be Alright on the bluidy Night every bluidy week! Baz, erza schedule forra Craigfieth stint, hae ye goat it yet?"

"Yea, O Master, thy unworthy handmaiden hath it right here," replied Ms Tinto heavily.

"Well cutra crap an let's hae it!"

Ms Tinto reached for the document with a practised air of bored efficiency.

"We have the Rev Gilleasbuig MacAndrew doing his bit, that's fifteen minutes approx, then we have the two hymns, of course, and the psalm —"

"Whit are they?"

"Er, let me see: The Church's One Foundation, Rock of Ages and Psalm 23."

"Well, erey'are! Psalm 23, that's a bugger, eh? Aw they harmonies, am I right? That's angles, shots, cross-fades and awra rest o' it, an that means wan theng — oot-takes! Whit else?"

"You're going to love this, Docherty. There's a procession by the Boys' Brigade, who are going to present their battalion colours to the Kirk Elders. Then there's a performance by the Maureen O'Rourke Dancers of a Floral Ballet, accompanied by the WRI Glee Singers and the Craigfieth High School Wind Band, and that's followed by a Pageant depicting a Century of Town Life, courtesy of the Ancient Order of Stags. And then there's the Lone Bugler."

"Whit inra name o' Gehenna's that?"

" 'That' is a youth called Stuart Stewart, who's going to stand on top of the church tower and sound the Last Post."

"Whitra fock faa?"

"VJ Day," replied Ms Tinto. "August the fifteenth. They think it'll be topical."

"Jeezis wept!" Dixie Docherty's voice rose to a sob. "An oor lairds an maisters expec' us tae get aa that inra can in *twa days?* Erra loada barmheids!"

"They do Trooping the Colour live," pointed out Ms Tinto.

"Ah ken that, Mizz Cluvverdick! Ersa perfeshenal ootfit, though, ent it? Ah mean, ersa troop o' sodjers aa ken whit they're at, no a bunch o' hicks wi straas inra heids. An ersanuther theng, whit're they gie'n us inra way o' a director?"

"Damian Colquhoun," replied Ms Tinto.

"*Whit?* Yon wee poof fae ra weans' programme, whitra heil's it caa'd?"

"Romper Suit," said ex-Fr Todd. "My children watch it."

"Jeezis fock anawra fockin sents," exclaimed Docherty. Ex-Fr Todd coughed gently.

"Sorry, Faither."

"Not at all," the consultant replied. "Actually, old chap, I was wondering if you had the loan of a fiver about you, I seem to have run a bit short this week."

In Craigfieth, preparations for the great day proceeded apace. In the Community Centre, the Boys' Brigade paraded their colours on Tuesday evenings between seven and nine o'clock until, with more than a fortnight to go, they were all but perfectly proficient in their drill. Of course it had to be admitted that the confined space of the Centre's main hall did not allow a full exposition of the routine, but Mr Maxwell (aye concerned, even in retirement, to pursue his interest in Youth) wisely decided that prolonged public exposure of the lads might blunt the keen edge of public interest, and devised instead a scaled-down version congruent with the hall's dimensions. All the Boys had to do on The Day was to remember to multiply each manoeuvre by five.

No such mathematical problems presented themselves to the O'Rourke Dancers: as a leading member of the Community Council when the Centre was built, Maureen herself had ensured that the measurements corresponded exactly to the maximum requirements of her choreography. The Dancers were required to meet every Monday, Wednesday and Friday to hone their balletic skills to the accompaniment, in the first few weeks, of the Misses Urquhart on the upright pianoforte, generously gifted by the late Lady Margoyle from the nursery of Lunie Castle. It was a magnificent instrument. Tuned a little sharp to allow for winter dampness, most of its hammers were in perfect working order and it had, as the Misses Urquhart said, a wonderful Tone. Miss Pollack had thought it prudent to hide the light of the WRI Glee Singers under a bushel for the time being, until the Dancers had perfected their routines; the same thought occurred to Miss Desirée Clocket, Principal Teacher of Music at the High School. In any case, since the majority of her Wind Banders were due to be away on holiday at the time, the few who remained could easily be accommodated for rehearsals in the drawing-room of her spacious villa on Lummock View. "We should feel sorry for our absent friends," she told them. "Stuck away there in their Majorcas and Morecambes, they don't know what they're missing!"

She was very probably right.

After a series of Extraordinary Moots in the Ben Almond Hotel (whose upstairs lounge became, on Thursday evenings, the Sacred Temple of the Craigfieth Lodge of the Ancient Order of Stags) the following programme had been devised for '100 Years On — A Craigfieth Pageant':

1 Death of Queen Victoria
2 War Declared (1914)
3 Silver Jubilee of King George V
4 War Declared (1939)
5 VJ Day; Departure of the Royal Hythe Regiment
6 Craigfieth Welcomes Mains Electricity
7 First Man On The Moon
8 Craigfieth Wins 'Scotland In Bloom' Contest For Fifth Year Running.

The last item had been specially devised by Bruce Waddell (Velvet Templar and Spoormaster Seneschal) to lead into his wife's Floral Ballet and was unanimously acclaimed by his fellow Stags — keen gardeners all — as a stroke of genius. Mr Glencairn Senior, Warden Royal and Honorary Life Rutter, generously offered to take the parts both of Lord Kitchener and His Majesty George V. As the leading man in countless productions of the Craigfieth Players he was sure he could manage the false whiskers. Rehearsals (without costume) were held on the McWhirter Playing Fields (weather permitting) every Saturday afternoon: they little hinted of the splendour of the spectacle to come, though the trial runs of Item One, using a demonstration casket kindly loaned by Mr Jolly of the Duncruddie Haven of Rest, caused a few eyebrows to be raised by those who were not, as they say, "in the know".

The Lone Bugler practised every night in the bathroom of his council house on Fleming Way.

No reasonable person could fault the town's careful mobilization for the Centennial, and no one with a pretence to Christian charity would dare to lay the blame for what transpired at any one particular door. Indeed, the most charitable epitaph* on the events of that memorable August day is also, surely, the most true: "Eh, but it's been a poor year for the town — first the Gala, and now this." Few would care·to disagree with this verdict.

Among the few who would, Mr Cyril Bullock found the weeks leading up to DD Day** an increasing source of frustration and dismay. The whole town seemed to him to have lost itself in idolatrous profanity. In vain did he preach against the barely concealed papistry of graven images, in vain did he discourse upon the ungodliness of vainglorious display; even his darkly transparent hints

---

* Overheard during a conversation on the following Monday in Mr Meiklejohn's shop.

** 'Dixie Docherty's Day', an acronym coined by the *Perthshire Gazette*.

anent the symbolic and paganistical connexion between towers and Those Parts which should be Kept Well Hidden fell, so it seemed, upon ears wilfully and sinfully deafened by the siren voice of honey-tongued Belial. In the end he was constrained to mount his assault against the cohorts of gaudy darkness with the aid of those few of his rural Brethren not entitled, however remotely, to participate in the forthcoming feast of blasphemy. It is possible he may have suspected their motives: certain it is that such thoughts, had they occurred to the Evangelist, would have been expeditiously dismissed, in the higher interest; certain, too, that the prospect of facing the legions of Beelzebub with but half a dozen foot-soldiers of the Elect was a depressing one indeed. It was all a long way from the sort of thing the authors of the *Praise The Lord* Handbook* evidently had in mind. Who can say but that his thoughts may have turned, as July gave way to August, to thoughts of emigration? It is a terrible thing to be without honour in one's own burgh.

Someone could have told him about things being always darkest before the dawn, but no one did: then again, it probably would not have done much good. He was in Manichean mood, and not inclined to be gospelled out of it.

It might have been of some small comfort to Mr Bullock to know that preparations for the Floral Ballet had hit an unexpected snag in one of the items on its programme, the terpsichorean interpretation of 'You Are The Honey, Honeysuckle, I Am The Bee'. The particular problem that arose concerned the Bee who, in the O'Rourke version, was choreographed to flit (wooingly) from one

* TM.

Bloom (Deidre) to another (Sharon) and so on (Kareen, Charlene, Joy-Anne and Marlene). The part of the Bee was rehearsed by Morag who, with but a week to go, planted her large hands on her hips in mid-routine and said:

"Ah'm no going to do the Bee, Mrs O'Rourke."

Time stood still a while, then Ms O'Rourke said:

"Good gracious, Morag, whatever do you mean?"

"Ah mean, Ah'm no going to do the Bee, Mrs O'Rourke. It's a boy's part."

Morag's dancing sisters stared at her with mute horror. Every Dancer understood that there were two things you didn't do, ever. One was to call Maureen 'Mrs O'Rourke', because it was (a) sexist, (b) élitist and (c) wrong, anyway. The other thing you didn't do was to contradict her.

Maureen O'Rourke looked long and hard at Morag, who had turned up (her leotard being in the wash that night) in tights and an Aran sweater.

"Really, Morag dear," she rasped, "I do think we're being a little silly, don't you? You took on the role of Bee several weeks ago and I think we would all agree — wouldn't we, Girls? — that you do it very nicely indeed, and besides, you're not exactly, well, how should we put it, dear . . ."

Suppressed giggling was heard from the other Girls.

"Ah ken," said Morag. "You think Ah'm flat chested, well I'm not, it's the leotard. Look!" she commanded and, adjusting her dress accordingly, gave Ms O'Rourke no option but to obey.

"So there! *And* Ah'm getting a new leotard tomorrow. So Ah'm no going to do the Bee, an' Mam says so too. It's not proper, Mam says, no at my time of life."

"I see, dear," Ms O'Rourke coughed. "Indeed we all do — yes, all right Morag, pull your jumper down — but who can we get instead? We can't do it without a Bee!"

Sharon nudged Joy-Anne, who prodded Kareen, who kicked Deidre.

"Please, Maureen," murmured Deidre, "there's Stewart."

More giggling, which Maureen silenced with a look before replying.

"Stuart who, Deidre dear?"

"Please, Maureen!" squawked Marlene, now emboldened. "Stuart Stewart! He could do the Bee!"

"Stuart Stewart? I don't think I know him, do I?"

"No, Mi—Maureen, I mean, he's new," said Charlene.

"He's doing the bugle in the show," added Sharon. "He stays on Fleming Way."

"I see," said Maureen, frowning. "Well, it sounds to me as though he's got quite enough to do already. Besides, the fact that he's a good bugler doesn't make him a good Dancer, does it?"

"Oh but he *is*!" Joy-Anne yelped. "You can tell!"

"Tell? How can you tell?"

This time the laughter was unrestrained.

"Well, he's — you know . . ."

"Yeah!"

"They only let him in the BBs 'cos he can do bugle."

"He reads poems. In the playground!"

"*And* he won't do rugby!"

"He makes his Mam take him to Dunbroath for a haircut!"

"He talks funny."

"I see," said Maureen. "Well, it seems I have no choice, doesn't it? I'll go and ask his mother tonight — Fleming Way, did you say?"

"Yeah," said Joy-Anne. "Number 15."

"Very well. We shall see what happens. And now, Girls, since we can't practise the Honeysuckle thanks to Morag's new leotard, we'll go on to number four, 'The Yellow Rose

Of Texas', Miss Urquhart and Miss Urquhart, if you're ready?"

Ms O'Rourke was admitted to the poky interior of 15 Fleming Way by an overwhelmingly plain woman who answered her request with the observation that there was no knowing what her Stuart might not agree to, he was a law unto himself and she (Mrs Stewart) was at her wits' end, sometimes, to know what to do with him. The muffled echoes of a bugle call came from somewhere upstairs. Pursuing them, Ms O'Rourke located their source seated upon the lavatory in the unlocked bathroom, his red tie and powder blue shirt clashing hideously with the restrained puce of the pedestal suite's fluffy accoutrements. He listened inscrutably to Ms O'Rourke's request and, to her surprise and no small discomfiture, immediately assented. She left him, rehearsing once again his mournful notes, feeling puzzled and not a little anxious: such a *strange* boy. Still, so long as he *could* dance . . .

He could. In fact, not only could he dance, he could dance like one possessed, obsessed . . . inspired, almost. To the relatively undemanding role of Bee he brought an intensity of emotion, purpose and artistic commitment such as is normally expected only of those who do the thing for money. While this undoubtedly had an inspirational effect on the WRI Glee Singers and the High School Wind Band (who, joining the Dancers for the final rehearsals, nightly reached undreamed of heights of musicological insight) it distinctly unsettled Maureen's Girls, unaccustomed as they were to being brought face to face — nay, limb to limb — with such purity of intent and execution. They did not like it: it wasn't what they were used to, and it wasn't right either, somehow. Still, since they themselves had suggested the strange youth, there was nothing they could do now about him. They galumphed through their routine as instructed, feeling the while both undeserving and resentful, and hoping their mentor would not employ his services on a permanent basis.

Stuart Stewart himself remained an absolute puzzle: according to the Girls (who, naturally enough in the circumstances, talked about him — indeed, talked of little else — for some time afterwards) he never said one word to anyone the whole time he was with them. All he did was dance. They were not to know that behind the masklike features a litany of contempt was being rehearsed, repeatedly and with feeling. And who could blame them for not knowing this? They were, after all, healthy, normal girls, their parents' daughters, products — as any Behaviourist will tell you at some length — of their environment. It is not reasonable to expect of such people they they should recognise the pain and ecstasy of adolescent intellect even when so closely confronted with it. It must be understood, therefore, that they are not in any way to blame for what happened. Nor is anybody else, of course, not in the least. Not, in fact, at all. It was, as Ms O'Rourke herself so succinctly put it, just one of these things that happen, that's all.

The exigencies of television — editing, splicing, mixing, dubbing and so forth — demanded that the parish of Craigfieth celebrate the tower's Centennial one week early. As the Minister explained, during the Intimations on the first Sabbath day of August, this was scarcely to be wondered at, television being one of the advanced marvels of the Age and consequently in need of sustained technical expertise to bring its fruits to the Scottish living-room. Nor, he stressed, was the Kirk Community to fear anything in the way of Divine disapproval for thus tinkering with the Kalends: for sure, he said, the God who commanded the sun to stand still in the heavens (Josh 10:xii, xiii) would cast a benign eye on these His faithful servants in their worshipful necessity.

Mr Cyril Bullock used the same text to prove, to a curiously depleted meeting at the Gospel Hall, the inevitability of the Almighty's condemnation of such profanity: was it not God's Will, and God's Will alone, that could command such disruptions in the Universal Order? And was it not mankind's place simply to obey? And was it not undeniable that the last man so to interfere with the Divine Ordinance was a Pope of Rome? He rested his case — but not his prayerful labours.

In the Religious Affairs Suite of Caledonian Television an atmosphere of dark foreboding prevailed. Dixie Docherty raged impotently at the callous stupidity of the company's executives; Ms Baz Tinto brooded on the corporate paternalism of life's institutions; ex-Fr Todd's latest little yankee hadn't come up, and the twins were teething. Only Damian Colquhoun was looking forward to the outing. It would be nice to get away, for a couple of days, from all those aggressive women in dungarees.

The last week of rehearsals saw a succession of cloudless days and record temperatures throughout the nation. A large anticyclone settled somewhere over Droitwich and showed no particular inclination to move, while a succession of Atlantic depressions was shrugged effortlessly away to Iceland and the Mediterranean resorts. While the wonderful weather brought one or two attendant problems — for the Southern Region of British Rail, for instance (expansion of points at East Croydon) and for the Northern Isles (fog) — it was difficult, as Mr Ingram remarked to his fellow Elders, not to believe that the good Lord Himself was smiling on the town's endeavours. The Stags rehearsed in full costume on the

McWhirter Playing Fields and although Mr Glencairn experienced some difficulty, even after five shots at it, in changing out of his Kitchener clothes in time to be George V in the next episode, everyone agreed that the eventual performance, screened all over Scotland, would be a credit to the town and a boost to its visitor industries. The floral display planned for the climax of the Pageant was rumoured to be of such unparalleled splendour as to defy the ability of mere words to describe it.

As for the Art which, transmitted as it is by Artistes for whom Language is a thing of bone and sinew, a Muse sheath'd in one-size stretch lurex, no one doubted dear Maureen's ability, once again, to pull out the Big One for the occasion: did not the nucleus of her floral team comprise the very Girls who had, only last autumn, taken the fiercely coveted Bronze Porringer of Coatbridge from all comers in the Intermediate Ladies' Section of DancePo Scotland '86? And had not the Wind Band and the Glee Singers been rehearsing so long that they must by now be capable of performing in their sleep? How, therefore, could any right-thinking person fear for one moment that Craigfieth's Tower Centenary would be anything other than a triumph for all concerned!

The collapse, late on Thursday night, of the anti-cyclone, its hasty retreat northwards — in the Northern Isles temperatures soared to the mid-sixties before falling back to their seasonal norm in time for the agricultural shows — and its eventual ignominious decease over the Faroes late on Friday afternoon may perhaps be explained by hubris on the part of the BBC's weather forecaster who, the night before, had spoken rashly of the prospects for the second day's play in the Old Trafford Test.

The television people arrived in Craigfieth at eleven o'clock on the morning of Friday, August 7th, in a large truck, two Range Rovers and three Sierras. At five past eleven the rain began, not spectacularly but with every indication of persistence. Neither drizzle nor torrent, it yet possessed a very *wetting* quality: it was, in the striking phrase of Mr Meiklejohn, as if someone had turned on a tap, but not very much. Nonetheless, a call by Ms Tinto at half past twelve to the Station with the Weather Situation for the Nation confirmed the unlikelihood of anyone turning it off. Shooting rehearsals were abandoned for the day, save for what the Director termed the all-weather worship component which, as a Second Assistant Key Grip helpfully explained to the Rev MacAndrew, meant his bit.

The Kirk Choir (or at any rate as many of them as could be spared by the WRI Glee Singers, who were grappling in the Community Centre with a tricky counterpoint in *The Bonnie Heather Braes O' Lunie*) was rounded up and powdered while a procession of dour menials trailed in reels of cable and, in less time than it takes to arbitrate a piecework bonus rate, festooned the gallery (which had once accommodated, on Empire Days, three generations of Lunie Moithers) with lights, slings, cameras and boom microphones. This accomplished, the menials then withdrew for their meal break, leaving the Minister and his quasi-congregation in something of a quandary, the latter being unwilling to go home in the rain for fear of spoiling their toilette and having to go through it all over again while the former, though he had so far escaped the make-up department through being too busy supervising in the gallery, did not feel it would be quite right to abandon his flock in their distress. Presently, however, their plight was relieved by Ms Tinto, who arranged for soup and rolls to be brought in from the Bide-a-Wee Tearooms in Mr Duff's taxi, at Caledonian's expense.

The Rev MacAndrew was led away to the Vestry by Damian Colquhoun and his friend Jock, the make-up supervisor, to be prepared for stardom. After barely half an hour they reappeared, the Johnstonian aspects of the Minister's countenance highlighted with such loving skill that he wanted only a grubby wig and a few gravy stains to make the illusion complete. The Director and his friend were plainly delighted with their achievement.

At last, promptly at three p.m., the rehearsal began.

For the Rev MacAndrew, who had precious little first-hand experience of alienation, it was undeniably an ordeal. To begin with, he was acutely aware of a fundamental disruption of all his natural rhythms: he had not made his usual substantial luncheon and was accustomed to spending this hour on a Friday afternoon in quiet contemplation of the Manse garden or, if wet, of one the many bound volumes of his grandfather's sermons. Secondly, he couldn't move his face properly without the discomfiting sensation that some vital part of it might fall off at any moment, and when he raised his eyebrows — as he often did to lend quiet emphasis to the burden of his argument — it felt as if his hair were responding to the movement by sliding, all in one piece, across his scalp. He was uncomfortably hot, and his collar felt too tight; the television lights seemed to throb and gong with pitiless intensity and when he looked down for relief at the body of the Kirk, relief was there none. He was in the habit of running his eyes along the pews and finding, if not respectful attention, then at least respectful abstraction, which in many ways was better. Now, however, the prospect below was utterly disturbing. His fellow Craigfiethans, looking like nothing so much as satiric waxworks of themselves, gazed boldly back at him, as if he were some sort of television programme devised for their entertainment: the real television people, on the other hand, simply went about their inscrutable business as though he did not exist. When they did acknowledge his presence it was only to point some instrument at him, or make their hands into a frame and squinny through it at him before hurrying off to communicate something to a colleague. Twice the Minister almost lost the thread of his discourse; towards the end he was shocked to find, on tuning in, as it were, to himself, that he appeared to be making no sense at all, and throughout the last page and a half of his notes he was distracted almost to the point of breakdown by an unpleasant-looking man in a blue cardigan who stood before the pulpit making frantic circular gestures with one hand while appearing to slit his throat with the index finger of the other. To his disordered senses it seemed at last as though he had been condemned to some subtle region of Hell wherein fallen clerics were doomed to preach for all eternity to the inmates of a bedlam-house.

He ceased at last and, for several slow seconds, nothing happened. His auditors continued gazing and gaping, the rude mechanicals continued to fidget and mutter. At last, Damian Colquhoun, who had been conducting a conversation with Ms Tinto by the hymnbook table throughout the Minister's ordeal, turned to him now in his ghastly isolation and called gaily up the aisle:

"Lovely, your Reverence — super, thank you — sound, was that all right for you? Lighting, cameras, any problem with the Reverence?"

Sound replied that the Minister's pitch and frequency were well within the limits of tolerance; lighting reported no problems with flare though they'd had a little trouble with the nostrils and could the Minister sort of crouch down just a little bit? Cameras expressed themselves pleased with all their angles but suggested the subject could do a little more with his hands.

"Great, super!" said Damian. "Just one *teeny* little thing though, love, and that's the content."

"The . . . content, Mr Colquhoun?"

"Yes, pet. Baz says, and I agree with her, that — only *as it stands*, mind you — it's just a tiny bit *preacherly* for the format."

"A bit — what did you say?" asked MacAndrew, his hands now finding something to do by gripping the pulpit rail.

"Preacherly, love — you know, *heavy*. Like a sermon, if you like."

The Minister frowned.

"But — I mean — it *is* a sermon, Mr Colquhoun."

"Oh yes, ha ha! Of course it is in that sense, as such, and we do appreciate that — don't we, Baz? — what we mean, love, is it's a bit of a *sermonly* sermon, you know what I mean?"

"I am bound to say, Mr Colquhoun," replied the Minister, to whom the act of grasping the pulpit rail had begun to put in mind of other grasping acts anent such things as nettles and bulls' horns, "that I do not. I do not see that your describing me as a preacherly preacher given to delivering sermonly sermons is any more illuminating than my describing you as a directorly director or your friend there as an assistantly assistant. A thing either is or it is not, in my experience."

The Director giggled. "Oh, you are a wag!" he said.

Ms Tinto intervened.

"What Damian means," she explained, "is that your sermon was sententious, platitudinous, semantically flaccid, intellectually vapid and five minutes too long, okay?"

"Oh," said the Rev MacAndrew.

"He was trying to be diplomatic," added Ms Tinto. "Weren't you, Damian?"

"Oh yes!" agreed the Director. "You know me, dear. Such a timid little thing, I am."

"Oh," said the Rev MacAndrew again.

"But you're not to worry about it, pet, all right? I'm sure you'll be able to do something before tomorrow, a clever man like you. All that stuff about the tower being a refuge and a haven, that was great, super, keep that in. Only lay off the righteousness a bit, okay? It's a family programme you see, my dear — that's why they get me to direct — and we don't like to give offence. Besides, Dixie's got this *lovely* commentary he's bringing tomorrow for the shooting sequences, all about the lovely hills and the pretty glens and the little town nestling 'neath the Kirk on the hill, and all that sort of thing. He's been reading all the guidebooks, and it'll sort of fit in, you see, love, if you concentrate on the idea of *tower* rather than those other controversial concepts, we rather tend to leave that sort of thing to the Beeb for late at night — yes, Mr Ibrahim dear, what can I do for you, not being harassed by those naughty circuits again, are you?"

The grim, Zapata-moustached figure of the Senior Electrician loomed over the diminutive Director.

"Ah'm no here in mah capacity as electrucian, Mr Perducer," he said. "Ah'm here in mah capacity as Senior Shoap Stewart. Ah've bin up the tooer!"

"Super!" said Damian.

"It's no super at aa! It's awash wi' watter!"

"That's all right, Mr Ibrahim," said Ms Tinto. "We've brought several pairs of green wellies, as per Chapel agreement. You and the lads can wear them when you rig up the OB equipment tomorrow, can't you?"

"Ah'm here tae tell ye," the Senior Shop Steward thundered, "that there'll be nae Union labour up yon tooer, no in wellies, no in wet suits, no in deep sea divin' gear, no at aa, no way!"

"Well that's not a very *nice* thing to say, Mr Ibrahim dear, is it? It's only water."

"It's no safe! Wan slip o' concentration wi' electrucal equipment an' woof! mah Union'll pute in the biggest compensation claim in th'entire hustory o'tullyvusion! As it is, Ah'm claimin' fae these troosers. They're ruined, as ye can see."

"Oh yes, dear, I do see, and I do so sympathise, believe me. You wouldn't *believe* the pairs I get through in those filthy studios. Okay, hearts, you all heard what the man said, no aerial shots tomorrow. That means, your Reverence — still there, love? Good! — that means you're all right for time again, okay? If you *could* just see to those things we were discussing, yes? Cut out the things Baz mentioned, okay, then it'll be fine — make it less, you know . . ."

"Less churchly?" said the Minister.

"Lovely man!" said the Director. "Now then, people, let's hear some singing, shall we?"

It was past five when the choir was eventually released, and still raining steadily. A dispirited air, an atmosphere almost of enervation, settled slowly on the little town as the evening wore wetly on. Sundry horticulturalists gloomily inspected their blooms and reflected that there might well be no Pageant to decorate, the way things were going. Half-heartedly they emptied water from the plastic awnings above their borders. Even the O'Rourke Dancers gave up at last and went their several ways home, leaving the air of the Community Centre heavy with their exertions.

Only behind the lace curtains of Jerusalem House did the true flame of Christian joy burn brightly in the soul of Mr Cyril Bullock as he relayed to Mrs Bullock the good news that the rain was still falling.

"God's Providence is at work in this town, Elspeth," he said. Nonetheless he continued to paste selected biblical verses on to placards, just in case.

Mr Bullock's Laodicean faith was not misplaced. Saturday dawned grey, it is true, and muggy — but dry. Indeed, as the Rev MacAndrew could testify, the rain had finally ceased shortly after two a.m. and a little before he fumbled his way to bed having completed (at untold mental, physical and spiritual cost) a complete reworking of his sermon, fiercely exterminating the last vestiges of preacherliness as the cruel adjectives of Ms Tinto rang and re-echoed in his tired cranium. He groped darkly into bed, taking care not to waken Jessie, breathed a silent prayerful apology to his Maker and his forefathers for the travesty he was bound to commit in a few hours' time, then fell profoundly asleep.

By ten o'clock the sun had begun to struggle through and the High Street was steaming gently. The Kirk Green sparkled as if putting on a last show of brave bejewelled defiance before the tramplings of the Stags and the Dancers.

At half past ten Dixie Docherty himself arrived in one of Caledonian's executive Audis and was introduced by Damian Colquhoun to the Centenary's principal participants among the crowd already assembled at the coned-off top end of the street forenent the Kirk Green. He smiled, clasped hands, signed autographs, exchanged pleasantries, laughed agreeably when told he looked smaller in real life: "Aren't we all though?" was his reply — one which, it was agreed, showed a very proper humility.

The Misses Urquhart evinced great interest in his origins.

"We *do* so love listening to your voice, Mr Docherty," they said. "So soothing, we think. Do tell us, do you come from Morningside by any chance?"

Dixie Docherty favoured the ladies with his warmest, most ecumenical smile.

"Bearsden, ectually," he replied.

Baz Tinto and Damian Colquhoun hung back tactfully from the focus of all this genteel adoration.

Ms Tinto shook her head. "You've got to hand it to the old bastard," she said. "He's a real pro."

Damian agreed. "My dear, a triumph of the art of the cosmetician and the elocutionist, I do declare. An asset to the god-box industry. Look how he's got those old dears cooing over him!"

" 'Every woman adores a fascist'," Ms Tinto quoted.

"Speak for yourself ducky, I'm sure," replied Damian archly.

Ms Tinto grinned, and kicked him playfully on the ankle.

The morning being fair, if somewhat close, and the forecast unpropitious, it was decided to transpose the order of events for the Centennial, filming the Pageant and the Floral Ballet while the light held before proceeding to what should have been (and, so far as next week's viewing public was concerned, would be) the opening Service of Rededication and Thanksgiving. Cameras were hoisted, microphones slung, and breaths held in anticipation of the emergence of Queen Victoria's funeral cortège from the forecourt of the Duff Garage.

It was at this point that Mr Cyril Bullock appeared, accompanied by six godfearing Christian Brethren from the tiny inbred hamlet of Bonquhars,* all bearing placards.

The Pageant was not a failure. Everything that the Stags' organising committee had planned to happen, did happen. The late Queen Empress's gun carriage (a flat

---

* Pop 32. Hotels, none. B&B, none. Features of Interest, none. (*Tourist Guide to the Lummocks, 1964*). Pron. as in Sanquhar.

trailer drawn, in the absence of sable horses, by Mr Duff's breakdown truck) processed to the Green, flanked by six Senior Stags in a very creditable approximation to Victorian mourning dress and draped in a Union Flag kindly loaned by Mr Snotter on behalf of the Lunie Estate; the First World War was declared by Mr Haq, who stood at the exact spot where the Mercat Cross used to be, while Mr Glencairn pointed a Kitchener finger at the children in the crowd; ten minutes later (for the Warden Royal and Honorary Life Rutter had practised the change of costume so often that he could achieve it now with lightning swiftness) he reappeared as George V acknowledging the cheers of his jubilant lieges with a very gracious wave, and his beard only came off twice. And so on, including Mr Glencairn (Junior) and Bruce Waddell, clad in foam rubber and baking foil, as Messrs Aldrin and Armstrong. There were small hitches, of course, minor unlooked-for mishaps: the giant light bulb (a novelty item purchased especially from a reputable firm of theatrical suppliers in West Yorkshire) failed to light up at the climax of Item Six, though the Stag chosen to switch it on (Mr Borden, the Butcher and Grand Wizard of Viands) did not lose his nerve and was seen by all to react as though it had done; the Declaration of War (1939), though similar to the striking tableau effected for the Declaration of War (1914), lacked somewhat in impact, possibly because of the slightly tarnished image acquired by Mr Chamberlain in later years. Also, the grass on the Kirk Green was treacherously slippery after Friday's rain; this rather spoiled the efforts of Bruce Waddell, hampered as he was by his lunar suiting, to take one giant leap for Mankind.

There was also the constant, inescapable and irritating presence of the town's Evangelist and the Six Men of Bonquhars whose placards, despite the best efforts of Caledonian's most experienced lensmen, formed a backdrop to most of the proceedings. Nor, it was felt, were their tidings quite in keeping with the spirit of the occasion, however holy their provenance. The messages of the Bonquhars Brethren ran as follows:

I WILL CURSE YOUR BLESSINGS; YEA, I HAVE CURSED THEM ALREADY (Mal. 2:ii)
YE ARE CURSED WITH A CURSE (Mal. 3:ix)
THE WAGES OF SIN IS DEATH (Rom. 6:xxiii)
SIN, WHEN IT IS FINISHED, BRINGETH FORTH DEATH (Jas. 1:xv)
THEIR DAMNATION SLUMBERETH NOT (II Pet. 2:iii)
LET THEM GO DOWN QUICK INTO HELL (Ps. 55:xv)

Mr Bullock's placard proclaimed THE DEVIL IS COME AMONG YOU, HAVING GREAT WRATH (Rev. 12:xii): as Damian Colquhoun remarked, *sotto voce*, to Baz Tinto at the time, "Lo! Six threats and one lapel badge!"

There was nothing anyone could do about them, of course; they were not creating an obstruction or causing a disturbance. Nonetheless, they did rather take the shine off things.

The last item, however, was as close to perfection as it was possible to be in this life: its hazard lights flashing, its paintwork gleaming, the Scotland In Bloom Trophy (a silver-plated watering can) proudly displayed on its roof, the smartest lorry in the fleet of Mr Poulson, the builder, made its stately way down the High Street, turned in at the Hearse Gate and parked at the Kirk door, laden with such herbaceous gorgeousness as to make the hearts of all Craigfiethans — men, women and children, gardeners and non-gardeners alike — swell with pride. Scarcely had the gasps of astonishment and admiration died away than, with a spine-tingling roll on the Boys'

Brigade drums, the floral spectacle exploded — there is no other word for it — and out leaped the pride of the Maureen O'Rourke Dancers ("the pick of the bunch" as their mentor wittily described them) ready to plunge into their first routine. The High School Wind Band blew a ragged chord, the WRI Glee singers cleared their throats, the two Dancers who had sustained sprained ankles upon alighting hobbled discreetly away, and the display began.

All the weeks of toil in the Community Centre found their reward at last, in the breathtaking execution of 'Mary, My Scotch Bluebell', 'Daisy, Daisy', 'My Darling Clementine', 'La Vie En Rose' and many, many others, but without doubt the jewel in dear Maureen's crown was the extraordinary performance of young Stuart Stewart as the Bee: that, as the Caledonian cameramen instantly recognised, was distinctly "something else". He danced with all the poignancy, all the artistry, of a mature performer at the apex of his powers. Where others slipped, he shimmered; where they stumbled, he transcended; where they suggested, he *was*. For the first time that day, Damian Colquhoun became intensely involved in the proceedings. The dazzling performance ended — all too soon — and was succeeded, with an almost audible breathing-out from the spectators, by 'The Yellow Rose of Texas'.

Stuart Stewart slipped away, unnoticed, through the church door and into the Vestry, where his uniform and bugle lay ready. He hauled off his Bee costume, shivering in the sudden dank chill and, his transformation complete, slung the bugle over his shoulder and began the long ascent to the summit of the tower, trembling now with excitement.

Outside, the applause for the Dancers died away and the Kirk Elders assembled outside the porch, the Rev MacAndrew in their midst, ready to inspect the colours of the town's Boys' Brigade. Mr Maxwell, resplendent in his officer's uniform, watched as his Sergeant-Major (who was also his nephew) lined the lads up. He was glad, on the whole, that the Company was incomplete: despite being the only boy in the history of the local Brigade who could bugle his way through the Last Post without hitting a wrong note, young Stewart was not, in his opinion, the stuff that a true BB is made of. The phrase 'too clever by half' occurred to him, as did other less savoury epithets. Mr Maxwell was a man's man.

The Caledonian crew struggled, though with no great enthusiasm, to position their cameras for the presentation; two cameras had in any case been taken temporarily out of service under instruction from Damian Colquhoun to prepare for tower shots. The Director was anxious: the light was fading by the minute. The drums rolled, the bags of the Kipplerigg Distillery Pipers swelled, but he was oblivious to them. He cast worried glances at the darkening sky, and hoped the next number would not last long.

Stuart Stewart made his way upward, upward. After a while, the stone spiral stair gave way to a succession of ladders and landings. He reached the clockworks, stilled and silent for nearly sixty years, and climbed on. He sweated. The bugle bumped awkwardly against his side, again and again refusing to stay where he shoved it. The ladders became narrower, the air warmer. He passed a colony of Pipistrelle bats, the floor below them thick with droppings. At last he reached the top, hearing the pipes skirl into action as he drew back the bolt from the trapdoor and pushed it open.

He emerged on to a small platform raised some two feet above the level of the tower's flat roof. All around him lay a lake of still water, its brim less than an inch below the lowest points in the shallow crenellations. At one point

— near, as he thankfully saw, to the porch door below — a block of masonry had fallen inwards, leaving a gap in the pattern, its upper surface just proud of the water. He waded across to it, not caring about his uniform or his shoes. The water felt surprisingly warm. His goal attained, he knelt on it and peered over the edge.

Below, the Director saw him and turned to his head cameraman.

"What do you think?" he asked.

The man consulted his lightmeter.

"Dodgy."

"Here, let's see the picture." The Director swung the camera upwards until its miniature screen displayed a neatly formed picture of the tower, the sky and, between them, the slight stooped figure of the boy.

"Christ!" he muttered, his mask of camp facetiousness momentarily slipping. "Dodgy perhaps, but a great picture. Like the Last Trump."

Stuart Stewart observed him, as he observed most things, with detachment, his perceptions sharpened to hideous intensity. What a place, he thought, what a pointless place this is: just look at them. He saw all the stupid girls — Dancers, they called themselves! — standing around the Green, pouting and giggling and nudging each other; he saw the Bonquhars Brethren, like day trippers from an asylum, standing with their placards, and their leader, the slippery-looking old bastard in the plastic mac, sidling round to be in the picture when the colours were presented. He watched his so-called pals — silly little boys all of them, silly little boys who would grow up to be silly little men leading silly little lives in shops and offices in their silly little town, marry silly little women, have silly little children and die silly little deaths, their silly little duty done — as they marched idiotically up the path, the noise of their feet on the wet gravel fractionally and hilariously just out of sync with the image. He saw it all, as in a map, and he seemed to see himself; caged — at bay — defiant.

Directly below him were the bared heads — some bald, some thinning — of the Elders, and the silver mane of the Minister. He thought of Mills bombs. He thought of spitting, of letting a nice big yellow glob of gob fall, splat! at the critical moment, but he did not act upon that thought. He was too old for that; he did not care, one way or the other, what anyone thought of him but he cared a great deal about what he thought of himself, and he had thought a lot lately, and his decision was taken. Very soon, They (for so he termed the hell of other people) would be in awe of him, probably; perhaps, even sorry for what they had done to him. Stuff them, though, whatever they thought. He knew what he was. He was a perfectionist: only one opinion mattered. He must get it *right*: that alone would be enough to make him unique in this dump: nothing less would do.

The fatuous ceremony was drawing to a close. Stuart Stewart stood up and lifted the bugle to his lips, moistening them in readiness for the dying fall of the pipes and the last beat of the drum. At his back, the leaden surface of the water was punctured by the first heavy drops of rain.

The whole town craned its neck, every eye strained to focus on the silhouetted figure. After two beats of perfectly timed silence, the first faultless notes of the Last Post sang out in the heavy summer air. Damian Colquhoun and Baz Tinto looked from boy to screen, from reality to image, then at each other in an instant of recognition which said: this is rare, this is what we say keeps us in the business: this is the diamond in the dross. The last four notes sounded, G and D, G and D, the last pair a melancholy echo, calling from sad shires. They saw the boy as he held the last, sweetly tapering note, raise his bugle skywards until it seemed to touch the very heavens. There followed an abyss of silence. Then he jumped.

At last there came the prosaic, manageable noise of screaming.

Damian gently turned Baz away from the spectacle, from the hubbub. Her shoulders were shaking.

"Come on, ducks," he said, "leave this to Docherty, it's what the bastard's paid for. We've got work to do before the news vultures get their claws on the tapes. I've got matches."

As they passed Mr Bullock they heard him talking to someone about York Minster.

The good folk of Craigfieth did their duty by the dead boy. A fund was set up, called the Lone Bugler Fund and, by a unanimous vote of the Chamber of Commerce, the proceeds were used to repair the church clock, which was dedicated in his honour at a service some six months later. Caledonian TV were invited, but did not attend.

Maureen O'Rourke bought a small silver cup, which she named the Stuart Stewart Trophy. It is competed for annually and awarded to the Dancer who gains most points for Inspiration.

Every year, on August 15th, the Boys' Brigade, uncapped, file past a glass case in the Community Centre, and salute it. In it is a crumpled bugle, last sounded by their honoured comrade before a tragic accident removed him from their midst.

Mr and Mrs Stewart moved away, but no one knows where to. Life, after all, goes on and as Mr Bullock knows, has a low tolerance of the divine prerogative of perfection.

5

Mister Right

One dreary Autumn afternoon in Craigfieth three young
ladies met, as was their weekly Thursday custom, in the
Bide-a-Wee Tearooms on the corner of High Street and
School Road. It was a long-standing arrangement between
them, one of the many things they had in common and
which bound them together in sisterhood. All three had
attended the High School together, leaving shortly after
their sixteenth birthdays (which fell within five weeks of
each other) with three Ordinary Grades apiece, in English,
Food and Nutrition, and Anatomy, Physiology and
Health. All three had been O'Rourke Girls and had forged
links of camaraderie that only leotard wearers can truly
know; all three were shop assistants. Each had chosen her
job on the grounds that it would be an easy one to leave,
when the time came; each, however, perhaps as a result of
nine years of meeting at the Bide-a-Wee on early closing
day, harboured an intense though unspoken desire to
work as a waitress in the genteel calm of the tearooms,
cosy amidst the brass and chintz and wicker. Each knew
this to be an impossible ambition. The Bide-a-Wee was
the inviolate universe of Miss Phemister, who brewed
and baked, and Mrs Spurtle, who wore the establishment's
public face, and who bore down now upon the trio, her
face glowing above the trolley in the warm, pink-shaded
light.

"Tea and fancies for the Three Graces," she said, as
always and, as always, the Three Graces giggled politely
until she heaved away.

The accident of their identical names had been the first bond, all those years ago at Primary School when they first started going around together in the playground. To their teachers they had been distinguished by their second initials as Grace J, Grace M, and Grace B; among themselves they were Gracie, Grace and Gray.

Today it was the turn of Gracie to pour, of Grace to choose the first cake, and of Gray to buy the *Perthshire Gazette*. They set about their duties with intense seriousness, these three, for transcending the ritual of the occasion was a higher purpose on whose perilous outcome depended their lives' fulfilment. While Gracie, straight-backed and proprietorial, manipulated the pot and strainer and Grace played her plump fingers over Miss Phemister's baking, both knew that it was Gray, peering obliquely at the paper, who alone could unlock for them the gates of delight. For they had reached the critical age of twenty-five, each with one vital finger unadorned.

Children of their age and place, they had known since puberty the path that fate and choice had mapped out for them, and had undertaken without complaint to tread it with unfailing purpose. Nine autumns running, they had moved out of their parents' houses into rooms on Lummock View, newly vacated by the tourists. For six months every year they organised their lives around the throbbing winter heart of Craigfieth; they hugged the walls at its dances and discos, they found partners for its annual socials, they even boarded buses to sample the markets in Dunkeld, Pitlochry and Crieff: all to no avail. Nine springs running, they had folded their independent tents and returned home for the summer season. No coy mistresses they, given certain assurances, yet worms threatened, with each passing year, to try what the male youth of Central Perthshire so inexplicably eschewed.

They knew their path, they followed it faithfully yet still it did not lead them to the promised land of wedlock. There had been temptations, of course: times when Gracie, or Grace, or even Gray had felt inclined, out of curiosity or sheer exhaustion, to say 'yes' without arranging the necessary insurance. But their companionship had saved them, their weekly confidences in the Bide-a-Wee, their superstitious belief that an uncommitted surrender of maidenhead would appear, writ large, on their guilty faces the following Thursday afternoon. Not for them, however stoic their determination, the joys of marriage; not for them the pretended effort of deferred gratification, the 'not yet, my darling', the dress, the mystery, the steady accumulation of soft furnishings and co-ordinated units that is the reward of wedded bliss. They began to feel wronged. They began to feel the pangs of unremunerated virtue. They began to wonder — privately, of course — if the novels they bought every week at Haq's might have got it wrong. They looked at the elders of their sex, at Mrs Smellie and Mrs Duff, at Mrs Ingram and — just imagine! — at Mrs Bullock, and wondered how on earth they had managed it.

Their quarter century attained, they began, in short, to feel the first intimations of despair.

It had been Grace's idea to try this exciting, dangerous remedy. The others had agreed without demur.

Now they watched, Gracie and Grace, while Gray's squinting eyes scanned the turning pages of the *Gazette*.

"Here it is!" she announced at last, her lips crimping in a prim smile. "Shall I read it out?"

Grace and Gracie nodded, mouths agape, across their cooling tea and untasted fancies. Gray cleared her throat schoolmarmishly.

" 'Datamate Services'," she began with nasal elocution.

"Shhh!" hissed her sisters, mutely indicating the open hatch to the kitchen.

"Sorry. 'Datamate Services'," she resumed in a low whisper of ghastly female confidentiality, " 'Select your partner the scientific way, in complete confidence. Love and Marriage go together in our memory banks, many satisfied customers. Send full personal details, interests, etc., and £20 joining fee, refundable if not compatible. Replies under plain wrapper.' Then a box number. There!" she concluded, her expressive features composing themselves in readiness for the lines of middle age.

"How about it, then?"

Before they could reply, the tearoom door pinged open to reveal, stepping in from the darkling air, the form of Hamish Ganglion, his skin problem burning lividly in the pink light.

The young proprietor of Sounds Good (formerly the Bonaventure Wireless Shop) ran his hungry eyes over the three young ladies. He really didn't know why he was here: they always took tea together. But he never seemed to get a chance of meeting any of them alone and could not deny himself the opportunity of viewing them, however briefly, en masse.

"Dark enough for you, eh?" he asked.

"Don't worry, we all wear something white," riposted Grace. She laughed, and her full figure bounced provocatively at the frustrated youth. The others joined in.

"Where would that be, then?" countered Hamish.

"Never you mind," said Gracie, crossing her thin legs under the table.

"Are you thirsty?" teased Gray, twisting her head round to squint at him.

"Bit peckish," he muttered miserably.

He tapped on the counter for two long minutes while behind his narrow back he heard venomous sussurations from the Three Graces. Finally Mrs Spurtle sold him a Kit-Kat and he departed with a jaunty, "See you around, then," that deceived nobody. Time was when they'd been only too eager to go out with the DJ of the Lummock Disco Roadshow. Never came to anything, though. He couldn't understand it at all.

The door closed behind him. The girls clicked their tongues and rolled their eyes.

"Really!" said Gracie.

"The cheek!" said Gray.

"Some men'll try anything," said Grace, with all the outraged propriety of the matron she hoped soon to become. "Honestly!"

The others tutted their acquiescence to this observation. Gracie said:

"I mean — Ganglion!"

"I know," said Gray. "Imagine it!"

"He says it's very old," commented Grace. "Old Scots, or something."

"Oh, he's tried that one on you too, has he?" asked Gracie. "About the lions?"

"And me," Gray added hastily. "'Gang wi' the Lion'. He told me his ancestors fought with Bonny Prince Charlie."

"No wonder he lost, then," Grace said, before Gracie could get it in. Her tall namesake had to be content with a parody instead:

"'Will ye no' come back again?' — let's hope not!"

All three capped this *bon mot* with a draught of lukewarm tea. Gray made a move for the cake stand.

"Naughty!" said Grace, taking the cream one.

They munched in silence, thinking of scientific consanguinity.

***

On Friday evening, Hamish Ganglion called on Gracie to ask her to the Hallowe'en Disco at the Ben Almond Hotel the following Saturday. She replied that she was going out with friends that night, but would not elaborate.

On Saturday evening, he called on Grace.

"The drummer's a good friend of mine," he added.

She said she was booked up that night, and left it at that.

On Sunday evening, he tried Gray.

"You should know better than to ask such a thing on the Lord's Day," she snapped, and slammed the door in his face.

For the three young ladies, Monday and Tuesday passed in a tremble of expectancy. Hamish Ganglion fumbled through his work in a frustrated stupor.

On Wednesday morning, Angus Monzie the postman delivered computer-addressed items to three houses in Lummock View, noting that each envelope bore an ordinary first-class stamp. Funny for business letters not to be machine-franked; still, he supposed everyone was using these micro things nowadays.

Miss G. J. Mathieson, Miss G. M. Wemyss, Miss G. B. Abernethy: he wished those three would settle down to one address. It would make his life so much easier.

"Who's yours?" asked all three Graces at once the next afternoon, as soon as Mrs Spurtle had gone.

Three brown envelopes were produced from three handbags, and their contents unfolded.

"You first," they all said.

Gray cleared her throat.

"Well, then. I've got John Steel. He's thirty, and a freelance chef. He's medium height, slim, blond hair, likes cinema and dancing, and he wants to go out with me on Monday night."

She looked triumphantly at her friends. Gracie smiled and read her letter.

"Ian Owen, thirty-one, runs his own business supplying office equipment. He's five foot-ten, muscular, dark hair, and enjoys theatre and the finer things of life. He's free next Wednesday."

Grace pouted and read hers out.

"Euan McKinnock, twenty-nine, a journalist. Red hair, blue eyes, says he's a bit of an individualist and likes discos. He's average height and he's taking me out on Friday, tomorrow week that is."

She pouted again. They smiled at each other, Gray poured the tea and Gracie chose the cream cake. Grace left the *Gazette* in her bag. When young Hamish entered the tearooms they seemed too deep in conversation to notice him. He quickly withdrew.

"Mine's got a car," said Gray.

"So's mine," replied the other two.

"And he lives in Dunbroath."

"Mine too."

A peal of giggles. Mrs Spurtle looked through the hatch to make sure nothing unsavoury was going on, and listened awhile before closing it and turning back to Miss Phemister, who was waiting to hear all about it.

"Well?"

"Just the three shopgirls, as usual," replied the widow. "Talking about *men*," she snorted.

"Ooh. Do you think there's any chance —?" Miss Phemister's hand trembled a little. Her sublimated domesticity in the tearoom kitchen still left some room for vicarious excitement. She loved weddings.

"All too likely, I should think, poor little idiots. They'll learn when it's too late. You'll drown that pastry if you're not careful."

Though she applauded her partner's ignorance of marriage, Mrs Spurtle found that it led sometimes to those annoying flutterings and twitterings. As she once told a startled Mr McMurtry in an unguarded moment while paying in the week's takings, it still gave her a frisson after all these years to think that she was charging for it. No use telling Phemister that, of course. She stumped out into the tearoom to collect the dirty crocks.

The Three Graces were still chittering over their bits of paper and hardly noticed her. She could tell them: all stomach and dirty underwear, that's what men were. That and Saturday nights, and look where that got you. She shuddered massively, making the trolley rattle.

In the kitchen, Miss Phemister began to sing.

Hamish Ganglion closed the shop half an hour early next evening, reasoning that the chances of anyone wanting to buy a hi-fi after five o'clock on a dark October night were too remote to bother about. He told Eric, his YTS assistant, to go home: he could watch the children's telly on his own set. Hamish had some thinking to do.

He switched off the shop lights and went upstairs to the flat. He'd been long enough in the tearooms yesterday to see what his unrequiting lovers had been up to. He'd seen the name at the top of Grace's bit of paper. He felt his face burn with pocked and flaky anger. The ingratitude of it! Here was he: young, successful, running his own business now that the old man was in the Eventide with his chronic weakness, with his own flat and everything, and a motorbike. All right, he had a slight skin condition, but so what? Anyway, he'd read in a magazine at the Young Idea Hair Salon the other day that his particular skin was a sign of sex-drive and would clear up on its own, given half a chance. And they were hardly raving beauties, any of them, Gracie with her tombstone teeth, Grace with her weight problem, especially at the back, and the crosseyed Gray. They should count themselves lucky but no, they had to write off to a computer place! He'd read about the sort of men who used those agencies, too. There'd been an article about it in his men's magazine. Serve them right if they did get what the magazine said: 'Taken For A Ride', the article was called.

Lucky devils.

It was as he sat forking in cold baked beans at the kitchenette table that the amorphous passions which had seethed around the crinkles of his brain for twenty-four hours crystallised suddenly into one rational thought of piercing clarity: *Why shouldn't he?* Before the thought had a chance to accumulate distracting illustrations he reached convulsively for paper, biro and the *Gazette*. Where was it, where was it? Dental Repairs, Double Glazing, Monumental Sculptors, Pensioners' Appliances . . . there! Wedding Bells . . . Caterers, Bridal Requisites . . . he found it, took up his pen, and wrote:

> 'Dear Datamate, I am a young business man with my own . . .' what? Shop? Sounds common . . . Business, no, can't use the same word twice . . . 'retail outlet. I am six foot tall' — well, almost — 'with hazel eyes and' — think about this one, brown, no, crinkly, no, that could be taken the wrong way, what's the phrase women are supposed to go for? Oh yes — 'darkly curling hair. I am' — add a couple — 'twenty-' — make it three — 'six years old, though' — this is a good one, I'm getting the hang of this — 'with a very youthful appearance . . .

Hamish wrote on, conjuring ideals of character, appearance and interest into shimmering actuality. He hadn't got his Grade B English for nothing. He finished an hour later with an irresistible invitation to sophisticated womankind, and a hyphen between the syllables of his ancient name.

He'd show them!

It was a pity about the tomato sauce on the envelope, but it was his last one.

Youth is (it may be recalled) another country, and in it news travels fast, even by Craigfieth standards. At the Hallowe'en Disco on Saturday night the news of the Three Graces' glamorous escorts was on everyone's lips, and the girls themselves the centre of an interest which they did not discourage. Not even Hamish's substitution of the Sex Pistols for the last waltz could spoil their triumph.

By six o'clock on Monday night, eight eyes were watching, afraid almost to blink, the strip of road outside the door of 'Four Wynds', Lummock View. Three pairs belonged to Gray, who was sitting by the window of the residents' lounge in 'Four Wynds' itself, and to Grace and Gracie who were looking down from their bed-sitting-rooms along the road. The fourth pair belonged to Hamish Ganglion, who had concealed himself in the dark shade of the Golf Shop on the opposite side.

They had not long to wait. At ten past six a very shiny car, which Hamish bitterly identified as an Escort XR3i, drew to a stylish halt outside 'Four Wynds' and a blond figure in a leather jacket sprang athletically from the driver's seat and was admitted to the house. A few moments later he appeared again, escorting Gray on his left arm. She had made her eyes up heavily, to draw attention away from the irises, and looked a little like an emaciated panda.

The courtesy light shone briefly on her thin nose, then car and occupants were gone.

Gray's return was logged at 12.43 a.m.

On Wednesday night, in steady, drenching rain that had been coming down since lunchtime, the miserable Ganglion noted that the car was an Opel Manta. It made a racing stop outside 'Fairholme' and a sheepskin-coated figure with dark executive hair disappeared inside. Grace and Gray, from their watchtowers, saw their friend wore a beatific smile which enabled her to keep her teeth well hidden. The roar of the departing engine drowned the volley of sneezing from across the road.

Gracie let herself in at ten to one the next morning. At opening time in Sounds Good (formerly the Bonaventure Wireless Shop) Eric was dispatched to Meiklejohn's to buy decongestants, linctus and tissues.

Gray and Gracie entered the Bide-a-Wee that afternoon to find Grace waiting impatiently for them. She had already poured the tea. Gray sat down and razored into the cream cake, while Gracie began ostentatiously to unfold the *Perthshire Gazette*. Grace could bear it no longer.

"Well?" she quivered.

"Well what?" asked Gray.

"Well, what about them?" Grace squeaked.

"Well —" began the other two together, then broke into sniggers.

Grace's fingers drummed plumply on the table.

"You first," she told Gray. "Tell us about John."

"He's *really* nice," gushed Gray, "I mean, *really* nice, you know? And he drives superbly of course, I mean we were in Dunbroath before I knew what was happening, well what with the velour seats and the eight-track stereo I hardly noticed we were moving, you know what I mean? Anyway, he took me to this *really* chic nightspot, Bangers it's called, and he danced like a dream, I mean really —

magic, I was over the moon. Of course, he's got contacts, he knows people everywhere, you know? So, they put on this special hologram display, just for us, and that was really, you know, special, and then we went to the bar and he ordered two specials — just like that, 'Two Specials, André', he said, you could tell he was a special client of theirs — and when they came they had these wee umbrella things in them and he had to show me how to drink mine so he leant in close, like you know, like . . . that."

Grace breathed heavily through her nose, and nodded.

"Go on!"

"Well, then he told me all about himself, how he does all these special chef things in all the posh restaurants and hotels, for when they want something special done, he has to work awfy hard of course, Monday's his only night off worse luck, but he's doing really well and he's hoping to open his own really special restaurant soon if he can find someone to, you know, be his right hand. But he's got all his recipes computerised, and he showed me how —"

She stopped suddenly, flushed and breathless. Grace gasped.

"You mean he — he *took you back to his place?*"

Grace squinted down the sharp line of her nose into her lap.

"What was it like?"

"Nice."

"And?"

"Just . . . nice."

"Oh Gray, you didn't . . . you didn't?"

"Of course not!" exclaimed Gray. "Not on the first date, he's too nice to expect that. Besides, we're not engaged. Yet."

"Ooh!" said Grace.

"He's going to give me something special next week, though. That he's done."

"Ooh!"

"Ian's special, too," said Gracie, a little sharply.

"Oh yes, tell me about Ian!"

"Well, he said he could see I appreciated the better things in life, so he took me to the Theatre Bistro, the special one I mean, where all the actors go afterwards. They've got pictures on the wall with their signatures on, you know, Dick Emery and Bruce Forsyth and, oh, everybody, and we ordered Green Rooms, that's very expensive drinks made with Crême de Menthe and things, and I noticed they seemed to be giving him special attention and he explained, he'd just equipped all their offices for them as a special favour to the boss of the Theatre, who's a friend of his, of course he must be able to afford to do favours like that, I mean, his car! You wouldn't believe, it's like being in your own private jet, only without wings of course. Anyway, we had a meal there as well. I had a First Night Platter and he had a Rave Review Grill, really high-class food, and wine, white *and* red, of course, to go with the different things on the plate, and he told me about his life. Oh, really tragic it's been. He was engaged to this girl five years ago and she left him at the last moment and went off with the secretary of the Dunbroath Young Socialists. And the worst thing was, he wouldn't, you know, that, until they were married, out of respect for her, then, when she went off, they started living together, this girl and the socialist I mean, and it really broke his heart so he threw himself into work instead, to forget. And he hasn't been out with anybody since, but he says I'm different, and he thinks, well, he thinks I'm different, as I say. And he's got a computer too, for his flows and projections. He showed me all about it."

"So you went —"

"Yes, and it was very nice. *Very* nice," she added, with a sharp glance at Gray.

"His pee der tear, he calls it. That's French, of course."

"Sounds German to me," said Gray, taking another cake.

"Oh, well," condescended Gracie.

"Ooh!" sighed Grace again. "I can't wait for Friday!"

Grace was ready by half past five, and standing by the bay window of 'Timbertops'. She did not dare sit down yet in case it spoiled her dress. She had chosen a long dress, slashed to show an apparent thinness of leg. It had a low neckline to complement her best features which, after three-quarters of an hour in the changing room of Madame's, were secured in such a way as to maximise swell and plunge while avoiding the risk of overspill. She still practised shallow breathing through her nose, though, just in case.

A full moon cast long cold shadows across the golf course and turned the wet road into a steel ruler. In a fathomless well of darkness at the gable end of the Golf Shop, Hamish Ganglion thought he could hear his eyelids creak when he blinked. Nonetheless, he diligently polished the lenses of his new binoculars (given free to all retailers of Haiku Audionics).

A car pulled off the High Street and hissed along Lummock View. Curtains twitched at 'Fairholme' and 'Four Wynds'; Hamish raised his glasses. A Cavalier RSi. Grace went to stand behind the front door, remembering to take small steps and keep herself tucked in at the back. Westminster chimes rang loud in the tiled hall. Grace counted ten, as slowly as she could, then turned the latch.

"Hello," she said.

He wore a suede safari jacket and a collared shirt left carelessly open at the throat, and was standing two steps down from the doorway. As he ascended to greet her, she saw his shoes had a handmade look, with little gold buckles on them.

"Hi!" he said, "I'm Euan, and you've just got to be Grace. No other name would do. I hope I'm not too late?"

He stood in the hall now, seeming to fill it with his presence, his crisply tonsured red hair lighting up the innermost recesses of her soul until she felt warmed, possessed by him.

"Euan's a nice name, too," she said, looking up into his perfect blue eyes, and falling in. A hand — she saw not where it came from — brushed her cheek. She breathed in deeply, and saw his eyes widen and engulf her utterly. He spoke softly, huskily:

"I don't want to waste one precious moment, Grace, do you?"

"No," she said. "I'll get my mac."

He helped her put it round her shoulders.

Cerebral rage etched on Hamish Ganglion's consciousness the sharp-focused features of his rival as the couple left the house. The flash clothes, the twinkling shoes, the hair like a picture at the barber's; above all, the face. A smooth face, a face that smiled, and smiled . . . a face unblemished by pock or zit, the face of a woman's man. He loathed it, instantly and unforgettably. It was still before him when he brought his binoculars to bear on the front of Grace's dress as she climbed into the car; it filled the black vacuum between those glistening moons.

And then the usurper turned to walk round the car and seemed to look straight at him with a leer of triumph as if to say: run along and play, spotty. His knuckles whitened and he trembled all over, ague-stricken. They drove away.

He took her first to Scene Around, where it was Lovers' Night. Secure in the gaze of those wonderful blue eyes, she danced without heed to her seams or her bust and, miraculously, all remained contained, even after she had eaten. A hasty but thorough inspection in the mirror of the Juliets' confirmed the complex webbing and submammarian wiring of her corsage to be intact. Breathless from dancing, they sat together in one of the Spooning Couches on the edge of the dance floor. He bought them two Snakebites, and she noticed he called the barman by his first name.

She asked him about his work.

"Oh dear," he sighed, his handsome face a little occluded suddenly, "work, work, work, there's no getting away from it, is there? Not even tonight."

He sighed again.

"Oh, I'm sorry," she stuttered, "I didn't mean to upset —"

"No, no, I'm the one who should say sorry, of course you want to know. I've told you I'm a journalist, and you're probably thinking, 'Euan McKinnock, I've never seen his stuff in the papers, I wonder if he's making it all up'."

"Oh, no!" Grace gasped, horrified that he should have suspected this so easily. "Of course I wouldn't think like that!"

"Well," he smiled, "I can see I was right, then — you really are one in a million. You see, I'm what they call an Investigative Journalist — I do all the stories the others are too frightened to touch. That's why I'm freelance, not tied to any one paper, you see. Sometimes I use a nom-de-plume — that's to say, a writer's name, as you know."

Grace nodded vigorously. She must remember that; it was definitely one up on pee der tear. Euan continued; he had to speak very close to her ear, because of the noise. She could feel his lips tickling her hair.

"Sometimes" — he glanced anxiously round — "sometimes I'm Uther Pendragon, and sometimes, for foreign news, I use a French name. So whenever you see a story signed 'U.P.' or 'France Presse', you'll know it's me. But — sssh! — don't tell anyone! It's what they call a professional secret."

Her heart beat wildly. That 'Sssh!' had sent the adrenalin mainlining through her system. She risked a glance at her bust: still safe, thank goodness.

"I won't tell a soul," she breathed.

"Oh Grace, I knew I could trust you," he murmured, and put his firm, manly hand on her knee. Beneath the taut fabric, she seemed to feel the joint begin to melt. She could melt in his arms, right now . . .

But he was speaking again, in a low conspiratorial voice.

"Listen Grace, I know tonight is our special night, but — well, now you're in on my secret, would you like to know more about my work? Find out what makes me tick?"

She was sure he must see her heart lurching, or at any rate the effect of it on her bodice. Quickly she said:

"Yes, oh yes, Euan, I'd love to."

So they left.

He drove quickly through a narrow maze of darkened streets until she gave up trying to work out where they were or where they were going. He did not speak, but turned to her often, and smiled reassuringly. At last they stopped, and he said:

"Here we are, then. The nerve centre."

As he bent to find her handbag on the floor — such consideration! — she could see that beneath his lovely exciting hair, his scalp was a perfect pink. She loved him then, for his lack of dandruff.

The building was on three storeys. A narrow stair disappeared behind a sinister-looking archway, but he took her hastily round the side.

"Top flat," he explained. "I'm on the first two floors."

He unlocked the door and led her past what appeared in the hall light to be a kitchen and a sitting-room, to the front room of the flat. It was lined with filing cabinets and cupboards. In the corner opposite the window was a large desk, and on it was a substantial amount of micro-processor accoutrements and a screen that winked greenly at them.

"Now, then," he said. He selected a disk from one of the dozens of labelled boxes on a shelf above the desk, and fed it in. The screen leaped at once into frenzied activity. Grace caught only odd phrases as the text rolled away off the top of the screen: floods, earthquakes, by-elections, conferences, death, plague, scandal, wars and the rumour of war . . . Euan clicked some keys, and the display was suddenly still.

Grace read: 'UK Sterling M3 Index: Treasury Forecasts To OECD' and a set of incomprehensible graphs and figures.

"You might call that Top Secret," said Euan, switching off and removing the disk. "See this?"

He held it out for her to read.

"Keesing's Contem- contemper . . . erary —"

"Precisely, yes," he said. "Sounds innocent enough, doesn't it? Computer code, of course: the sort of precaution I have to take, I'm afraid, in this wicked world. What it really means is, Keep Concealed Away. KCA, get it? I'm the only one who has the program for accessing all the data on this. So," he smiled, "now you know!"

She smiled weakly back: he seemed so tall suddenly, as if he were going to fall on her . . .

"Grace? Grace! Oh my darling, I'm so sorry, I shouldn't have frightened you like that. Here, lean on me, that's right, come into the other room and sit down."

He put his strong arm round her waist, or some of it at least, and straight away she felt better, felt . . . healed.

She nudged him with her thigh, but not enough to knock him over.

"I'm all right," she said. "Really."

The sitting-room was clean, but not a lot else. Grace felt she had to say something.

"That's a nice, er . . . rug."

Euan laughed ruefully.

"I know," he said. "Not very homely, is it? I just don't have the time, you see, always so busy, always working. Hardly even eat, actually, except when I have to. What I need's a — oh well, never mind."

"I know what you need!" Grace announced, playfully squeezing his arm. "Let me see your kitchen."

She was mistress of the situation, as, after ten years preparing for it, who would not be? She tutted over the sink, sighed knowingly at the food cupboards, ran her finger coquettishly over the surfaces, yet contrived nevertheless, with professionally feminine sleight of hand, to create two cups of coffee and a bowl of tinned fruit salad out of the culinary chaos. The latter Euan placed carefully in the fridge, "to remind me of you when I eat it".

They took their coffee into the lounge, where they sat deliciously close together on a two-seater settee in front of the gas fire. Grace kicked off her shoes and wiggled her toes inside the nylon. She knew just the suite to go in this room . . .

They drove out of Dunbroath in dreamy silence, Grace gazing through the window at the necklaces of twinkling neon lights.

"Yes," said Euan, reading her thoughts, "my town. I love it. Next time, I'd like to walk with you through the streets, late at night, just breathing it all in. Oh!"

He braked suddenly, causing Grace's seat belt to dig in painfully and almost catastrophically.

"I'm sorry! There I go, taking you for granted . . . Grace, please say there'll be a next time. You — you do like me, don't you, just a little bit?"

"Silly boy!" She ruffled his hair. In the dark, she interpreted his indrawn breath as a sigh of relief. "Of course!"

And then he kissed her.

It was past one o'clock when she got in. Gracie and Gray were almost asleep on their feet. She stood in her room, looking round it as if for the last time, as she was sure it nearly was.

She heaved a deep, contented sigh of pleasure and, its dynamic tension no longer needed, her bust flowed gratefully out of its twin prisons.

On Saturday morning the post once again failed to bring Hamish Ganglion any data on his putative intended. He wrote to Datamate again, reminding them that they had cashed his cheque the previous Monday.

Grace could not contain her news until her half day at Mr Smellie's. She hurried back to Lummock View straight after work on Saturday evening to call on Gracie at 'Fairholme', and found Gray there, too. The two friends were sitting on Gracie's bed, studying a copy of *Brides* magazine. Gracie's Snoopy poster had been taken down; in its place was a photograph of a large expanse of sandy beach, lit only by the rays of the setting sun, and deserted except for a couple holding hands on the distant shoreline.

She told them everything; or, rather, nearly everything. She kept her promise of reticence about his work, even though this meant telling them less about the visit to the flat than she would like to have told. She mentioned the computer, though, and went into great detail about Euan's wonderful eyes.

"So blue, you'd think you could swim in them," she concluded.

"Mmm," said Gray. "John's got the same, only of course they go with his honey-blond hair."

"Personally, I think blue eyes with brown hair are more appealing," interjected Gracie, looking up from an article entitled 'How To Make That First Night One To Remember'.

"Especially Ian's. They're fantastically blue."

Grace smiled, feeling no animosity towards her companions. She knew no eyes could be bluer than Euan's, and no hair more striking nor more clean. Nonetheless, as the talk wore on and the pages of the magazine were turned, each became conscious that the cement of their friendship was beginning to crumble. There were reticences and evasions that had never been there before. Each noted the phenomenon, though none particularly regretted it; after all, they assured themselves, they were about to become properly grown-up at last, and that was bound to change things.

The bonds of friendship had been renewed by Thursday, however, at least between Gray and Gracie, by a significant and unexpected breakthrough in their pre-nuptial foreplay. Each had, apparently, contrived to steer her escort past certain important shop windows during their second evening out, and this triumph of navigation had led to a kindling of mutual interest in domestic comforts.

In short — and, unable to continue teasing Grace for long, they came swiftly to the point — Gray's John had shown a most satisfactory enthusiasm for a fitted carpet offer in the window of Floored Again, while Gracie's Ian had warmly approved her taste in kitchen units in the showroom of Cookerama. Major progress had been made towards a decision to purchase these symbolic items, both of which were considerably cheaper in Dunbroath than they were at the Craigfieth Centre.

"Even so, they must be terribly expensive?" suggested Grace.

"Oh, well," said Gray coyly, glancing across to Gracie, "things are different now, aren't they? I mean, this is the age of Women's Lib. People share things nowadays, especially if they're going to — well . . ."

"Yes," agreed Grace. If they expected her to be disappointed or jealous she was going to prove them wrong. Hadn't Euan mentioned walking through the streets? She'd just have to make sure their romantic journey took them past a representative selection of three-piece suites.

"So you're going to buy them together?"

Both shook their heads.

"It's easier if John does it," explained Gray. "I can't get off work, can I? Anyway, he knows a few people in the trade. We can save money for . . . something else."

"Same with Ian. I'll pay my share next Wednesday and he'll have it fitted."

They sighed happily. Gray said, "You'll have to get your Euan interested too."

"Don't worry," Grace replied firmly. "I'll see to that. Hey, wouldn't it be great to — I mean, when *it* happens, if we all did *it* together? The six of us!"

"Oh yes!" they breathed, and Gracie added:

"Won't the Reverend MacAndrew be surprised? Three weddings, all at once!"

"And we'll let Hamish be an usher!" shrieked Gray.

In the kitchen, Mrs Spurtle heard their manic giggling. She dumped the washing-up disgustedly in the sink, breaking two cups. Phemister never stopped singing these days. It was beginning to get on her nerves.

"Oh, I forgot to ask," said Grace as they were putting on their coats. "What was your special present?"

"Oh yes!" exclaimed Gray. "I nearly forgot. Well, John had done this special dessert for a very posh do at Gleneagles — I think he said Gleneagles — and he did one extra, just for, mmmm, *us*!"

"What was it called?" asked Gracie.

"Let me think, now. It was a very long name, and all foreign." She mimed an elaborate pretence of recollection.

"Oh, yes. 'Fruites de Cannes avec Syrop Munchausen'." she announced. "Lots of naughty calories, of course, but then I don't have to worry, do I?"

Even this cruel barb could not wound Grace now. It was obvious what Euan liked, and anyway, who wanted to go round looking like a lot of coathangers? She remembered how they used to tease Gray in the changing room at school, when she was still wearing a vest in second year. At least she'd never had to worry about that! She waddled quickly home to look through her club books.

Her faith was not misplaced. The next night, Euan behaved as though she had rehearsed him herself. They paused to kiss outside Suite 'n' Low . . . and there it was. They anatomised its dralon fabric, its frilly valances, the practical wooden inserts on the arms . . . and the bargain was struck.

"Leave it to me," said Euan. "I know the guy who imports these."

They kissed again, and walked on hand in hand.

On Monday morning, his letters unanswered, Hamish Ganglion telephoned the *Perthshire Gazette*. After some minutes, the switchboard answered.

"Hello? Oh good. Can I speak to Slim Beauly, please? What? Slim Beauly. He's your Contemporary Music Critic."

"One moment please," said the switchboard.

Several hundred moments later, a voice said, "Hi, this is Slim Beauly, what's your rap?"

"Mungo, hi, this is Hamish, remember? In Craigfieth."

"Oh, Hamish, hi, how are you man, still truckin'?"

"Yeah, sort of. Listen, do us a favour, will you? I need to track down a box number in the paper."

"Ssss! Dat's privi'lidged information, boy! What's the handle?"

"Datamate — Datamate Services, find your scientific partner, you know. They advertise every week."

He heard a burst of cackling laughter.

"Datamate? Jeez, I'm surprised we print that. Hey, what's your interest, then? You're not married, are you?"

"No — well, never mind. Just find me that address. That's all."

"Okay, Okay, cool it. Personally, I've never had to pay for it. Still, I'll do what I can. Take a day or two, though. I might have to come heavy with one of the Classified Girls, know what I mean?"

"Thanks, Mungo," gritted Hamish and hung up.

A casual observer, were such a creature to exist in Craigfieth at two o'clock on a Tuesday morning in November, would have been bemused to see, outside a house in Lummock View, a young lady standing under a street light and waving her left hand frantically to the seemingly blank windows above. As it happened, there were two observers behind those ubiquitous net curtains, and they understood perfectly.

They understood at the same hour on Thursday morning, too.

Some eight hours earlier, just as he was shutting the shop, Hamish Ganglion received the news he had been waiting for.

"Hi, Hamish, still containin' yourself? OK, here's the location. 171 Forfar Road, got that? Guy by the name of J. Callaghan. Sounds like a shaky outfit to me, still I'm just the messenger. Seems he took up a three-ads-for-the-price-of-two offer but he hasn't paid yet. OK, that's it — oh, by the way ole buddy, this'll cost you two dinners and one helluva lot of drinks, you get me?"

"Aye, thanks," said Hamish. "I'll make it up to you. I'll play all your crappy demo tapes at the Christmas Disco. Cheers."

He left Eric to mind the shop on Thursday. He might need the whole day: Callaghan could turn nasty, and the Honda 90 had never been all that fast.

He found Forfar Road just before midday, parked the bike and followed the numbers down from 247.

It did not look like an office, more like a small tenement struggling to look like a large house and, since there was no number on it, he could only assume that the memory banks of Datamate were somewhere in this block between 173 and 169. There was some sort of mutated shrub in the unweeded garden, its leaves like blackened tinfoil scraping in the breeze. Hamish swallowed, and mounted the smelly stair to the left of it. He may as well start at the top and work down. His binoculars banged against his ribs as he went up. He didn't really know why he'd brought them.

It was gloomy at the top of the stair and he almost had to feel his way forward. Thus it was that he made the acquaintance of a large lady who introduced herself as Mrs Corbie. She was standing by the undrawn curtain of the landing window, almost as if she had been spying through it on his arrival.

"Friend o' his, are ye?" she growled.

"Wh-wha' . . . pardon?" he gulped.

"Yon creature." She tugged the curtain open and nodded to the grey emptiness.

Hamish peered through the window, as if expecting Yon Creature to be hovering outside.

"Do you by any chance mean Mr Callaghan?"

She laughed, a harsh bronchitic bark that had aeons of poor landlord-tenant relations behind it.

"Aye, that I do," she snarled. "I mean oor Mr Callaghan. Only crawled oot o's pit abute an hour ago, but I mussed him. But I'll no' muss him when he gangs back."

"Have you, is he . . . I mean, does he owe you money then?" Perhaps, thought Hamish, she was another dissatisfied customer, though it seemed rather unlikely; after all, who —

"Aye, that he does. A month's rent, for one thing, and a fortnight's worth o' sleepless nights, wi's on-carryings. Thunks he's a real Bonny Prunce Cherming, wi's fancy cars an's wugs, but he disnae fule me!"

"Wugs —?" began Hamish. But then he saw, crossing the street below, a figure whose upturned, supercilious face at once froze and boiled his blood, just as it had done two weeks before in his dark, shivering hour behind the Golf Shop. Whatever he did, he must not let Mrs Corbie see him: he must get to the bastard first. He drew the curtain shut.

"Well, er — thanks!" he piped, and clattered off downstairs.

He was too late. He rounded the corner of the house in time to see his quarry's gold-buckled foot disappear through the side entrance, then he heard the unmistakable sound of a Yale latch clunking into place.

But Hamish Ganglion — Gang wi' the Lion — was not to be defeated. He crept stealthily back to the front of the house, ducking under the sooty branches of the hideous bush. Through the uncurtained window of the front room he saw a green, flickering screen, and the red-haired man seated before it, his fingers on a keyboard.

Hamish blessed his foresight. Easing himself as silently as possible through the sharp unhealthy leaves he found purchase for his elbow in the fork of a branch, and brought the binoculars slowly, slowly, like a stalker on the hill, to his watering eyes.

It was him: the same smooth, sculpted chops, the same smiling, sensual lips, the same manikin's hair . . . the same. Hamish blinked, focused the glasses on the VDU screen, and began to read what was on it.

There were three columns, with a name at the head of each. At the foot of the first two was a simple arithmetical calculation, in which a small sum of money was subtracted from a much larger figure. Hamish did not need to look at what lay in between. The names alone told him enough.

The red-haired man switched off the screen, leaned back in his chair, and scratched his head.

It is not unusual for a man to scratch his head. It is, however, uncommon for him first to remove his hair in order to do it, revealing a scalp of repulsive maggoty whiteness, filmed with mousey stubble.

Hamish closed his eyes and stifled the desire to cry out loud. When he looked again, the man was standing before a large metallic grey cupboard, just visible to Hamish between the branch he was wedged against and the window frame. He was fitting a key into the lock. Then he took off his suede jacket.

He hung the red wig next to the blond one and the brown one. He arranged the suede jacket carefully on a hanger, and hung it in front of the sheepskin coat. Then he locked up and left the room.

Hamish began to disentangle himself from the ghastly foliage, his heart pounding and his throat dry. Then he froze, for he saw that the man had re-entered the room.

He sent up a silent prayer for invisibility.

He need not have worried. Callaghan, if that was his name, was too busy with what he was doing to glance out of the window. He was bringing in suitcases and piling them on the floor.

The intrepid youth's last sight of the offices of Datamate was of the grim, toadlike face of Mrs Corbie, eerily disembodied by the curtains at the upstairs window.

Hamish kicked his Honda into spluttering life and rode off. A sharp, icy singleness of purpose had taken over from his earlier palpitating outrage. He knew precisely what he had to do. By one o'clock he had located the premises of the *Perthshire Gazette* and had blustered his way into an office containing a typewriter, a photocopying machine and Mungo 'Slim' Beauly, critic, cub reporter, unrecorded pop idol and friend in need.

Miss Phemister had hung two corn dollies (purchased earlier in the day from the Craft Corner out of her own money) above the corner table, on whose embroidered surface rested two elegantly arranged left hands, third fingers prominent. Grace held both hers in her lap.

Nobody could remember whose turn it was to pour the tea. They helped themselves, and no one complained when Grace took the cream cake.

"Of course, it's not the real ring," said Gray, squinting lovingly at it and not caring how many times she had said it before.

"We're going to choose that together. John wants a single diamond, but I fancy a cluster. He says a single stone will show everyone I'm his single love. He's terribly romantic."

"I'm going to have a sapphire, I think," said Gracie. "To match Ian's blue eyes."

Grace winced a little, thought of rubies and red hair, and was comforted.

"And where did yours come from?" she asked Gracie again, just to show friendliness.

"From his own little finger, bless him," crooned Gracie. "And it fitted nearly perfectly, just like that!"

"So did mine," said Gray, "only it wasn't his own one, it belonged to his grannie. It's terribly old!" She kissed it.

Grace made an appropriate noise. She looked again at the corn dollies dangling obscenely from the light fitting.

She had to ask.

"Did it . . . was he — you know?"

"Mmmm!" they replied, and took a sip of tea each. It had, quite a lot, and he wasn't, particularly, but it didn't do to let on. Besides, you had to give them something in return, didn't you, every now and then. Bless them.

Hamish slept long and deeply that night. He was physically exhausted, for one thing, the suspension on the Honda not being what it once was, and for another, he was untroubled in his mind. It was all up to the Post Office now.

Mr Smellie had been fussy all day, and at five o'clock had insisted on double-checking Grace's till. It was gone half past by the time she got home, and she wouldn't have bothered opening her mail if it hadn't been for the Dunbroath postmark. But it couldn't be from him; there were two sheets of typeface, stapled together. She began to skim through on her way upstairs.

Dear Miss Wemyss . . . apologise profoundly . . . chance in a million . . . never occurred before. Enquiries . . .

She halted on the second landing.

. . . assumed name . . . false identity . . . James Harold Wilson . . . Mrs Wilson . . . in the office . . . four children under six years . . . babe in arms. In view of this . . . good name of Datamate . . .

She clutched at the banister for support. Then she read on.

... in lieu of refund, alternative selection . . . new to our files . . . double-checked . . . details enclosed . . . Yours sincerely, R. MacDonald (Manager).

Mechanically, Grace turned the page.

'I am a young single businessman with my own Retail Outlet. I am five foot eleven and three-quarters, with brown eyes and curly hair . . .

She finished reading, then went upstairs to change.

"Small world, eh?" remarked Hamish, half an hour later.

"I brought a spare helmet."

Four eyes watched their departure. Then Gray and Gracie sat up half the night wondering what it might mean.

Hamish Gang-Lion's little trouble cleared up early in the new year, at the same rate as Grace Wemyss' weight loss. The weekly gatherings at the Bide-a-Wee ceased abruptly in November, and she doesn't see much of Gray and Gracie these days.

After all, as Hamish remarked one evening as they were relaxing on the new sofa, waiting for their favourite serial to come on, people change when they're engaged, don't they? Particularly when it's a long engagement.

6

The Old Folks at Home

We have, at the latter end of this century, made great strides in our provision of care for the elderly. Gone are the days of insanitary domestic muddle, when grandparents sat mumbling in the chimney corner, gobbing in the embers as they handled a drooling infant, while around them the filthy tide of life swept in and out, reminding them of the burden they were laying on the rising generations. We have dispensed with all that guilt and irksomeness in these nuclear days.

Gone, too, is the workhouse. Nowadays, the institutionalised aged have their own rooms, and in the Craigfieth Eventide Home there are forty-eight of them, arranged on two floors in four blocks of a dozen each. It is a modern building, one of the first to be erected in an access of conspicuous provision by the new Regional Authority back in 1973. It is conveniently sited on what used to be the allotments of the now defunct Vale of Lummock Council.

The four residential units are arranged, dice-wise, around a central administrative pod, and joined to it by glass-covered walkways. While each block has its own lounge facilities, which residents are free to make use of if they wish, this middle building is also the social centre of the Home, providing as it does not only the canteen area but also the main lounge-cum-concert room. These two facilities lie to the right of the main entrance; both feature a long, double-glazed wall of windows, so that the inmates may enjoy, while they are eating, a panoramic vista of

160

School Road and, while resting or enjoying a sing-song, a private prospect of the long back gardens of Lummock View. To the left of the main entrance lie the offices of the various medical, administrative and secretarial support services and, of course, the headquarters and furnished apartments of Matron herself.

Miss Hilda Dowie was seated at her desk. A native of Craigfieth, she had lived and worked all her life in the area, first at the Strathlummock Cottage Hospital and then, when that was rationalised and turned into a leisure centre, here at the Eventide. To begin with she had been in charge of Bailie Douglas (each residential unit was named after a noted municipal councillor and magistrate; the other three were Bailies Alexander, Home and Botha) then, five years previously, Matron McKneispey had retired and gone to live with her married daughter in Tain, and Miss Dowie had succeeded to the tasteful grey and cream décor of the office and the whitewood furnishings of the flat. She was proud of her position, proud of the Home itself: her own widowed mother had been among the first beneficiaries of the new regime. Now, at the age of 52, her still ungreying hair securely bunned, her full unravaged figure encased in its starched uniform, she presided over what she liked to call a Tight Ship In Calm Waters. If there was a cloud in the offing, it was no bigger than a man's hand, and on a very distant horizon.

Before her sat a couple in their mid-thirties: Mr and Mrs Ochilree, of Newbiggings Farm which, it had been established, lay just within the Home's catchment area.

Mrs Ochilree she knew as a teacher at Craigfieth Primary School; a pert, forceful woman who carried over her crisp, didactic enunciation from the classroom into real life, her trim, no-nonsense outline only a little blurred by the first intimations of pregnancy. The husband she had not met before, but recognised in him the unmistakable signs of the progressive farmer: the bespoke woollen suit, the face tanned by sunlight filtered through the tinted glass of the tractor cab, the ears reddened from long hours wearing headphones, the neatly manicured fingers. Both seemed utterly at ease with their surroundings. They were there to arrange the admission of Mr Ochilree's father, at Matron's earliest convenience.

"Well, now," she said, and checked her list. "I think I've got everything I need to know, for the time being. Let's see — dietary foibles, yes, well we soon sort those out, toilet habits, regular and clean, good, medical problems, nothing we can't control here — oh, I forgot to ask, Mr Ochilree: does the prospective resident *drink*, at all?"

The young man grinned brightly and then winced as his wife kicked his ankle.

"Erm, no, not really, I mean, well sometimes, you know? Just occasionally."

"I see."

Matron made a note on the form. "Because we have a peaceful community here, Mr Ochilree, and we don't want it disturbed by immoderacy. Do you understand?"

"Oh aye," he replied sheepishly. His wife pursed her lips and nodded.

"Now then, where was I? Glasses, yes, teeth, yes, ambulatory aids, not applicable as such. Would you say he has any interests?"

"Oh, aye, he's always been very —"

"Because if so, the library van calls once a week and he'll be able to take out up to two books at a time, and then there's always the television of course, I sometimes think it's stuck on button three! But there, they seem to like it. Now, we're nearly there — hearing problems: you say 'only when he wants them' and I do so understand what you mean, Mrs Ochilree, believe me, but we conquer them in time, I can assure you — and anti-social attitudes, just the usual. Well!"

She smiled and rose from her chair.

"If you'd like to follow me, I'll give you a look around and you can meet some of Mr Ochilree's new neighbours — Mr Ochilree *Senior's*, that is" — she laughed shortly — "and then you can see his room over in Botha. He'll have a lovely view of the High Street from there, you'll be able to tell him how lucky he is. Dear Mr Bleaney used to spend hours by his window every day, just watching."

She led them across the corridor into the Main Lounge where, cocooned in warm air, six elderly persons sat in a broken semi-circle round a very large and barely audible television set. The chairs seemed of gargantuan size to the visitors, the high backs dwarfing their occupants, some of whom were barely able to reach the floor with their feet. Another, empty, semi-circle fronted the huge south window, beyond which the October afternoon had settled like a grey crepuscular shroud over the dying gardens. Mr Ochilree shuddered a little; his wife smiled bravely. Matron spoke to her:

"You'll see we like to keep the seating arrangements as socially informal as possible, Mrs Ochilree: no sitting-out here! Except for that one, of course, which is for one of our friends who has, well, a little weakness. Isn't that right, Mrs Bonar?" she suddenly shouted.

The frail old lady thus addressed shrank back into her chair and replied with a stream of palsied nods while continuing to knit something very long and purple in her lap.

"Poor dear!" exclaimed Matron only a little less audibly. "Heaven knows what she thinks she's knitting, but she's always at it. I tell her it wouldn't fit a giraffe, whatever it is, but she takes no notice. Do you, Mrs Bonar?"

Mrs Bonar shrank still further, smiling weakly with moist, bruised lips. Mr Ochilree noticed she was almost bald.

His wife expressed an interest in the potted plants, and while Matron was showing them to her (each, apparently, had been donated by grateful families of the residents) Mr Ochilree read the large handwritten notice above the gas fire. "We would prefer you not to smoke," it said. "Smoking causes cancer, bronchitis, emphysema, heart disease and premature birth. If you really must fill your lungs with tar, please sit by the extractor in the corner. Thank you, H. Dowie, Matron." He saw that the two scruffiest chairs on the end of the crescent had been placed under a fan in the window. There were no ashtrays.

His wife and Matron were leaving the lounge. He was just in time to catch the big glass fire door before it swung shut.

". . . as I say, if they were eating I'd show you, but at this time of day there's no point. Oh there you are, Mr Ochilree, I thought we'd lost you. I see you read my little notice. It's never too late, you know, to form good health habits."

"Oh, aye. No," he replied.

They followed her along the walkway to the Bailie Botha Unit, moving in single file at one point to allow a wheelchair to pass. "Out for a spin again, Mr Carr?" bellowed Matron, and he gargled by way of reply. His eyes, Mr Ochilree noticed, had the same look of furtive apprehension as Mrs Bonar's.

They passed through more heavy swing doors into the Unit, and looked inside the Botha Residents' Lounge. The windows here afforded an unrelieved prospect of the backs of shops across a patch of worn-out scrubby grass in sharp contrast to the mown immaculacy of the Eventide lawns. A stark sign in the room simply said 'No Smoking'.

The television played to empty chairs.

"We like them to rest a little before their tea," explained Matron. "Otherwise they can get excited."

She rang for the lift, stooping to press the call button.

"Designed for the residents, as you see," she grunted, straightening. "Now, I'll take you up to the gentlemen's floor." She tittered briefly. "We let the gentlemen go on top," she said.

They clattered up in silence.

"What happens if it gets stuck?" asked Mr Ochilree as they stepped out.

"There's an emergency button," Matron snapped. "And a direct line to the engineers in Dunbroath. But it's never happened in my time."

She clacked off down the linoleum and opened a door.

"Bathroom. Toilets, low unit of course, shower, assisted shower, and bath. Notice the safety grips. We have a strict bath rota, which is pinned to every door. You understand there can be no exceptions, except of course in the one case we already have. There have been no complaints, as far as I know. Now then, I'll show you one of the occupied rooms so you'll have an idea of how our residents live here. This one, I think."

She flung open the door next to the bathroom and switched on the light. A large, red-faced gentleman was revealed in the act of turning away to button his trousers.

"Now then, Mr Sproat, that's not resting before tea, is it? I can see we'll have to keep an eye on you. I'm just showing this lady and gentleman what the rooms look like with your bits and pieces in. We tidy them up every day, of course," she explained, as the hapless Mr Sproat continued his fumbling. "But they still get their things everywhere. Still, as you can see, the rooms are quite homely and provided it's kept within reason we don't discourage them from bringing in some of their own belongings. So long as we don't hide them away in our sock drawer, though, eh Mr Sproat?"

But Mr Sproat said nothing. He merely breathed heavily, and kept his back turned.

"You should see the laundry we get sometimes," muttered Matron darkly as they left. "Not my province, thank goodness, but some of our auxiliaries are straight out of school and very impressionable. Still, I don't think we'll have any more trouble with our Mr Sproat. Now, here we are."

She halted outside room fourteen and selected a key from her belt.

"This is the room, Mr Bleaney's that was. You'll notice, by the way, that the rooms can only be locked from the outside; that's for fire regulations as well as helping with the smooth running of the Home. We only allow Mr — well, one of our guests here, to put a bolt on, and that's for our own protection, except when he forgets to do it. . . . Well, as you can see, Mrs Ochilree, your father-in-law will have every comfort here: there's a wardrobe and a wee chest, a chair, bedside cabinet with urinal drawer, wash-hand basin, tooth glass bracket, and bed. The floor is a special non-slip material, so no rugs, please, some of our old folks look so sad when we have to take them away. And of course, there's the view! Mr Bleaney was *so* fond of it! You can't see much at the moment, but on a fine day you can see right through between the Post Office and the Craft Corner, and watch all the busy folk, and the traffic. Used to count the lorries, he did, and tell me every day how many he'd seen. Such an easy guest! Still, I mustn't go on like this—are there any questions you'd like to ask me?"

Mrs Ochilree turned from the window.

"Are they allowed out?" she asked.

"By special arrangement with the families concerned, of course, and we have outings every week in the Community bus to the Chiropodist in Dunkeld and sometimes treats as well, at Christmas and other times. Naturally, we cannot prevent the more able ones from going out on their own, but it's not encouraged, really. We like to think we can create a community atmosphere here and there's lots to do, thanks to our Occupational Therapist. I don't think you need to worry too much, Mrs Ochilree."

"Good," she said. "Come on then, Angus, my legs are getting tired."

"Oh. Aye, right," he replied, and followed his wife into the corridor.

"Are you sure there's nothing else you want to know, Mr Ochilree?"

He blushed a little. He never had been any good at asking questions until long after they could be answered. He cast around for something to ask about, and pointed to the next door along.

"Erm, what's that for?"

They all looked at the red triangle sticker, high up on door thirteen.

"That's a resident with, er, special needs. He has a particular weakness. We put that up to alert our student nurses to use their discretion."

"Oh, I see. Is he the one with the chair, the one we saw downstairs?"

"Yes," replied Matron grimly. "When he condescends to use it. And he has a bolt, and a bath rota exemption. And . . . other things. And now, if you'll excuse me, I *am* rather busy . . ."

"Of course," said Mrs Ochilree. "We'll write and confirm tomorrow. Thank you very much indeed, Matron, you've quite put our minds at rest. Hasn't she, Angus?"

"Oh aye, erm thanks a lot," he confirmed, and followed his wife to the lift.

***

Oswald Ochilree sat by the window of Room Fourteen, Bailie Botha Unit, looking at the traffic. Every evening that week, Matron had asked him how many lorries he had seen, and every time he replied that he did not know. Now here he was, counting them. Perhaps it was some kind of test they gave new residents.

There did not seem to be anything else to do. There was still over an hour to go before tea.

Two. A green one and a red one, going in opposite directions.

The first night, he had felt too miserable to leave his room. Instead he got into bed, closed his eyes, and slept.

After breakfast the next morning, which had not been porridge, he had made the acquaintance of some of his fellow-inmates in the Main Lounge; it had not been easy, confined as he was to the smokers' corner, but he had tried.

He had a short conversation about the weather with Mrs Bonar, and agreed with her that it was chilly, and likely to get chillier before it got warmer, and that the wind seemed to cut right through you sometimes, though it was warmer when the sun was out and they had much to be thankful for, really. He had wondered how, in the tropical heat of the Eventide Home, she could know anything about the wind: however, since on the second and subsequent mornings Mrs Bonar had imparted the same meteorological information in the same words, he soon stopped wondering and she, for her part, relapsed into her knitting. That seemed to be all there was to Mrs Bonar.

Mr Sproat had asked him if he had any magazines to lend. He had replied that he had the *Scottish Farmer*, if Mr Sproat was interested. Mr Sproat had snorted and fallen monumentally silent. Mr Carr had laughed (at least, he thought it was a laugh) and then he too had closed down communications.

Then Mr Mealie, a pile of seed catalogues in his lap, had observed that it was never too early to propagate. Mr Sproat had excused himself from the Lounge at that point, and Miss Abercrombie's shakes had become more violent.

Miss Gourock had smiled remorselessly at him until, after half an hour, he had been forced to leave.

Three. A big brown one with a trailer. Ought that to count as two? "Please, Matron, I saw three, or four if you count the trailer. Can I count the trailer, please, Matron?"

Pull yourself together, man.

Don't give way. Nil carborundum.

On Wednesday, Occupational Therapy day, he had tried to paint a stone. He had chosen stone painting from a list of activities which included basket weaving, rug hooking, and cleaning the cutlery. He had begun to paint Fergie, his prize cross Hereford bull (Supreme Champion, Central Scottish Fatstock Show 1954) trying to capture every well-remembered curve and wrinkle of the beloved beast, until Miss Farquhar, the Therapist, had passed by and said, "Jings, what a fierce-looking cow, Mr Ochilree! I wouldn't like to milk her."

He had given up then.

Thursday was bath day, but Matron had pinned up a notice saying, 'Rota suspended'. He did not bother to find out why.

On Friday he'd gone to the Chiropodist, who said he'd got splendid feet for his age, and not to bother going again.

The minibus had passed by the farm entrance. He'd closed his eyes for that bit.

On Saturday afternoon, the Maureen O'Rourke Dancers (Junior Section) had given a performance of 'Little Red

Riding Hood' in the Main Lounge. Matron had sharply reminded Mr Sproat that they already had a wolf, and eventually ordered him to leave.

Four, five. Or five, six. Number five, or six, was a cattle transporter all the way from Harrison and Hetherington in Carlisle. He'd always had good luck there . . . stop it! His knuckles whitened on the sill.

On Sunday, all the immobile residents were wheeled in to be treated for an hour to the Gospel Choir's selections from the *Evangelical Songbook*.

Not a dram all week.

Now it was Monday again.

And still an hour to go before tea, which would be sloppy, and taste of tin.

If it hadn't been for Maggie, he'd have cracked up already, and the steak he'd filched from Margo's fridge would not last beyond tomorrow. It was a wonder no one had smelt it yet.

There was a knock on the door. He sat bewildered for some seconds, already accustomed to having his door flung open without ceremonial courtesy. There was a second knock. He turned himself round and wheeled over to open it. Another few weeks and he'd give up bothering to walk altogether.

An alarming figure stood in the corridor. It wore bright tartan trousers, a combat jacket and a balaclava helmet which revealed only the wearer's eyes and a grinful of small brown teeth.

"Gonner let me in, mate? I'm yer next-door nayber. Ganglion by name, an' never-mind-wot by naitchewer."

Oswald wheeled back a circumference, but his visitor did not enter the room. Instead he put his head round the door, said, "Blahdyorrible, like livininer bleedin' frigidaire. Come ter my place, scosier," and withdrew. Oswald followed him.

Ganglion raised a hand outside the door of Room Thirteen.

"Angonnersec, gotter do suffink firse," he said, and shut the door behind him.

He reappeared within a minute, and with a cryptic "Juscoverinup me prosthesis," wheeled Oswald in.

Not Quartermain in the mines of Solomon nor Evans at the opened sarcophagus could have been as astonished as was Oswald Ochilree at that moment.

There were velvet curtains at the window. There was a desk, with a green leather top and an agreeable clutter of pipes, knives, books, glasses and small brass ornaments. There was a dark oak dresser. There was an armchair, very old and sagging and, Oswald was sure, very comfortable. The bed had a padded headboard and a thick mattress, and black sheets. There was a carpet, deep enough to make wheeling an effort. An imposing oak wardrobe loomed in the hole in the wall where the fitted unit must once have been. And there were pictures . . . oh, my goodness! There were pictures . . .

"Like me prints, dew yer? Very artistic, ent they? Pickedem up in the Edgware Road, firty-seven, no I tell a lie, firty-eight it musterbin, cos of where I went in firty-six. Nah, then, wots yore poison ter be? Muggerale, glassergargle, or boaf? Better make it boaf, yerlookasthough yer could dew wivit. Mind if I try yore chariot ferrabit? Yew can give yer bummertreat onnat fing."

Ganglion had removed his balaclava. Nothing about his face, so far as Oswald could see, was quite as it should be. The whites of the eyes were yellow, the skin was like a walnut's and the ears seemed blessed with more than the usual quota of folds and interstices. Only the eyes, pale piercing blue, appeared half way normal.

"Gotter keep up me image when I goes aht," he explained. While Oswald negotiated himself into the armchair — his grateful buttocks seemed to sigh as they met the cushion — Ganglion fiddled about under a sort of shroud in the corner, under the washbasin, and reappeared with a large glass of something dark and a small glass of something pale.

"Pinter Baillie's Best ana glasser Matron's Ruin. Ere's lead in yer penciw!"

Some time later, Matron found Room Fourteen dark and unoccupied. She listened next door. She heard voices, and laughter, and the clink of glass on glass. She sniffed, pursed her lips, crimped her buttocks and scowled. She tried the door, expecting to find it bolted, and was not disappointed. She stumped off down the corridor. That little cloud was threatening to grow bigger.

"Okay," said Ganglion, "she's gawn. Tha's yore card marked, me boy. Nah then, wot wozyew sayin'? Oh yus, yore accident. Go on."

"Och, well," said Oswald. "That's it all really. After the bull got me in the pens they took me to the hospital, and when I got out they gave me yon chair and told me to take it easy. Well, you can't take it easy and be a farmer, so I signed everything over to the lad. He'd been on at me to do it anyway, because of death duties. And then, och, he just sold the lot, as I was saying, breeders, in-store, the lot. He said cereals were the only future now we were in the EEC. I won't deny he's done well enough out of it, as far as that goes."

He stared into his glass.

"But he seemed to get busier and busier, what with the accounts and the investments and dear knows what else besides, and now there's Margo expecting and saying they can't cope. Oh, I don't blame Angus really, he's a good lad but he's kind of weak, you know? She's got a grant, like, for the tourists, and she can't manage without the space. So that's me."

"I'll put some wet inat glass, mate, afore yew dew. Gizzitere."

Ganglion took their glasses over to the shroud.

"You're not Scottish, are you?" asked Oswald.

A volley of muffled cackling came from under the washbasin.

"Jeezers, not likely! Nah, bahtas Scotch asser Jappernese whisky, me. Beffnaw Green's where I come from. Tellyerorlabahtit later. Ere yer go. Get that dahn yer while I fix us some dinner."

"Oh, my goodness!" exclaimed the guest. "I'd completely forgotten!"

"Not difficult *ter* ferget, that crap. Nah just sit tight ani'll gerrus some peanut butter sammiches, wiv brahn bread, Sorl yew need, is that. An no bleedin bromide in it neiver. By the way, not meaninter be rude or nuffink, but wots that movin abaht under yore rug?"

Downstairs, tea was corned beef hash with prunes and custard to follow. It made an interesting, though unappetising, combination in the bibs of the more confused diners, but as Matron said, eating together helped to reinforce the sense of community within the Home. She took her meals in her flat.

Angus and Margo Ochilree stood in the recently vacated downstairs room at Newbiggings Farmhouse. Margo held a kitchen catalogue open for Angus to look at. Despite her condition, she had somehow summoned the energy to help him shift the furniture out into the yard, to give the builders a clear run the next day.

The small intelligent face peered round a statuette of Shiva on the desk.

"So yore Maggie, are yer?" Ganglion asked the creature. "Ere Maggie, averbirrer sammich, thassit, there yer go. Cworr! Lookatem fangs, wiw yer? Glad I'm norrarabbit. Yewadderere orl week then, aveyer?"

"Aye, that I have, Mr Ganglion. In the fork o' my trousers. I've been training her to think of it as home since they told me I was coming here. Had to leave the rest behind, though. I couldna bring enough meat for all o' them."

"Ar, well, dontcherworry abaht that, we'w sort that aht in the mornin'. Blahdyell, she polished that lot off quick, dint she? Berrergivver the crust next, I reckon."

They watched while the ferret did full justice to the last of the Mother's Pride, thickly smeared with best butter and the crunchy ambrosia of the Deep South.

"Reckon she could be the world's first vedgytarian ferret," observed the chef. "We orter give that Attenburger bloke a ring."

Later, after they had devoured their own meal in companionable silence, Ganglion said:

"Well, me ole mate, time yew woz makin' tracks fer beddlybylode. I need ter give me prosthesis an airin' an I don't reckon yore quite up ter that yet."

"Oh, I'm sorry," said Oswald. "Have I been here too long? You should have said earlier, and I'd —"

"Naw, naw, honist, I've bin fine. Sides, I went afore yew came, not tharri go ser much as meet meself comin' back, if yer sees wot I mean. Only it's a bit of a shocker, me gadget. Andy enough fer brewin' up Matron's Ruin in between times, though. Djew wannerleave Maggie May erewiv me? Berrerforer than banginabaht in yore goolies, I'd of fort. I could clear aht a dror ferer."

"Oh . . . well — I don't rightly know about that. Will she be safe here, do you think?"

Ganglion leaned conspiratorially in.

"Listen, mate, nobody, but *nobody*, gets inere wivaht I wantem to, yew get me? Right as rine she'w be inere, anyew can visit *anytime*, savvy? Nah, come on ole son or it'll be pop goes the weasuw. Thas it, easy duzzit . . ."

As his host helped him to his wheelchair, Oswald felt the weakness in his legs in a way he had not known for a long time.

"How do you do it, man?" he asked. "I mean, all this, and locking your door, and — and — everything?"

"Ah, secrits, those are, secrits of the dyin' sepoy. Naw, not reely. I'll tew yer termorrer. Nah run along, there's a good boy, me fuse is burnin' low."

Back in his bleak cell, where his framed photographs of fatstock winners languished against the skirting board under Matron's edict forbidding holes in the plaster, Oswald retrieved the last shreds of stinking steak from under the mattress and pushed them through the narrow aperture of the window. Fixed that way to prevent suicides, probably, he thought. He wondered again if his purloining of the steak had spoiled Margo's celebratory meal. Then he realised he was beginning not to care.

Tuesday dawned fine over Craigfieth, stirring its dull tubers into commercial activity. A van drove out of the yard of Poulson the Builders, crossed the Fieth Bridge, still wreathed in thinning mist, and took the north road for Newbiggings Farm.

In the rear office of Sounds Good (formerly the Bonaventure Wireless Shop) young Hamish Ganglion wrote his weekly cheque, sealed it in an envelope, and addressed it. He would have to go to the Post Office for a stamp: an extra expense, but worth it not to have to deliver the thing himself. He wondered how much longer he could keep it a secret from Grace, now that she had all but taken him over. He would have to tell her one day, he supposed, or he might lose her altogether and get his old problem back. But it was going to be tricky when it happened, and it would be just like him to turn up at the wedding . . .

Matron had risen early after a disturbed night, and come to a decision regarding the choice that lay before her. On the one hand lay tranquillity, of a sort; on the other, authority. She could let the apparent deterioration of the new inmate continue and hope, as before, to contain it, or she could assert herself, hoping to reduce the miscreant to the proper state of grateful, quiet, senescent mansuetude. All night she had toiled between the two; now, in the golden morning light, she saw each clearly for what it was. The complicating factor of the Inspection, due shortly, she laid aside for the moment, since it bore equally on both courses.

So, she would hedge her bets for the time being. She drafted a letter to Mr and Mrs Ochilree, using the phrases that had served so well once before: extra care, strained resources, financial stringencies, sliding scales of familial contribution to ensure secure provision . . . She filed it away for future use and set off for the dining-room.

She was relieved to find Mr Ochilree unaccompanied, seated with his back to the window and spooning up the last of his Fibrebisks. She waited, unseen, until he had wheeled his empty bowl back to the hatch, then pounced.

"Ah, Mr Ochilree, and how are we this morning?" she fluted shrilly.

He beamed vacantly up at her. From where he was, her head above the adamantine breasts looked like a small clock on a very large mantelpiece.

Encouraged by this response, she bellowed, "We missed you last night, Mr Ochilree!"

He beamed again, wagging his head a little this time.

"We never said how many lorries we'd seen through our window, Mr Ochilree, did we now? Always Mr Beasley's busiest day, Monday was!"

Oswald gargled and cupped his hand to his ear.

"*How many was it, Mr Ochilree?*"

"Oh, aye, very nice, thank you, Matron. Keep me going all morning, that will," he piped, and wheeled off back to Botha, crooning happily to himself. Matron stood still for some minutes, looking — as indeed she was — deeply thoughtful.

"Howdit go, chum?" asked Ganglion, sliding back the bolt.

"Very well, I think," replied Oswald. "I think I managed to puzzle her a bit."

"Used the ga-ga ole twit routine, did yer, like I said?"

"Aye. And deafness. Deaf ga-ga old twit, and I slavered a bit as well. Just came to me, that did, as I went along."

"Triffic! That oughter keeper worried ferrabit, she won't know what ter maker that lot orl at once. Nah then, lookerthis lot 'ere. Know wot this is, ole buddy?"

Oswald looked inside the paper package held out to him.

"Meat," he said finally. "Of some kind."

"Gercher! 'Meat', is that orl yew can say? Gawd, I'm glad I never bought nuffinkorf yore farm. This, yew dear daft ole bugger, is venison, swot this is. Wot the eighty-four per cent get screwed for so's the uvver seven can shoot it, if I've got me facks kerrect. Suffink like that, anyway. Couldn't get rabbit. Sorl right, I 'aven't fed Maggie yet, fort yew'd prefer ter."

"Thank you, that's very — my goodness, it *is* good meat!"

"Bleedin' well oughterbe! Cost Lord flymin' Margoyle enough ter rear, dinnit?"

"The Laird? Goodness gracious,. Ganglion, however did you . . . I mean . . . how?"

Ganglion patted his combat jacket and grinned cariously.

"Cordless tellyphone, wunner the wonders of the age. Gavermaterminer bell lars nigh, arter I'd finished wiv me doo-dah. Good pal, 'e is, anafrienter the oppressed masses, like wot we are. Can orlways be relied on ter be in the right plice at the right time, like when wunner the monarckserthe glen azzer little accident. Fahnd this on the step this smornin', wiv the miwk. Nah, put yore Maggie ahterer misery, plonk yore arse dahn over there, get yerself rahnd that mugger tea, and I'll tell yer me life 'istory, leastways orl the interestin' bits."

They watched while Maggie, who seemed to be growing visibly sleeker by the minute, devoured a good quarter-pound of Caledonia's curse. Oswald sipped his tea. It was strong and sweet, and slid down his rejoicing throat like liquid velvet. Ganglion spoke:

"Nah then, first orf, I speck yore wunnerin 'ow someone oo's more Cockney than the ole bleedin' BBC put tergether comes ter be in this snooty dump innerfirs plice. Wew, I'll tell yer. I woz in Orkney durina Woah, right, an' incidentally if yer ever up there, don't go callin' it the Orkneys, wiw yer, cost it makesem go bleedinairless. Any road up, I'd like to've styed reely, only I gorrinterabirrerbovver, see, an' I 'ad ter scarper quick. Wew I'd bin a sparks fer six bleedin' yeers, so I fort, right, I fort, firs place I comes ter ant gorrer wireless shop, I'll open one. So Gawdelpme, I cumere. I opened up on the Igh Street wiv me wossname, discharge money, plus a bit extra's we won't go inter nah, an' Fanny's yer bleedin' arnt. I corled it the Bonnervencher Wireless Shop cos I cottoned on that sounded Scottish like, an' I did very well though I sesitas shouldn't. An then I gorrinteranuvver

little birrerbovver, luverly she woz, only I inadvertently
puter up the stick, dinni? Wew, I arsk yew, wot could I
do? She dint wonner marry me, cos she woz arf my age or
less an we woz only avinabirrerfun, like — this woz afore
me weakness come on, ercourst — an anyway, oo wants
ter be corled Mrs Ganglion, I arst yer?"

"It's, erm, an unusual name, certainly."

"Yew said it, mate, yew bleedin' said it. Andoncher go
believin' wot me sprog sez abaht ganglin' wiv lions niever.
Fahnd aht tharrin Orkney, cos there's lots of ole names
there, like Langskaill, that's long skull, an' they aren't
arf long too, summervem, an' Merriman, thass Moor
Man, dark skin, see? An' eapseruvvers, goin' right back.
So, sobvious wot Ganglion is, innit? Narmean? Neiver
morenerless than wot yew fink it is. Must've bin a bleedin'
big one though, ooever it woz. Anyway, I wanted ter dew
the decent fing, so she popped orf dahn Sahf ferabit ter
stay wiv friends, saver bein gorped at like she'd got free
eads or suffink, an when she comes back I sez, see ere gurl,
I sez, yew don't want all that palarver wiv nappies anat,
norrayore ige, yore a bright gurl, goanave some fun an'
I'll bring the blighter up. Ave 'im back liter if yer want,
only give yerself time ter fink, is wot I'm sayin'."

"Goodness mercy, man! However did you manage? It
must have been awfy hard going."

"Nah, not reely. I meanter say, any ole fool can flog
wireless sets, can't they? Anit's as easy ter fix valves anat
aht the back wiv a babby arahnd as it is ter dew anyfink
else, ironinan so on. Swot most wimmin dew, arteraw.
Anyway, cut a long story short, Amish grew up — she
wonninim cawed that, wozen't nuffink ter dew wiv me
— an I started ter get me birrertrouble, I mean this
birrertrouble wot I've stiw got nah, an djew know wot?
We dint pertickly like each uvver. Nah, that's not quite
it reely. See, I've allis bin a loner, right? an' e's orl right

reely is Amish, cept I jus' don't like livvinwivim much, narmean? So I fort, right I fort, taker long 'ard look at yerself, mate. So I did, anen I fort, right wotcher want is a cushy billet somewhere, getcherself wew stuck in an no nonsense, an' let the lad gerronwivit. So I cumere, dinni?"

"She never came back, then?"

"Oo? Oh, 'er. Nah, she never did. Carn't blamer, reely, can yew? Oo'd wanner come back terranarsole plice like Craigfeef? Speshly when she woz doin' serwew ferrerself. Nah!"

"But I still don't understand — I mean — all this!"

Oswald waved an arm around the room.

"How do you get away with it all?"

Ganglion cackled.

"Same way allis gorrerway wiv fings, I spect. Nah, listen, cos yew could dew wiver tipper two, yew could. From wot yew've said, yore ballsanchaines've gorrerlorrerackers, right?"

"I beg pardon?"

"Ackers. Spondoolicks, greenancrinklies, flexible friens, narmean?"

"Oh. Money . . . Aye, I suppose they will have."

"Yew betcher they dew. Same wiv my Amish, I made surerthat. Right. Now, are Matronere, in addition ter bein' as big a fret ter the yuman ricerswot footan mouf is ter, wottever it is footan mouf is a fret ter, is also a big fat greedy pig, geddit? An she as these ere slidin scales, see, which means that yore deerly biluvvid pays a little extra wot they can afford feryew ter be buried alive inere, anner little extra on topper that if they reely loves yer an wants yer ter be appy in yer decayin yeers, djewget worri'monabaht?"

"I think so, aye. But surely that's not legal, is it?"

"Oo cares? Stuff me if I know wevver it's legal or not, sjust a facterlife, mate, anat'sat. So, Amish puts is ortergrarf onner birrer paper every week, sends it in, an everyfink's sweetnessanlight. Cos if 'e duzzern't, I comome, right? Anat leads ter the secanfing. Yew've gorreravver Weakness. Snow problem, we orl ave, at ar age, only yew camp it up, narmean? The narstier the better. Ercourst, I dunnaffter bovver, me, mine's narsty enough wivaht campin. Only, if yer make it reely disgustin, an I mean *reely*, thenat duz two fings, dunnit: one, they leavesyeralone inere, two, they don't wantcher back at ome, which means they goes on appily shellinaht feryewter live the lifer Reilly. Simpuw! I reckon it stopsyer goin ga-ga ackcherly, I mean it's bleedinard work sometimes, beiner disgustin ole man. Keeps yer on yer toes. Or yer front wheews, in yore case. Avvernuvvercuppertea!"

Time passed. The great globe continued its controlled spin into the shadows and in Craigfieth the days grew perceptibly shorter.

Mr Poulson's men worked for three days at Newbiggings, making several large holes in the internal kitchen wall, and then departed for three weeks, during which the ravaged masonry seemed daily to exhale dust: ornament, shelf and coffee table appeared to glow with a rose-red aura, half as old as time. A letter arrived from the Matron of the Eventide Home, hinting at difficulties in the provision of the full range of caring support services for one of her residents. Mr and Mrs Ochilree increased their weekly contribution to the Friends of Botha Fund (No. 2 Account). Mrs Ochiltree telephoned Mr Poulson to ask whether it would all be over by Christmas. The builder assured her it would.

"As Earl Haig said to the actress," he muttered, replacing the receiver.

A week later the men returned and made another hole. The new units arrived from the Finnish Design

Workshops in Dundee, and were stowed conveniently in the downstairs passage, where they, too, acquired patina.

The men found a pipe in the wall, and turned the water off. Their discovery helped to settle the dust a little. Then they went away to find a plumber.

Bonfire night came and went. The O'Rourke Dancers, dressed as rockets, gave a display in the Main Lounge for those residents unable to view the fun on the McWhirter Playing Fields from their cell windows.

Ganglion concocted a mulled punch called a Botha Blitzkrieg, which he and Oswald enjoyed with their indoor fireworks in Room Thirteen. Maggie the ferret took an intelligent interest in the display. She seemed to have grown to half the size again on her diet of venison shaved from the steaks that Ganglion cooked for them on his Baby Belling. She seemed to appreciate the punch, too.

Two mornings later, Ganglion burst unexpectedly into Oswald's room without knocking.

"Sorry mate, but yew'd berrercum quick, suffink's appeninter Maggie!"

"Oh, merciful heavens, whatever is it? Is she ill?"

"I should cocoa," gasped Ganglion as he wheeled his friend outside. "She's crappin suffink orrible, like the stuffat comes ahter yew-bends, it is. Sorl over my Y-fronts."

"My Lord goodness, whatever can it be?"

"Blimey, I dunno mate, yore the livestock merchantare-ahndere. There. See worrimean?"

Later, when all four pups were suckling nicely, and the midwives too were enjoying a liquid breakfast, Oswald said:

"It must have been Sir Alec, before I left. I was that trachled with coming here, I couldn't have noticed them going about it. Well, what a business! Ye ken, I was at the calving-down o' my Bessie, when she had Angus. It came on quick, and we hadn't the phone in for to call the doctor. My, that was a job! I had to get the soap flakes in her afore I could slip the wee fellow out. And I was hoping to be there when Margo had hers. But — ye ken this? — I won't miss that now, Margo's bairn. Ferrets are more rewarding, somehow, if ye take my meaning."

"Abso-blahdy-lutely, mate. Abso-flamin-well-lutely. Gizzerglass. Blah-dy wunnerfew, that woz. Marvel o'nay-chewer. Jus lookater nah, bleedin' wunnerfuw. Privvy-lidge ter watch it, wonnit? Like bein' in a caffedreal. Bet ar Maggie beats yore Angussis bint inera cocked 'at. Ere. Ere's ter ar Maggie, anawat sails inner."

Later still, Oswald said: "We'll have to watch them later on, and keep that door shut. They're wee buggers afore they're properly trained. Oh, and ye'll be letting me get you some new underpants."

"Nah, thassorlright, I'll bungem in the lorndry, they'll never notice the difference."

By Saturday, Oswald had sexed the young ferrets and Ganglion had named them. They sat together, Ganglion rocking gently backwards and forwards in Oswald's conveyance, watching young Tebbit, Edwina, Maxwell and Princess Michael concentratedly fuelling themselves for the great game of life. Oswald sighed happily.

"Reminds me of home, this does, when I was a lad and our Flora had her first. Have ye ever seen a collie bitch with her pups? Gentle as anything, they are. She stayed out in the sheds normally, but my father was that soft-hearted he took her in for the whelping."

Ganglion sniffed a little.

"Yew woz lucky, yew woz. Dragged up orl over the place, me, probly accahnts fer me bein' such a solitary bastard ever since. Least yew knew yore farver, anis farver too, I expect. Never knew mine. I get the Ganglion from me muvver's side, Gawd rester. Don't tell me, I bet yore dad builtisahse wivisownands, dint e?"

"Och, well, not quite, no. He extended it when I was still a lad. Just a but-and-ben it was, before that, but he built on. Took him over a year, what with everything to see to on the farm as well, but he managed it. Of course, there weren't the planning regulations then, he just made it up as he went along."

Ganglion sniffed again.

"Luverly. Luverly, ter be settled like that. I mean lookat me, I never bin settled in me life, not reely. Longest I've bin anywhere was over the Wireless Shop, anat felt like campinaht, mostovertime. Yew dunno yore bawn, mate, thachew don't."

Oswald was disturbed by Ganglion's sudden mood.

"Oh, well, it didn't feel very settled at the time! No, indeed, we all had to stay living in the house while he toiled away round us. He never bothered doing anything much to the place as it stood, just built out and up, working away. It ruined his health, though, poor father. He burned himself out on it. Ah well, at least Angus won't have to worry about that."

Tebbit raised his head, his milky face blindly sensing the strain in the atmosphere.

"Thassorlright, mate, everyfink's orl right. Just yer ole nuncle avin a wobbly terimself. Back ter work, nah."

The little ferret obeyed.

"Yer know," said Ganglion, "I ennarf glad yew cummalong. Only wunnaswoz arfway different till then woz ole Wanker Sproat, aneewozern't no use. I mean, I couldn'taviminere, could I? One look at me art prints, eedof blown up."

Oswald raised himself determinedly to his feet.

"My turn to make the tea," he said.

The year slid towards its crisis. In ages past, bonfires had been lit, at Johnsmas and Midwinter's Eve, on the summit of Ben Gunn, the most majestic of the Lummocks. Now, the town below contented itself with the Gala, and the Christmas light in the High Street windows.

Young Hamish Ganglion was glad he had Grace with him this year, even if it did mean Christmas dinner with Mr and Mrs Wemyss, and thinly veiled references to bridesmaids. Like his father, he enjoyed a degree of privacy but, unlike the elder Ganglion, did not know the first thing to do with a turkey. He wound a string of fairy lights around his window display, and switched on. Fortunately, he did know about fuses and was able, half an hour later, to restore light to his darkened premises.

Nor was the festive season ignored at the Eventide Home. Matron had expressly ordered, as she did every year, a large roll of slicing chicken for the groaning geriatric board. She was now busy dismantling four dozen crackers: they should have their paper hats, but the bangs might alarm them. She carefully assigned the mottos which, as always, were edifying passages from the Scriptures, to those best suited to them. For Mr Sproat she chose' "And the thing which he did displeased the LORD: wherefore he slew him also (Gen. 38:x)." She could not find one to suit Mr Ganglion.

Streamers were unpacked and rehung from the corners of the social areas; in the entrance lobby, the portraits of the four Bailies were garlanded with tinsel. For not only was Christmas coming, but the visit of the Health Board Inspectors was due the morrow morn, and Matron was anxious to give the most favourable impression of her little community.

The young ferrets thrived, threatening to outgrow their natal home.

By half past eight on the morning of the Inspection, everything was ready. The residents, roused half an hour early for the purpose, were scrubbed, polished, shining and wearing their best party manners. Rugs were draped over the Lounge chairs to conceal the splits in the vinyl and the heavy fire doors, normally closed for the sake of fuel economy, were kept open by the electronic agency of the fail-safe system installed after the previous Inspection. All the plants had been washed. The whole Home reeked hygienically of polish and disinfectant.

Oswald was taken aback on entering Ganglion's room to find his friend dressed soberly. He wore a pair of dark trousers, which had once been pressed, an off-white shirt, brown tie, fawn cardigan and a tweed jacket that almost matched the trousers. He looked quite ten years older.

"Good heavens!" said Oswald. "You're looking very, erm, different today. Special occasion?"

"Sort of," Ganglion replied. "Terday's the day I pay me dues, or discharges me debt ter serciety, whichever way yew looks at it. Smatron's big day, innit?"

"Oh, you mean the Inspection, aye, I'd heard about it. But why the change of clothes?"

"Becawz, ole son, if I'mer good boy terday, I goes on wiv me special privilidges fer annuvver six munfs. Wot the Inspectors want ter see is a lot of wew-behaved ole crumblies lookin respeckful, annerslong as I don't step outer line while they're ere, I'm allowed ter go on as before, wiv me bolt, an me bitser furnichewer, an me noods onner waw. An yore ferrets, which, I might add, suffinkle affter be dunwiv soon. I've adtergivvem the run of the room, that dror's not big enough no more anidursen't lettem in me wardrobe. Anyway, serficient unter the day, anaw that. Cahm on, I've bin psychin meself up arf the night fer this bleedin' breakfas. Lessgerrit overrandunwiv."

Disconsolately, he wheeled Oswald out, letting the door swing shut behind him.

Downstairs in the dining-room, the Health Board Inspectors were standing, as they thought, unobtrusively by the grey curtains in the corner. There were three of them, two leaden gentlemen in their early fifties and a hatchet-faced lady of approximately similar vintage. Oswald gave them his best vacant smile as he was trolleyed to his place at the table.

Miss Abercrombie, he noticed, was shaking well this morning, with a regularity of tremens that caused her to miss one mouthful in three. Mr Sproat was dangerously crimson.

"Very chilly this morning, isn't it?" observed Mrs Bonar. Oswald was so socially out of practice that he almost forgot not to answer. One of the leaden men made a note on his clipboard: Mrs Bonar had scored a Social Interaction Point. Ganglion saw him.

"Wouldn'terve said so, meself. Sweatin cobs, I woz, lars night."

"Yes, yeees," drawled Mrs Bonar in reply. "And Ay don't doubt it will become chillier before it becomes warmer."

"Ir stickin ter me legs, my jim-jams woz, smornin. Fair put the wind up me, it did."

"Oh yes," agreed the old lady, "and it's so cutting, Ay find."

"Stiw, sbahnd ter get warmer if yer sticks yereadina-noven, innit?"

"Oh mai word, yes, but colder when it goes in!"

"Silly ole boot!" grinned Ganglion. "Finished yer shroud yet, ave yer?"

"Oh yes, we have much to be thankful for," smiled Mrs Bonar, and took up her needles.

The Inspector with the clipboard scribbled furiously. His companion caught the eye of the hatchet-faced lady, who wrote something on a pink slip which she then passed to the note-taker. He read it, nodded, and copied the details.

Matron smiled a smile of professional indulgence at them all.

Ganglion fixed his eye on Mr Sproat.

"Finished wiv that maggerzeen I lent yer, aveyer? Yew know, Strenf Fru Joy Annewal, 1961, the one wiv the hula-hoops?"

Mr Sproat choked and turned the colour of a brick wall.

"Well now!" ejaculated Matron hastily. "I think it's time we went into the Lounge, don't you? Mr Sproat, perhaps you could lead the way."

She propelled him through the connecting door to the Main Lounge. The others followed, in their various bedraggled ways. The Inspectors slipped greyly in behind them as Oswald and Ganglion were taking up their station below the fan.

The inmates settled into the unaccustomed luxury of their rug-lined chairs.

"Now then!" said Matron brightly, clasping her hands beneath her bosom.

"How about starting the day with a nice sing-song, shall we? Who's going to get us going, I wonder: Mr Mealie, perhaps you'd like to sing a song for us? We all know you know lots of songs, Mr Mealie," she wheedled, "don't we, boys and girls?"

A chorus of affirmative croaks and gargles robbed Mr Mealie of the will to resist.

"We plough the fields and scatter," he droned, and the others took it up.

"The good seed on the land," warbled Matron. Mr Sproat blenched.

They all joined in. Oswald could not prevent himself, and Ganglion seemed to be relishing his own performance, which sounded not unlike a Gregorian chant through comb-and-paper.

They began the second verse without the benefit of Mrs Abercrombie, whose intensifying tremblings had reduced her contribution from a thin vibrato to quivering incoherence, and finally to silence. Her hands flapped frantically at her withered lap.

Then Miss Gourock, too, stopped singing; though she remained smiling, her eyes took on a glazed expression. Mr Sproat followed her into soundless abstraction. He squirmed convulsively, bringing the rug down around his ears so that he looked like one of the grosser Saudi princes.

It was Mrs Bonar's scream, though, that finished it, halfway through the third chorus. As Matron stepped forward to investigate, the old lady's knitting writhed on her knees and then uncoiled itself, like some exorcised daemon, across the floor.

Alone of all in the Lounge, Oswald, with his stockman's prescience, knew what was going to happen next, and it came as no surprise to him to see Princess Michael emerge from the purple comforter. Nor was he unduly amazed when, to the accompaniment of the sort of noise a picture by Hieronymus Bosch would make if it could talk, she was joined on the carpet by Tebbit, Edwina and Maxwell. A pair of dentures flew, cartoon-like, from an anonymous gaping mouth. The adolescent ferrets began to worry them, playfully.

It was Matron who reacted first. While all around her continued to prove the old fallacy about hypnotised rabbits, she broke her trance and waded in with a strong left leg, uncompromisingly tipped with sensible NHS footwear. Tebbit was suddenly airborne: he described a lithe arc across the Lounge before landing in the glossy embrace of the most overpowering of the rubber plants. The others scattered in fright.

Oswald had been wondering when Maggie would put in an appearance. Now he found out. Intelligent for their species, ferrets exist nonetheless in the state of mind memorably ascribed to certain American Presidents as that of being unable to think and chew gum at the same time. Maternal atavism triggered adrenal aggression; long hours of careful training dictated the route. Teeth bared, claws extended, she scaled the nylon heights of the offending leg and disappeared above its skirted hem in simultaneous pursuit of haven and revenge.

This much, it must be allowed, was unpreventable. It was, however, mere capricious misfortune that, in her time of crisis, it was Mr Sproat whom Matron fell upon for relief.

It was a busy day for the Ambulance Service. No sooner had they ferried the last casualty from the Home to the District Hospitalisation Facility than they were required to return yet again to Craigfieth, or, rather, to the Craigfieth area. Mr Poulson's men stood in an uneasy knot by the ruined building as they watched the vehicle bump away down the farm track. At length, the silence was broken by the foreman, Paddy O'Hare, whose homely Hibernian wisdom belied his Hawick origins.

"Well, well, boys," he lilted. "Whoever would have tort dat was a load-bearin' wall, at all?"

"Well, mate," observed Ganglion the next day, "this is it then innit? Once again, the lickle tramp totters orf dahn the road inter the sunset. Nice while it larsted, wonnit?"

"Och, don't, man. It's all my fault."

"Nah, nah, nunnerthat. Woz me wot left the bleedin door open, wonnit? Spec I wonnid ter, reely, in me subconscience. Allis woz me own wurs ennimy. Nah, it's yew I feew sorry fer. Wotchergonnado?"

"Well, Ganglion ——" Oswald drew a deep breath, then a thought occurred to him.

"May I call you by your first name?"

"I'd rarver yew dint. Ganglion suits me better, anitswot I'm used ter. Same as I carn't finkeryew as an Ockilree, blahdy silly name, no offenceanawat."

"Well, then — Ganglion — I've been doing a bit of thinking lately, and especially since yesterday. We get on all right, the two of us, don't we? I may tell you — and I'm not an emotional man, mind, I've learned not to be — that you're the closest friend I've ever had. And I can't bear to think of it all ending, like this."

Oswald turned his right wheel and looked tactfully out of the window. He had noticed the other man's eyes beginning to water.

"Oh, Gawd!" Ganglion choked. "Donchew start. Sbadennuf wot I've bin finking, wivvaht yew chiminin."

"Aye, but listen!" Oswald swivelled round to face his friend, who was wiping his face with the back of his hand.

"There's something I didn't tell ye, indeed I didn't tell anyone. When my Bessie passed on, I thought about the future, and I saw myself as a lonely old man, nae use to anybody excepting myself. And I bought a wee cottage away up in the Lummocks. I thought I could maybe retire up there and fouter about, looking after myself, and die in my bed without being a bother to anybody. Then when I had my accident, well, that was that, I knew I couldn't. Many's the time I thought to tell Angus, but something always held me back and, well, there we are, I didn't. But I've still got it. The cottage. It's nothing much, a twa-three roomed place just, and a' facilities, but it's got running water, and

Hydro, and a wee bit shed foreby. What do you think, my friend? Could you bear that, the two of us, there?"

"Oh, Jeezerz!" Ganglion groaned. "Listen, yew luverly ole bugger, yew fink yew know me, doncher? Butchew don't, my friend, yew dunno the arf of it. I'm not jus private fer the sakervit. I've got me weakness, an when I sez weakness, I effinwell *means* weakness. I'm the only one wot can bear ter deal wiv it."

"Tell me about it."

Oswald's words came calmly, untrammelled by any professional obligations.

Ganglion told him.

"God man, is that all? I can deal with that, I'm the right height too! Why, it's no more than I used to do for the cattle!"

Let the cynical reader pause at this point, and ponder this: be they ever so farcically engendered, there are no tears at all like the tears of age.

And cursed be they that deny their right to flow.

Hamish moved them to the cottage, in his van. They took all Ganglion's furniture, and his art prints, and other needments purchased by Ganglion *fils* for their comfort. Grace was there, too. She had made a meal for their homecoming, and there was a bright fire in the grate. The ferrets' button eyes winked and sparkled in its dancing light. The swift midwinter dusk was turning the surrounding hills to silhouettes of blued steel as the young couple took their tactful leave.

"Well, dad," said Hamish at the door. "I expect we'll be seeing you around, from time to time, in Craigfieth."

But it was Oswald who replied.

"You bet you, Hamish old mate. We'll be back. Oh aye, we'll be back!"

7

Caveat Elector

The politics of the Burgh of Craigfieth have always
been, like so many other aspects of its life, a settled and
orderly affair. Down the years, the town has, in its own
estimation at least, managed to get along nicely without
giving hostages to the chimeras of mandate, pledge and
policy. When it comes to voting, Craigfiethans prefer to
keep politics out of it. Let others shout their slogans: if
Craigfieth were ever to indulge in such an activity —
which, of course, it never would — it would have to be
that most reassuring of rallying cries, 'No Change!'

It is a remarkable fact, though seldom remarked, that
between them, the town's elected representatives have
chalked up one hundred and fifty-six years of dedicated
service to the community. Heading the list, with forty-one
years under his belt, is the MP, Sir Ashley Foutret,
whose unswerving loyalty to his constituency, his Party
and his Country has at last earned him recognition at
the Scottish Office, where he is a Junior Spokesman on
White Fish Industries, Higher Education and Sport. An
active Parliamentarian — he has led delegations of his
colleagues to the Turks and Caicos Islands, Singapore and
Liechtenstein and is an energetic member of the House
of Commons Catering Committee — he has never failed
to put in an appearance at election time in Craigfieth,
where his appeal to the virtues of stability and continuity
has never gone unanswered. At the other end of the scale
of democratic longevity, sitting in the same interest as Sir
Ashley and related, like him, to the Laird of Lunie on

the distaff side, is the Euro-MP, a Perthshire man, cereal producer and Past President of the Area NFU; his tally so far is one summer short of a decade.

At the bottom of the representative heap is the Community Council or, as an embittered Political Editor of the *Perthshire Gazette* once put it, the political wing of the Maureen O'Rourke Dancers. Its six members (only four of whom are, in fact, in any way related to the town's famous troupe) have served continually, since its inception, recording a total of sixty-six years between them. In his nineteen years, eight of them spent on the old Burgh Council, District Councillor Duff (brother of the proprietor of Craigfieth's eponymous garage) has overseen the smooth running of the Library Van, the upkeep of the McWhirter Playing Fields and nine consecutive years of successful competition in the Scotland In Bloom contest.

Forty-one years plus nine, plus sixty-six, plus nineteen: total, one hundred and thirty-five. Twenty-one years remain unaccounted for, and they were buried on Burns' Night along with the mortal remains of Regional Councillor Hector Smeddum, BEM.

Old Stonewall Smeddum, as he was affectionately known to his colleagues, was one of the few members of the old Perthshire County Council to withstand successfully the chill wind of change that blew into existence Scotland's Eastern Region. Indeed, when news of his untimely death at the age of seventy-six reached his electors, many blamed that upheaval for hastening his end. If that is the case, then it is certain that old Smeddum himself would be the last to point an accusing finger. Having retired as Head Stalker on Lord Margoyle's estate ten years previously in order to shoulder the burden of Councillorship, he became an enthusiastic supporter of local government reform. He it was who led the delegation of welcome when, in 1973, Mr Jim Woodlowes performed the opening ceremony at Eastern House, the new Regional Headquarters in Dunbroath (described by the *Financial Times*, in a special Scottish feature, as the Brasilia of the North). The building itself, erected for barely three times the cost of refurbishing the County Offices in Perth, and thrown up almost overnight on land owned by Tarantula Investments International, a Woodlowes subsidiary, still stands today: repaired, of course, over the years, its roof replaced and its floors reinforced, but still an object of local pride and economic confidence.

Nor was Councillor Smeddum inactive thereafter: he chaired the subcommittee set up to design the Regional logo and was inspirational in drawing up the guidelines for its final appearance as a symbolic representation of the Region's positive characteristics. Subsequently he served as Vice-Chairman of the Policy and Resources Committee, with special responsibility for twinning with the EEC. It was his proudest boast, however, that throughout his tenure he remained staunchly Independent, not only by name but by nature also. Indeed, at the end, he was the only Councillor so self-designated. After a decade in which, regrettably, local government slid inexorably into the slough of politicisation, he found that on the rare occasions when he did not abstain, he was left raising his hand as a minority of one. Behind the scenes, however, his influence was widely felt. In informal discussions among the various caucuses, his opinion was sought. 'See what Stonewall thinks first' became a catchphrase among Party managers at Eastern House, and it was largely thanks to the aids to his mental process that they supplied that he was able to live his latter months in any degree of material comfort, for he resolutely eschewed the allowances enjoyed by his colleagues.

For the truth of the matter — and the reason for the unprecedented politicking that followed his decease — is that Councillor Smeddum found himself at last in a position of real power in the manoeuvrings of local government, for the last elections had produced the following psephological impasse: Con, 23; Lab, 19; Alliance, 3; SNP, 1; Ind, 1. And Hector Smeddum BEM had, in the eighteen months prior to his collapse at a reception in honour of the new Prune Computers factory in Kirriemuir, been the Ind.

It may seem surprising — it certainly amazed the reporters, analysts, commentators and assorted experts who followed the subsequent by-election campaign — that for the last three elections of his career Councillor Smeddum had been returned unopposed. The fact was variously explained by the savants of the press as being attributable to his former association with the local landowner, his firm stand against the depredations of fluoridisation and the permissive society, and his perennial opposition to rate increases. The truth was, however, that his constituents came to regard him in time as an institution. He was as much a part of the Regional scene as Forfar Athletic Football Club: he did not blaze across the firmament, his name did not make the nation's pulse beat faster, but he was — always — there, and that was a comfort.

And then, suddenly last January, he wasn't. And even before the Convener had thrown the first handful of earth in the kirkyard of Smeddum's native parish of Duncruddie Mains, the campaign had begun to find a successor to the vacant seat of Mid Lummock. For, as the *Glasgow Herald* put it the next morning, Brasilia stood by to receive a new power broker. Craigfieth was set to become the fulcrum of a political apparatus whose operation would trouble the counsels of the great and the wise.

At first, however, there was nothing to suggest to the town itself that the forthcoming poll would be anything out of the ordinary. Although it was agreed that to have four candidates to choose from was unusual (few now remembered Mr Ganglion Senior's attempt to become the first ever Anarcho-Syndicalist MP in the General Election of 1950) the motives of the would-be Councillors were generally understood. Thus it was assumed that Mr Meiklejohn was standing because he had achieved eminence in the Chamber of Commerce, and Mr Smellie because he had not; Mr Haq because he was naturally a hard worker and Mrs Pitt-Holyoake for want of something to occupy her during the long period of commercial hibernation between tourist seasons. Like all received truths, these confident assumptions were good enough as far as they went, but they did not paint the whole picture.

For behind their familiar bland Craigfiethan faces there pulsed a will to power undreamt of even in the smoke-free rooms of Eastern House. These four worthies were not merely candidates in a genteel local ballot. They were ideas whose time had come.

The candidacy of Mr Haq was not so much a matter of choice as of divine revelation. Sitting in his private office, its walls hung with framed photographs, cut from magazines, of Margaret Thatcher, Ray Honeyford, Paul Johnson and Samuel Smiles, his desk tidily stacked with back numbers of *The Salisbury Review* and selected *Times* leaders carefully pasted in scrapbooks from the shop, his eyes rested again on that morning's *Scotsman* spread out before him and on its short centre page feature entitled 'All Eyes On The Mid Lummock Crucible'.

He knew the article almost by heart already. Eastern Region was, it pointed out, a classic 'hung' council, the abstentionism of its lately deceased Independent member having brought it, in the last eighteen months, to a state of feverish inertia. The three Opposition parties had combined in an uneasy confederacy to produce on almost every issue something which the area president of the SDP described as 'creative stalemate'. Since the previous summer, the Region's Convener had been more often in hospital than out of it.

What followed was, of course, matter for speculation, but informed sources (the paper said) were agreed on one thing only: that the next elected tribune of the people of Mid Lummock would describe himself, or herself, as an Independent; Independence was as much a political reflex in Mid Lummock as was Liberalism in Orkney and Shetland or Socialism on the Clyde. What would matter, therefore, would not be the label but the person: it would be foolish these days, and especially in Scotland, to assume that the Conservatives still had first call on the services of Councillors so designated. The four main parties, the writer insisted, would be making discreet overtures to each candidate, hoping, when the time came, to ensure that the ideals of the newly elected member coincided as closely as possible with the practical aims of their organisations.

For what was at stake in what the paper called 'the manicured heartland of Middle Scotland' was not merely the breaking of a deadlock at Eastern House, vital though this was: there were wider issues involved. Whoever was sent forth from the fastness of Dunbroath to represent his fellows at the counsels of the Confederation of Scottish Local Authorities would be glad to be spared such taunts from his colleagues as 'Which side are you on today?' and 'Look out, here come the Swiss'. Should the election produce an Independent of the Right, the outcome would be clear: COSLA would gain a champion of poll tax, self-reliance, council house ownership and nuclear deterrence. Should, however, the ballot go any of three other ways, a kaleidoscope of possibilities appeared, almost too awesomely dazzling to contemplate, though the writer had a good stab at it nonetheless. Labour might try to go it alone and form an administration with the covert support of the smaller parties: what midnight hagglings might not then precede every vote? Or a Grand Coalition might be attempted, as the Alliance had already hinted: what price then might they charge for their support? And would the People's Party tear itself apart in its attempt to decide whether or not it was worth paying?

Nobody, the writer allowed, needed reminding that a General Election was imminent. Conservatives would be hoping that the likelihood of a third term in Westminster would be accompanied by the possibility of having enough MPs to staff the Scottish Office; Labour would be looking to tighten its grip on the hearts and minds of mainstream Scots. The Alliance badly needed to bring the supply lines closer to its beleaguered redoubt at Hillhead, while the SNP were seeking a torch with which to rekindle the flame of Hamilton. No auld wife, the commentator confidently concluded, ever scrutinised the tea leaves with such intensity as the party managers would bring to bear on the election addresses shortly to be distributed in Central Perthshire.

This intelligence Mr Haq now digested all at once, such was his familiarity with the text. He liked the phrase 'Independent of the Right': it seemed to him to illuminate the whole and, like Saul, he was blinded to reborn sight by the light therefrom, in one epiphanic instant. He would stand. He would pull his last limb clear of the ravening wolves below, the carrion of poverty and alienation: then let others sue him to let down the ladder. He would so outgrow Craigfieth that he could, in course of time, affectionately acknowledge his debt to the little town . . . in the meantime, he must personify the place to his fingertips, slipping in his political message in terms which would, though unmistakable at Conservative Central Office, pass consciously unnoticed among the electors, like vaccine on a sugarlump. He must start work now on his Address; there was no time to lose. He smiled, and lit a cheroot. Old Chisholm would be glad of a change from raffle tickets, Gala programmes and the High School magazine. It was a nice feeling already to be in a position to provide employment . . .

It was Mr Meiklejohn's practice, during daylight hours, never to leave the Dispensary unless under dire provocation, such as the near-débâcle of last year's Gala. Consequently, lunchtime that fateful day found him eating tuna sandwiches amid the shelves of his witch's kitchen, the *Scotsman* propped against a well-thumbed copy of *Pharmacopoeia,* with enough drugs to hand to enliven and obliterate the lives of his fellow-townsfolk. If the truth be told, the diminutive pharmacist secretly relished the sensation of latent power he derived from this occupation. It gave him a frisson.

He smiled — wryly, inwardly — at the phrase 'manicured heartland'. Fierce emotions fought within his narrow breast. He thought of Craigfieth, his cradle and haven these fifty-odd years. He thought of Mother and her fabled acquaintance with Sir Alec, of her years of selfless devotion to the Unionist cause and of all the hundreds of thousands of election address envelopes she had licked in its service; of her untimely demise, hastened as it had been by the shattering news of the ill fortune of that nice young Fairbairn man.

And what return had all this service brought her? Nothing. Not an ounce, not a scruple, not a grain.

He thought of the cruel blow struck at the very heart of his profession by the removal from NHS prescription of his most profitable branded placebos. It would have killed Mother, that Act, had she still been alive. He folded the paper with uncharacteristic disregard for its natural creases.

A terrible beauty was born.

He would offer himself, and he would incline to the Socialists.

Mother would understand . . .

Mrs Pitt-Holyoake did not take the *Scotsman*, distrusting anything that allied itself, however ludicrously, to the illusion of nationalism. However, the Northern edition of the *Daily Telegraph* had done full justice to the possibilities inherent in the forthcoming struggle for the votes of Mid Lummock. Forgotten ancestral ideals stirred within her; of her maternal grandfather, a Fabian of the William Morris school, who met and married a girl who helped — with what transcendent joyousness had she risen above that dirty word 'worked' — with the Kelmscott Press. That it should come to this, she thought, looking round her displays of Scottish crafts: trinkets and tourists, artless manufactures for the philistine bourgeoisie, and a native populace seduced by the latent fascism of the Wha's Like Us Nationalists. How she had laboured in this barren vineyard! She had tried — heaven knew she had tried — to engender the Spirit of the Movement in the dull clay of Craigfieth. For eight years she had run for them her Art and Craft classes, hoping to attract worshippers at the shrine of true socialism, with her offer of a retail outlet for their creativity: to no avail. Now, she did what she could, with her water-colours, her batik work and her macramé

and they, for their part, languished long unsold. She had
to scrape along on souvenirs and tartan geegaws.

True Fabianism was dead, alas! along with Art Nouveau
and dear old GBS. No matter: here at last was Hope.

Those nice Liberals would recognise her worth: they
alone could claim to have inherited the mantle of Beatrice
Webb. And this year's Regional Grant to Visitor Industries
was, as she knew only too well, pitifully inadequate . . .

Such trivia as local politics in Central Perthshire are not
the concern of the *Sun*, so it was not until Grace Wemyss
brought in the old papers for wrapping the brassicas that
Mr Smellie was made aware of the golden opportunity that
offered to raise him from the obscurity of greengrocery to
the reforging of Scotia's pride. Too long had he shivered
in the shadows, like some timorous crofter in awe of the
landowning Saxon filth. Hail Caledonia! Floreat Smellie!
And let the Craigfieth Chamber of Commerce mourn
the loss of the best Honorary Life President it never
had.

The light burned long above the Emporium that night,
yet it was a sprightly and elated Mr Haq who presented
himself at the Craigfieth Printers the next day. He
found the front office, with its yellowing clutter of old
Gala programmes and sepia tint postcards, deserted.
From beyond the bead curtain behind the counter came
the rattle of machinery.

Mr Haq rang for attention. Nothing happened. He
rang again, shaking the little brass bell until the clapper
flew off and rolled out of sight below the curtain. Still there
was no result, except that the noise from within seemed
to grow louder. He leaned over the counter and shouted
above it:

"Mr Chisholm? Mr Chisholm! Are you there? Shop!"

The racket expired suddenly with a bang, a whirr and a long exhausted wheeze.

Mr Haq called again: this time a voice replied.

"Ready Tuesday," it said.

"What?"

"Tuesday," came the voice again. "Can't do it before then, I'm afraid, it's my busy time of year."

The prospective candidate considered this remark before framing a suitable reply.

"Could you come out here, please?" he called.

After much unseen shuffling the melancholy ink-smudged face of Mr Solly Chisholm appeared in the parted screen.

"I'm rushed off my feet just now," it said. "I'm sorry Miss — oh, beg pardon Mr, er, just hold on a moment while I, now where did I put them?"

"On your head," said Mr Haq, who had now restored himself to the vertical.

"What? On my . . . oh, aye, right enough. Now then, that's better . . . oh, Mr Haq, it's you. For a moment I thought it was that poetry lady, you sound just like her, you know. Well, and what can I do for you, Mr Haq? Paper bags again, is it? Invoices?"

"No, no, no. I have an urgent order for you, Mr Chisholm. I want you to print my Address."

"Oh, aye, fine enough at that, Mr Haq. You just write it down for me on that wee pad on the counter there, and mind to put your postcode, and I'll see what I can do, though I can't promise —"

"No, no, not that sort of address, I mean an Election Address, for my leaflet, Mr Chisholm. I'm standing in the Council Election. Here it is, look."

Mr Haq handed the printer three sheets of closely written foolscap.

"The underlined bits are for italics," he explained.

"Oh dear me, goodness, I don't know about this at all, the way things are at the moment. You want me to do all this for May next year?"

Mr Haq blinked.

"May? Why May?"

"That's when they are, isn't it? The Council Elections? It's gey queer, I could have sworn I voted for somebody only last —"

"Oh no, Mr Chisholm, no, you misunderstand me. This is a *by*-election, in four weeks' time . . . mind your thumb there, please, you'll spoil the photograph."

Mr Chisholm blanched beneath his ink and clutched the counter for support.

"Four weeks, Mr Haq? Oh dear me, I can't possibly . . . and a photograph, I'll have to send that away, you know. Oh no, Mr Haq, I'm sorry, you should have told me earlier, before the New Year at the latest. I've had that poetry woman on at me since November last as it is . . ."

But Mr Haq had not got where he was without learning how to get what he wanted, and as a local man standing in a local election, he wanted the name of the local printer on his Address. They concluded the negotiations a quarter of an hour later: Mr Chisholm was to fend off the poetry woman with some technical excuses while Mr Haq was to pay slightly less than double the normal charge for five thousand leaflets, guaranteed to be ready in a fortnight, plus envelopes. He also undertook, by the following morning to reduce his Address to the Electors of Mid Lummock to a single side of A4 paper, with a biography to go with the photo on the reverse.

He left the shop in an abstraction of composition and nearly collided with Mr Smellie as the latter hurried in, a sheaf of papers protruding from the pocket of his brown overalls.

The greengrocer drove a hard bargain; having grimly overcome Mr Chisholm's initial refusal he beat him down to a price which represented only a trifling increase on that already quoted to Mr Haq. Nor did the printer fare much better at lunchtime with Mrs Pitt-Holyoake, who settled in the end for little more than Mr Smellie: really, when he considered what would be involved, he might as well be giving the things away. It was left to Mr Meiklejohn to restore his faith in the business. So anxious did the pharmacist appear to leave the works as quickly as possible that Mr Chisholm was able to demand at once a sum which, taken together with his receipts from the other three, represented enough to fix up the old Kleinwort-Benson in time to finish that awful woman's poems and still have something left over for a little holiday later on.

He locked up, and regarded his machine, its slumbering mass silent since his last running repair had given way that morning, halfway through a run of tickets for the Carpet Bowls Grand Prize Draw. He stroked it affectionately on the platen.

"There, there, old lady, don't you worry now. Daddy's going to make you all better, just as soon as he's found his Yellow Pages."

A week later, the papers printed the bald statement that, at the close of nominations for the Eastern Region By-Election in Mid Lummock, the four declared candidates were Mahommed Haq, 42 (Ind), Aeneas Quentin Meiklejohn, 53 (Ind), Audrey Rossetti Pitt-Holyoake, 59 (Ind), and Wallace Gladstone Smellie, 52 (Ind). Beyond the fact that all four were local tradespersons, nothing further was known. However, as Mr James Naughtie pointed out that evening on 'Left, Right and Centre', it was no accident that the following three weeks were to witness the stirrings of the Party machines from their winter slumber; for the Alliance, Dr David Owen was set to make a Midlothian Tour that would undoubtedly manage, forby the topographical inappropriateness, to include parts of Perthshire, while the SNP had booked the Crieff Tearooms for the first of this year's season of Special Extraordinary General Conferences to dispel false rumours of a split in the Party hierarchy, and the Labour Party in Scotland had announced the publication of a policy document entitled 'Profits Are Good For You: Socialism And Small Business'. Its cover showed a man selling red roses. Meanwhile, the corridors of St Andrew's House were alive with speculation that the eagerly awaited Rate Support Grant Re-revaluation would benefit Eastern Region at the expense of Strathclyde. Interviewed via satellite link from the International Congress of Business Technologists in Palm Springs, Sir Ashley Foutret MP described himself as 'quietly confident'.

In Craigfieth, however, the four persons at the quiet centre of all this attention were finding that they had no time to feel any of its excitement. Each had collected from Mr Chisholm five thousand envelopes in advance of their contents, each was alarmed to discover that electoral law demanded the addressing of one envelope per elector, and each was finding it an uphill job. Mr Haq had found the number of his domestic helpers reduced by two, Sayeed and Benazir maintaining that their preparations for Highers and O Grades respectively were of supreme importance, an argument to which, having advanced it so many times himself, their father had no adequate reply. Mr Smellie had slipped a little extra into Grace's pay packet and given her two thousand envelopes each for herself and the Ganglion boy, but was finding his own task hampered by the unhelpful attitude of Mrs Smellie. Even Mrs Pitt-Holyoake, who had little else to do all day — or all night either, for that matter — had fallen behind schedule since she would not sacrifice the elegance of her italic hand for the sake of speed.

Poor Mr Meiklejohn, though, was suffering worst. An unseasonal spell of mild weather had brought the town down with disorders of the nose and chest; every morning the pharmacist brought a large stack of envelopes and a copy of the Electoral Register to his dispensary and every evening took it all home again, scarcely touched. How could the wretched people ever vote for him if they insisted on being ill all the time? Alone of the four, he had no one to help him: the Chamber of Commerce had, for the sake of harmony and the Gala, adopted a stance of strict neutrality, and he dared not ask Miss Reekie, for obvious reasons. The days slid inexorably by until, utterly exhausted, he fell asleep one night in mid-envelope. When he awoke in the early hours of the morning he felt stiff and chilled, and knew he had a cold coming on.

Solly Chisholm drove carefully back to Craigfieth ten days after receiving the eight sheets of manuscript which, carefully typed by him, clipped together in four pairs, dispatched by Royal Mail Special Delivery and transformed by the new technology of Messrs Printitkwik of Dunbroath into twenty thousand folded leaflets, were to be the visible proof of the democratic process in action in Mid Lummock. Collecting the finished product in his own van had partly offset the cost of having 'Printed by Chisholm, Craigfieth' on the bottom of each leaflet; they had been unwilling at first, and had talked of electoral malpractice. But Mr Chisholm had found, in this cashless age of computerised banking, that a liberal application of unattributable folding currency did much to oil the machinery of commerce. Besides, it might not do if a rival firm's transport had been spotted making a delivery to his High Street premises and he had a little errand of his own to run in Dunbroath, or rather, four little errands: the delivery, to the city headquarters of the Conservative Party, the Labour Party, the SNP and the Alliance of one copy of each candidate's Address. The expenses he received for this favour corrected the imbalance caused by his wee token of appreciation to Messrs Printitkwik.

He had also found time to purchase a reconditioned Schroder-Wagg unit for the dear old Kleinwort-Benson. He would get her going tonight, and no one would ever know.

And there would still be enough to pay for that package trip to Gothenburg.

Mr Chisholm's van made three deliveries in the High Street that evening before heading out on the Lunie Road on the last leg of its mission. Half a mile out of town, the printer helped Mrs Pitt-Holyoake unload her order and stack it in the tiny hallway of Dante Cottage. This accomplished, he drove home, the van seeming to float along on its relieved springs. Pausing only to make and consume a sandwich, he was off again, this time to the works with the precious spare part. He knelt reverentially by the silent hulk of the press, carefully removed the Hambro arm (worn around its joints but good for another few years yet) before stripping out the damaged unit. The replacement fitted perfectly.

His sigh of satisfaction was drowned as the press lumbered into action and the interrupted flow of raffle tickets resumed. He leaned against the bench by the wall and fished in his coat pockets for the four leaflets he had kept for himself: he'd been that busy he hadn't found time yet to look at them.

It would be as well to check that Printitkwik had done a decent job on his behalf . . .

Those who have at some time in their lives offered themselves for election to public office will appreciate that the last thing any candidate wants, halfway through the campaign, is to spend a night of sleepless worry. Yet this unhappy fate is exactly what now befell three of the four hopefuls. It was not that there was anything wrong with their Election Addresses, *as such*: far from it. The photos had come out very well, especially Mrs Pitt-Holyoake's, which had been taken in Salzburg back in the carefree days of '58. The facsimile signatures were very convincing: in general, the quality of the printing far exceeded their expectations. That was not the worry . . . Of course, it had all been a terrible rush, and it all seemed years ago, that carefully composed statement of belief and policy and its subsequent hurried revision between visits to Mr Chisholm's. Much had to be left out, the rest compressed, abbreviated, simplified . . . but surely well . . . had they *really* written that? Were those their own phrases? 'Strike a blow for enterprise and economic freedom'? 'Raise our heads again in the pride of identity'? 'Small is beautiful'? The last was a particular worry to Mr Smellie: his wife, snoring lustily at his side, would make hay with that in the morning . . .

And what if the worst happened and they were elected? Ah, what then! What horrors had they let themselves in for? Could they . . . should they . . . withdraw?

Only Mr Haq slept soundly. He had a copy of his original Address, and it did not take him long to work out what had happened. Also, he had checked the documents from the Returning Officer: the deadline for withdrawal had come and gone. In any case, it was a perfectly good statement, as far as it went. Of course he was for the people; who was not? Naturally, he believed in fair shares for them; it was simply a question of gauging the degree of fairness. No one abhorred the rapacious greed of others more than he. There was no disputing the ends: the means, he reckoned, would be his affair, after he was elected. After all, was not politics the art of the possible? And when in Rome . . .

Bill Smith and John Brown, President and Vice-President respectively of the Scottish National Party (Eastern Region), sat together in the office of the organisation's Area Headquarters, the back parlour of the Vice-President's furnished flat in Alloa Avenue, Dunbroath.

"That's settled, then," said the President. "We go for the woman."

"Aye, I suppose so," his lieutenant replied unhappily. "But I'm still no' happy . . . d'ye not think we should hae askit Robinson what he thocht?"

"Bugger Robinson," Smith said. "He's a bloody faction-alist, let's leave him out of this."

He dialled a Craigfieth number . . .

. . . The ringing woke Mr Meiklejohn abruptly from the profound sleep he had at last achieved. Something was terribly wrong: it ought to be too early in the morning even for this feeble light . . . he struggled out of bed and picked up the receiver; as he did so, he saw the clock. Saints alive! He knew who that must be . . .

"Oh, Miss Reekie, I'm terribly sorry, I must have over— pardon? Who? Sir Ashley Fou— in Miami! But isn't there, I mean, have I got you out of . . . what? . . . What service? . . . Well, that's very kind of you, thank you very much, but I don't see how . . . a few what? . . . Well, yes, I *am* a little behind with my envelopes, as a matter of fact, but . . . today? Well, er, yes. Yes! . . . And thank you, Sir Ashley, I don't suppose you'd remember my Mother, but she always — hello? Hello? Oh. Good gracious!"

It was all very puzzling, he thought as he pulled his trousers up under his nightshirt. He couldn't exactly remember writing that bit about the competitive society, but he should have thought its meaning was clear enough. That Sir Ashley Foutret of all people should . . . oh well, it was probably just politics. Meanwhile he had a more serious and immediate problem to deal with. He hurried down to the shop, his laces clicking on the stairs.

It had been a trying morning for the greengrocer. He had opened the shop, his helpmeet's derisive laughter still ringing in his ears, to find that half the sprouts had turned a brilliant cadmium yellow overnight. He had barely enough time to turn them to the bottom of the box before Grace arrived with the best part of three thousand unaddressed envelopes and a demand for more biro money: that Ganglion wretch was putting ideas into the young chit's head these days.

Now she was calling him through to the phone. He straightened painfully from the potato sack, wiped most of the noisome glair on the seat of his trousers, and took the instrument from her.

"Smellie Provisions," he snarled.

"Good morning," said a female voice. "Hold the line, please, I have a personal pre-recorded message for you from Dr David Owen . . ."

Mrs Pitt-Holyoake frowned vigorously. What an extraordinary conversation; really, it had been more like talking to some fugitive anarchist than a serious discussion with a once-great national party. She was quite sure her grandfather had not found it so in

Campbell-Bannerman's day, but there: everything was so different then. People had appreciated good handicraft, for one thing. She supposed it was merely another sign of these troubled times that her call from the Alliance should come from a public 'phone box and that her caller should have been unable to finish what he was saying about the way forward before his last ten pence ran out.

Still, at least she would be getting help, on the next bus, with the ghastly addressing business. So long as they had legible handwriting, that was all . . .

Mr Haq dealt coolly and professionally with his call from Maxton House. Yes, he would indeed be grateful for any assistance with some of the less appetising chores of candidacy and no, he had no personal dislike of Young Socialists, provided they *were* young, ha, ha, nor had he (after instantaneous consultation with his political conscience) any reason to suppose his attitudes any more discriminatory than the next person's with regard to age, gender, disability or sexual orientation: "It is untrue that my people do it facing Mecca!" he quipped. He was glad he'd mentioned that: ethnic origin was very important to these people, for some reason.

He looked up at his mentors' gallery, winked at Roger Scruton and saluted Chief Constable Anderton.

"This time *we'll* be the enemy within, eh James!" he said. The custodian of order in Greater Manchester stared pontifically back.

During the next two weeks of that crucial campaign, the candidates were at least able to enjoy a measure of the celebrity they had hoped for. Freed from the deadly chores of their democratic inheritance, they were entertained to a special tour of the Kipplerigg Distillery (which, having just found itself to be one of several dozen disparate enterprises newly acquired by Genghis International Holdings plc, was eager for all the help it could get) and were further courted, sometimes singly, sometimes en masse, by the NFU (who plied them with hospitality in the VIP tent at the Central Perthshire Poultry Show) and by sundry other bodies ranging in variety from the Strathlummock Leisure Centre to the Tayside Committee of Families For Defence. They began to revel in the sensation, new to all of them save Mr Haq, of having at all times an audience willing to hang on every word they said, no matter what the subject. As the days sped gorgeously by, a feeling of warm camaraderie developed between them as whatever imagined political differences they might have had evaporated like hoar frost in May. Were they not, after all, Independents? — and Craigfiethans? What else mattered?

There were, it is true, occasional flies in this balmy ointment. Mr Haq was obliged, after complaints from certain of his fellow-townsfolk, to deny himself the canvassing support of the Stirling University Wimmins' Consciousness Workshop, and Mr Smellie allowed himself, in an interview with the political correspondent of the *Perthshire Gazette*, to contradict certain of the points made by the leader of the SDP in his address to an SWRI conference in Kilmahog the night before. Mungo 'Slim' Beauly (whose turn it was that week to fill the post) sold his story to *Scotland Now!* who splashed it on the front page beneath the tricoloured headline, 'SDP SPLIT ROW LOOMS', but the fuss soon blew over. Mrs Pitt-Holyoake caused some consternation when she told a reporter from BBC Radio Lummock that she 'didn't give a damn' about the SNP Extraordinary General Meeting in Crieff, but an aide hastily explained that she was of course referring to the factionalists, and left it to the commentators to decide which factionalists she might have been referring to. On the whole, though, amicability prevailed and when the four candidates sat together to watch the Caledonian eve-of-poll special on the 24-inch colour stereo set in the Lounge of the Ben Almond Hotel it was in an atmosphere of decorous conviviality. No one minded in the least when Mr Meiklejohn was referred to as 'Maggie's Great White Hope North of the Border'; no one looked accusingly at Mr Haq when the presenter, over a picture of their adopted townsfellow, observed that Mr Kinnock's pink rose had found fertile soil in Craigfieth High Street; nor was there even the merest hint of a blench when Mrs Pitt-Holyoake was described as 'a pin-up very much in the mould of Winnie and Margo', or when Mr Smellie was eulogised by a duet of Alliance spokespersons as being 'just what the Doctor ordered'.

The truth was, they had all got used to this sort of nonsense by now. What if it had all turned out quite differently from the way they had first imagined: it didn't really matter. Only Mr Haq, it may be suspected, thought otherwise, and a lifetime in the retail trade as well as nearly two years' residence in Craigfieth, had taught him how to feign a mask of inoffensive inscrutability.

Polling day dawned bright and calm over the gentle hectares of Mid Lummock. Little was seen of the candidates until lunchtime when, Thursday being early closing day in the town, they were able to shut up shop and circulate among their people. They found they had little to do apart from stroll up and down the High Street, often in each other's company, and be pleasant. The diligent and discreet ministrations of their assistants (augmented by the rather less discreet help of the more partisan primary pupils, who had been given a day off to

enable their school to be used as a Polling Place)
ensured that a steady stream of Craigfiethans presented
themselves throughout the day to perform their civic
duty. Indeed, by the time these unofficial party workers
got round to visiting the farms and picturesque hovels
on Lord Margoyle's estate, which comprised the greater
part of the rural area of the constituency, they found that
every qualified person there had already been to the polls,
in a fleet of Landrovers thoughtfully provided by their
beneficent Laird.

A heavy poll was predicted. Even the candidates
themselves remembered to vote.

The result came too late for the morning papers,
which had to content themselves with headlines such as
'Independent Victory Forecast In Vital Mid Lummock
Test' and leave it to the broadcasters to break the news,
which they themselves did not receive until after four
o'clock on Friday morning, all four candidates having
demanded a recount. The figures, when they came, were
not disappointing, providing as they did sufficient fuel
for days of in-depth analysis. They were:

Meiklejohn, A.Q. (Ind)	832
Smellie, W.G. (Ind)	802
Pitt-Holyoake, Mrs A.R. (Ind)	793
Haq, M. (Ind)	767
	—
Maj.	30

Electorate: 4,890 Votes cast: 3,194
% Poll: 65.3   Winner's Share: 26%

A spokesman for Mr Malcolm Rifkind described the
Secretary of State as being 'very satisfied' with the result;
his opposite number in the House was reported to be
'encouraged', and pointed out that the overwhelming

majority of the people of Mid Lummock had rejected Thatcherism. All eight wings of the SNP were agreed on the imminence of a revival, and hoped the other seven were not going to spoil it. In a ten-minute interview on *The World At One*, Dr Owen forecast a coalition government by the end of the year.

Mr Meiklejohn advertised for a locum pharmacist, hoped his Councillor's expenses would cover the cost, and wondered how he would arrange things so that the interviewees did not meet Miss Reekie until it was too late.

Craigfieth, the unwonted excitement over, quickly reverted to normality. The Gala Committee began its preparations in high hopes of grant assistance and a memorable display which would go some way to redeeming the previous year's unfortunate incident. At least the Grand Opener would not be a problem this time: tendering his resignation, for reasons of public probity, from the office of Committee Chairman, Councillor Meiklejohn intimated that he would be happy to have the honour of performing that duty himself.

It says much for his high principles that he was, unfortunately, unable to.

This unhappy state of affairs might never have come about had it not been for Mr Meiklejohn's political conscience — that commodity so often demanded of our masters, and so often shunned and despised on those rare occasions when it is exercised. For his colleagues at Eastern House it was all the more shocking that Councillor Meiklejohn should have taken this fit after such a promising start.

Arriving for his first meeting, the new Councillor had been gratified to recognise among his fellow tribunes many familiar faces; it seemed that quite half a dozen of the helpful young men who had assisted him in his campaign were also Conservative Councillors. Whatever his ideals before, the chemist was determined now to set his face firmly towards the goal of Independence, and as far as he was concerned this meant supporting those who had supported him, and, ipso facto, supported his electors. It may be seen that Mr Meiklejohn, however new to the game, was an apt student of the more important of its unwritten rules. Within the day he had twice supported his friends in the Council Chamber, and had found himself installed on the Leisure and Recreation Committee which, he was given every reason to believe, would shortly be formulating a policy of active support for the Region's cultural base. It was not, he reflected as he drove home that night, that he ruled out the possibility of support for the Labour group per se. It was just that, as things stood, they could be of little use to his people. Time might alter that but then, as an Independent, he had little to fear from Time, had he? For the true Independent, a week in politics is much the same as a week in any other occupation. Indeed, if today's evidence was anything to go by, it could be a deal less stressful than a week in pharmacy. He wondered how the locum had managed on her first day, then decided he was too busy to find out.

No, if there had been times when he wondered if standing for election might not have been an awful mistake (the size of Mr Chisholm's bill had been particularly alarming, for instance) those times were past. He now knew that it was the best thing he had ever done. He parked his car carefully and decided to treat himself to an early night. He would take the Leisure and Recreation Committee agenda to bed with him and study how to raise the Gala at the next meeting. One had, after all, one's responsibilities, and it would always pay to have an eye to re-election.

He was not aware — since he had no reason to be — that one of the nice young men had received a

potentially disturbing letter from a certain gentleman, a
retail tradesman in the parish of Craigfieth and elector
of Mid Lummock, alleging that he (the writer) had been
unwittingly deprived of the democratic right to fly his
true political colours, and enclosing what purported to
be documentary proof. The nice young man consulted
with certain of his nice young colleagues, and one or
two of his older ones, and decided that, at this stage, no
acknowledgement need be made nor action taken. The
new bug, whatever he might think he was, was doing
tolerably nicely.

And indeed, the new bug did rather more than tolerably
nicely in the weeks that followed, allowing the Convener at
long last to hope that his peers throughout Scotland might
begin to take him seriously. Not even the best-regulated
Councils could guarantee their leaders two whole months
of restful nights, as his had done. A good chap, that little
chemist man. Backbone of the Party.

And then, quite unexpectedly, the backbone slipped a
disc, with crippling consequences for the body politic. To
Councillor Meiklejohn, his intervention in what *Scotland
Now!* dubbed the AIDS Crisis Drama was a simple matter
of professional pride coupled with an Independent outlook. To speak out in the Council's debate on community
services was part of the natural function of a freely
elected representative; to move an amendment for the
granting of immediate cash aid to retail pharmacists in
order to allow them to issue free condoms on demand
to the sexually active was a question of simple common
sense; to carry the amendment by twenty-four votes to
twenty-three, a matter for congratulation rather than
censure.

His erstwhile colleagues at Eastern House did not, alas,
agree. They saw beyond the superficial attractions of the
scheme, to the devastating long-term consequences for

themselves and, through them, for their Region. What had now become Council policy—and God help the Convener at the next meeting of COSLA — went wildly and unforgivably beyond the spending limits which months of painstaking negotiation, together with the recent by-election, had at last wrung from St Andrew's House, as the opposition parties well knew. There would now be no alternative—to coin a memorable phrase—to the instant clawback, to the rate-capping, to the imminent blasting of several very promising political careers. To hell, as one senior Tory put it, with this Queers' Clap, or whatever it was: the wretched little man had buggered them all up, and must be made to pay for it.

An ad hoc committee of nice young men was formed, and they in turn chose the very nicest of their number, Cllr. Adrian Hartley-Drummond, to deliver the blow.

He found the unsuspecting Meiklejohn at the Cocktail Bar of the Wee Drappie O't, which had become his favourite haunt in recent weeks, when not engaged in Council business, and took him on one side.

"I thought I ought to tell you," said Hartley-Drummond, "what a little bird told me a little while ago."

"Oh yes?" replied Mr Meiklejohn, as the nice young man guided him to a secluded seat in the corner. "Is it about the Gala?"

"No-ooh, not as such, my dear, no. Actually, it's about your election expenses. My little bird tells me you've been just a teensy-weensy bit overgenerous to your friendly neighbourhood printer."

"Oh, old Solly!" Mr Meiklejohn laughed. "Yes, I know, daylight robbery, wasn't it? Never mind though, it did the trick."

"Ah, well, and there's the rub, my dear, you see. All very boring and tiresome I know, but there's a little law our big brothers have made, just to give the plebs the illusion of fairness and make them feel glad they're not Americans. It's called the Representation of the People Act, and if you read the small print *ve-ery* carefully you'll see it says you're not supposed to spend more than two point nine pee per elector, plus a hundred and, for some reason, forty-four pounds. That would make your limit something in the region of, let's see, about fifteen hundred, give or take a pony or two. Are we following my little drift?"

"Fifteen hundred?" spluttered the outraged representative. "But that's much less than I paid! Do you mean to say Chisholm charged me more than he was allowed to?"

"Not quite, my dear, no. You see, it works the other way round, don't you know. Mr Chisholm is competing in a free market and can charge what he likes, as I'm sure you'll appreciate. No, I'm afraid *you're* the one who's been a naughty boy. A very naughty boy, in fact. A very *very* naughty boy! I wouldn't like to be in your shoes — nice as they are, my dear, you must tell me where you buy them — if the plods ever come to hear of it."

Mr Meiklejohn trembled.

"Wh-what would they do?"

"Oh dear, my friend, what wouldn't they! It's the one thing we all try to avoid, you see, because the Grundys call it corruption, and that's bad news all round. It's simple enough to avoid, of course, especially since we've done so much to help the black economy in only two terms: a little cash here, a little there, and no questions asked. But we didn't do that, did we? Oh dear me, no. We paid with a little checky-poo and sent the receipt in, all nice and tidy, to the Returning Officer. We have a few friends in that department, I'm glad to say, but I'm afraid they can't keep it a secret for long. And then, well . . .!"

"What'll . . . happen?"

The nice Mr Hartley-Drummond tutted painfully.

"Slapped wrists, my dear; smacked botties. Appearances in Court. And then . . ."

He drew the wretched man closer in.

"Prison!" he hissed. "Durance vile. And believe me, my dear, they don't call it being Banged Up for nothing, oh dear no. I should know, some of my best friends have been there. No condoms in Dunbroath Gaol, my friend, not even for ready money!"

There was an awful, reverberant silence. Then Mr Meiklejohn had a desperate idea. He put it to his young friend.

"Very wise, my dear, very wise," purred Mr Hartley-Drummond. "Yes, I believe we could stem the flood if you did that, provided you did it right away, of course. For professional reasons, shall we say?"

A terrible thought occurred to Mr Meiklejohn as he rose, unsteadily, to leave.

"But that'll let Smellie in! We can't have that, the man's a lunatic!"

"No it won't, my dear, they'll have to have another election, and then who knows? Besides, I don't think you need worry about any nasty Smellies. Or any nasty Pitt-Holyoakes either. They've been naughty too, poor things, not as naughty as naughty old you, of course, but naughty enough. I must say, if it was up to me, I'd co-opt Mr Chisholm straight away, but there we are, *mutatis mutandis* as my dear old Housemaster used to say, there's a fair chance we'll have our first tinted Councillor very soon. They're all the rage these days, apparently."

The second Mid Lummock by-election was very much in the tradition of the community. For one thing, the political media were far too busy consoling one of the London Parties on the apparent voodoo which had attached itself, yet again, to the office of its Honorary

Assistant Deputy Vice-President to concern themselves with anything that went on above the Watford
Gap or, for that matter, above the waist. And for another
thing, the worrying variety of choice which had exercised
the minds of the electorate in February did not recur in
May, which is to say that, at his second attempt, Mr Haq
did not require the services of Mr Chisholm. And that was
just as well. The Kleinwort-Benson finally succumbed to a
surfeit of bad poetry and hurled its Hambro arm into the
Ansbacher assembly, with consequences beyond repair.
Gothenburg was deferred indefinitely.

As the sole candidate, Councillor-designate Mahommed Haq was able to celebrate his election on the evening
of nomination day. He was guest of honour at a little soirée
organised by his constituency colleagues, including all the
nice young men, in the drawing-room of Lunie Castle,
and he was received into their midst (having graciously
relaxed his religious scruples for the sake of his host's
amour propre) with a glass of South African sherry.

He had restored normality to his town, order to his
Region, and faith to his ideals. He had arrived. He allowed
himself a rare smile, and a second glass of sherry.

8

The Strange Destiny of

Wallace Smellie

. . . and he took of the stones of that place, and put them for his pillows . . . —Gen 28: xi

Since he had won home, his numbed feet blistered, nearly a year before, Mr Kirkpatrick of the Craigfieth DIY Centre had not let a day pass without thinking — puny word for the puissance of the occupation! — of the Hon Davinia Moither. Her appearances in the crinkles of the cerebellum wherein such exotica are engendered, were not so much thoughts as apprehensions, unbidden and undeniable, vivid despite their evanescence, which interfered drastically with the channels of communication between him and his appointed task. He might be vending a flat-pack lounge suit or arranging a display of bathroom accessories when the visions struck. There was no predicting their occurrence, and no accounting, on any rational plane, for the chain of connexion between, say, the particular design of a shower fixture and the sudden manifestation of the Lunie heiress, accompanied as she always was by the full range of sensory apparatus. Had she but retained the teaching of her long-dead dominies, well might Mrs Gloagie have observed, like Banquo, 'Look, how our partner's rapt' to each puzzled customer on these occasions. For Wayne Kirkpatrick, in the months following his baptism in the back of the old van, did not live on his erotic imaginings alone. New honours came upon him.

While the Hon Davinia was kept busy at the vocation into which she had been born — attending premieres of Lloyd-Webber musicals, for instance, and the opening parties of new nightclubs, doing her bit for the Distressed Estate Managers' Benevolent Fund and the British Film Industry, providing occasional copy for the social diarists of the *Daily Mail* and the *Spectator* (both High and Low) and all this on top of the workaday obligations of Ascot, Henley, Cowes and so on — she did not neglect her faithful swain in faraway Central Perthshire.

Once every six weeks, on average, the telephone would warble amidst the executive furnishings of Mr Kirkpatrick's bungaloid abode, and the siren voice would say, "It's me, Wayne darling. Guess a man's gotta do . . ." And the words would bring flooding back, like a tactile video, the memory of that Second Time, that incident of post-coital near oblivion . . . and, as often as not, Mr Kirkpatrick's reply as his copy of *Management Today* fell, detumescent, to the floor, would be what can only be inadequately represented in print as "Ahh-hh!"

And for several days thereafter Mrs Gloagie would be compelled to carry on the enterprise of the Craigfieth DIY Centre alone and without benefit of a diploma in Management Studies. Her singlehanded stewardship of the business during these periods speaks volumes for her grim loyalty to the dear dead days of Mawhinney's Ironmongers.

As far as Mr Kirkpatrick was concerned, the only disquieting aspect of these blissful assignations was their location. For in what he supposed to be a touching allusion to their first dalliance, his enjoyment of his beloved took place, at her insistence, in the most unlikely places and in the most physically taxing ways. Adored for his athleticism and slimness of figure, Mr Kirkpatrick found himself engaging in exploits for which his adolescent perusal of the *Kama Sutra* had but scantily prepared him. In the breeding pens of the Laird's pheasantry, atop the bathroom annexe of the Dower House, aloft in the branches of the Great Deodar of Lunie, nipple deep in the slimily clinging waters of the Castle moat . . . Although he found his stamina more than equal to his partner's inventiveness, he found his thoughts tending, of late, fondly towards double beds or, at a pinch, hearthrugs. If the Hon Davinia divined these whims at all, she resolutely ignored them. Inflamed by weeks of abstinence he was unable to demur and she, for her part, seemed unlikely to run short of novelties just yet.

Thus it was, one soft June evening, that Mr Smellie, concealed below the lip of the third bunker, observed the impassioned couple making their way across the Golf Course to their latest trysting place.

It should be averred at once that spying on the priapic excursions of his fellow-citizens was not a regular pursuit of Mr Smellie's, although he might be forgiven for it in view of his own domestic arrangements. For one thing, it was a hobby unlikely to find much in the way of fulfilment in the environs of Craigfieth, despite the best efforts to the contrary of the town's Homewear entrepreneur, and, for another, twenty-seven years of marriage to Mrs Smellie had reduced the greengrocer's interest in that area of human activity to mere academic levels. That is to say, for instance, that his awareness of the liaison between his assistant, Grace Wemyss, and the Ganglion youth was confined to periodic irritation at her lateness in the mornings and occasional listlessness at work and this, he noted, was happening with less frequency as time went by. Vicarious salacity was not for him; even the stramash, two years before, over the business of Mr Haq's magazines had largely passed him by. Had Fate decreed for Mr Smellie a career in used cars, say, or advertising, there is no telling what heights his libido might have attained in sympathy: as things stood, however, it was his experience that sex, in whatever shape or form, had nothing in common with the successful merchandising of fruit and vegetables. The blooming of Miss Wemyss into consummated womanhood left him, in that respect, unmoved.

So why, it may be asked, was he lurking thus embunkered? Why did he, at a safe distance, begin to follow this couple, whose imminent intentions would have been obvious even to a blind castrato, so pregnant was the still air with throbbing sensuality? Strange indeed are the ways of destiny, as Mr Smellie was to shortly discover for himself.

The simple facts of the matter are that the greengrocer had, over the years, evolved various strategies to fill his leisure hours, the latest of which had been his almost successful bid for elected office. In the winter he attended meetings of the town's Men's Debating Society and Burns Club, and combed the *Concise Scots Dictionary* for solecisms and misguided etymology; during the clement seasons he played solitary golf. His presence on the Craigfieth course in the magical later hours of June daylight is thus prosaically explained. And it happened, on this particular night, that his efforts to avoid the third bunker had been rewarded by the sight of his ball glowing briefly ruddy as it arced through the perfumed air into the miniature downland of the Rough.

The territory into which his ball had fallen had long been the subject of dispute between the managing committee of the Craigfieth Links and the Factors of the Lunie Estate, a dispute which, after seventy years, showed no sign of ever being settled. Agents for the Estate (Messrs Drubber and Dunning, W.S., of Edinburgh) claimed ancient lights of reversionary socage granted by James

IV in grateful recognition of the service rendered His Majesty by Lord Archibald 'Hogsbreath' Campbell, the only begetter of the Lummock sept of that great Clan, with which a farsighted ancestral Moither had made politic union through the agency of an otherwise unmarketable younger daughter. Against this formidable legal evidence successive Golf Club Committees could only argue that their course offered little in the way of genuine rough land save this one piece of oddly hummocked ground, and they needed it. Though both sides had in their possession copies of the sale agreed between Sir Tarquin Moither and the Club, the palsied hand of the cartographer employed to draw the plan had ensured that recourse to it was doomed to be forever useless. Meanwhile (and possibly for all Eternity) the area remained unfenced. It might also have remained uncontroversial—Lord Margoyle having lost the desire, if he ever had it, to exercise his feudal rights thereon—had it not been for the irritating habit of certain of the Laird's house guests to conceal themselves in the place in order to steal golf balls, for a lark, whenever some unfortunate practitioner of the Royal and Ancient Art miscued a drive.

It was Mr Smellie's good fortune to be Golf Treasurer — and his bad luck to be one of the persons so frequently discomfited by this childish practice; hence his interest in the amorous couple that momentous evening. It was not erotomania that drove him; it was his balls and his honour. He left his clubs in the bunker, the better to stalk his quarry.

Let it be said, once more and for all time, that there was as little of the voyeur in Mr Smellie as in the child unborn. Of course he noticed where Miss Moither had her hand; naturally (since a lifetime's greengrocery had trained his eye to Nature's symmetries) he saw that Mr Kirkpatrick's was likewise engaged, as if each were about to give the

other a helpful shove over a stile. He could not help it
if, as the lady turned to address some pleasantry to her
partner, the dying rays of the westering sun turned her
flimsy summer dress to gossamer translucence; neither
was it his fault when, in the interests of his quest, he had
perforce to witness the scene when the lady dispensed
even with this passing nod to modesty before helping her
friend, rather more cumbrously, to do the same. All this,
and what inevitably followed, was of so little interest to the
misogynistic Mr Smellie that he was reduced to adjusting
the focus of his field glasses, just to pass the time.

The loving couple, unwitting in their engorged passion,
had led him for fully ten minutes through a landscape
that might have been formed from the rejected produce
of some giant's bakery. Scattered around on the gently
rising ground, these loaf-like outcrops, grassed and
spangled with daisies, tormentil and clover, provided
excellent cover for Mr Smellie's stalking activities. Despite
his years he was able, on his hands and knees, to follow the
progress of the pair while remaining unobserved himself.
As they rounded each hillock, watched by him from the
one behind, he crept out of hiding and scuttled like some
ocean floor crustacean across the intervening space before
regaining cover. They came at last to a protuberance quite
unlike the others. Its western face contained a hollow,
half way up, whose turf was shorter, and greener, than
the rest. With the slope continuing above it and falling
away on either side, it resembled not so much a miniature
amphitheatre as a large armchair: or, to take the analogy
as far as it can possibly go, if the entire mound had been
a bean-bag this hollow could well have been the impression left, in its hidden polystyrene nubules, by someone
recently seated therein.

It is doubtful if Mr Smellie was struck by the comparison: connubiality as he knew it had certainly never

found such uses for a chair as Mr Kirkpatrick and the Hon Davinia Moither, after certain urgently playful preliminaries, now demonstrated in their little green place. The shopkeeper would not have believed it possible had he not, fortuitously, had binocular assistance to hand. And the climax — so to speak — was quite outwith his admittedly restricted experience.

There is a manifest incidence of situational cliché in what we unthinkingly refer to as 'real life'; Freud made a career out of it, and Murphy gave his name to the Law which embodies it: Life, it seems, is a great breeder of the thing, and as long as Life endures, so will it prosper. Yet, cruelly, let the humble fictionmonger but use it once, and he is doomed. Fiction, we are told by those who presumably ought to know, is supposed to mirror Life with a super-real (though not slavish) exactitude, or at any rate distort it authentically enough to satisfy the craving for realism in the breast of the averagely literate bookbuyer; yet it is never so much at risk of critical excoriation as when, faithful as it is to the tyrant Life, it stands guilty in the Courts of Review of the supposed sin of cliché. It is not fair, really. It is especially galling, for the conscientious storyteller, to run up against an incident which can only be related in one way. You — dear Reader — and thou — gentle Critic — may blame Mr Ernest Hemingway for what will be perpetrated in the next paragraph. For were it not for his shameful wasting of a perfectly good phrase on a situation which so patently did not warrant it, the description of what Mr Smellie saw, through his pin-sharp lenses, would deserve only critical acclaim or, at worst, uncritical indifference.

The earth moved.

. . . And when Mr Smellie crawled over to investigate the sudden disappearance of the lovers he found it moved for him, too. The intensity of the surprise this gave him had a certain anaesthetic effect, so that the shock of his landing shortly afterwards was not as severe as might be imagined. After that, he rolled and slithered for a while and when he finally came to rest it was, for him at least, a very soft landing indeed.

It was very dark; he might, for aught he knew, be in the very barrenmost depths of space, such was the numbing effect of the dark airlessness of the place. At times like this the individual human soul, however atrophied, cries out for companionship.

"Where are you?" he whispered.

"Under you, mostly," came a muffled female voice.

Mr Smellie half-raised himself awkwardly (it is surprising how very difficult and puzzling even the simplest movement becomes in the total absence of light) and placed his hand below him for support. Then he hastily withdrew it.

"Sorry," he gulped.

"Why?" said the voice, wetly, in his right ear.

This time Mr Smellie tried to roll off his human cushion, blanking his mind as best he could to the tactile and pneumatic sensations necessitated by this manoeuvre, and at length he succeeded.

Somebody struck a match (since only one of the three persons present was blessed with pockets, it is not difficult to work out who it was). Thankfully, he saw the lady was lying on her front; he also saw the gentleman, wild of eye and muddy of countenance, emerging from behind a rectangular boulder which seemed, in the fitful light of Mr Smellie's vesta, to glisten, though the atmosphere down here was dry. Then he felt his fingers burning, and threw the match away.

"Ow!" said the lady.

"Sorry!" gulped Mr Smellie again.

His clumsy fingers eventually found another match, and struck it. The lady had now arranged herself in a position which owed more to comfort than to propriety. She was seated with her back to the boulder; her companion still goggled from his former location. However, long ages — so it seemed to the astounded Smellie — before his second match went out, it was the fourth occupant of the underground chamber that engaged his exclusive attention. He gasped as the match failed though not, this time, with pain. In the renewed darkness, the Hon Davinia made a conversational overture.

"You're trespassing," she said.

Mr Smellie's third match illuminated the heiress of Lunie in a pose of brazen arrogance, commensurate with her class and occupation. The greengrocer crawled past, cradling his feeble light, with as little regard for the naked nymphomaniac as if she had been a sack of remaindered carrots, and laid his hand on the bevelled smoothness of the boulder. It seemed to thrill beneath his warm palm, like a slumberous wife stirred to vibrant passion by her good man's touch in the unexpected watches of the night. Even this simile, had it occurred to him, would not have taken the shine off the experience for Mr Smellie.

Match after match he kindled, heedless of the pornographic absurdities perpetrated by the retreating pair as they made their way, on all fours, out of the chamber. Let them resume their business elsewhere, or dress and go home: he did not care. Even his lost ball was forgotten.

He lingered in the chambers of the earth until his last match was spent; later, he returned with a torch and a notebook.

Less than a mile away, in the lounge area of Mr Kirkpatrick's bungalow, the lovers sat facing each other across the synthetic logs of a gas fire. Both had bathed and changed; the Hon Davinia was wearing a pair of Wayne's designer denims, rolled up at the bottom, and a Gala '86 sweatshirt bought cheaply at the Misses Urquhart's the Christmas before. She looked overwhelmingly attractive and desirable. He suggested an adjournment to the bedroom.

"Mmm?" the lady replied. "Oh no, not now darling, too tedious. Besides, I have some thinking to do."

Puzzled and hurt, the entrepreneur sat in shocked silence.

Few sensible people nowadays entertain the illusion that the lump of dull sandstone built into the ugly coronation chair of that unattractively physical Plantagenet monarch Edward I, and displayed to the vulgar gaze in Westminster Abbey, is the original and genuine Stone of Destiny on which ancient Scots kings were accustomed to sit during their anointment. (It is, incidentally, a little-known fact, and one which has nothing whatever to do with this tale, that the initials 'J.G.' prominently carved on proud Edward's throne belong to one Jeremiah Ganglion, a cordwainer of Southwark, who incised them there one afternoon in 1851 on his bibulous way home from the Great Exhibition.)

Among the majority from whose eyes the scales have fallen, there are two schools of thought. The first teaches that the real Stone, which was spirited (if that is the right word for the action of removing a 400lb block) from the Abbey in 1950, has never been returned. Instead it was exchanged for a replica by the sponsor of the theft (or repossession), one Bailie Robert Gray, a monumental mason of the City of Glasgow, whose principal recreations appear to have been Scottish Nationalism and the manufacture of duplicate Destiny Stones, in roughly equal proportions. This, they aver, can be proved by the fact that the real Stone was dropped during its removal:

a corner broke off, and was afterwards repaired. The block now in Westminster shows no sign of mending, while that on display in St Columba's Church, Dundee, does. Furthermore, the puckish Gray is said to have assured the Minister of that parish that the Stone he was receiving was the real thing. It rests there still, in a sort of monumental iron maiden, with a wee plaque to proclaim its provenance. Finally, as if to clinch their case, they tell of a third Stone, 'hidden somewhere outside Arbroath' and presumably intended, like the placebo in a pharmacological experiment, to act as a sort of control on the other two, and generally confuse the wretched English.

So far, so clear. But the second school hold that the real joke — assuming you are a Scot, that is, or, if such a thing is possible, neutral — consists in the fact that the thing which Auld Ned abstracted from Scottish soil in 1296 was not It anyway, oh no, not It at all. For in a fit of overweening hubris the bigheaded old poltroon, believing his word to be universal writ, gave the Abbot of Scone six weeks' notice of his intention to run off with the Luck of Scotland, *without taking the precaution of looking at it first*. The good Abbot, blessed with a fine sense of the ridiculous all too rare in today's Church, thereupon had his monks hack out a chunk of the local pink sandstone and rough it up a bit until it looked sufficiently sat upon to fool the silly man and send him crowing back to his own midden: which thing, being no more, after all, than a mere tool in the Hand of Providence, he duly did. The parishioners of St Columba's, Dundee, must therefore content themselves with possessing an original fake, albeit more venerable by some seven hundred and sixty years than Bailie Gray's one in London.

But what, then, of the *real* Real Stone? What happened to that black meteorite, used by Jacob as a pillow in the wilderness, set up by him as a pillar the next morning and anointed with oil, at the place called Beth-el? That sacred boulder which, while the descendants of the prolific progenitor were multiplying all over Israel, was brought to Perthshire via Egypt, Spain and Ireland? What precautions did the holy jester of Scone take against being found out by the Southern filth?

Not surprisingly, he hid it: so well, in fact, that it was not rediscovered until the year of grace 1826, when two braw lads fell upon it, quite literally, in a cavern on Dunsinane Hill. They described it as being 'carved with Hieroglyphs' and it says a lot for the state of Scottish Education at that time that two such folk should know what a hieroglyph was, even if they did not recognise the markings as Hebraic script. The thing caused quite a local sensation: it is reliably reported that even the owner of the land on which the Stone was found came to have a proprietorial peek.

And then it disappeared again.

Not a wink did Mr Smellie sleep that night; how, indeed, could such a thing be expected of him? He was transported beyond such ordinariness.

He left Miss Wemyss to mind the shop while, fuelled by Fate's adrenalin, he began putting into action the fruits of his long night's planning . . .

The Hon Davinia Moither woke refreshed from her chaste sleep; next to her, Wayne Kirkpatrick was somewhat less refreshed from his. As he stumbled off to the blinding steel and melamine cave of his kitchen, Davinia tried to marshal some order to her thinking on the events of the night before. While she could, no doubt, be accused of many things, being a fool was not one of them, and she knew from long experience that mere misogyny was no defence against her charms, particularly when they were so obtrusively displayed. In order to resist — nay, ignore — such a spectacle, a man must have his mind concentrated with total exclusivity on something else, something so compelling that her siren signals could find no receptors even on the most lickerish level of the unconscious mind. Here, admittedly, she was straying into realms of theory, such a phenomenon being outwith her ken, but she was sure the hypothesis was sound, and the knowledge annoyed her intensely. Something down there had enthralled the little tradesman to such an extent that her allurements had been passed by, unregarded. Even her little exercise in *noblesse s'excuse* had fallen flat: this, then, was serious.

It could not have been Wayne, of that she was sure. The Smellie man could not possibly — she giggled inwardly at the peculiar inappropriateness of the adjective — be gay. It was not that she desired the man — well, not really — it was the principle of the thing. After all those years at Roedean she was very hot on Principles, and quite determined that, in this case, as in all previous cases, hers should prevail. *Il faut chercher,* she thought (Roedean had been quite good at teaching French, too) *il faut chercher* . . .

But what was there? Only that lump of rock . . .

She bit her lip thoughtfully, while her lately thwarted lover banged about in the kitchen.

Mr Smellie could not bring himself to wait for the cheaper rate, and made all his phone calls before noon. Very soon, representatives of the various patriotic organisations — the Bannockburn Society, the Killiecrankie Club, the League of Prestonpans, the Philabeg Brotherhood and the Knichts of Alba — would be flocking to Craigfieth. He made his purposeful way to the Golf Course, stopping only at Haq's for new torch batteries.

It was easy to see, in full daylight, what had happened the night before and to work out from that the events of long ago. Mr Smellie's rapid deduction owed more, it is true, to his obsessive interest in the icons of his Faith than to any native quickness of mind: nonetheless it may be assumed to be correct. A tunnel had been driven into the side of the hillock, sloping down to an excavated cavern. Its entrance had been covered over with wooden stakes, whose rotted remains were still visible, and then with turf which must have been carefully laid aside at the breaking-in. As the stakes decayed, so the surface soil slowly collapsed inward, creating the hollow. Last night's activities had been sufficient to burst this earthy hymen, tumbling the despoilers into the secret place below.

He crawled in, following the tracks already made by three pairs of knees, his torch beam flashing wildly ahead. There it still was, and there beside it was the heap of charred matches. It had not been a dream. Wishing he had thought to bring a trowel he set to work with his hands at scraping away the earth from the base of the monolith. It was bigger than he expected, and after the best part of an hour's grubbing, he saw that it had been laid, not on its base as he had first supposed, but on its side. At last, and with the batteries failing, he had the thing exposed, the dry earth falling away easily from its polished sides. He took the torch from its lodgment and, stooping Neanderthally, examined the treasure from all sides.

Aeons ago it had hurtled earthwards from the wheeling stellar immensities. It had survived the unimaginable abrasion of the last, atmospheric leg of its long voyage. It had buried itself in the sands of Palestine, then, slowly, so slowly, worked its way to the surface to the light of the Old Testament, to be used as a pillow by the second son of Isaac. And he, the next morning, took the stone (how? wondered Mr Smellie; he must have been a giant of a man, for all his smoothness) and raised it for a pillar, and poured oil upon the top of it, and called the name of that place Beth-el, though it had been called Luz at the first.

What furtive labours had brought it halfway round the world to Scotland, Mr Smellie could not imagine, but here it was in the parish of Craigfieth, its upper side worn only slightly by a succession of regal buttocks: The Stone of Destiny. The Real One.

His torch went out. Undeterred, he made a reverential exit, rump first, into the June afternoon, thus giving the Hon Davinia Moither time both to stifle her sniggers and to conceal herself behind a nearby mound. She waited for the grubby little man to pass safely out of sight. Then she went underground, with less reverence though with somewhat more elegance than her predecessor. Her light source being a great deal more expensive than the greengrocer's, she was able to remain some two hours at her work. She then returned to Lunie Castle to continue her investigations.

"Oh, there you are!" grunted Mrs Smellie on her husband's return. "Stay just where you are, Wallace Smellie, till you get those clothes off!"

"Oh dear, not now, surely?" he wailed.

"I was thinking of my floor," she replied sourly.

"But . . . the shop . . ."

"The shop can mind itself. Yon young madam seems to be doing well enough, and anyway you know fine well you only spend your days there to avoid me. Now, then. Off!"

When he had complied, and put all his dirty clothes in the washing machine, Mrs Smellie folded her brawny arms, fixed him with a hard stare, and said:

"And now you're going to tell me what you've been up to all day and half the night. Parliament this time, is it? Or a big debate at the United Nations?"

Mr Smellie swallowed. Mrs Smellie was not an easy woman to be interrogated by, particularly when one was naked.

"Well, I, erm, that is to say . . . Winnie my love. I've been — doing something. Something . . . very important. Oh, yes. Very important . . ."

He shifted his feet, stickily, on the cold clean lino. His wife snorted. He continued:

"Very important indeed, as a matter of fact. And I'll tell you all about it. Oh yes. But not now. I have to wait for a certain . . . well, confirmation, first — and then I'll let you know, I promise I will. When I know for certain."

Winifred Smellie took two slow, ponderous, menacing steps towards her trembling spouse. Her voice sledge-hammered in his ears.

"Wallace Gladstone Smellie, what have you been up to? Is this one of these pregnancy tests you're talking about? Because if it is, I tell you now, you needn't —"

"Oh no, no! Good gracious, my dear! Whatever gives you that idea? I'd never, well, I'd never . . ."

"No," she said. "No, you wouldn't, would you? I should ken that well enough. Oh well, I expect you'll tell me when you've scraped up the courage. Just don't expect me to be interested, that's all."

She released her gaze; Mr Smellie relaxed a little, and looked at the floor.

"No dear, of course not — I mean, erm, yes, yes of course. Erm, by the way, I've got some people coming tomorrow, I hope you don't —"

But she had gone. Oh well, he had tried to warn her . . .

He felt suddenly weak.

He took a long bath, went to bed and slept so soundly that he never noticed when his life's partner heaved herself contemptuously next to him some hours later.

Abandoning her lover to questions unanswered and her father to questions unasked, the Hon Davinia Moither drove, the next morning, to Edinburgh to interview the Hon Hudibras Finlayson, an old nursery chum who now occupied a position of some eminence in the Lyon Court, though whether couchant or rampant she really did not know or, for that matter, care. The drip had been quite settled in his perverse inclinations even at the potty stage.

She found him, pale and studious, poring over a tome in his dingy office. They exchanged pleasantries: he enquired after Lord Margoyle's health and was anxious to know if he was still happy with his coat of arms (a pair of braches passant at dexter chief and sinister base, with a tower at sinister chief and a twelve-bore at dexter base, parted by lines potent) or whether he required some refinement: the odd estoile, perhaps, or some martlets disposed around a cross crosslet fitchy.

She replied that Daddy was fine, as far as she knew, and quite happy with his Achievement, having had it printed on several thousand letterheads already.

Then she told her tale, reasonably expurgated, and showed him the drawings she had made the previous afternoon.

He boggled awhile, then thought, then boggled again. Then he took her out to lunch. It was a very successful expedition.

Mr Smellie's important guests arrived a little after two that afternoon and all together. A natural sharing of obsessions, combined with the fact that the Hon Sec of the Knichts of Alba operated a minibus hire firm, contrived to bring them to Craigfieth in one distinguished load. Judging from their expressions on disembarking outside Mr Smellie's shop, they did not seem to have enjoyed a particularly harmonious journey. On each disparate face, animosity was writ large. Sharing transport was one thing: sharing purity of ideals quite another, and evidently quite impossible. Nor did their expressions alter for the better when the harassed greengrocer told them they had not, after all, reached journey's end, owing to domestic circumstances beyond his control.

Fortunately, the Ben Almond Hotel had that morning received a cancellation from a party of Americans forced to curtail their tour owing to the sudden collapse of the dollar in the wake of the latest revelations from the Oval Office, and was willing to accommodate the chauvinist crew at short notice and at party rates.

After some discussion, Mr Smellie agreed to pay half their bill. This settlement notwithstanding, the gathering that then took place in the upstairs Lounge, with its idyllic prospect of the main road and the Eastern Region Transportation Facilities Department's gravel storage depot, was not a happy one. Strange tensions thickened the already pregnant air.

It was left to Mr Smellie, whose moment of gregarious triumph this should have been, to pierce the silence.

"Well, erm," he began.

Five hostile faces turned to him in a bristling semicircle, faces whose names had for so long been talismans to the humble shopkeeper: Domhaill Mhic Domhaill Dubh of the Brotherhood, his five receding chins hidden beneath a jungle of hirsute black, glared most balefully at him, abetted by the twitching goatee of the Bannockburn Society's Professor Crawford Sims, lately of the University of Moose Jaw. Three razored faces completed the silent chorus, those of Alpin Prigpenny (Killiecrankie Club),

Melvyn Runcieman (League of Prestonpans) and the bus driver, His Mysterious Pissance Elvis Paisley, the Knicht of Alba.

"Thank you," said Mr Smellie. "Erm, any questions?"

"Before we go any further," piped Professor Sims, "I should make it clear to all concerned that my organisation in no way accepts the provenance of this alleged stone, nor —"

"Nor mine," growled Domhaill Mhic Domhaill Dubh. "No way."

The two enthusiasts turned to each other and snarled silently.

"Well . . . gentlemen!" exclaimed Mr Smellie hoarsely. "I mean . . . after all, you haven't seen it yet!"

"Maks no differ!" snapped the Brother.

"Quite!" sniffed the Bannockburnian.

"As far as we're concerned, we reject it!"

"As do we. After careful consideration, of course," added the little academic.

"So stick that up yer erse an fart it!"

"An ye're aa erse an pooches!" interjected the representative of the Killiecrankie Club, "for aa yer pleats an yer wulliewarmers!"

"Please, gentlemen!" wailed Mr Smellie, forced to exercise the chairman's function lest he be called upon to separate the delegates by physical means.

"Please — thank you. We don't want the management here, do we?"

He smiled wanly at the tartan-trewsered Prigpenny.

"You have another opinion?"

The wiry Killiecrankian squared his thin shoulders.

"We hold the original Stone to be concealed near Arbroath, actually," he said, reverting to his wonted committee dialect. "Though we're open to suggestions."

Someone said "Pah!" Mr Smellie looked hopefully at the other two.

"Dundee," said Mr Runcieman.

"Westminster Abbey," said Elvis Paisley.

"Oh," said Mr Smellie. "Oh."

"Perhaps it would be useful were I to elucidate," smiled the Professor. Ignoring the rumbles behind him, he continued. "You see, my dear Smellie, we of the Bannockburn Society hold singular store by the theft of the Stone by the tyrant Edward, whose effete offspring was so roundly trounced in 1320. It is an article of faith with us that, one day, an expeditionary force will be mounted to seize the emblem of our Nation back from the offending English, that is, assuming that the Stone in Westminster Abbey is the real one which, with apologies to my friend here —" he leered at the Mysterious Knicht — "I very much doubt. I hope that makes my position clear."

"Havers!" exploded Mhic Domhaill Dubh.

"Shut yir face!" the Professor lapsed.

"If I might be permitted a word?" asked Mr Runcieman. "Thank you. We have irrefutable proof that the Stone of Scone resides in Dundee. It was dropped in Westminster Abbey, you see, and Bailie Gray —"

"That old yarn!" scoffed Alpin Prigpenny, tossing his distinguished grey locks in skittish dismissal. "Everyone knows the old bugger made dozens of copies, dropped them all over the place, stuck notes in them and heaven knows what else. Giving that one to old McKay Nimmo at St Columba's was just another of his little jokes, that's all."

"If he ever had it in the first place," said the Pissance.

"Wha'?"

Mr Prigpenny gaped at him.

"Did I ken ye richt?"

"Yeah," bridled the young bus driver. "Wanna make something of it?"

Mr Smellie coughed nervously.

"See, it's like this, right? These two students, the ones who took it, they never brought it to Glasgow at all. They hid it somewhere in Northamptonshire, and Bailie Gray pretended his copy was the real one to throw the pigs off the trail. Then they put it back, only by then nobody knew which was which, and that was the whole point. Simple, really. You can forget Arbroath, and Dundee, and all the rest. It's in London."

Mr Prigpenny curled his lip at the speaker, then addressed Mr Smellie.

"What young Elvis here doesn't tell you," he purred, "is that our parfit gentil knicht here has an uncle who used to have a petrol station on the A1. He filled the lads' tank up for them on their way down. It's become a matter of family pride to squeeze everyone else out."

"That's not true!" Young Paisley turned angrily on his accuser. "Just because no one's ever seen your Stone, you have to knock everyone else's. 'Somewhere outside Arbroath' — what a load of crap! You've just got to be different, that's the trouble with your lot!"

"Which doesn't alter the fact," shouted Mr Runcieman over the ensuing din, "that the Dundee one has a bloody great crack in it! How do you explain that, eh, you and your mysterious pisspots?"

Ducking under the knightly blow that the man from Prestonpans earned himself for this sally, Professor Sims rubbed it home with some academic salt.

"An illogical syllogism, my dear fellow, quite illogical. Here, use my handkerchief. All Chinamen wear bowler hats, my father wears a bowler hat, therefore my father is a Chinaman ... it won't work, you know, it simply won't — no, it's all right, keep it — you've quite failed to establish the causal connexion, you see."

"What's your explanation then, smerty-breeks?" enquired Mr Prigpenny.

A sudden silence fell: in Scotland, even today, a little learning still has the power to engender awe.

"Quite simple, gentlemen, really. Either the Stone is in Westminster, or it is not. You are with me so far? Let us suppose, hypothetically, that it is not: well, then the Stone in Westminster is a fake. Where there is one fake, there will be others — the existence of A and B positing C, you see, and so forth naturally — and there is nothing objective to prove the *unspeciousness* of Dundee or Arbroath, or any of the infinite series of replicas that may arguably have emanated from the workshops of Bailie Gray. And the same thesis would hold, obviously, in the event of the Westminster Stone being the real one after all: except that it would then become Stone A rather than Stone B, of course, or perhaps I should say, Stone X rather than Stone Y, to avoid confusion. In the sense that all this *is* hypothetical, it doesn't matter, and I needn't insult your intelligence by explaining why. What *does* matter — and I'm sure we can all agree on this, gentlemen — is to make sure it *stays* hypothetical. Once we are forced to admit certainty, we are lost."

A round of throat-clearing followed this exegesis. Professor Sims smiled gently, his eyes hooded, and stroked his beard.

"Bollocks!" said Domhaill Mhic Domhaill Dubh.

Four pairs of hostile eyes turned to their kilted compatriot.

"I beg your pardon?" said the Professor icily.

"Ach, I don't mean about keeping it hypothetical, we all ken that, I mean about the other. Yon thing of Smellie's is the genuine article, no doubt about it. There's no sandstone in Judaea, and no meteorites in Perthshire, Keweedee, right?"

Mr Runcieman permitted himself a superior smile whose effect was somewhat spoiled by blood and swollen flesh.

"Perhaps our friend could explain how Dunsinane Hill managed to walk to Craigfieth?" he spiered.

Professor Sims giggled scholastically.

"Whaur's yer Wully Shakespeare noo?" he quipped.

"Simple," the Brother replied. "They moved the Stone, the one they found in 1826. They hid it somewhere else."

"Why?" asked Mr Smellie. The others stared at him, united in their incredulity.

" 'Why', Mr Smellie, 'Why'?" said the Professor. "Good heavens man, haven't you been listening to a word I've said? What our colleague says is perfectly understandable, I should have thought!"

"But . . . but . . . oh help! I don't understand any of it!" spluttered the hapless greengrocer. "Do you mean to say you agree with Mr Dubh — with Mr Dom . . . with this gentleman?"

The Professor smiled patronisingly back; Mr Runcieman shrugged, then winced; Mr Prigpenny coughed.

"Aye. Why not?" said Elvis Paisley.

Mr Smellie threw caution to the winds.

"Then what the devil have you all been arguing about?" he croaked.

"Aw, that!" grinned His Mysterious Pissance. "That's different, isn't it?"

"Aye!"

"Absolutely!"

"Naturally!"

"Quite."

"*Why?*"

Elvis Paisley sighed. "Och, I give up! You tell him Prof, you were last in school."

The retired pedant rose to the occasion, though not to his feet. He held the greengrocer with his glittering eye.

"My dear Smellie, you must not confuse disputation over one thing with agreement on another. We may have our own ideas — our own hobbyhorses even, some of us — about what became of the Stone the English stole in 1296 — incidentally, I am planning a symposium to coincide with the seven hundredth anniversary of the outrage, I hope you will all attend if spared — but we're quite ready to believe it wasn't the real one. It may well be the one you found. I expect they took it away from Dunsinane and hid it here; they might even have made a replica to put back in the ground on Dunsinane Hill. It wouldn't surprise me, though it would have to have been made of some other black rock: jet, probably, or one of the ligneous metamorphosites. Unless it was the other way round, of course, and this one . . . anyway, it doesn't matter: the point is — the point Mr Paisley was trying to make — the point I'm sure we're all agreed on — the point *is*, Mr Smellie, that we must do everything in our power to get rid of the thing as quickly as possible, before the press gets wind of it!"

Mr Smellie pressed both hands to his temples and groaned softly.

"I'm sorry," he said at last. "This isn't at all what I expected. You're saying that the Stone of Destiny is the one in London, or it's the one in Dundee, or Arbroath, or wherever; and you're saying it isn't any of these because it's the one I found or the one I found is a copy of it and the real one is buried somewhere on Dunsinane Hill, but whatever it is, we mustn't tell anyone. Is that right?"

"It'll do," said Elvis Paisley.

"But *why*?"

Mr Runcieman snorted bloodily.

" 'Why', he says. Help ma boab!"

"But surely," Mr Smellie persisted, "if you think the one I found is the real thing — and they can do tests, can't they, to find out? — if it is, then why can't we say so? I mean, it would be a great thing for Scotland, wouldn't it? Isn't that what it's all about?"

His audience shifted uncomfortably; Elvis Paisley shook his head in disbelief and Domhaill Mhic Domhaill Dubh muttered something about parcels of rogues. Alpin Prigpenny at last spoke up.

"Really, Mr Smellie, I'm surprised you call yourself a Nationalist at all! In fact, I wonder if you haven't lured us all here under false pretences!"

"Glencoe!" growled Domhaill Mhic Domhaill Dubh.

Mr Prigpenny held up a hand.

"One moment, my friend: stay your wrath. It may be we are dealing with ignorance rather than treachery. Mr Smellie, I will give you one last chance: tell me, are you a Christian?"

It was the greengrocer's turn to look affronted. He flushed.

"I go to the Kirk every Sabbath Day, and so does Mrs Smellie!" he asserted.

"Aye, well, that'll do I suppose. All right, listen: supposing they found God, yes? Sitting at His desk on a cloud somewhere, making memos: Earthquake in Peru, Wednesday; Outbreak of VD in Kelvinside, Thursday; Appointment with James Anderton, Friday a.m. and see Satan re Khomeini; NB book harp tuners, that sort of thing. What do you suppose that would mean?"

Mr Smellie looked dumbfounded.

"Well . . . it would mean God exists, wouldn't it?"

"Precisely, Mr Smellie. *Precisely.* And then where would Christianity be?"

"Vindicated?" he suggested.

"Maybe, yes — but *at what cost*, Mr Smellie? Mmm? Think about it: everyone would queue up to see Him, wouldn't they? 'Please God, do something about famine.' 'God, why have I got Parkinson's Disease?' 'What happens to Buddhists when they die?' 'Can you tell me, God, which is right: U.F.s or F.P.s?' Can you imagine it? Oh, sure, you'd get answers right enough, though you might not like them: 'Sorry, old chap, as a matter of fact I'm rather fond of sex Myself, one of My better ideas, I've always thought, now run along to Hell and don't not do it again.' Or, 'Actually, some of My best friends are Popes.' And what do you think it would mean for the Churches? Eh, Mr Smellie?"

"Well, erm . . . well . . ."

"Yes, Mr Smellie?"

"Well, I suppose we wouldn't need them."

"Quite so, Mr Smellie, and then where would we be, eh? Vindicated, oh yes, for all the good it would do us! Imagine it! No more interpretations, no more sermons, no more theology — no more Ministers! Imagine what that would mean — churches falling down, thousands out of work with nowhere to go, and nothing for the rest of us to speculate about or look forward to! Consider all the religious conflicts that would become mere base bloodlettings! Remember the Highlands and Islands! Think — well, just *think*, man, for God's sake!"

Mr Smellie thought. Then he said:

"And it's the same with the Stone, you say?"

"Exactly so, Mr Smellie. The very same. It should be ours, it might not be theirs: let's keep it that way, eh? For Scotland's sake."

"Like North Sea Oil, you mean?"

There was a perceptible slackening of atmospheric tension. Sounds filtered back into the room: birds singing, the four o'clock Dunkeld bus, a hoover working on the floor beneath. The company was all smiles.

"An aptly chosen simile, Mr Smellie, if I may say so," observed the Professor.

"Bang on!" said Elvis Paisley, and winked at Mr Runcieman, who indicated his agreement.

"Right boys," said Domhaill Mhic Domhaill Dubh. "Now for problem number two: we can't let it fall into the hands of the propertied classes, least of all that Margoyle bastard. How do we get rid of it?"

Mr Smellie cleared his throat.

"I've got an idea," he said.

Wayne Kirkpatrick was being stubborn.

"I still don't see why it's important," he repeated. "It's just a bit of rock, when you come down to it."

Davinia sighed: really, he was being excessively tedious lately. She hushed him and went to check that Mrs Gloagie was not listening at the office door. Then she made him sit at his desk while she perched on it, tantalisingly out of reach, and said:

"Now listen: listen very hard and then forget what you've heard, because this is very important. I'm not altogether what I seem, you see. You think you know all about me, but you don't. I'm not just an easy lay, you know."

It was on the tip of Mr Kirkpatrick's tongue to utter something of the 'Not even that, lately' variety but he thought better of it as she anticipated the remark.

"And there's something I want to say to you about that as well — later. Now, then. What you call 'just a bit of rock' is much more than that to the people I work for —no, don't interrupt, let me finish. I'm not going to tell you who they are, because it's Secret and we don't go round telling everybody all about our Secret Services like those silly Americans do, but let's just say, between ourselves, that it concerns the National Interest."

"You mean . . . MI5? MI6?"

"Mmm, if that's what you want to believe, yes, something like that anyway. Now then, you've heard about the Stone of Destiny, haven't you?"

"Oh aye, there was a programme on telly about it a while back."

"Precisely. Well, that's what you were hiding your tackle behind the other night, when that Smellie man fell on us."

"That thing? Aw, come on, it couldn't have been — the one they showed on telly didn't look a bit like that!"

"No, stupid, of course not, and that's because the one they showed was a fake. We've known for years that the one those two students ran off with wasn't the original. I expect Edward I knew it himself. Besides, they made a copy for Westminster Abbey in 1939, in case it got bombed, only the place where they hid the original — which wasn't the original, of course — got bombed instead, and they couldn't find it afterwards. It's probably under a tower block somewhere. Anyway, I happen to know that the Smellie now has his hands on the genuine article, and he's got all sorts of unsavoury little men in a minibus — subversives, the lot of them: never mind how I know — ready to make a big thing of it. That's where you come in. We've got to stop them."

"Me? Oh, help."

"Oh come on, Tooly! Be a man!"

"Chance'd be a fine — oh, never mind. Look here, I don't see where the National Interest comes in, I mean it's Scotland's Stone, isn't it? What's wrong with it being in Scotland?"

"Nothing, you silly boy, so long as all those grubby little revolutionaries think it isn't, or think it might not be, and keep the squabble going among themselves, along with the ones who think it is. It's divide and conquer, don't you see? They're all the same, these people; tell a Commie with a bomb that his pal with the detonator's a Trot and they'll blow each other up and save you the bother. And that's the way we want to keep it, thank you very much. Besides, it's the principle of the thing: the Government would no more think of letting the Nats have their Stone back than of sending the Elgin Marbles back to those horrible Greek socialist types. Anyway," she pouted, "there's another reason, a personal one, to do with Us."

"Oh?"

"Well, use your head, darling — no! Stop it, can't you keep your mind on the job? Don't answer that. Listen, if it leaks out that they've found the Stone here, the whole place'll be crawling with press and TV and trippers. We wouldn't have any privacy then, would we? And I know how much our little picnics mean to you."

Wayne Kirkpatrick sniffed.

"Ordinary people manage with a bed," he muttered.

"Well thank you, Mister Shop Man, now I know what *I* am! Funny, I always thought I might be a bit special to you. Well, you can bloody well do-it-yourself from now on, as far as I'm concerned! That won't be too way out for you, will it? Mind you lock the bathroom door first though, won't you!"

She began to stalk out of the office.

"No!" wailed Mr Kirkpatrick. "Please don't, I . . ." he sighed heavily. "Okay, then, what do you want me to do?"

The loveliness of a clear June evening — so dear to the hearts of golfers, anglers, adulterers and romantically inclined people generally — finds little echoing appreciation among conspirators of an outdoor persuasion. It was well past one o'clock in the morning before the Hon Davinia Moither drove Scrymgeour's Landrover through the back roads of the Lunie Estate to the edge of the Craigfieth Golf Course. Wayne Kirkpatrick sat next to her, a large coil of nylon rope in his lap.

"Jings, I hope this works," he said as they made their furtive way among the tumps.

"Of course it will," Davinia replied. "All we've got to do is tow the bloody thing out of the hole, jack it up till it's level with the back of the jeep, then shove it in. Easy."

"I wasn't thinking of that."

She reversed the vehicle carefully up the slope and parked some feet from the tunnel entrance, a black yawning patch in the circumambient gloom. She switched off the headlights.

"Just one thing," said her companion. "What're we going to do with it afterwards?"

"Ah-ha!" she teased. "Wait and see."

A casual and perhaps inebriated passer-by might, during the next minutes, have imagined he had trespassed on a subterranean convocation of the Commonwealth of Fairies. A curiously amplified yet muffled noise emanated from beneath the mound into the still June air, a blending of low notes and high notes, halfway between human speech and earth music. A mellow light spilled upwards from within, fitfully occluded as if by secret celebrants far below; sometimes a peal of liquid laughter floated out. At this point, surely, our observer would have fled the scene of these awful festivities clutching whatever mortal comforts he had to hand: his Bible, perhaps, and his carry-oot. He would not have witnessed the emergence of the Hon Davinia Moither, clad in charmingly beguttered dungarees, nor of her companion, who stood with rope in hand beside her.

Others, however, did.

Her Majesty's two secret servants saw they were fenced in by a semicircle of hooded figures silhouetted against the blazing headlamps of a vehicle. They appeared to be carrying spades. One of them, rather unnecessarily but perhaps for purely sadistic purposes, shone a powerful flashlight into the eyes of the intrepid pair. Then, slowly, casting threatening shadows before them, they began to advance.

It was Davinia who acted first. While her partner stood still entranced, she retaliated with her own torch: as luck would have it, the feeble beam struck the features of the one advancing figure not in balaclava'd anonymity.

"Ah, Smellie!" she fluted. "I want a word with you."

And before the greengrocer could protest or his companions intervene, she had taken his arm, bundled him down the tunnel and followed in his earthy wake.

Outside, the air turned palpably chill. Mr Kirkpatrick grinned foolishly and shuffled his feet.

"Fine night, eh?" he squeaked.

The silent aggressors halted their advance and leaned on their spades, obliging Mr Kirkpatrick to remain where he was, though he had nothing to lean on at all. There they remained for some ages, in mute immobile confrontation, like an assembly of Easter Islanders or a suicidal brotherhood of trolls, waiting for sunrise. Once Mr Kirkpatrick thought he heard, from below, what might have been a cough, but he could not be sure. In time, the pounding of his own blood occupied his senses entirely. The others, too, stayed rooted to the ground; none dared stir to switch off the dimming headlights. An agony of time crawled by. One statue at least began to wish itself beardless.

Davinia resurfaced first before turning to help the enfeebled Mr Smellie to his feet of clay. His companions gathered round him urgently. Davinia tickled Mr Kirkpatrick's ear before whispering into it:

"It's all right, he gave in!"

Some yards away, Mr Smellie caught his breath at last.

"I persuaded her," he muttered.

Later, as the first pale harbingers of the Perthshire dawn were appearing over Fife, a strange vehicular procession inched its way, lights extinguished, across the Craigfieth Golf Course, led by a hooded figure with a torch. It halted at the very foxhole wherein the strange destiny of Wallace Smellie had first begun to unravel. A digging party, eight strong, then set to work, as if grimly determined on the realisation of that ultimate golfer's nightmare, the bottomless bunker, or, perhaps, the grave of the Unknown Caddie. Into this lair was laid, after one or two false starts and with as much reverence as was possible in the circumstances, that most potent of the Nation's totems, the one and only True Stone of Destiny: there to lie, unseen and undisturbed, until the Repeal of the Act of Union or, failing that, the dissolution of the Links at dusk on the Last Day.

The diggers stood awhile in thoughtful silence around the hole, heads bowed in their various sure and certain hopes, respectfully and impenetrably deaf to the clamant ironies of their hurried sextonship. Then they set to work to cover the wretched thing up.

They worked swiftly and with manic energy, and were nearly done when Auld Murdo came upon them in the full splendour of his wrath and the first pale rays of morning.

An answer to his imperious demand came sweetly up, at length, from the sandy pit below.

"I lost my ball yesterday," it trilled, "and these gentlemen have very kindly helped me find it."

The Greenkeeper's savage breast was soothed eventually with libations from Mr Prigpenny's flask and Miss Moither's wallet.

The company split up then: Mr Smellie to his loveless home, his *confrères*, trusty guardians of Caledonia's honour, to their hotel and Wayne and Davinia to the DIY Centre for, as Wayne said on the way, there had been an unexpected demand for garden tools the day before and theirs were the last of his stock. Once they'd cleaned the sand off they'd be as near new as made no difference.

Professor Sims and Messrs Prigpenny, Runcieman, Paisley and Domhaill Mhic Domhaill Dubh settled down in the minibus while they waited for the Ben Almond to open. Some enjoyed a brief uneasy doze in the strengthening light; others scratched wakefully.

Mr Smellie found an empty house and a note on the kitchen dresser. He scanned it briefly, not daring to read attentively, fearful of what it might tell him. Then he conned it properly. He made himself a cup of tea, laced it with the last of Mr Prigpenny's flask, which seemed to have found its way into his pocket at some stage, then wrote a note of his own to Miss Wemyss and left it for her to find on the till.

He slipped lightly into bed and ventured first one tentative foot, then the whole blaspheming leg, into formerly forbidden territory, wincing in anticipation of the blow. None came.

He hoped Miss Wemyss would accept the Managership; he hoped he had offered her enough, and that the Ganglion boy would not cause trouble. He hoped Winnie and her Friend in Auchtermuchty would be very happy together.

It had been a good night's work.

He slept, and dreamed he was shooting the Falls of Killiecrankie astride the Stone of Destiny. He plunged low, the clean wind streaming out his thin greengrocer's hair . . . as he soared up again he saw, falling away below him at the bottom of the Falls, the golden glint of the lost Eagle of the Ninth Legion. A sign in the air read 'Tir nan Og': he passed through it into the mists of golden revenance.

Meanwhile, in the Leisure And Garden section at the back of Mr Kirkpatrick's enterprise, the owner stood, white-faced and open-mouthed in the unflattering strip lighting, frozen in mid-protest.

"*Me* take *you* for granted?" he hooted at last. "Me *use* you? Crivens, that's a good one! What about you? What about when I was stuck on that fish hook? Or in the van?"

His voice rose to a crescendent shriek.

"*What about that tree?*"

His audience exhibited scornful hauteur.

"You don't understand, do you? Typical! You've never even noticed that it's different for a woman, that we have our times, our moods, our *seasons*, for God's sake? You're supposed to stand to and wait for them — show a little finesse, a little consideration — a little *tenderness* between-times, a little maturity — catch the mood, let it happen. Not sit there, all ape and trouser. 'Fancy the bedroom now, hen?' My God!" she snorted. "You carry on as though you've the God-given right to ram away at anything that moves every time you feel . . . My God!"

Mr Kirkpatrick looked miserably at the floor. This was it, then. Finished.

"I'm very sorry," he mumbled. "I didn't realise. I won't do it again, promise. Oh. There won't be an again, though, will there?"

"My God!"

Mr Kirkpatrick raised his eyes, but she was not looking at him now. She was staring, wide-eyed, at a point beyond and above his left shoulder. She stirred, zombie-like. He felt a hand slip inside his waistband.

"Is that really a *hammock*?" she breathed.

9

Of Culture, Curios and Conversation

Craigfieth is proud of its museum. Housed within the impressive exterior of a large Victorian building on the main Dunbroath road, the museum — or, to give it its full original title, the Craigfieth Collection of Antiquity and Natural History — was founded in 1912 under the auspices of the Central Perthshire Antiquarian Society whose President, Sir Hector Rae, owner of the Kipplerigg Distillery and distant relative of the Arctic explorer, provided the funds for the purchase of the premises from a failed medical practitioner in the town. Despite his failure to secure the burgh for the Liberal interest in the elections that followed the museum's opening, Sir Hector remained assiduous in his search for items of local and historical interest to place therein. He encouraged teams of enthusiastic Craigfiethans to take up their spades and picks in an unremitting quest for archaeological plunder. Though a self-taught practitioner of the science of excavation, Sir Hector personally supervised much of the work and with a keen eye for treasures matched only by his disregard for the finer points of land ownership, brought to light the bulk of the collection in those early days. Nor did he stop there: he it was who, with the aid of rapidly growing library, personally identified the hauls of ancient refuse unearthed by the volunteers. In cabinet after cabinet his work lives on: Craigfieth must surely have the richest single collection of miscellaneous fragments in the whole of Scotland, but it does not stop at that. Here, for instance, you will find the atrophied remains of a sandal (?Roman) which, Sir Hector wrote at the time in one of his many pamphlets, may bear dumb witness to the slaughter of the ill-fated Ninth Legion, and there, stretching the full length of one wall on the ground floor, is abundant evidence that the Vale of Lummock was to the earthenware pot industry what Detroit is to motor cars.

Nor, even today, does his pioneering work go unrecognised: only last year, Craigfieth and its environs were prominently featured by *Archaeology Today* in an article entitled 'Forerunners of the JCB'. Particular emphasis was laid on the rich crop of disarticulated skeletons and disembodied skulls which is now housed in a special gallery to which entrance by unaccompanied persons under sixteen is forbidden, and to the small collection of unidentifiable statuettes described by Sir Hector as 'primitive (?Bronze Age) fertility figures' to which children below the age of reason are denied access altogether.

The great man passed away in 1920, bequeathing to the museum his by now exhaustive library and the small pot-still, its copper worm still intact, with which the water of life had first been made, albeit illegally, from the Well of Kipplerigg. He thus missed, by a bare twelve months, the discovery of what instantly became the pride of the whole collection, the Pictish Symbol Stone. The post-war government having decreed (for reasons as inexplicable now as they doubtless were then) that Craigfieth was an ideal place for returning heroes and that homes fit for them should be built there, a workman's shovel uncovered the thing within sight of the distillery, under what is now the corner of John Knox Road and Logie Baird Avenue. Seven feet high and entirely covered on one side with a jumble of strange devices, it dominates the museum's main gallery, roped off and spotlit on its specially constructed concrete plinth.

Successive generations of primary school children have gaped at it with expressions variously indicative of awe as they strive to gain inspiration for the school's annual creative writing competition, whose theme since the monolith was first exhibited has been the imaginative recreation of the origin and meaning of the symbols. Notwithstanding — or rather, so to speak, withstanding — this annual assault of juvenile intellect, the stone, like so much else pertaining to these strange distant people, retains its mystery.

Strangely, despite all the excitement over the discovery of the stone, the Antiquarian Society did not long survive the passing of its benefactor, and in 1923 the museum was taken over by the old County Council, who in turn handed it to Eastern Region fifty years later. Between these dates the collection continued to grow, though not, it is true, with quite the evangelical zeal of yore, its two most notable acquisitions being an extensive collection, the gift of Lord Margoyle himself, of birds and mammals exterminated as vermin by Lunie gamekeepers down the decades and lovingly stuffed by four generations of the Fingal family, of which 'Wrens In A Bush' (c 1911) and 'Otters At Home' (1936) are probably the most striking, and Craigfieth's own Mercat Cross, presented to the museum by Eastern Region following its removal from the High Street under the improvement scheme in 1975. A framed photograph on the wall behind the cross records the memorable scene when it was formally presented to the curator by the then Convener, Councillor Archibald Jobbie, MBE. (In the background, standing between Cllr Hector Smeddum, BEM and Miss Pollack of the WRI, are the two plain-clothes Fraud Squad officers who arrested him immediately afterwards.)

The curator himself, Mr Campsie, whose countless years of service to the museum have made him almost kin to the exhibits in his care, resides, as our story begins, in a commodious flat above the public galleries. His apartments have two exits to the outside world: one is a door marked 'Private' between the osprey and the red squirrels in the stuffed fauna collection on the first floor and the other gives directly on to the yard at the back of the building. It is hardly used, except for the putting-out of rubbish on Monday mornings. For Mr Campsie is a shy man, rarely venturing far into the world of animate life except to attend occasional convocations of his profession and, apart from the three-week period in 1979 when the museum was closed for refurbishment, never taking a holiday. On that one occasion his visit was in response to a long-standing invitation from a visitor to Craigfieth, a Mr Duane Edsel Chrysler III, of Atlanta, Georgia, to come for himself and see the gentleman's Institute of Fine Arts over there. Returning after his sojourn, Mr Campsie would only say that they did things differently there, to be sure.

A home help, Mrs Kininmonth from MacAlpine Way, cleans and cooks and brings him his few material needs; it would be fair to describe her as Mr Campsie's window on the world since, according to her, he does not possess a TV set and his wireless remains permanently tuned to Radio Three. Not that Mrs Kininmonth is a gossip: as she says, there is nothing really to gossip about, Mr Campsie being such a tidy man about himself, and given to locking things.

During working hours Mr Campsie is diligently occupied among his treasures and, despite his retiring nature, prepared with a commentary as accurate as any tape-recorded message whenever he is asked about this or that exhibit. His pale head, round and almost completely bald, may be seen bobbing around among the cabinets between 10 a.m. and 4 p.m., six days a week, as, with a distant smile and half-closed eyes, he discharges his duty.

Seldom has he been known to speak unprompted; thus it was a severe shock to Miss Pleat — almost as if the Mercat Cross itself had waved its arms and walked across the floor — when, as she led her Primary Seven class on its annual pilgrimage one May morning, the curator emerged from behind an early mechanical farm implement looking paler than ever and uttering the fateful words that were to strike chill in every loyal Craigfiethan heart.

"The barbarians are at the gate, Miss Pleat," he said. "Read this."

The letter was brief, and blunt almost to the point of brutality. The Archaeological Services Support Unit of Eastern Region, it said, was conducting an ongoing overview of its district-based resources and had decided as a matter of immediacy to remove a number of items of particular heritage interest to its headquarters in Dunbroath, where they would benefit from the superior facilities. Replicas of the items concerned (see attached list) would be placed in the contributing Resources Sub-Centres. The addressee was asked for his/her co-operation and reminded of his/her obligations under the Conditions of Service of Eastern Regional Council, paragraph seven, subsection two, as amended.

Mr Campsie stood by in mounting agitation while the schoolmistress read the letter.

"Do they mean to say," she said at last, "that they want to take some of our exhibits away to Dunbroath? And give us *plastic models* instead?"

"That's the gist of it," the curator confirmed.

Behind Miss Pleat, the class stood in frozen silence. They well recognised the danger signals of their Mistress's mounting indignation.

"But this is terrible, Mr Campsie!" she spluttered. "It's — it's an outrage!"

"That's nothing," the curator flushed suddenly. "Look at the list."

Miss Pleat turned the page, and gasped.

"No!" she breathed. "Not our Symbol Stone — never!"

"That's what it says." Mr Campsie began to hop from one foot to the other: an unsettling sight, but then he had good cause to be unsettled. "And not just that, look — *the statuettes*!"

There was a burst of hysterical giggling from twenty juvenile throats. Miss Pleat silenced it with a single gorgon glare, then folded the letter viciously into its creases and gestured with it at the curator, the class and the universe in general.

"It shall not happen, Mr Campsie," she declared. "We must organise! They shall not pass! Now children, come with me to see the Pictish Stone which, I may remind you, is Craigfieth's own stone and shall aye remain so. This stone —"

"Please, Miss!" interrupted a small boy with large ears.

Miss Pleat sighed.

"What is it, Lance?"

"Please, Miss, are they going to take the willy men away?"

A sharp percussive noise rang round the distempered walls.

"As I was saying, class, this stone . . ." Miss Pleat continued her exposition while young Lance Sproat nursed his glowing ear.

The schoolmistress was as good as her word. Two nights later a meeting was organised. Out of deference to the curator's known reclusive habits it was held in the museum itself, in the very shadow of the mysterious monolith whose image was shortly to become synonymous with Central Perthshire. All the town's leading opinion-formers were there, and both wings of the Christian tendency, in the bulky form of the Rev MacAndrew and the leanly zealous figure of Mr Cyril Bullock. Not since the affair of the salacious matter at Haq's had such a righteous collocation taken place, and it says as much for his assimilation into the mainstream of the community as it does about the ironies of history that it was Councillor Haq himself who took the lead in these proceedings.

Mr Campsie was on hand, naturally, to lend professional advice, but it was Craigfieth's tribune in the distant fastness of Dunbroath who grasped the vital issues most firmly and exposed them to his fellow-townsfolk. Mungo 'Slim' Beauly, summoned to cover the meeting for the *Gazette*, scribbled furiously in a corner and wished he had learned shorthand.

"The issue, as I see it, is this," said Cllr Haq. "Are we to let our heritage be taken away by the faceless bureaucrats of Dunbroath, or are we going to fight?"

"Hear, hear!" said the Misses Urquhart warmly.

"Thank you, ladies. For let us be under no doubt of what is at stake with regard to this, ladies and gentlemen. This isn't just an interesting piece of old remains, as Mr Campsie has so eloquently described it to us; this . . . monument" — he nodded at the thing — "is, for us, the very essence of the town itself — it *is* Craigfieth. I have often wondered why we do not make more of it. Mrs Pitt-Holyoake, for instance, I'm sure, could sell tasteful models in the Craft Centre, and the museum could do postcards."

Mr Campsie coughed.

"We did, as a matter of fact," he murmured. "Only we ran out, in 1981."

"Well, there you are then!" beamed the Councillor. "What we have here, friends, is an asset! You follow what I mean?"

Mr Bullock spoke.

"I do indeed, Mr Haq. I'll have a word with my son Stafford tonight about putting the stone on his lemonade labels. As part of the publicity for our campaign, of course."

"Quite so, Mr Bullock, an excellent idea. And that's just the beginning! We've got the Gala coming up, and an ideal opportunity to, er, impress on our visitors what a fine relic we have in our museum. Can you see people wanting to come here just to look at a plastic replica?"

There was a rumbling and a shaking of heads.

Miss Pleat, forgetting her surroundings for a moment, put her hand up excitedly.

"I've got an idea!" she shrilled. "You know my class — that's P7 of course — always does some nice little stories about how the stone came to be made? Well, I could collect the best of them, and make them into a wee book for folks to buy!"

Amid the chorus of approval for this idea, Hamish Ganglion lowered his head and blushed deeply. He had not forgotten his own contribution to this annual ritual, nor Miss Pleat's dark censures of his unhealthy domestic influences after she had read it. But his embarrassment passed unnoticed as a volley of ideas echoed round him: Mr Bullock and Mr Glencairn discussed the possibilities and technical difficulties inherent in the production of Pictish Fudge and a Pictish Loaf, Mrs Pitt-Holyoake made lightning sketches of the stone with a view to their transformation into tasteful watercolours and handy ivorette paperweights while Ms Maureen O'Rourke engaged the Misses Urquhart in urgent negotiations towards the rigging out of the Girls in authentic costume for the Gala parade, and Mr Chisholm offered Miss Pleat discount on a bulk printing of her nice collection.

Cllr Haq, smiling expansively, brought them at last to order.

"Well, ladies and gentlemen! I can see Craigfieth will never be found wanting in enterprise. But we must not forget the other aspects of our campaign, must we? We must have a petition, and write letters. I have a petition form here, if you would like to hear it? 'We the under-signed call on Eastern Regional Council to leave the Pictish Symbol Stone of Craigfieth in the local museum where it belongs.' Any objections on that one, no? Then if it is the will of the meeting, I will hand that in to the Con-vener personally when we have collected the signatures."

"Hear, hear!" said the Misses Urquhart.

"Thank you again, ladies. And I have copies of a letter I have written to our MP, Sir Ashley Foutret, which I'll pass round. Now, another idea would be to go through the museum visitors' book and write to famous people who have been here over the years — perhaps, Mr Campsie, you could oblige us with regard to this one?"

"Er — yes, yes I er, I could," stammered the curator. "Hm, there's just one thing, though." His head began to wobble precariously, as if threatening to spill into the lap of Ms O'Rourke seated beside him.

"It's, um, not just the stone though, is it? I mean, there are the statuettes as well."

There was a short, nervous hush and an outburst of coughing from the Misses Urquhart. They had sneaked in to look at the statuettes on their sixteenth birthday and were still prone to nightmares about them.

A raucous voice called from the back row of the meeting.

"Hear, hear!" it said.

Everyone turned to behold Mrs Kininmonth, who had not spoken before and whose presence was inexplicable to the others, though they were far too polite to say so, of course. Cllr Haq smiled at her.

"Mr Campsie's quite right," she continued. "Yon figgereens are much more important than ony stane — they're ten a penny, half the dykes in Scotland are full o' them, and there's nothing special about yon yin that *I* can see!"

She glared back at her disapproving auditors, and went on, "But they figgereens are yewneek! There's nothing like them onywhere, leastways not in Scottish aboriginal culture. *They're* the things ye should a' be getting agitated about!"

Even Cllr Haq was a little taken aback by this sudden outburst of scholarly philistinism. It took him some moments to recover his public face.

"Well, erm, I'm sure we're all grateful to Mrs Kininmonth for her contribution," he purred. "I must say I'm sure we've never thought of them in quite that way, eh Mr Campsie?"

Two spots of colour appeared on the curator's billiard ball features.

"The statuettes are, as Mrs Kininmonth says, unique. Their provenance has never been fully established; Sir Hector Rae's thesis that they prove the land bridge theory whereby the artefacts of oriental culture found their way to prehistoric Caledonia has yet to be proved or, indeed, disproved."

"They're disgusting, I do know that!" shouted Miss Pleat.

"Hear, hear!" agreed the Misses Urquhart, somewhat tremulously.

"They are indeed, um, explicit, in a crude way, it is true, being, as they are, primitive. What is more to the point, they are priceless in archaeological terms, and they belong in my — in this, I should say — museum in Craigfieth. And they are fragile. I won't even touch them myself, far less feel happy about moving them."

"Fragile?" queried Hamish Ganglion. "They're solid stone, aren't they?"

"Bits," explained the curator, "could break off."

"Oh," said Hamish, and crossed his legs.

There was a brief silence while the meeting digested the import of the longest and most forceful extempore utterance anyone had ever heard from the lips of Mr Campsie.

Cllr Haq's political instincts came at last to the rescue.

"Perhaps I could suggest a compromise? Let us amend our petition so that it reads, 'Pictish Symbol Stone of Craigfieth *and other artefacts*, di dum di dum di dum, where they belong.' I am sure we all understand why these figures would not be suitable for any other sort of exposure, eh Mr Bullock? Minister?"

"Quite!" agreed the Evangelist.

"Indeed, Mr Haq. You have it exactly," rumbled the Rev MacAndrew.

Mungo Beauly remained as the gathering dispersed, until Mr Campsie had finished an urgent conversation with his home help.

"Er, excuse me," he said. "Slim Beauly, *Perthshire Gazette*. I wonder if I could ask you a little more about these statuettes?"

"What, in particular?" snapped the curator.

"Well, I mean, er — what are they like?"

Mr Campsie adopted his informative pose.

"There are four figures altogether," he droned. "Two male and two female, carved from metamorphic rock, probably with a metal instrument, and ranging in height between fourteen and eighteen inches. The single male and female figures are hyperbolically redolent of the outward features of concupiscence. The other two are joined."

"Crivens!" exclaimed the reporter. "Can I see them?"

Mr Campsie blinked.

"It would be most irregular," he said. "The museum is closed."

"Aw, but I have to get back to Dunbroath tonight. To meet my deadline."

"Oh . . . very well, then. No photographs, mind. Museum regulations do not permit photographs."

He unlocked the door and led the reporter inside a small room, in the centre of which was a padlocked glass case housing the venereal display.

"Christ!" gasped Beauly.

"At least a thousand years earlier, I should say," replied the curator.

"Eh? Oh, aye. Still — Christ! I mean, fancy this lot in Craigfieth, eh? I see what you mean about breaking bits off."

"Any damage at all," replied the curator, "would have disastrous consequences."

"Aye, no kidding. Help ma boab! Is this what they looked like, then, these Picts?"

Mr Campsie sniffed.

"Certain things have been exaggerated, Mr Beauly, for symbolic reasons. And we are by no means certain that these are Pictish artefacts. Their discovery is something of a mystery."

"Oh, yeah," Mungo Beauly nodded. "Like, bragging about it, eh? Well, thanks pal, these'll help the story a lot."

"I would advise you to use a certain amount of, er, professional reticence, Mr Beauly, about these figures."

"Eh? But I thought you wanted to make more of a thing of these. Back there, like, when you said they were unique and all that."

"I merely tried to remind the meeting that the threat from Archaeological Services in Dunbroath did not apply only to the symbol stone. I was not suggesting turning the museum into a peep-show."

"Oh, yeah, I get you now. Dinna fash, pal, I'll be very discreet."

"Thank you, Mr Beauly. And now, it is getting rather late . . ."

"Sure. Time I hit the trail anyway. Cheers, then."

He looked back wistfully as they left the room.

"Still, I bet they'd sell a lot more lemonade if they stuck one of those on the label!"

"Good night, Mr Beauly."

Mr Campsie locked up and went wearily upstairs to his flat, past the dead accusing eyes of Lunie's slaughtered innocents. It had been an exhausting evening, he had missed a concert of Bartok and Maxwell Davies, and there were, he was certain, trying times to come.

Mungo 'Slim' Beauly was, however, as good as his word. That week's edition of the *Perthshire Gazette* carried a report of the meeting, it is true, but the main thrust of the reporter's copy concerned the town's campaign to save its monolith. There was a picture of the stone, reproduced from a rather fanciful steel engraving in a copy of an Antiquarian Society pamphlet on file in the Editor's office. There was a map, showing the approximate location of the stone's discovery, and a paraphrase of Cllr Haq's speech clearly demonstrating the significance of the stone to the town's economic health as well as to its cultural life. All those present at the gathering were named, only four of them incorrectly; there was a potted history of the

Picts by the paper's Ancient Affairs Correspondent, Old Potsherd, and an imaginative (in the sense of untrue) recreation of life in Pictish Craigfieth by Lad o' the Lummocks, the well-known rambler. Only two short paragraphs at the end of the report made passing reference to 'other curios', including a set of 'crude figures of unknown origin which, some experts say, may have been intended as wedding presents'.

Mr Campsie may not have liked the journalistic inaccuracy of the phrase, but he had to admit it was unlikely to bring the voyeurs of Perthshire flocking in their charabancs to his door. A spokesperson for the Archaeological Resource Support Unit refused to comment on the issue beyond a bald statement that the decision to call in the relics had, like all other decisions, been democratically arrived at through the usual procedures, was part of an ongoing process of reallocation within the authority's duly constituted parameters, and would be implemented in due course.

The intrepid Beauly did, in fact, send another, somewhat different, report to *Scotland Now!* but the editor of that august journal decided not only that it would be irresponsible to print the story while the paper was running its daily eight-page AIDS pull-out but that the whole thing was probably too erudite for the Scottish tabloid-reading public, and in any case there wasn't a picture.

Other aspects of the campaign proceeded with varying degrees of success. The search for famous names in the visitors' book threw up a rather short list, comprising Derek Jameson, Councillor Archibald Jobbie, the King of Siam and Pope John Paul II, who had given his telephone number as Vat 69. None of these persons, for various and obvious reasons (as Miss Pleat said) could be approached. The petition, however, was coming along

nicely, though an ad hoc meeting of the Craigfieth Heritage Campaign decided to keep it open until after the Gala,
during which they hoped at least to double the number
of signatures. Cllr Haq, as Chairman of the Campaign
Committee, wrote to Sir Ashley Foutret, MP, and to
the Director of Archaeological Services, and entertained
his committee, while they waited for replies, with weekly
verbatim accounts of his lobbying of the Convener at
Eastern House.

Meanwhile, Stafford Bullock had decided to launch a
completely new product on the strength of the issue and,
after barely a fortnight's delay while he experimented
with various combinations of permitted colourants and
waited for the labels to be printed, Picta-Cola made its
assault on the unsuspecting palates of Central Perthshire, where it soon attained a steady eight per cent market
share in school playgrounds, fast food outlets and Senior
Citizens' Day Centres.

His father had rather less success with his project,
discovering after much frustrating effort that his dairy
confection was not susceptible to holding its integrity in
anything other than the conventional rectangular shape.
Instead he ordered, at some expense, a set of moulds
embossed with an image of the stone (or, at any rate,
something remarkably like it) in bas-relief, and comforted
himself with the thought that production would be ready
for the tourist season. Mrs Pitt-Holyoake, too, was
storing up her riches in anticipation of this annual
millenium. Having given the artistic problem some
thought, she had cut out a hardboard stencil of the stone
to save the repetitive tedium of drawing it afresh each
time. The problem of background she quickly overcame
with a selection of heathery pastel shades and some paint
rollers from the DIY Centre: with a little practice she soon
attained a production rate of six tasteful watercolours

every evening on the draining board of Dante Cottage's tiny kitchen. She thought £30 each a not unreasonable price to ask, given their subject's topicality, their own creative originality, and their size: £5 per square foot was little enough, these days, heaven knew.

A gentleman signing himself 'Pro Alba' wrote to the *Perthshire Gazette* from Penrith to point out that the spot where the stone had been discovered was now the exact site of the public telephone box on John Knox Road, and that the telephone, gas and Hydro supplies under the pavement coincided precisely with routes that, if extended north-west and south-east, would unquestionably constitute a ley-line forming one side of an equilateral triangle whose foci were the Long Man of Strathspittle, the Twa Kizzens o' Ben Hirple and the U.P. Church at Duncruddie Mains. Eastern Region, he warned, ignored these portents at their peril.

The Rev Gilleasbuig MacAndrew preached a sermon on graven images, which went down very well.

Preparations for the Gala proceeded apace, inspired not only by the stone but also by the museum's item of atrophied footwear (which, thank goodness, the vandals of Dunbroath seemed to have passed over). Ms O'Rourke had devised an episode from the pageant of Scotland's history in which all the town's available talent was to be employed. The Boys' Brigade, it was understood, were to be the Romans. An organisation calling itself the Brethren Of The Picts wrote to offer, free of charge, a multi-media display entitled, somewhat confusingly, The True Scots, during the whole of Gala week, and was booked immediately. It all promised to be most exciting and memorable.

The surface of Mr Campsie's life seemed scarcely to have been ruffled by these events. He, too, received a letter from Pro Alba enquiring urgently into the positioning of the stone in the main gallery and foretelling doom if it were not in strict sidereal alignment. Mr Campsie replied that since it was set in concrete there was very little he could do about that and wondered how much, if anything, its makers had actually known of the subject. Three days later he received another, indignant letter in which Pro Alba revealed himself as Mr Bartholomew Goodwit, President of the Cumbrian Enlightenment. He regretted, 'in no uncertain terms' as he put it, that his work as a weights and measures officer made it impossible to journey to Craigfieth in order to say certain things too dangerous to put in writing. The curator threw the letter away, and thought no more about it.

Even Mrs Kininmonth seemed, eventually, to calm down. She had been most unsettled the day after the meeting and her mood worsened considerably when she discovered that her employer had allowed a reporter into the Statuette Room. "I fear you've ruined everything!" she said and, despite Mr Campsie's reassurances, she went on muttering it for days afterwards. However, as day followed uneventful day, the mutterings ceased. Besides, as Mr Campsie reminded her, he would very shortly be able to take early retirement and then all their worries would be over.

He did not hear again from Eastern House.

Cllr Haq, however, did. In a long letter which the Councillor read to his committee that evening, the Director of Archaeological Services explained in detail the reasons for his department's requisition. He likened the situation to the difference between ornithological research, on the one hand, and egg-collecting, on the other. Experts in the field had identified, he said, dozens of items of great scientific interest languishing (to use his word) unrecognised in museum cases all round the region. Much invaluable knowledge could be gained by exhaustive laboratory studies of these specimens, and this was only possible at a very few specialist centres of which Dunbroath was fortunate to be one. The science of Archaeology, he concluded, had long since moved on from the days of curio collecting, and it was time their region caught up.

Cllr Haq put the letter down, his hand trembling. Miss Pleat spoke for them all:

"Who does he think he is?" she demanded. "And where does he think he'd be now if Craigfiethans hadn't dug all those things up in the first place? That's what I'd like to know! Why, he says there he isn't even going to put them on show! They're just going to be stuffed away in a basement somewhere and forgotten about!"

"Like the Vatican treasures," rumbled the Rev Mac-Andrew.

"And we all know what happened to the last Pope, don't we, when he started giving them away!" observed one half of the Misses Urquhart.

"Poor man!" sighed the other half. "Such a lovely smile."

Mr Bullock gazed distractedly at the blotchy ceiling, planning to use the phrase 'Scarlet Woman of Dunbroath' at his next Mission.

"It is indeed an undemocratic attitude," agreed Cllr Haq, "and I shall tell the Convener so tomorrow. And quite out of keeping with the times we live in, I need hardly add. We all have a considerable, er, community investment in our symbol stone, don't we? How is the loaf proving, Mr Glencairn?"

"Difficult to cut," replied the baker, "but selling well, for all that."

"Stafford tells me sales of Picta-Cola have over-taken Lummockade," said Mr Bullock, coming out of his Reformationist reverie.

"The costumes are nearly finished," said a Miss Urquhart. "We've found just the right sort of merino for the hair."

"Precisely!" said Cllr Haq. "And I have been privileged to have a sneak preview of Mrs Pitt-Holyoake's watercolours. Quite enchanting."

The artist simpered and gazed modestly at her lap.

"In short, friends, we have everything to fight for!"

"Not forgetting the statuettes, of course," said Mr Campsie.

"Naturally, not forgetting those, my friend," the Councillor allowed. "Now, what I propose to do is this: I will suggest to this Director fellow that if he wants a little bit, just a slice, say, off our exhibits for scientific research, if that's all he wants them for, then he is welcome as far as we're concerned. They can find out everything they want that way, can't they, these boffin types?"

There was a growl from Mrs Kininmonth at the back of the room, and Mr Campsie twitched alarmingly in his seat.

"Out of the question!" he declared. "The stone maybe, but not the statuettes. Far too brittle. The slightest touch — disaster! I cannot permit it."

"Come now, surely, Mr Campsie," the politician wheedled, "these days that wouldn't be the case, would it? Think what they do to people."

"I'm sorry, Mr Haq, but there it is. I am the curator here, and I intend to do everything the word implies: to care for, look after, protect. What you suggest is quite unacceptable."

"I agree with Mr Campsie," Hamish Ganglion unexpectedly broke in. "We should stick out for our position. Always demand more than you're prepared to settle for; don't let them think you'll give an inch. Standard union practice."

Miss Pleat coughed.

"I am glad to say I have no personal experience of what Mr Ganglion says, as parents of my pupils well know. But on this occasion I agree with him. Let them do the compromising."

"Hear, hear!" said the Misses Urquhart.

Cllr Haq smiled, reminding himself that politics must always be the art of the possible.

"Very well then," he said. "It's agreed we stand firm."

Mungo Beauly was halfway back to Dunbroath before the meeting broke up. He had stopped taking notes after Cllr Haq read the letter. This time he had just the line he needed, and if he stepped on the gas he'd just have time to knock it out and phone it through. He hummed the *Ride of the Valkyries* as the wind whistled past his crash helmet.

He was not disappointed.

Mrs Kininmonth arrived early the next morning, her face as grim as the stone itself. She covered the curator's muesli with a copy of *Scotland Now!* folded back to the fourth page. Mr Campsie choked as he read:

SAVE OUR SEXY STATUES, SAYS TOWN
by *Scotland Now!* Reporters

The little town of Craigfieth in Central Perth-shire is fighting to stop the prudes of Eastern Region locking up the local folk's most famous tourist attractions . . . a sizzling set of sexy statues.

Mr Campsie read on, gulping, while Mrs Kininmonth breathed heavily across the table.

. . . curvaceous curios and meaty models dug up seventy years ago. "They're certainly well hung," said one visitor, "except that they don't exactly hang!"

"Who said that?" the curator demanded. Mrs Kininmonth remained thunderously silent.

> . . . "It's ridiculous," say residents campaigning to keep the randy relics in the town's museum. "After all, these are the Eighties."

"That's not what they meant!" he exclaimed.

"Got to your bit yet?" asked Mrs Kininmonth.

> . . . museum curator said: "I won't allow anyone else to touch them."

Mr Campsie looked up in horror.

"This is dreadful!" he groaned.

"Aye, so it is, but it's done. You'll have to think of something."

He hurried from the room, wishing he had been born a year earlier, or not at all.

He opened the museum at ten. Shortly afterwards a party from the Eventide Home arrived, escorted by the Matron, who was conversing animatedly with a young man who wore a suit and carried a briefcase, and made their slow way to the Skeleton Room. Tabloid newspapers, with the exception of the *Mail* and the *Scottish Daily Express*, were not permitted in the Eventide.

The *Sun* reporter arrived at eleven, escorted by Cllr Haq.

"Ah, Mr Campsie!" beamed the Councillor. "This is Gryce Goudie, I've been telling him all about our stone. Well, there it is, Mr Goudie. Impressive, don't you think?"

"Yeah, really big," remarked the reporter. "Now then, Mr Campsie, about these statues of yours —"

"You must be under some misapprehension Mr, er," replied the curator, striking what he hoped was a pose suggestive of restrained aggression. His head, extended and uptilted on its long neck, reminded the journalist of the nodding mascot in his wife's car.

"They do not belong to me, but to the public. I am their custodian."

"Okay, fine. Can I see them?"

"No."

"Now see here, Campsie, that's no way to speak to a member of the public, is it? I pay my rates, same as anyone, I've got my rights."

"You aren't a member of the public. Not in that sense."

Cllr Haq poured an oleaginous smile on the troubled proceedings.

"Surely, my friend, there can be no harm in the gentleman seeing the exhibits?"

"Put it this way, pal," snarled the newshound, scratching a spot on the back of his neck and leering at the two Craigfiethans, "there's going to be a lot of harm if I don't. A *lot* of harm. Public Denied Access To Public Property. Craigfieth Cover-Up. The *Sun* Says, What Are They Hiding? Look bad, all that will."

Cllr Haq shot a worried glance at the curator. This was not the way he had planned things to happen, at all. But Mr Campsie merely gave the reporter a superior smile.

"Perhaps it would clarify the position, Mr er, if I were to inform you that the museum does not permit the taking of photographs. At all. Under any circumstances. Let us say that I, er, have reason to believe that your presence in the Statuette Room might lead to a breach of the regulations. Or to a breach of the peace, even. Is that any help to you."

Gryce Goudie stepped back a pace and spread out his hands, palms upward. He bared his yellow teeth in a worldly grin.

"Okay, okay pal, no offence, right? Nothing personal I hope. Perhaps you could describe them to me?"

"Certainly." Mr Campsie coughed, blinked, adjusted his head and began:

"The four statuettes were discovered in 1912 by Sir Hector Rae during the course of excavations in a field near what is now the Strathlummock Leisure Centre and presented to the museum in September of that year. Though their origin remains disputed they are undoubtedly intended to symbolise prosperity to the tribe who fashioned them and may be associated with primitive fertility rites designed to ensure the next season's harvest. Though crudely fashioned, there is evidence in their workmanship of a stylistic form normally associated with the artefacts of the early Viking era and some experts, notably Professor Julius K. Shuyster of Colorado, have suggested a link between the holarctic cultures of the late Bronze Age and influences of Eastern or Near-Eastern origin. This in turn would suggest —"

"Yeah, great stuff, thanks. What size are the dicks?"

"I beg your pardon?"

"Dicks. Dongs. Their ladyfrighteners."

"Really, Mr er, I . . . hardly think —"

"Aw, c'mon pal, gie's a break, eh?"

"You wish to know the penile dimensions?"

"Yeah, if you wanna put it like that."

"Well, really, I mean . . . they are not lifesize, you know."

"Well, relative then, like, I mean — here," the reporter placed a hand in the middle of his paunch, "or here?" He raised it to nipple height.

Mr Campsie pursed his lips.

"Nearer the second," he said. "Allowing for the angle, that is."

"Great!" The reporter scribbled in his notebook "And the other one?"

"Impossible to say. And now, if you'll —"

"How do you mean, impossible? Snapped off, has it?"

Mr Campsie reddened.

"Not at all! It's . . . well, employed."

"Employed? Jesus, you mean there's a couple *bonking* in there?"

"If by that you mean what archaeoethnoculturologists call significant encoupling, yes."

"Great! Sensational!" He scribbled furiously. "What position? Straight? Or — *dirty*?"

But Mr Campsie's reply — if indeed he had been about to make one — was lost in a geriatric babble as the party from the Eventide shuffled out of the Skeleton Room. The reporter waved suggestively at Matron and winked at her young companion.

"Why don't you take the old dears in there, girly?" he leered. "You'd all get a thrill, know what I mean?"

The Matron, Miss Dowie's young replacement, halted and blushed angrily. To Gryce Goudie this was as the bleating of the kid: the tiger was excited.

"Aw, go on, gie'm a thrill! Show 'em what they're missing! Hey, I bet you don't put bromide in *your* tea, eh sweetie? Better watch out!"

Cllr Haq coughed nervously and attempted to distance himself from the source of these outrageous remarks, not wishing to be associated, in Craigfieth, with such an affront to uniformed maidenhood.

The offended maiden, however, at last spoke for herself.

"You filthy beast!" she cried.

"Yeah, that's what they all say, lassie," replied the reporter, unabashed. "Don't tell me you've been starched all the way through, though, eh? Oh, I know — you've seen it all before, eh, is that it, eh, eh?"

Some of the walking frames began to creak excitedly. Mr Campsie felt faint. Meanwhile, unobserved by all except Gryce Goudie, the young man with the briefcase had slipped through the door of the Statuette Room. Cllr Haq blinked and, glad of the diversion, exclaimed:

"Goodness gracious! A thunderstorm!"

But there was no answering peal. Instead there were more noiseless flashes and then, before anyone knew what had happened, Gryce Goudie was making a hasty exit from the museum in the company of the young man with the briefcase, who now had a camera slung over one shoulder.

The reporter turned to leer farewell to the dumbstruck company.

"All in a day's work!" he grinned. "Great story! *Ciao,* folks!"

And they left.

Matron's face turned from brick red to flour white.

"He — he said he was from the DHSS," she whispered. "Researching Stimulation Therapy."

She looked apologetically at Cllr Haq and Mr Campsie.

"I would never have brought them here otherwise, I promise," she said.

There was an appalling crash, and a long expiring groan. Mr Sproat, bent on achieving stimulation in the Statuette Room, had tripped over his ambulatory aid.

No one in Great Britain could be forgiven, the next morning, their ignorance of the existence of the town of Craigfieth. The front page of Gryce Goudie's newspaper announced, in addition to the latest Bingo game, exotic lingerie offer and centre page feature on Why Tory Men Bed Better, the shocking story of the attempt by the killjoys of Scotland's Eastern Region to deprive the ratepaying public of their right to take a mature and adult view of their ancestors' sexual awareness. At the foot of the story was the breathtaking announcement: EXCLUSIVE PICTURE: PAGE 2.

And there it was.

The figure had been arranged as if in priapic contemplation of Red-Hot Rhoda, 17, whose hobbies included aerobics and whose photograph appeared on the opposite page, and its caption made witty reference to things being worn under a Scotsman's kilt. Readers were invited to agree that this was just a phallus-y.

Alongside the picture was a fearless editorial. 'The *Sun* Says — Hands Off These Naughty Novelties' it declared. The *Sun*, it added, would not, for reasons of public decency (43 per cent of *Sun* readers being below the age of reason) publish photographs of what it terms 'the other sexhibits'. Instead, readers were offered the chance to claim glossy 10 inches by 8 inches prints of the full set by collecting coupons in next week's editions.

Mr Campsie closed the museum Until Further Notice and took sick leave. This action did not, however, stop the *Star* ('Hoots, Mon! Rude Relics Set 'Em Reeling'), *Scotland Now!* ('Dig Those Dirty Devils!') or the *Daily Record* ('Sex Statue Storm Sensation') printing their own versions of the hottest story of the week, though they were obliged to do so with the benefit of artists' impressions of the *Sun* picture.

Mr Robert Maxwell offered to buy the museum.

The following weekend, the *Sunday Times* carried a leader deploring the trivialisation of the serious issue of archaeological conservation, and a readers' Culture Club introductory offer of a set of handcrafted pine replicas at £19.99 each plus VAT and postage. By then the curator had received several sackfuls of mail, from which Mrs Kininmonth winnowed two items of serious concern to them both: one was a letter from the Director of Archaeological Services ordering him to attend an extraordinary meeting at Eastern House next Monday; the other was from a P. J. B. Haig Gore-Ligature (Lt-Col Ret'd) who recalled that, in his youth, he had been acquainted with Sir Hector Rae. The great man had been, while stationed there in 1911 with the 19th Punjab Lancers, a frequent visitor to his father's bungalow in Pispore whence had vanished, it subsequently transpired, a number of native curios from his father's extensive collection. Could there, the curator's correspondent wondered, be a connexion? He had, understandably enough, only chanced on a copy of the yellow press because his cook's niece's young man had left one in the summerhouse, but he had been struck by the resemblance between the photograph therein and a dim boyhood memory of the ornaments in his father's den all those years ago.

Mr Campsie read the letters, and groaned aloud. Mrs Kininmonth remained threateningly silent. Nemesis, her grey granite presence seemed to say, was nigh.

Monday's mail brought fresh intelligence. To Cllr Haq it brought a letter from the House of Commons. Signed in Sir Ashley Foutret's unavoidable absence by his secretary, it regretted that the MP could not become personally involved in affairs which rightly concerned the responsible authorities though it assured the addressee that the best interests of Craigfieth were, as always, dear to the heart of its elected tribune. To Mr Campsie, who had taken his telephone off the hook the previous Thursday, it brought an international telegram from Duane Edsel Chrysler III of the Atlanta Institute of Fine Arts Inc. It read, simply: PREVIOUS ASSURANCES INOPERATIVE STOP YOU'RE ON YOUR OWN PUNK STOP EXPEDITE IMMEDIATELY AND ADVISE.

The curator looked from the telegram to Mrs Kininmonth.

"What are we going to do?" he asked.

She smiled horribly, hands on hips.

"I'll tell you," she said, "on one condition."

"Oh dear. What is it?"

"I'm sick fed up of being a widow," she answered. "Ye ken my meaning?"

"But the pension — I mean, we agreed . . ."

"That was before all this. I told ye at the time, my brother might be a time-served monumental mason but he's no' an Ancient Pict. They were bound to find out one day, and just because old Rae got away wi' it once doesnae mean ye'll no' be found out this time. Ye're no' the man he was, if my Granny, God rest her soul, is tae be believed."

Mr Campsie sighed.

"Very well then. I agree. Now tell me what we're going to do."

Mrs Kininmonth sat heavily on the curator's bed.

"This'll no' hurt too much," she said.

Neither Mr Campsie nor Mrs Kininmonth was present at the festivities when the Forty-First Annual Craigfieth Shopping Gala got under way at eleven o'clock that morning. They missed the Grand Opening by that year's Miss Kipplerigg Single Malt (who was utterly charming and whose interests included promoting tourism and caring for senior citizens) and they missed, perforce, the Great Procession, in which the Maureen O'Rourke Dancers and the Craigfieth and District Boys' Brigade realised in strict choreography the imaginary Battle of Lunie Muir, and the Gospel Choir, by way of contrast, sang selections from the *Creationist Songbook,* including such anthems as *Six Days To Make This Vale Of Tears* and, on a lighter note, *'Don't Go Monkeying With Jesus*. They did not join the queue to buy the eagerly awaited Pictish Fudge at the dairy shop, they lost their chance to be among the first to purchase a Pitt-Holyoake original of the Symbol Stone of Craigfieth and, almost alone among the population of the burgh, would never be able to tell generations to come how they had witnessed the unfortunate collapse of its thirty-foot replica, lovingly constructed in their leisure hours by the stalwarts of the WRI without, alas, due regard to July's prevailing east wind. They failed to secure one of the limited edition of five hundred signed copies (soon to become collectors' items) of Miss Pleat's tasteful anthology of essays by pupils of Craigfieth Primary School.

In short, they were not there.

As the opening ceremony drew to a close and the Strathlummock Leisure Centre donkey drew the Gala Queen away in her gaily painted tumbril, Cllr Haq surveyed the scene with satisfaction from his vantage point on the podium. Never, surely, had the Gala Opening Day brought such crowds to the little town as now choked the doorways of the High Street, fingers twitching on their holiday pursestrings. And what a year for displays! Papiermâché Picts enjoyed a carnivorous feast in Borden's Family Butcher, the DIY Superstore showed what transformations could be wrought on the average broch by the addition of the latest in state-of-the-art Homeware and Smellie's, its 'Under New Management' notice scarcely more than a week old, had filled the window with the simple slogan: SAVE OUR STONE! Its exclamation mark was extravagantly picked out in kiwi fruit.

Really, thought Cllr Haq, the town was a model of organised creative enterprise. Then a frown clouded his beatific features: one element, albeit a small one, was missing. Mr Campsie had promised to favour the Emporium, at a fraction over cost, with a supply of Craigfieth Stone postcards as soon as they were ready, which should have been days ago. Cllr Haq knew that the curator had his own peculiar problems but really that did not excuse such slackness. Business was business, after all. He resolved to slip away for a few minutes and clear the matter up.

It seemed to the Councillor, as he made his way to the museum, that all human life was this day concentrated in Craigfieth High Street. By the time he fought his way to the crossroads his suit was sticky from the press of fellow mortals savouring their purchases of toffee apples, candy-floss and the Craigfieth Pictish Fudge. The Dunbroath Road, in contrast, shimmered emptily in the July heat and Logie Baird Avenue, as he passed the junction, might have been a thoroughfare on a deserted film set. He turned in at the museum entrance as a listless wind, exhausted in its efforts to destroy the WRI's handiwork, stirred the leaves on the twin sycamores that flanked the gateway. Cllr Haq shivered, despite the heat; it was quite eerie, that weary sighing. Knowing the public entrance would be closed against reporters, he was making his way round to the fire escape which led to Mr Campsie's private back door when a movement in the corner of his vision caused him to halt. Again the breeze fluttered fitfully in the branches overhead, and he saw what had attracted his attention.

The main door of the museum was ajar.

Cllr Haq stood for a moment, wondering, as the wind caught the door again and fanned it gently to and fro. There was no reason why the museum should not be unlocked, except that it was supposed to be closed and the notice informing the public of this temporary inconvenience was still in place, sellotaped to the fanlight. There again, there was no reason why the door should not be ajar, except that it was normally pinned back during opening hours.

Cllr Haq advanced slowly towards it, bringing into view as he did so the broken window on the far side of the porch.

Not for nothing had the Councillor spent his formative years in Pollokshaws. He burst through the inner door to the main gallery, ready for combat, but the place was empty of aggressors. There was only the long line of pottery fragments, the farm machinery, the illicit still, the tweed loom . . . the splintered remains of the Statuette Room door and slumped against the Stone itself, the bound, gagged and blindfolded figure of Mr Campsie, his swathed head wobbling grotesquely on its scrawny pivot as he struggled vainly to free himself.

He gasped as the Councillor ripped off his elastoplast gag.

". . . room . . ." he wheezed. "In . . . the room . . . heard . . . smashing!"

Cllr Haq was sufficiently well versed in the ways of detective fiction not to touch anything in the Statuette Room, nor to linger long. He stayed just long enough to ascertain that Craigfieth's naughty novelties would be naughty no longer. Their fragments lay strewn in a drift of broken glass.

He unbound the curator and called the police.

BBC Radio Lummock reported the local constabulary as 'baffled'. This was not entirely fair. Sergeant MacEachran might not have been used to criminal damage on so violent a scale, but he was not an unintelligent man. From Mr Campsie's own lips he learned that the curator had been surprised in his private apartments by four masked and hooded men of medium height and build, forced downstairs, made to surrender his keys and then tied to the symbol stone in the manner in which Cllr Haq had, some two hours later, found him. His own wits told him that the intruders must have gained access by the window and egress through the door. No further could he go, however, in his investigations. Mrs Kininmonth, bedridden since early that morning with a migraine, could not help. To that extent he was, indeed, baffled. But it must be said that the officers of Eastern Region CID were, despite exhaustive investigations, no more enlightened than their uniformed colleague. There were no fingerprints of known villains, only those of Mr Campsie himself, naturally enough. No one — understandably, since this had after all been the day of the Gala opening — had seen any suspicious persons entering or leaving the premises. In a town whose streets had been crammed with strangers' cars, no one had remarked on any vehicle.

Nor could the police make any headway with consideration of the motive: who would want to go to all that trouble just to smash and grind beyond repair a collection of prehistoric erotica? Rev MacAndrew's suggestion, that it might be the work of Hezbollah or some similarly extreme Shi'ite grouping, was not found helpful by Superintendent Bruce from Dunbroath. He suspected, he told the Minister, that Central Perthshire was unlikely to be viewed in such quarters as a vital ingredient in the Middle East melting pot.

The shattered remains of the figures were removed by grim-faced officials from the Archaeological Services Support Unit.

The police — privately, of course — added the case to the two-thirds majority marked 'unlikely to be capable of solution at this moment in time'.

Mr Campsie got his pension after all.

He had many comforters in the days following his nasty experience. His colleagues on the Campaign Committee flocked to his bedside, where he was being nursed by the dourly efficient Mrs Kininmonth, to offer their condolences and their fruit which, appropriately enough, had been bought at discount from the window of the greengrocer's.

Not until, by their estimation, the curator was restored to a semblance of health did they break the news that responsibility for the outrage had been claimed by a mysterious organisation calling itself the Moral Brigade, in a letter to the *Perthshire Gazette*. 'SO PERISH', the letter said, in capital letters cut, according to the police, from more than one copy of *Life And Work*, 'ALL ENEMIES OF CHRISTIAN CHASTITY'.

The envelope bore a Craigfieth postmark. The police re-interviewed Mr Bullock and Rev MacAndrew, but their enquiries came, again, to nothing.

Poor Mr Campsie was visibly shaken by this intelligence. He sank back in his pillows, a banana (formerly half the U of SAVE OUR STONE) slipping from his limp hand. Mrs Kininmonth suggested that it might be appropriate for the visitors to leave.

Afterwards, the curator opened one watery eye and regarded the stern features of his nurse.

"Well," he murmured, "I suppose this is it, then."

"Aye," Mrs Kininmonth agreed. "It surely is, hen."

No one in Craigfieth was unduly surprised to hear that Mr Campsie, demoralised as he was by recent events, had applied to his employers for early retirement on the grounds of ill-health. One or two eyebrows, it is true, were raised when his departure from the town was accompanied by that of his home help, and when reports filtered back to the town that both had been spied boarding a flight bound from Prestwick to the States. Eventually the town had other things to think about, and the pair were forgotten.

Some weeks later a spokesperson for Eastern Region announced that restoration of the notorious statuettes was not considered appropriate in the prevailing financial climate. The news did not come as much of a surprise to the guardians of the town's cultural heritage, most of whom had never liked the things anyway. If the Director of Archaeological Services ever ordered a radiocarbon dating test on the surviving morsels, he wisely kept the results to himself.

There was, however, much rejoicing over the final paragraph of the Region's communiqué: the stone, it had been decided, could stay where it was, pending privatisation of the town's heritage facility.

Cllr Haq knew a good investment when he saw one. Craigfieth, after all, has always been proud of its museum.

10

The Cost of Loving

The cow-bells above the door of the Bide-a-Wee Tea-rooms clunked and jangled as the door swung shut. Mrs Spurtle slid the hatch open a fraction, peered Medusa-like through the narrow aperture for a few seconds, then pushed it firmly home again.

"Gone at last!" she grunted.

The remaining customers in Craigfieth's premier refreshment outlet continued their luncheons without disturbing themselves. They had grown accustomed, over the last few weeks, to this daily occurrence.

Behind the scenes, Miss Phemister sniffed over her washing-up. Of all the various forms of Anglo-Scots phatic communion, the sniff is perhaps the most expressive and few sniffs, surely, can be more eloquent than that of Miss Honoria Phemister. Nonetheless she repeated it on this occasion.

"Don't you sniff at me, Phemister!" growled the widow. "I know what he's up to, believe you me, and I've told you: I'm not interested. You can have him, ha!"

Miss Phemister sniffed again, then began to twitter.

"Pah!" her partner snorted.

Mr McMurtry of the Craigfieth branch of the Scottish Amiable and Providential Bank closed the door behind him, lingeringly and with a dying fall, and crossed the quiet road to his place of vocation. The church clock wanted a little of half-past one; the town was still in a state of commercial interregnum but it was time for Mr McMurtry to return to work. He paused at the sported oaks of the bank to gaze beseechingly back at the country of his desires, then his watch bleeped a peremptory summons and he turned reluctantly back to his Monday afternoon chores.

Somewhere, carelessly, a lovesick cuckoo plied his tedious burden, piercing the banker's heart as he passed into the air-conditioned penumbra beyond the doors and acknowledged the greetings of his acned counter staff, all of whom, as always, were engaged to be married. Wearily he raised a limp right hand in salutatory response, then passed through the double chipboard doors to his managerial suite. He chewed an indigestion tablet while he scanned his appointment book.

Grace Wemyss had transformed the flat above Sounds Good (formerly The Bonaventure Wireless Shop) from its slough of sloppy bachelordom to a symphony of cohabited niceness. The main theme, stated boldly by the washable vinyl section in the opening movement of the hall, was floral. This was echoed by arpeggios throughout the work: by the moquette in the lounge, the lino in the kitchen and the crocheted spare roll cover in the Littlest Room. While major revisions — such as the stained four-legged bathtub and the obscenely porous stone kitchen sink — still required to be undertaken, the composer's stamp was firmly impressed on such cadenzas, minuets and trios as the 'Love Is . . .' poster on the wardrobe door, the gounie-case on the bed and the wipe-clean cruet set on the kitchen table. Grace's opus was well advanced: today would decide the fate of the major unimproved fixtures in her little nest; would determine whether they were to be torn out and replaced in the interest of taste, propriety and hygiene, or abandoned for the sake of their mistress's larger mission.

She straightened Hamish Ganglion's tie, brushed the flakes off his shoulders and adjusted the handkerchief card in the breast pocket of his new suit, bought the week before from Grace's club book. Its owner trembled beneath the affectionate urgency of the blows and attempted one last resistance.

"I still think we should ask my father," he bleated.

"No, Hamish, we've decided. We're not going to ask to borrow money off him, it's his money and he needs it for his old age. Besides, we'll get it anyway when he's passed on, won't we. No, sweetheart, we've got to do this on our own. It is important to you, doing things on our own, together, isn't it?"

"Yeah, spose so — yes, yes, of course . . . darling. It's just, well . . . why can't you go?"

Grace primped her lips and tweaked her master playfully by the earlobes.

"Because it's not my place, silly! You're the man, you've got to make the decisions and do the important things. Now, off you go, and remember all the things I told you to say."

Hamish drew breath to sigh, then, feeling the suit pinch, abandoned the attempt. He kissed her on the forehead, which was as far as he could bend, and shambled stiffly out on to the landing. Grace's bosom swelled, albeit strictly within bounds beneath her polyester jumper, and she flushed. She felt so proud of him, sometimes.

Mrs Spurtle stomped into the kitchen with a tray of dirty bowls and plates.

"Two more soups de jour, Phemister," she grunted, "with fresh baked rolls."

Miss Phemister took a packet of rolls from the freezer and put them in the microwave.

"Not enough soup here for two, Ay'm afraid," she said, replacing the lid on the simmering pan. "Ay'll have to open another tin."

Mrs Spurtle lifted the lid.

"Nonsense, woman! Put some water in and boil it up again. It's only for a couple of silly shopgirls."

Miss Phemister obeyed the order, though she managed to sneak in a little stock cube, to make it taste of something. She sniffed.

"Ay think you're being terribly hard on poor Mr McMurtry," she ventured. "He's only traying to be nayce."

"Pooh! Don't you believe it, Phemister, you don't known what men are like. I can see through that man's smarminess and sweet talk, the nasty old goat."

"Well, Ay think he's a very nayce man, Joan, whatever you say. He always gives me a nayce smayle when Ay go in the bank, and he asks after may feet."

"There you are!" said the widow. "That just proves it, doesn't it? He can't control himself! He's no more than a . . . than an *animal*, Phemister. Spurtle was just the same you know, oh yes. Coming home from his Lodge every Saturday night and asking me how I felt, and making me look at photographs of his sister's latest brat, year after year. Animals, Phemister, that's all they are! Twelve years it took me to tame Spurtle and then what did he do? Went and died on me, that's what! I'm not going through that again, least of all with McMurtry, pension or no pension. Do you know what he said to me today?"

"No, Joan, what?" Miss Phemister's eyes shone in the steam of the raging broth.

"He looked at me very shiftily, as if he were trying to ravage me there and then, and complimented me on my cock-a-leekie! Just like that! 'Very fine soup this, Mistress Spurtle,' he said — you could tell that wasn't what he meant at all — then he said, 'You must give me the recipe for Miss Finlay.' Hah! I soon told him, in no uncertain terms!"

"Oh dear, Joan — you didn't tell him it all came out of tins, did you?"

"Don't be a bigger fool than you already are, Phemister. Of course I didn't. I said you'd made it. Do you know your rolls are on fire?"

Hamish Ganglion was early for his appointment, and had to wait in the foyer of the bank, in full view of such of his townsfellows who had business to transact at the counters. He perched uncomfortably in his too-tight trousers on the edge of one of the bank's newly installed seating modules in the open-plan waiting area. After a few minutes he tired of looking at the rubber plant and tried to find visual relief instead in the range of Customer Service leaflets at his elbow, starting in first on 'Plan Ahead — Protect And Survive With An Amiable And Providential Nuclear Shelter Loan'.

A few feet from Hamish was a door leading to a passage, leading to another door, beyond which was the Manager's office. Seated therein, at twenty to two on this Monday afternoon, were Mr McMurtry and the first of his after-lunch clients, Cllr Haq, proprietor of Haq's Universal Emporium and newly elected Vice-Chairman of the Leisure Industries Support Subcommittee of Eastern Regional Council. He had only half an hour to spare for the meeting, being due to check in at Dunbroath Airport at half-past three for his official visit to study artificial ski slopes in Münchengladbach, but the matter was an urgent one and would not await his return. Fortunately, Mr McMurtry had everything at his fingertips and the interview was as brief as it was productive.

"A very wise move, Mr Haq, if I may say so." The banker inclined himself a little in order to call up the necessary information on his Seac Brokerlink VDU. The screen leapt into green life with the appropriate data.

"Yes, there we are now, Mr Haq. As a long-term shot it shows very encouraging signs, very encouraging indeed; there's your free fuel bonus after one year's ownership and a one-for-three offer if you hang on for two. Market projections are optimistic: I'm sure you read in last week's *Investor's Chronicle* that the new Board have indicated their determination to streamline the business and shed all capacity that they deem surplus to the paramountcy of the immediate demands of the shareholders, so that's all to the good. You wouldn't want to buy into a charity now, would you?"

"No indeed, Mr McMurtry," the Councillor grinned. "Charity begins at home!"

"Quite so, Mr Haq, that's very well put. And you'll note that privatisation will also boost profitability by removing all those antiquated restraints — so-called safety rules and so on—which have made the industry suffer in recent years at the hands of its competitors in America and Poland. After all, you can't make an omelette without breaking eggs, that's what I always say, and the unions can hardly complain about their working conditions when they're being offered such generous terms to leave their jobs, can they? So I think you're on a very sound investment here, in every way, and I'm glad you've come to us to manage it for you."

Mr Haq lowered his head to indicate modest acknowledgement of the banker's gratitude. Then he said:

"How much will I make if I flog them straight away?"

Mr McMurtry did not blink. He smiled.

"Ah, well, there the indicators are even better, I'm glad to say. Yes, we've been keeping our ear very close to the ground in the grey market these last few days — you know what the grey market is, Mr Haq? Of course you do, you're a veteran of Telecom and TSB after all — well, the trading there is very brisk at the moment, very brisk indeed. Of course, I wouldn't recommend you risk your money there — we like to think of it as a necessary evil, actually— but the indications are your shares would trade at a premium of, oh, at least eighty per cent and possibly as much as a hundred and twenty in the first few days."

"Really, Mr McMurtry? As much as that?"

"Oh yes, all the signs are there you see. There'll be heavy buying by the oil companies, of course, and British Nuclear Fuels too."

"Oh, I see." Mr Haq lit a cheroot. "If you can't beat 'em — own 'em, eh?"

Mr McMurtry permitted himself a dry banker's chuckle.

"Oh, very good Mr Haq, very good. I'm sure Jimmy Gulliver would agree with you there! Naturally, they'll be wanting to look after the interests of their own investors, and it all adds up to a very attractive stag market, as we call it. So — no problems, really."

"That's good news! Now, as regards finance, Mr McMurtry, you understand I have reasons for not wishing to liquidate my assets at this moment in time with regard to this?"

"Of course, Mr Haq, naturally we see our role here as being the protector of your interests in every respect. No, no, don't you worry about that. We'll see you right for a week or two and we look forward to acting for you in the resale — I've prepared a paper for you to sign to give me the power to act while you're away working for our community in Germany. It's quite straightforward — powers of attorney and so on, and the usual brokerage rates — if you'll just put your signature against the x on the bottom? That's fine, Mr Haq."

The investor signed and rose to shake the manager's outstretched hand.

"We'll expedite this straight away for you, then," said Mr McMurtry. "Twenty-five thousand shares in Britcoal, fifty per cent payable on application, and we'll let you know the good news as soon as we've got it."

Mr Haq's gaze lingered on the bank manager's terminal.

"A handy little gadget," he observed.

"This? Oh yes! All thanks to the Big Bang, of course. The shape of things to come, Mr Haq, make no mistake. Do you know, I was reading the other day that there are more people employed in financial services in Scotland than there are in steel, shipbuilding and coal put together?"

Mr Haq nodded.

"Rejoice!" he said.

"Oh, for goodness' sake stop twittering, Phemister! Really, sometimes I despair of you."

"Well Ay'm sorry Joan, Ay can't help it, Ay mean if Mr McMurtry is thinking of settling down, whay shouldn't he? And if you're quayte sure you do not want him, well . . ."

"Want him!" hooted Mrs Spurtle. "My dear Phemister, the idea is grotesque! Can you possibly imagine why any woman should want to make herself a slave *again*? Cooking, cleaning, washing, tidying up all the time?"

"Ay don't see what's wrong with that," insisted Miss Phemister. "After all, it's no different from what Ay do at the moment, is it?"

Mrs Spurtle's heavy features registered shock.

"Of course it is, you silly woman!" she snapped. "Quite different. We're women. We're a partnership."

"Oh well, if you say so dear, Ay suppose you must be right."

" Course I am. Besides, as I keep telling you, it's absurd to be thinking of throwing away what you've been hanging on to all this time. Especially at your age. I mean — look at you!"

"Aay can't help the way Ay look, Joan. None of us can."

Poor Miss Phemister's desiccated body sagged against the sink. Mrs Spurtle began to worry in case her partner should not be finished with the lunchtime washing-up before it was time for High Teas. She laid a meaty hand on her companion's thin, trembling shoulder.

"Come on now, Phemmy! Pull yourself together. You're just disturbed, that's all, I expect it's those silly old hormones again. Have you been taking those tablets Dr Bodkin gave you the last time?"

"Y-yes," sobbed the spinster.

"Well, then! Now, make yourself a nice cup of tea and you'll soon feel a lot better, mmm?"

"Yes — thank you dear — yes, Ay'll do that. Oh dear! It's just that Ay . . . well, Ay —"

"Yes?" sighed Mrs Spurtle. "What did you just?"

"Ay, well, Ay thought perhaps . . . Ay mean, a man like Mr McMurtry, a respectable man, in a good position . . . you promise you won't laugh at me, Joan?"

"I can assure you, Phemister, that laughter is the last thing on my mind. Go on, woman, spit it out!"

"Well, all right then. Ay thought his mind might be on Higher Things, that's all."

Mrs Spurtle's bray set the foam quivering in the sink. Miss Phemister began to wail.

"No! Oh no!" gasped the widow. "I wasn't — hooo! nyaaagh! — I wasn't laughing, I promise. Pfffpschsch! No, really, honestly. Oh, do shut up! Phemister, listen to me: men simply don't know what Higher Things are, do you hear? They're not like us. As far as they're concerned, a little bit of empty flattery now and again and they think they can do what they like with you, treat you like a — like a *servant*, or worse. Day *and* night! I wasn't laughing at you, you old silly, I was laughing at them! Believe me, it's the only way to deal with them."

"Yes . . . all right, Joan, Ay'm all right now, Ay think."

"Good, that's settled then. Now be a good girl and get that washing-up finished while I do the till. And then you can set the Tearooms out for this afternoon, like you do so well."

"Yes. Ay'm fine now, thank you Joan. You're very good to me, Ay know, and Ay am a trouble to you."

Mrs Spurtle patted her partner affectionately on the back.

"There, there," she growled. "Silly old thing!"

The telephone began to ring.

Five minutes after Mr Haq left the bank, Hamish Ganglion was informed by a counter clerk that Mr McMurtry would see him in five minutes. He looked anxiously at his watch. Grace would be at Smellie's by now, leaving Eric the YTS in charge of Sounds Good. He hoped this Monday afternoon would run true to form, and be slack. He picked up a leaflet entitled 'Stable Relationship? Insure Your Life With The A&P Now!' and began to read it.

Mr McMurtry waited impatiently while the number rang. Passion made his wait seem endless: in fact, it was only long enough for Miss Phemister to dry the suds off her hands, acknowledge Mrs Spurtle's hissed *'I'm not here!'* and lift the wicker cover off the instrument in the Bide-a-Wee office.

"Yes? Hello?" she trembled. Telephones always made her a little nervous.

"Ah," said Mr McMurtry. "Um, who is that speaking, please?"

Now she remembered: there was a correct way of answering the telephone, and she had not used it.

"This is the Bide-a-Wee Tearooms, Craigfieth," she answered.

"Ah," sad Mr McMurtry. "Yes. Good. Um, this is McMurtry here, at the bank."

"Oh, Mr McMurtry!" she twittered. "It's you!"

Mrs Spurtle hissed through from the kitchen with redoubled intensity.

"Pardon. Ay couldn't hear what you said."

"I said, is that Miss Phemister?"

The spinster's heart fluttered faster.

"Yes," she whispered.

"Ah," said Mr McMurtry.

"Is, um, is Mrs Spurtle there, please, by any chance?"

"No," croaked Miss Phemister.

"Oh. Are you sure?"

"No, Mr McMurtry. Ay mean yes, yes Ay am quayte sure. She's not here. She's out."

"Oh," said Mr McMurtry.

Then, in a flash of unwonted efficiency, Miss Phemister said:

"Can Ay take a message?"

"Ah," said Mr McMurtry. Here was a problem. He had steeled himself to telephone the object of his desires, trusting that he would think of something to say when she answered. Faced with Miss Phemister, his amorous muse picked up her skirts and fled, leaving only the banker's professional reflexes to aid him.

"Hello?" said Miss Phemister.

"Oh, yes, hello, um, McMurtry still here. Yes, would you tell your um, that is, Mrs Spurtle, I mean would you ask her, please, to c-come into the bank tomorrow and see me? A little matter of um, well a little matter. Say eleven o'clock."

"Oh mai guidness! Is anything wrong?"

"Oh, no, nonono. I just need to see her, that's all. I mean, that is to say, the bank does, in my capacity and um, in my office. You see."

"Oh, my! Very well then, Mr McMurtry, Ay'll tell her that."

"Right, fine. Oh, and — Miss Phemister?"

She started violently.

"Yes?"

"Congratulations on the soup. First class."

He replaced the receiver abruptly, its shiny plastic surface cloudy with damp. His hand shook: really, this would not do! He was a bank manager; he must pull himself together. Still, he'd done all right; handled it rather well, very well, in fact, considering. Very well indeed. He stopped shaking.

McMurtry, Man of Mystery. Fergus the Ladykiller. Mrs Spurtle could not fail to be intrigued. He must take advantage of that: must make sure she came to rely on him for advice, for guidance, for *security*. Yes, that was the way to do it . . . he slid into a cosy reverie. It was evening. He and Joan sat together before the fire, her head trustingly on his shoulder while he handled her portfolio . . .

The buzzer on his desk sounded rudely.

"Yes?" he snapped.

"Mr Ganglion's still here, Mr McMurtry."

"Who? Oh, that one. Very well, Mrs Oxter, tell him to come in."

"Mr McMurtry will see you now, Mr Ganglion," she said.

Hamish stuffed 'Where There's A Will There's The AmiProv Way' into his jacket pocket, breathed deeply, and went in.

Grace bridled.

"Is that all he said?" she demanded.

"Yeah," Hamish sighed. "I told you, it was a very short interview."

"But it doesn't make *sense*!" Had she not been sitting down, she would have stamped her foot.

"Makes sense to him, I suppose," observed Hamish.

"You're *sure* you told him everything?"

"Yeah, yeah, like I said. I told him you'd been running Smellie's for months since he went away, and now he'd decided to put the house and shop up for sale, we wanted to buy it. Then he asked me how much we'd got, and I told him, and showed him the books, but I needn't have bothered. He hardly looked at them, really."

"And you didn't forget the other things, about making it a Scottish Only Produce Centre, and getting a grant, and turning the top floor into guest rooms, and selling herbs we'd grown ourselves, and —"

"No, I *told* you. I said all that. Might as well've been talking to myself. Felt dead lonely by the end of it."

"He didn't say *anything*?"

"Nope. Not till right at the end. Then he sort of grunted, like he was waking up or something, and asked if we'd got anyone who'd guarantee the loan and I said no, and he said in that case he was afraid it wasn't the bank's policy to lend money for speculative ventures, Mr Ganglion, and that was it."

Grace flushed. "Oh!" she exclaimed. "He's a real . . . a real —"

"Banker, yeah," Hamish quipped.

"Naughty!" she said, and pinched his arm, but the mood did not last. The fell shadow of Mr McMurtry lay between them still.

Then, "That's daft!" Grace declared.

"What, particularly?"

"Well, if he'd only lend us money if someone else guaranteed the loan, that'd mean we'd already found someone else to lend us the money, wouldn't it? Someone who knew and trusted us, like a friend or a relation. And if we *had* got someone like that, we wouldn't be asking him in the first place, would we?"

"No — no, spose not."

"So who *do* they lend money to?"

Hamish fished in his pocket and showed her the Scottish Amiable and Providential Bank's nuclear shelter leaflet.

"People with big gardens, I suppose."

Grace glanced briefly at it before hurling it to the floor.

"Speculative ventures — huh!"

Her shoulders began to shake. She had yet to forgive the world its habit of denying the pursuit of happiness to those who deserve it most.

Downstairs, someone started to hammer on the door.

"Aw, shit!" Hamish groaned. "Spose I'll have to —" He touched her shoulder, but she waved him away, sobbing uncontrollably now, as the hammering was renewed.

Hamish slid back the bolt and opened the door.

"Oh, hi Dad, Oswald. How did you get here?"

The senior Ganglion grinned.

"In Lady Lazarus there!"

He pointed to an elderly taxicab parked outside the shop.

"What's that?" asked Hamish.

"*That*, my ole son, issan Orstin Eff Ex Free, a noble breed wot used ter ply the streetser London when yew woz nuffink but a wossname in the infinite cosmos. Pickederup froo a mater yeruncle Ernie's, dahn Ammersmiff way, an gorrer converted fer Oswaldere wiv a Mobility Grant. Nah, yewgonner lerrusin, or wot?"

Grace had finished crying by the time they carried Oswald in his chair up the narrow stairs to the flat. She kissed her father-in-law-to-be and went off to make coffee, which Ganglion Senior laced with a new invention of his called a Lummock Lumberjack.

He took a lingering sip at the hot cocktail and sighed with satisfaction.

"Ka-aaah! Smyopinion that beats even Matron's Ruin! Nah then, yew tew, wotsamarrer then? Yew look like yew've bitten on suffink narsty at yer own funeral tea."

They told him.

"Barstud!"

"Aye, right enough," agreed Oswald. "Yon Prigpenny tried to sell my farm out from under me one time, when I had the Brucellosis."

"There y'are, then," Ganglion commented. "Right blahdy barstud. Beteez makiner packet outer this privatisation lark, anaw. Dunno wot this bleedin country's comin tew, sometimes, prats like im in charge. Snuffter make yer wanner gerran Access card so's yew can join the SDP, innit?"

Grace smiled at last.

"Oh well," she said, "we'll just have to think of something else, that's all."

"Attergirl! Never say die, as Lloyd George said ter the actress. Nah lissen. I carn't promise yer anyfink, right? So don't start gerrinaw upsadaisy. Burri'llavvergo for yer. Salong shot, mind, annit proberly won't come off. Burri'll try, anat's orl I'm gunner say abaht it. Nah then, afore we orl drinks tew much as per usual, an gets nicked by Sergeant Macrinhanish, ow abaht a lickuw spin in Lady Lazarus: I've bin tryin ter teach Ozzie owter do wheelies burreez gorn orl po faced abaht it, aventcher, yew ole fart?"

Oswald grinned. "Take no notice of him, it's just sour grapes because I said he couldn't drive unless he passed his test first."

"Passed his —?" Hamish gulped. "But Dad, you always drove everywhere!"

"Yeah, wew, fings woz diffrent then, wonney? Sides, I knew a fing or tew abaht the local bobby an e wouldn't dare lay a finger on me. I never eard no complaints, anyway."

"A case of ignorance being bliss," said Oswald. "Come on then, if we're going."

Later, Ganglion took advantage of the diesel cacophony to murmur to his son, "I meant it abaht tryinterelp, and I wiw, ok? Only dunnarskow, and dunnexpeck miracles, right?"

"Right, Dad. Thanks."

"Asserboy."

Their return, after a tour of the environs of the town, was greeted by Craigfieth's own version of the Mexican Wave. The Craigfieth Wave, performed upon twitching net curtains, and extending the full length of the High Street, provided a visual accompaniment to the rorting progress of Lady Lazarus, her running boards and hubcaps glinting in the late sunlight. Only the lately abandoned apartments of Mr and Mrs Smellie broke, momentarily, the diaphanous ripple of the town's salute.

Ganglion Senior excused himself on the grounds of prosthetic arrangements and, locking himself in the bathroom, keyed in a number on his cordless telephone while perching gingerly on the pedestal seat, which Grace had covered with pink nylon fluff. Time, and possibly his telephone call, would discover whether her civilising hand would extend further into the Ganglion toilet . . .

"Ello? Izzat Miss . . . oh, good. Sme, Ganglion."

The earpiece made noises of distant incredulity.

"Yeah, yeah, I know I never rung before. Orlwiz wrote, though, dinni? Yeah, wew, if yer must know I woz a bit frightened ter ring, arfter everyfink, anat. Stiw, I'm ringin nah, enni?"

A little later, he said, "Lissen luv, I berrer gerronwivit, cos ackcherly I'm supposed ter be aviner crap — yeah, asright, I'm in the karzi . . . salong story, tell yer someday . . . sabout Amish, e needser birrerelp. Yeah, gorritinone, e needs money. E's gorrinself a gurw . . . no, she ain't, leastways if she is it don't show. No, she's orl right reely, a bit My Weekly but berrer than moster them in this dump. Yeah, wew, I'll tell yer . . ."

He did so.

"Fanks, luv, I knew yer'd try. An yew'll let me . . . Yeah, right. Wew, then. I'd, er . . . berrer say tara then, anni? Yeah, wew, then . . . tara. Wot? Oh, yeah. Fer now. Tara fer now . . . tara, luv."

He flushed the lavatory, washed his hands, and rejoined the others. Grace made more coffee, and he produced the Lumberjack. He needed it.

Mr McMurtry had prepared meticulously for his eleven o'clock appointment with the Widow Spurtle. He washed thoroughly, once with soap and again with emollient lotion to produce that shiny translucence of skin so essential for one who seeks to engender an aura of fiscal probity; he applied a modicum of salon mousse to his thinning hair to lend his face an illusion of length and businesslike sagacity; he selected his best dark blue suit, the one he wore to seminars at Head Office, and a red and white striped shirt with a white collar, to indicate his place at the thrusting forefront of Enterprise Britain. His tie proudly proclaimed the winning, in 1979, of the Queen's Award to Industry by the Corporate Management Team of the Scottish Amiable and Providential Bank. His toecaps threw back twin images of the scudding clouds as if daring them to drop their despoiling burden on the wearer. He bent to pick a selection of flowers from his borders, hoping his gardener would not notice. Murdoch could become quite uppity at times: God willing, he'd soon be able to dispose of the tiresome man's expensive services. Mr McMurtry's experience as treasurer of the town's Brighter Gardens and Neater Wynds Action Group had taught him that Craigfieth women of a certain age set great value on a floral display.

He arrived early, to avoid the staff, arranged a bouquet in a Manticore And MacVitie's Bank cream jug, a relic of more expansive, pre-merger days, and whiled away the two hours remaining to him by improving his knowledge of Mrs Spurtle's assets and perfecting his plans for their productive investment.

By half past ten, Miss Phemister was in what Mrs Spurtle called a state of Extreme Flutter, and was attempting to alleviate the condition by frantic polishing of the tea urn.

"Oh dear, Ay *do* hope it's nothing serious!" she said for the umpteenth time that morning.

Mrs Spurtle gave vent to a sound, halfway between a growl and a groan, that was reminiscent in its lower range of the noise a dead sheep makes when it is turned over.

"Oh, Ay know what you're going to say Joan dear, but may dear father always used to say, always make sure you ask to see your banker because when a banker asks to see you it means he's booked your bed in bridewell. Of course, it was may brothers he used to say it to, but Ay'm sure it's still true. And Ay can't think how Ay'm going to manage here on may own all the time you're away."

"Good Lord Phemister, how many years do you think they'll send me down for?"

"Oh! Don't!" Miss Phemister wailed.

"Oh, for heaven's sake stop worrying, they don't send debtors to prison these days; they give them credit cards instead. Besides, you silly woman, we're not *in* debt, thanks to Uncle Ramsay. I can't for the life of me imagine what McMurtry *does* want to see me about, but whatever it is it shouldn't take more than half an hour. Surely you can manage the tables for thirty minutes?"

Miss Phemister sniffed vigorously and polished a little harder.

"Ay'll tray," she whispered.

"Yes dear, you tray, and then the place will be all nice and neat for the Sheriff's men when they come to poind us, won't it?"

She shut the door on her partner's strangled sobs and went out through the Tearooms. Two startled matrons looked anxiously at her as she bore down on their table.

"Miss Phemister will attend to you shortly, ladies. If she does not then bang on the hatch. Hard."

She galleoned out into the street, her steely blue hair striking splinters from the morning sun.

Whatever shortcomings Mr McMurtry might be accused of, want of effort in the wooing of the Widow Spurtle would not be one of them. With his VDU as mute advocate, he displayed his affections. He sought her with stocks, he sought her with shares; he pursued her with unit trusts. He threatened her viduity with a joint high-income bond; he charmed her with endowments and gilts. Throughout it all Mrs Spurtle sat, vast and impassive, like a ship's figurehead, as wave after amorous wave of judicious advice broke ineffectually over her and dribbled away, figuratively, into the carpet. Little beads of unbankerly sweat began to form on his forehead. At last he ran out of things to say: his screen went blank; love's cupboard was bare.

There was a long, heavy, muffled silence. Mrs Spurtle stirred, Kraken-like above her massive ballast. Her tweedy bosom swelling, her square jaw set firm, she spoke:

"The late Spurtle, Mr McMurtry, whom God has been pleased to part from me these three-and-twenty years, was a man of many faults which it was my heavy burden to correct. He once attempted to speculate, behind my back of course, in a scheme for farming edible snails in Wester Ross. Fortunately I was able, on that occasion, to nip his incontinence in the bud. I reminded him of what my grandfather said, the day he passed on: two per cent Consols, he told me, were more than sufficient for any Christian soul. I made sure my Spurtle heeded those good words, Mr McMurtry, and I'm sure he had no reason to regret them while he lived. Thank you for showing me your little toy: now if you have no more important matters to attend to, I can assure you that I have. I recommend you dismiss the girl who does your desk. These pansies are limp. Good day to you."

Mr McMurtry had been present when Poulson's men poured the cement for his office floor: he still had the photo in that month's issue of *Banker's World* to prove it. Yet now he could have sworn that it trembled with the widow's passing.

Something told him he had not created a very favourable impression.

Mrs Spurtle stamped across the street and cycloned through the Tearooms. The cowbells were still proclaiming her entry as she made her exit through the door to the kitchen, where Miss Phemister was dithering between the till, the urn, the soup and the sink. Time was suspended for a few moments as the trembling Phemister waited for the storm to break.

"Men!" thundered Mrs Spurtle at last.

Miss Phemister uttered a little bleat. She was holding two soup bowls; their contents began to dribble, unheeded, to the floor.

"Oh dear!" she squeaked, not meaning the soup.

"I have discovered, Phemister," boomed the widow, "that there is one thing worse in this wicked world than the shameless libertine."

"Oh, no!"

"Oh, yes! He at least can be ... neutralised." She allowed herself a brief and silent recollection of the proof of this assertion. "Yes, eventually a strong woman — and I mean a *strong* woman, Phemister — can persuade him to lose interest. She can reform him. You, of course, will simply have to take my word for that."

"Yes, dear, Ay know," Phemister agreed meekly.

"But there is a worse, Phemister – *there is a worse!*"

"You mean Mr McMurtry — did he ... was he ...?"

"I mean that Mr McMurtry — whose name will not be mentioned again in this establishment, Phemister; remember that, please — I mean that *that Creature* is — is — *Otherwise!*"

Miss Phemister dropped the empty bowls.

"*Otherwise?*"

"*Otherwise!* Do you know what I mean, Phemister, by 'Otherwise'?"

"Y-yes dear, I think so."

"Good. Then you will understand that some of these ... Otherwise Creatures sometimes need to pretend that they are not."

"Yes, dear. Yes. N-not what?"

"Not Otherwise of course, you fool!"

"Oh. Yes, of course, sorry, dear."

"And I, Phemister — *I*, mark you — was to be chosen as the vehicle for this disgusting charade."

"Oh, Joan, whatever did you do?"

"Dealt with it, Phemister. Oh yes, I dealt with it all right. I almost wish that Spurtle, God rest his soul, had been alive to see it."

"Oh, Joan!"

"Never mind that now. We will say no more about it. Unfortunately we cannot bar The Creature from our public doors: that would cause comment, and be bad for business. But we will take our account to Mr Saunders, who is at least securely married, at Melmotte's Bank, in the South End. It is further to walk, but worth the inconvenience. And henceforth you will take over my duties in the Tearooms for the hour when The Creature's bank is closed for luncheon."

"Oh! . . . Yes, Joan, dear, if you say so. Oh, dear!"

A smile arranged itself on the dominant partner's squarely determined features.

"Brace up, Phemister! There's nothing for you to worry about. You're not his type."

If the rest of that day was a miserable one for the banker, it was scarcely any happier for Hamish Ganglion, his victim of the day before. Although his father's promise, the previous evening, to see what he could do had seemed to cheer Grace up a little, the morning had seen her in a mood whose distant gloominess could not be wholly due to an excess of Lummock Lumberjack. She had drifted somnambulistically off to work at Smellie's with none of her usual brisk managerial cheeriness. Not only that, she had rung him up, once in the morning and once in the afternoon, to cry down the telephone at him, while remaining silent throughout their lunch. For almost the first time in their relationship he began to dread the evening and the night to come. He felt like an exhausted mountaineer in the foothills of a massif whose summit was unknown and whose route was unguessable.

***

Fergus McMurtry drooped sadly home a little after four o'clock that afternoon. Normally he relished the quiet time after closing: the soft moneyed hush, as his reduced minions worked with silent concentration behind their closed counters, adding and bundling and balancing, the air of calm and orderliness at close of business, the occasional civilised interviews with privileged clients permitted to breach his Inner Sanctum for the purpose of mutual benefit. Today, however, had gone sour on him. Mrs Spurtle had been unimpressed; his flowers had wilted altogether in the afternoon and he had been obliged to smuggle them out under his jacket and then spend nearly a quarter of an hour in the managerial staff lavatory trying to flush them away. Finally, just on closing time, had come news from the Stock Exchange of the disastrous first day's trading in the Britcoal flotation. A combination of overnight events, all unnoticed by him in his ardour for the admiration of the Widow Spurtle, had conspired to dash the hopes of small investors the length and breadth of Britain, not to mention Jersey and the Isle of Man. The break-up of OPEC and the instantaneous fall of $10 a barrel in the world oil price; the election to the Commons of Mr Arthur Scargill in the Slagthorpe East by-election and the relegation of the Conservative candidate to a derisory fourth place in the poll; the latest wave of resignations and revelations from the Board of Ghengis International and its Merchant Bankers, Meider-Bahnhof, and the run on sterling induced by these events: all had combined to give poor Mr Haq a pitiful premium of, at most, 2p per share on his equity holding. It would barely be enough, Mr McMurtry calculated, to cover the bank and interest charges he would now feel compelled to levy on his unfortunate customer. It was indeed dispiriting to reflect that such confident enterprise as Mr

Haq had shown should be so cruelly rewarded, especially in the 1980s.

He trudged up the weedless path to his front door, a solid-looking affair of mahoganette and brassite standard to the dwellings of AmiProv managers. Inside it he found his housekeeper, Miss Finlay, wringing her hands and looking inwardly ravaged.

"What is it, Miss Finlay?" he demanded.

"Indeed I'm sorry, Mr McMurtry, but there's a visitor. I tried to say you were not available but it was no use. She just walked past me and said she would wait for you. I couldn't stop her, sir."

She? Could it be . . . had his true colours shone through after all? Had that massive heart softened?

With a perfunctory 'Thank you, Miss Finlay, that will be all', he brushed past her and opened the sitting-room door.

Then he stood in the opening, his jaw hanging slack as he gazed fishily at the occupant of the room.

A lithe female figure uncoiled herself gracefully from the settee and advanced to greet him.

"Well Fergus," it said, "I can honestly say you don't look a day older than when I left you — mind you, you looked quite fifty-two then. How are you?"

Mr McMurtry was nothing if not a temperate man. There are, however, certain shocks which even the most extremely moderate cannot be expected to bear without fortification. As far as the banker was concerned, meeting one's ex-wife, unexpectedly and in one's own sitting-room, was one of them, especially when it came as the coda to a day that had seen financial disappointment and romantic impasse.

He poured himself a second glass of Voortrekker Medium Dry.

"How did you find me?" he asked.

The lady improvised plausibly.

"Through the bank, of course. I asked old Stuffie at the Princes Street branch."

"Stuffie? Good heavens, is he still there?"

"Still there, still Chief Accountant, still smelling of Mintoes. He told me where you'd gone. I must say, I think it was deliciously ironic of you to come here, of all places."

Mr McMurtry frowned.

"I go where the bank sends me," he said stiffly.

"Of course, silly of me to forget. Always the loyal servant, weren't you Fergus? Always obeying the Bank Rules. One point four times per week, with the light off: page thirty-two, paragraph (e), subsection (ii) d."

"Please don't bring that up again, Fiona."

She giggled.

"As the actress said . . . Sorry. You're right, it was all too long ago. Pour me another glass of Kaffirbasher, Fergus, if that's all you've got, and we'll drink damnation to old times together."

They drank in silence. Then he said:

"So. What are you doing now? Are you . . .?"

"No, I'm not. I decided it didn't suit me. I'm a career lady now."

"Oh? What line of business?"

"I'm in the book game. I spent about a year trying to write one, then decided all I really wanted to do was read them and get paid for it. So I got a job with a publisher and then turned myself into a Literary Agent."

"Oh, I see. Afraid I don't know much about books."

She laughed softly. "No, I know. Do you remember that awful row we had — well, I suppose I had it, really — when I found you'd used Samuel Beckett to prop up the wardrobe?"

Mr McMurtry thought hard.

"No, I'm afraid I don't," he said at length. "Anyway, how's it going, this book game of yours?"

"All right. No, really, all right. I pulled off quite a coup last year, actually — I got John Gorse."

"Oh. Is that good then, getting John Gorse?"

"Good? I should say! The poor dear didn't know anything about contracts and royalties. You should see how grateful he is now! Laughs all the way to my bank."

"I see. Well, good for you." He frowned. "Wait a minute . . . John Gorse, isn't he the one who wrote all those scurrilous stories, the one that court case was about?"

"The very one. Do you know, he was actually going to rewrite all the bits that awful MP was objecting to? Incredible, isn't it? Thank God I talked him out of it — the sales shot up!"

Mr McMurtry sniffed.

"Oh dear, don't you approve?"

"I grant you it was good for business," the banker allowed. "But I can't approve of that sort of book, and never will."

"Have you read it?"

"Of course not."

"No, dear, of course not. Well, never mind anyway — it keeps me, more or less."

Even after three glasses of Voortrekker, Mr McMurtry's senses were keen.

"Ah! Now we come to it. What exactly do you want from me, Fiona?"

"Dear Fergus! Always quick on that sort of uptake. Well, as a matter of fact, about forty thousand pounds, unless I've done my sums wrong."

"Forty th—?" He spluttered as the last of his Voortrekker went the wrong way.

"Did you say forty thousand? How on earth do you expect me to have that sort of money?"

"I don't. Because it's not really yours — erm, well, I don't think it is, but God knows whose it is if it isn't mine."

Mr McMurtry felt faint. He closed his eyes and whispered, "I think you'd better tell me about it."

She patted his arm.

"Poor Fergus! I didn't mean to shock you, really. Don't you remember the first birthday present you gave me after we were married?"

He tried to focus on the event.

"Flowers?"

"Wrong, that was all the other ones, dear. You gave me a receipt from the Incredibly Rich Bastards' Management Fund or some such. You'd invested five hundred pounds with them and they were going to hold it in trust for me until I was forty-five. Ring any bells?"

"Yes! Yes, of course, I remember now. You were very annoyed about it."

"Bloody right I was! Five hundred quid and I couldn't spend it! Not that it was the bloody money I was so angry about, of course."

"No, it wasn't, was it? I never could understand that. You said you'd have been happy just to get a bunch of . . . oh."

"Which is just what I did get after that — chrysanths, every time. Well, I expect you remember there was the little matter of a signature to release the money when the time came. You said it would pay for some nice holidays for us when the ch— . . . when we were on our own again. And then, when we split up, you started fussing about it, and *I* said —"

Mr McMurtry achieved full recall.

"You said I could, er, stuff the bloody money, and keep it in a box under the bed when I was a lonely old man, and count it on Christmas Eve."

"Oh dear, did I say all that? That was very rude and mostly uncalled for. I'm sorry."

"Apology accepted: I daresay from your point of view, at the time, and given the state you were in, there might have seemed some justification for saying it."

"Well." She remained forcibly calm. "Let's assume that's a sort of *mea culpa* on the marriage, shall we?"

Mr McMurtry began to protest.

"*Mea culpa*? I certainly didn't mean —"

"Never mind, for Christ's sake, what you meant, all right? I don't want to argue, I just want to say — well, I'm forty-five now, you are Fergus McMurtry and I claim my money. Please."

The banker smiled sourly.

"The book game not going so well after all, eh?"

"On the contrary, the book game is going fine. I want the money for something else, to help a — well, let's say a relation. Someone who needs a little leg up in these troubled times. Not that it's any of your business, really, is it?"

"No — thank goodness! Very well then. It seems there's nothing else I can do, so — I agree. I'll sign the document for you."

"Thank you, Fergus. Thank you very much. And now — you can tell me who the lady is!"

"Lady? What lady? What are you talking about?"

"Come on dear: people don't really change, you know, and I haven't forgotten what sexual passion does to your dress sense, even if it was all so very, very long ago. It must be pretty devastating to get you out of white shirts. Tell me all about it."

He prevaricated a little more, then he told her.

"Poor Fergus! Is she very rich?"

Mr McMurtry, mindful of his Banker's Oath, gave her a reasonably approximate idea of the current trading and capital account of the Bide-a-Wee Tearooms.

"Dear me," she said, "how frustrating for you! Perhaps I could help? If your inamorata always does the serving, maybe I could have a little chat — without giving anything away, of course. Just, well, help things along a bit, perhaps? You could think of it as my thank-you for the money."

Mr McMurtry agreed, heartily and gratefully. Then he asked, "Mm, where are you, er, that is, tonight. Are you . . .?"

She laughed in the old way, the way Fergus McMurtry had never known was meant to be with him and not at him, and never would.

"It's all right! I'm at the Ben Almond. One star and a green stain in the bath. Why don't you join me? — for dinner, I mean."

"Oh, no, no I couldn't really, you see Miss Finlay — that's my housekeeper — will have some nice liver for tonight. I don't want to put her out."

"No? Oh well, then, I'll leave you to Miss Finlay's offal. Goodnight. I'll see you tomorrow evening, and let you know how I got on. Oh, and Fergus? The paper, perhaps, before I go . . .?"

But Fiona Gourlay did not return directly to the Ben Almond Hotel. Instead, following carefully the directions Ganglion had given her, she drove her BMW coupé into the Lummocks, and arrived at the little whitewashed cottage some twenty minutes later.

Oswald greeted her warmly before making himself tactfully scarce with his ferrets in the other room. Ganglion and Fiona sat awhile, smiling shyly at each other.

Finally, "I got it," she said.

"Yew dint? Yew did! Oh, yew beautiful lady! But lissen, I do know it wozzer blahdy liberty arskin yew."

"Nonsense, it was a pleasure. Besides, it wouldn't be the first liberty, would it?"

Ganglion agreed, "It bleedin well wouldn't —"

"And that was a pleasure too, in case I was too callow to say so before."

"Yew did, an it woz, an yer can say it as often as yew like, ter remind me. Blimey! We ad some times, dint we?"

They remembered some of them.

"An if," Ganglion concluded, "I ad me time agen, I'd do the bleedin same, I can tell yer!"

She smiled sadly. "I wouldn't," she said. "I'd stay with you. I might turn out a better person."

"Nah, gercher! Don't get orl silly now. Lissen, I reckon we boaf did wot woz best. Wozzern't no joke bringing Amish up, sometimes, but I orlwiz ad the advantage of not bein contradicted, dinni? Weed of quarrelled like buggery if you'd stayed."

"Oh, well," she smiled again. "Maybe."

"Nah, then!" Ganglion roared. "Yore not gointer mooch back ter that stiffs' waitin room in Craigfeef till yer've ad suffink goodanot inside yer. Goan get Ozzie froo an I'll make us suffink. I'll do a Scarper Flo."

Ganglion kept them both entertained while he prepared the meal, which turned out to be clapshot, followed by more clapshot, and very nice too.

Afterwards, he saw her to her car.

"Remember now," she said, "no telling who it is. Promise?"

"Promise. Only — well, keep in touch, narmean?"

"Narmean, guv," she said, then became serious. "I have to ask you. Look — do you think we could . . . well, could we?"

Ganglion kissed her.

"Course we could. Could do anyfink. Only, I don't fink we should, do yew? You got yore life, I got Oswald, narmean? But see each uvver agen: yus. A fahsand times yus. Wotcher say?"

"I say yus to that, my dear. Soon. Soon and often, yes?"

"Right. Hey, maybe I could write a book, owabaht that?"

"I think that's a marvellous idea! You could give Gorse a hand, too. Some of his plots have become a bit contrived, lately."

"Right, yerron! Nah then — off yew go, an come back soon. I'm gointer phone the good noos froo ter Amish."

"Cheerio then, darling."

"Slong, luv. Drive carefully."

He found it was some time before he could focus properly on the telephone.

Despite her bed, Fiona slept in the next day and it was past noon before she ventured out on her mission. She could not resist a visit to some of the shops she remembered from youth: not being recognised was such fun. When she reached the Tearooms she was obliged to order a Bide-a-Wee Luncheon.

She could not at first bring herself to believe that the lady who served her could possibly be Fergus's type: then, as she realised that such a thing could not possibly exist, in the normal way, she found it no problem to engage her in conversation. She knew how to flatter (most of her authors, indeed, lived on flattery for want of anything more material) and soon had the presumed object of her ex-husband's desire in voluble communion. Leading the talk round to the subject of Fergus McMurtry, however, would not be so easy. She decided to broach the matter indirectly, and spoke with simulated knowledgeability about business.

They agreed that redecoration would be nice, not to mention expansion: the Bide-a-Wee Bistro, perhaps, or even Brasserie.

"Of course," Fiona cleverly concluded, "it all costs money, doesn't it! Banks can be so difficult these days, I find. But I believe I know just the man you need — he was *so* helpful to a friend of mine a little while ago — you wouldn't believe how supportive he was when it came to capital!"

"Oh, well," her interlocutor interrupted, "that wouldn't be may worry, thank guidness! It's may Partner who deals with all that sort of thing."

She leaned close to whisper coyly, "Her money, you see, may dear!"

"Oh!" said Fiona.

"Now, was there anything else?"

"What? Oh, no, no thank you. No."

Miss Phemister tripped gaily through to the kitchen, where her partner was grumbling at the sink.

"Such a nayce wee chat Ay was having with a Lady Customer!" she trilled.

"Any sign of The Beast?" growled Mrs Spurtle.

"No dear, none at all. Anyway, as Ay was saying —"

"If this goes on much longer," the widow said, "I'll damn well have to buy a dishwasher."

"Bad news, Fergus, I'm afraid," Fiona announced that evening.

"Bad news? You mean she still spurns me?"

"Up to a point. Well, no actually, I mean no, that's not what I mean, not no, she doesn't — look, you'd better sit down."

He did so.

"Now Fergus: you'll have to brace yourself for a shock, I'm afraid."

"You did speak to her, didn't you?"

"Oh yes, we spoke all right. There she was, bringing the orders out just like you said; I started a conversation about the business and we chatted away like anything. Then she rather dropped a bombshell."

"You don't mean — you don't mean she's . . . engaged already?"

"No dear, nothing like that. Leastways, as far as I know. No, it's worse than that. *She hasn't got any money!*"

"Wh-what? But that's ridiculous! The business has thousands, just lying idle."

"Yes; but not hers — it's all the partner's you see."

"The *partner's*? You mean to tell me *Miss Phemister* . . . Fiona?"

But she was giggling too helplessly to reply.

The next day, Hamish Ganglion enjoyed a longer interview at the Scottish Amiable and Providential Bank: long enough, at any rate, to agree a loan with the rather distant manager. He showed Mr McMurtry the letter of guarantee. Mr McMurtry did not ask for further details which, since Hamish did not know them, was just as well.

Hamish smiled broadly at Mr Haq as he left the office, but the latter for some reason seemed abstracted and did not respond.

He returned to the flat and told Grace the good news: now they could buy Smellie's, now they could move house. Grace could make their nest, they could run the two businesses: all would be as they had willed it to be.

But Grace's reaction seemed strangely low key, and Hamish grew anxious.

"This is what you wanted, isn't it?" he asked.

"Mmm? Yes, oh yes Hamish, it's wonderful, really. Well done. I'm really very pleased, honestly."

"You don't sound it," Hamish said. "There's nothing wrong, is there?"

"No . . . no, nothing. Only . . . it's just that . . . Hamish, you know I've been taking Misogynon, don't you?"

"No, what's that then? A new magazine?"

"Oh *Hamish*, really! It shows how much you care!"

"Care? I like that! Aw, hell, don't cry, I'm sorry. Tell me about Misogynon."

"It's — it's what I went to Dr Ghouleagh for," she sniffed, "two months ago, when you said you were fed up of going to Meiklejohn's for, you know, those : . . things."

"Oh, yeah, I get you now. It's great not having to ask Miss Reekie for twelve-packs any more. So, what about it?"

"I don't think it's worked very well, Hamish," she said.

11

Matrimonial Causes

Grace Wemyss' misgivings in regard to the efficacy of the Misogynon pill (prescribed by the good Dr Ghouleagh in order to spare her swain the awkwardness of demanding alternative prophylaxis from Miss Reekie at the chemist) seemed eventually to be well founded. For a few weeks after her suspicions were first roused she did nothing: for one thing, there was all the excitement of buying the shop, of ordering a new sign — SCOTTISH PRODUCE CENTRE AND HERB GARDEN — to replace SMELLIE G EENG OCE , of going through her club books to choose from the tempting array of bedroom suites, lounge furnishings and bathroom accessories for the new house, of generally fixing and securing the new frontier of the Ganglion-Wemyss business empire, and for another there was Hamish's own advice that embarking on a course of oral contraception often resulted in hormonal changes which had the effect of temporarily disrupting the menstrual cycle. He spoke with authority and conviction, having but recently read an article to this effect in a magazine at the dentist's.

Indeed, a whole month slipped by before her unease returned with redoubled force. The phenomenon known to Maureen O'Rourke's senior dancing sorority as 'The Monthly Visitors' failed, once again, to appear, and this time, as she told me herself, she went to the doctor about it.

Thaddeus Ghouleagh M.B., Ch.B., listened attentively, the nervous tic below his left eye more or less completely under control, as his patient unfolded her anxieties, helping her over the occasional hurdle of embarrassment with a soothing grunt of encouragement. By the time she had finished, Grace already felt a lot better. There had always been something about talking to kind old Dr Ghouleagh that made her feel this way.

The physician smiled warmly, "Well my dear," he said. "I think we'd better just have a little look round first, don't you? Just to be on the safe side. Just slip behind the screen, my dear, like the good girl you are."

Grace willingly assented: ever since that nasty dose of 'flu — which turned out not to be 'flu at all in the end — when she was fourteen, she had been accustomed to these examinations. It was because he was always so thorough, she realised, that he was such a good doctor. That, and his lovely warm hands. After a lengthy and painstaking investigation Dr Ghouleagh professed himself completely satisfied. She dressed and resumed her seat, feeling curiously suffused with healthy vitality.

"Now then my dear, what exactly is the nature of your little trouble, did you say?"

She briefly recapitulated and produced from her handbag the blister-pack in current use.

"I've been very careful, doctor," she said. "I've never missed a day, as you can see."

"Hmmm," said Dr Ghouleagh, turning the packet over and over with his elegant fingers. "Aah, Misogynon, Misogynon, purple packet, now let me see, there was something . . . now then where did I see it at all I wonder? Just a few weeks ago it was, dear knows there's so much to read these days and all the new names . . . let me see now . . ." He stood up, a little stiffly, and shuffled across to the filing cabinets.

"I'm certain sure about the colour of it, though," he muttered. "Don't often get purple stuff these days, for some reason."

The modern physician exercises his vocation in conditions that would be unrecognisable to such antediluvian practitioners as Finlay and Cameron, or even Snoddie, for whom effective treatment — or its reverse — was for most of the time a simple enough matter of striking the right balance between the dosage of a trusted nostrum and the application of horse sense. While there are still the good old-fashioned ailments like the bad back and the streaming cold, and while it is true that they remain, happily, as impervious to cure as they ever were, the managing director of the present-day Primary Health Care Agency has to cope with a veritable pantheon of pathogeny and pathognomy, a myriad of maladies ranging in ineluctable variety from aphasia to zymosis. Thankfully he is not alone in his Promethean struggle: he has the drug companies, whose products seem sometimes almost to precede the ailments for which they may be prescribed, to help him and they in turn, thank goodness, have the support of the many promotional agencies whose mission it is to ensure that nobody in the developed world should feel unprofitably poorly. To this end they see to it that the average British GP receives a fair-sized rain forest's worth of instruction, enlightenment and reasonable inducement, all so that we — the assets, as it were, of the whole Caring business — may fulfil our moral, social and economic duty to be, within agreed parameters, healthy.

The Craigfieth practice of Drs Bodkin and Ghouleagh has evolved its own strategy for dealing with this daily tide of promotional material. Eschewing such faddishnesses as medical secretaries, and being too busy working, so to speak, at the heather-roots of their profession to indulge in such distractions as refresher courses, they have instituted instead an in-house filing system into which, so sophisticated have their skills become, much of what thunders through their letterbox may be placed unopened. This uniquely simple system consists of three large drawers labelled respectively S (for Samples), F (for Freebies), and B (for Bumf). The first drawer, thanks to the foolproof instructions attending each tube, vial or sachet, enjoys a rapid turnover; the second has provided the fortunate denizens of Mid Lummock with physicians who have profited (for instance) from their experience on fact-finding missions to Bangkok (Venereal Disease Control — Dr Ghouleagh) and Tibet (Altitude Sickness — Dr Bodkin). The third drawer is kept in manageable order by the simple expedient, when it is full, of throwing out from the back in order to make room at the front. Proceeds from the sale of material thus discarded to a collector from Eco-Cycle plc, Dunbroath, furnish the practice with a useful source of secondary income.

It was in this drawer that Dr Ghouleagh now rummaged, with much grunting and muttering, and from which he at length produced a circular from Messrs HelvetiaChem which bore an illustration instantly recognised by Grace Wemyss as being that of her particular brand of pharmaceutical marvel.

"Now then!" beamed the good doctor, resuming his seat, "let's see what it says, shall we? Where's my reading glasses now . . . ah, good, here we are then. Der, derum, derderderder, deriphm, zzzz, zzz, hmm, oh! 'Unfortunate transposition on an unattended capsuling belt', ur, derderum, drummmn, umm, 'resulting in the dispatch to suppliers in your sales area of', erm, hrmm, der, oh sweet Jesus! Wait till I have a look at one of dese little devils now, come on out wit you, now then . . . oh dear! Oh, goodness gracious now who'd have thought it, eh? Well now I'll be jiggered with an oily feather! Just goes to show, my dear, doesn't it now?"

"What, Dr Ghouleagh? What does it say?"

"Eh? Oh, yes, yes of course! Well, my dear, what seems to have happened is that there's been this little mix-up, you see, at the factory. You've been taking something else by mistake, that's all."

"?!" said Grace.

"Just one of these little mistakes, my dear, that reminds us we're only human after all!"

Finding speech at last Grace whispered, "What . . . what is it that I've been taking, Doctor? Is it . . . something bad?"

"Good gracious girl! Something bad? Now whatever makes you think that I, who brought you into the world all naked and helpless, should want to bundle you out of it? Eh? Not lost your faith in your good old Uncle Ghouleagh after all these years now, have you?"

"Oh no — no, Doctor, of course not! It's just, well, some of these drugs, I mean . . . if they're not, you know . . . suitable?"

"Tush girl! You've been reading too many newspapers! A dangerous thing I've always thought, reading, in the wrong hands. No, I expect it's something quite harmless, let's see now, what do they say . . . ah yes, here we are: Mammogynon, that's what it is and there you are, you see? Worrying your pretty head over nothing, just like I said!"

"Oh!" Grace laughed nervously. "Good! Erm, what's Mammo–, Mam-mal–. . . what you said, what is it, Doctor?"

"Eh? Oh well it's just, it's . . . where are we? Ah! Oh well now, look at that, just six and two trees all along! It's another wee Pill, my dear, just a different horse for the same course as you might say, only this one's for nursing mothers, you see!"

"Oh," said Grace.

"So that's nothing to worry about, now is it?"

"No, I suppose it isn't, Doctor, only . . ."

"Only what, my dear?"

"Only I thought, well . . . Mam said, once, when she was . . . you know, telling me . . . things, she said women who were . . . doing that, with babies I mean, didn't, I mean couldn't . . . you know, if they — with their husbands of course — if they . . . well, if they did."

"Ho, ho! That's what we modern medicos call a popular fallacy, as the Art master's wife said to the gardener. No, I'm afraid the Holy Father and I have to part company on that one. In my experience it's only true for ladies who've had a long delivery and only then if they've had episiotomy as well, in which case the question hardly arises, as Cleopatra said to the eunuch. No, apparently this little Mammogynon devil is a low-dosage precaution, just to take care of things until life gets back to normal."

"Low dosage? Oh, but surely — I mean, what you're saying is then I could be, I mean I could *really* be — oh dear, what am I going to do?"

"Why, have the little brute I expect! That is, if you *are*, of course. Why, what are the tears for now? Come along, me dear, there's no call for all that now is there, eh? A fine healthy girl like you, why you'll just sail through it no bother! And you'll have your good old Uncle Ghouleagh to look after ye and give ye lots of check-ups, won't you now, hmmm? So what's there to cry about in that?"

"N-nothing, Doctor," Grace sobbed. "I — I always wanted to ha—, have one one day. B-but it's Hamish and me Doctor, we're . . . we're — oh dear!"

"You're what?" snapped Dr Ghouleagh. "What are you? Don't tell me you're brother and sister for I've a very acute memory and I've got your good Mamma down for three sockets and not a spigot in sight! Come along now girl, spit it out!"

"We're not married!" wailed Grace.

"Great plates of ambrosia!" wheezed the physician. "Is that all? Well good gracious now that's easily remedied isn't it? I suppose you can bear to put up with him for another forty years or so?"

"Oh!" Grace pondered this awhile. "Yes, yes, I suppose so."

"Well, there y'are, then! I take it you've no theosophical animadversions to the grand old institution of matrimonial bondage?"

"Oh no, Doctor, never!" Grace looked shocked. "We don't like that sort of thing."

"Well, then. Away ye go, me dear, and make an honest man of him! Only, before you do that, perhaps you'll be so kind as to make me a little water and bring it into surgery, a jam jar'll do if ye wash it out first, and then we'll see if your journey's really necessary, won't we?"

"Yes of course, Doctor. I'll do everything you say."

"That's the girl! Now away you skip and we'll see you in a day or so with a nice pot of wee-wee and I'll give you a good, long examination. Would ye like that?"

"Oh yes, thank you Doctor! You're very kind."

"Just pursuin' me vocation, me dear," replied Dr Ghouleagh and, patting Grace affectionately on the head, the shoulder and the right buttock, he saw her out.

Grace found a nearly-empty 2lb mincemeat jar left over from her Christmas shopping at the Bonnie Braes Cash 'n' Carry, washed it out and found it just big enough for her requirements the next morning. A sample of this sample was sent off and Grace was thoroughly examined just in case; in due course the result came back and Dr Ghouleagh was able to examine her in earnest.

"And if it's half as bonny as ye were yerself, me dear, then ye can be well pleased!" he said.

Grace and Hamish talked it over that night. The first part of their discussion proceeded roughly as follows:

(a) It didn't really matter one way or the other, did it, because

(b) They loved each other, didn't they?

(c) Well, then.

(d) In that case . . .

(e) Aye, right enough.

(f) It was bound to happen sooner or later, and besides,

(g) They were what really mattered, weren't they?

(h) Oh, aye.

(i) Well, then.

(j) So.

(k) So this was it then, eh?

(l) Yes, this was it.

(m) Oh well, why not?

(n) Darling!

(o) Now, she meant?

(p) That's what they'd decided, wasn't it?

(q) Suppose so . . .

(r) . . . he meant yes, of course!

(s) Darling!

(t) Right, then. Right.

After all, this was Craigfieth.

In the second part of their disussion they decided against a church wedding because churches made Hamish feel peculiar and he wasn't sure they would let you do it there anyway if you hadn't been christened, and because Grace did not feel she could wear white and feel completely clean inside, and there wasn't any point in it, really, if you didn't wear white that is.

They resolved to see the Registrar first thing in the morning. At three o'clock that afternoon — it being Thursday, and early closing — they came to see me.

"It's the way he said it, Mr MacIain, that's what was really hurtful!" Grace said.

"Aye, that's right," agreed Hamish.

"I felt like he thought I was just *dirt* — oh, it was horrible!"

She started to sniff.

"It shouldn't be allowed, Mr MacIain, that's what we think. Not in this day and age. Here pet, use mine."

Grace blew her nose. "Can you do anything about it, Mr MacIain?"

They had visited Mr Cyril Bullock, Craigfieth's Registrar, having first left their shops in the charge, respectively, of Eric the YTS and Dolina the JTS. Their reception had been frosty: it turned out that Mr Bullock knew all about the reason for their visit, his sister-in-law being the surgery's receptionist. He even quoted the precise date of Grace's anticipated parturition.

"Oh!" Hamish had said. "So when do you think you'll be able to do it, Mr Bullock?"

Mr Bullock smiled thinly.

"That is a rather difficult question, young man."

Grace burst in. "Oh, I know there'll have to be banns posted and all that, Mr Bullock. We'd have come before — a long time ago — but we sort of kept putting it off, didn't we, Hamish, and well, you know how it is Mr Bullock, don't you. Anyway, we're here now and that's what matters, isn't it?" she smiled.

"Indeed, *Miss* Wemyss," replied the evangelical Registrar, "it is quite clear to me that you know not what matters at all, or you would *not* be here now."

"Oh . . . I'm sorry, Mr Bullock, is there something we should have done first, someone else we should have seen?" asked Grace.

Mr Bullock laughed mirthlessly. "You may well ask, my girl, aye, and you may ask for all Eternity and still not heed the answer!"

"I'm s-s-sorry," Grace stammered. "I don't quite understand."

"No!" rang out the reply. "No, you do not, and your sinful ignorance is manifest in the eyes of the Lord! Do not imagine, my girl, that He who knows the number of hairs on thy head should allow His faithful servants here below to let thy transgressions pass unchastised!"

"Hey, hang about!" Hamish intervened. "What's all this got to do with us getting married?"

"Hold your peace, young man! You also are not without blame in this sorry business! Those who fall are not without their portion of damnation."

Grace reached for Hamish's arm. "What's he talking about, Hamish?" she asked.

"Do not feign innocence to me, my girl! I speak of the serpent Lust, and of Eve's uncleanliness that first brought Sin on earth. Aye, blush for shame! Thy redness will become thee when thou'rt chained in the brimstone lake!"

Grace burst into tears. Encumbered as he was, Hamish stepped forward.

"Now look here," he protested. "You can't say that sort of thing, you're a Registrar!"

"I know my duty," replied Mr Bullock primly.

"Well then, are you going to do it? I mean, that's what Registrars are for, isn't it, marrying people? Not carrying on like the Spanish Inquisition!"

Mr Bullock hissed.

"There is no call to be offensive, young man," he said.

"No call — jings! I like that! Look, Mr Bullock, you just give us a straight answer: are you going to marry us, or not?"

"I think you would do well to reconsider," replied Mr Bullock. "You may decide it would be better to go elsewhere. I shall be happy to give you a list of other Registrars in the region."

"But we don't want to go somewhere else!" wailed Grace. "Do we, Hamish? We want to be married here, it's our home! Won't you do it for us?"

"It is a dirty bird that defiles its own nest," was the Registrar's reply. "Let us just say, shall we, that I should be most reluctant. Look into your hearts. Good day to you." He began to close the door.

"Hey!" exclaimed Hamish. "That's no answer! Will you or won't you?"

"My conscience is clear, young man," said Mr Bullock. "I shall do my duty."

He shut the door.

"It was awful," said Grace. "He was so — so *horrible!*"

"Yes," I said. "I quite see what you mean. It's not the sort of thing you expect, is it? The point is, what do you want me to do about it?"

"Well —" began Grace, then looked at Hamish.

"Well," said Hamish. "I mean, well, get him to do it, I suppose. I mean, he's got to, hasn't he?"

"Oh yes. The law is quite clear on that, as far as I know, provided you both satisfy the requirement of residence, which you do, and so long as you are both free to marry, which you are, aren't you?"

"Does that mean your Mam and Dad agreeing to it?" asked Grace.

"Gracious no! That doesn't enter into it except in England, where they're still a bit scared of sex, and then only if you're under eighteen. No, it means so long as you aren't married already."

"That'd be daft, though?" said Hamish. "I mean, if you were married already, you wouldn't need to, would you?"

"To someone else," I said.

"Oh," said Hamish.

"What a funny idea!" said Grace. "Who'd want to do a thing like that?"

I shrugged. "Well, it takes all sorts you know, Miss Wemyss, and the law has to cater for them all, in its way."

"Just imagine!" Grace commented.

"Anyway, the point is you're quite right, he *will* have to marry you, and that is what Registrars are for — marrying people who either can't have a church wedding or don't want one. Only what I ought to ask you is —"

"What, Mr MacIain?"

"Well, I was going to say . . . no. No, it can wait. Let's ring Mr Bullock first, shall we, and see if it hasn't all been a big mistake."

It had not.

Mr Bullock was deferential at first, indeed almost unctuously so, a reaction not uncommon among inhabitants of petty office who are unexpectedly confronted with one of the minor secular deities. He was pleased, indeed humbly honoured, to confirm that he was indeed Registrar of Births, Deaths and Marriages for the District of Craigfieth and yes, certainly he would be most gratified to assist me in any capacity with my enquiries and, oh, not at all, it was nothing, and so on. Thereafter his manner changed abruptly. Scarcely had the name of Ganglion been spoken than the Registrar was addressing me as a jumped-up little whippersnapper the like of whom it was beneath his dignity to talk to. Then, to employ a euphemism, he replaced his receiver.

There then remained only one thing to be done. It is a cardinal rule of legal practitioners never to commit cursor to screen without first securing the Fee. The firm of Crawford, Crawford and Potts is not, after all, a charitable institution, and work had been rather thin on the ground lately, at least for its junior member.

They signed the appropriate form, Hamish with an indecipherable flourish, Grace in the carefully rounded hand she had doubtless perfected in her third year at Craigfieth High School (English: Neat Worker, C+).

"What are you going to do?" she asked.

"Well, I shall write to the Registrar General in Edinburgh to register a formal complaint on your behalf, and I shall write to Mr Bullock advising him of this letter and inviting him to reconsider his decision. The only trouble is . . ."

"Yes?"

"The only trouble is that these things take time. The mills of bureaucracy grind slowly, when they grind at all, and I don't expect Bullock to do anything at all until he feels he has to. How long can you — I mean, how long could you stand waiting?"

"Oh!" Grace exclaimed. "But we've got to . . . that is, well, no one wants to wait longer than they have to, do they?"

"We'd not want it to look obvious," Hamish translated. "Not in the photos, anyway."

"Quite so," I said. "In that case I must ask you, are you sure you don't want a church wedding?"

"No." Grace was firm.

"You don't want one?"

"No!" she said. "It wouldn't seem right, now. Folk would know why we were doing it. It would be like admitting we'd been — been . . . bad. We want to do it properly, don't we Hamish?"

"I see. And you're absolutely determined on being married by Mr Bullock, are you?"

They looked puzzled.

"This is what I was going to say earlier, you see. The point is, given that he's been horrible to you, are you really sure you want *him* to marry you?"

"Well . . . but," Grace began.

Hamish was a little quicker on the uptake. "Why, who else is there?"

"A depute, presumably," I said.

"Oh!" said Grace. "You mean Mr Bullock has . . . that there's someone else who could do it?"

"Oh, yes. Every Registrar has an appointed depute, in case of emergency. If the Registrar was off on holiday and there was a baby to be registered, someone would have to do it or the parents would be breaking the law."

"Mr Bullock never goes away," Grace muttered gloomily.

"All the same," I persisted, "he has to have a depute, just in case. You see, I'm thinking it might just be possible, without going through all the long-drawn-out business of the law, to persuade him to let his depute do it, if we knew who he was. Or she. Do you?"

They shook their heads, although Grace looked hopeful.

"You could find out though, couldn't you?"

"Oh I expect so, yes. I could —"

"No!" Hamish interrupted. "No, we don't want that. Bullock's got to take back what he said; he's got to do what he's supposed to, hasn't he pet?"

"We-ell," began Grace.

"You do want us to get married properly, don't you?"

"Oh yes! Yes, Hamish, of course I do!"

"Well, then, that's settled. We leave it to you, Mr MacIain. Don't we, Grace?"

She gave way before her patriarch.

"Yes, Hamish, if you say so," she cooed.

"Right, then," I said. "One more thing — for how long has Bullock been the Registrar, do you know?"

They looked blank. "Always, I think," said Grace.

I saw them out.

There is a school of thought which teaches that the pomp and ceremony attendant on any institution is inversely proportional to its own perception of its right to exercise authority. Adherents of this philosophy argue their case with reference, for example, to organised religion. The Roman Catholic hierarchy, they say, being historically the more intellectual Christian faction, recognise the fundamental implausibility of their professed faith and so surround it with a beguiling wealth of costume and ritual while the Protestants, in ascending order of Scriptural rigour and descending order of cerebral endowment, strip away the saving layers of ceremonial until the basic tenets are exposed to the ridicule of all save themselves alone. That, they say, is why the Romists offer a good show, bags of mumbo-jumbo and the option of deathbed repentance while the Reformists insist on a regimen of plain worship, unequivocal language and a lifetime of tedious good works — indeed it explains (they maintain) why the most extreme Calvinist groupuscules are reduced to the gloomy certainties of predestination, and why the Papists, realising that no movement can survive long without new recruits, attack contraception while their opponents attempt instead to wipe out sex.

Within this framework of outlook, so the argument goes on, it can be seen that schools which insist upon discipline and uniform are, in fact, hotbeds of anarchy with no belief in the redeeming value of education, while those that cheerfully abolish rules and let their pupils wear whatever they like are fundamentally secure societies dedicated to the perfectibility of the human race: the unfortunate tendency towards unquestioning uniformity among the products of such liberated establishments is a predictable, if somewhat unfortunate outcome of this rationalistic outlook. Look, say these iconophiles, at Parliament itself: the ermined Peer knows that he is participating in an agreeably harmless nonsense but the lounge-suited backbench MP, poor sap, actually believes he is doing something Important and Worthwhile.

It is tempting, when contemplating the Law, to subscribe to these teachings, for certain it is that those who yoke their fortunes to it become members of a society whose gorgeous flummery makes even the most arcane Freemason appear positively subfusc by comparison. Moreover, when it comes down to practicalities, its ability to aid the average citizen faced with the average injustice is roughly equivalent to that of a rabbit with terminal *taedium vitae* faced with a really determined ferret.

There is, in short, virtually no legal remedy against what the majority of folk not hampered by a Law degree would instantly recognise as a breach of natural justice (which, as we all learn in our freshman lecture, There Is No Such Thing As). Against the twin evils of incompetence and bigotry there is no recourse save to the relevant professional organisations who, existing as they do in a state of collegiate rectitude and accustomed as they are to pursuing courses of action which make Death itself seem quite a stimulating affair, are unlikely to deliver judgments satisfactory to any but their own easily satisfied selves. This is known as 'self-regulation'. Should you happen to be raped by your dentist while under anaesthetic, you may eventually succeed in having him put away for a year or two; should, however, you happen to experience the not uncommon misfortune of having the wrong tooth pulled, or your nerve drilled, or your perfectly healthy wisdom teeth extracted in a fit of misguided dental zeal, you may as well abandon immediately all thought of compensation: content yourself instead with having yet another grisly anecdote with which to bore people at parties.

I did not, therefore, entertain any sanguine hope of bringing Mr Bullock to book though I would, in consideration of the pecuniary undertaking entered into by Hamish Ganglion, go through the motions of an attempt, knowing as I did so what the outcome would be.

There are, however, more ways of killing a cat than by prosecuting it for crossing a motorway without due care and attention to other road users. The question of which comes first, the propensity for suspecting and exploiting human turpitude or the Diploma in Legal Practice, is a nice one and not within the competence of this tale to explore, the reader having suffered enough ersatz philosophy already. Suffice it to say that I made two telephone calls: the first to a friend who had, for my purposes, the good fortune to live within walking distance of the Public Records Office in leafy Kew and the second to the office of the Registrar General for Scotland where a very personable voice answering to the name of Ishbel informed me, after an efficient pause to check the microfiche, that the previous occupant of the post of Registrar of Births, Marriages and Deaths for the District of Craigfieth had been a Major Godfrey Pitt-Holyoake.

I drove to Craigfieth the next day, dropping my speed involuntarily as I passed the sign welcoming me as A Careful Driver, and pulled up outside the Craft Corner behind a minibus proclaiming itself the flagship of Duff Tours, Tel C'fth 263.

A kilted gentleman was leaving the shop with his mate, a deeply tanned lady in a tartan trouser suit.

"Fergit it, Martha," he was telling her. "It's just another goddam schlock store."

They boarded the bus and sped off to photograph the Standing Stones of Muckle Dull.

Mrs Pitt-Holyoake was still bristling behind her counter.

"That man," she said, "just said the most dreadful thing about my Coos!"

I looked around: there was no one else in the shop.

"Your — Coos?"

"Yes, my Coos! Really, for a man whose country gave us the cabbage patch doll, to criticise my Craigfieth Coos is a bit much, don't you think?"

She held one up for inspection.

"You can't see anything wrong with it, can you?"

Fluency in doublethink is one of the first proficiencies acquired by the practising lawyer. The article held up by Mrs Pitt-Holyoake was pre-eminently the sort of thing a first-time Tory voter in the West Midlands of England might dangle from the driving mirror of his Ford Escort.

"Nothing at all, Mrs Pitt-Holyoake," I said. "It's charming, of its kind, isn't it?"

"And very popular with our *discerning* visitors too, I'm glad to say. Such fashionable colours, aren't they?"

"I believe they are, yes."

"Some lengths of velour," the craftswoman explained, "left over from Maureen's Girls' last refit. So handy! Now, then, what can I be doing for you?"

"As a matter of fact," I said, "I haven't actually come here to buy anything, I'm afraid. It's just a little bit of research that's cropped up in the office — I believe your late husband was Registrar here for some years?"

Mrs Pitt-Holyoake replaced the Coo with the others in their hand-woven wicker ashet (£4.95) and assumed a wistful expression.

"Indeed he was, Mr MacIain, in fact it was almost the first thing that happened after we removed here — it was just after the War, you know, and the specialists had recommended Perthshire for poor Godfrey's wound — we came down one morning, or rather I did, poor Godfrey was down all the time, of course, to find quite a little deputation at the door and, well, believe me Mr MacIain, they practically begged Godfrey to take on the responsibility and — oh! poor Godfrey, he never could bring himself to be brutal with people, you know, and say no — he agreed right away. No thought for himself, naturally, but then that was my Godfrey all over, bless him. It Hastened His End, of course."

She sniffed.

"Such a fine man you know, Mr MacIain, my Godfrey, though he never got any thanks for it as you may imagine."

We mused awhile on the distressing phenomenon of human ingratitude. Then I said:

"I don't suppose you'd happen to remember, would you, whether your husband appointed an Assistant, to take over from him in case of . . . unavailability?"

She replied with vehemence: "Indeed I do, Mr MacIain, and it just goes to show what a fine man he was! Believe me, I tried to talk him out of it, I told him, 'No one will thank you for it,' I said, ' least of all the man himself!' But of course, being Godfrey, he just said, 'Well, m'dear, we're not put on this earth for that, you know' — those were his very words to me, Mr MacIain — so there it was, the appointment went through! It was because he was a brother-in-arms, you see, that's what Godfrey said, with his way to make in the world, so of course Godfrey had to help him."

"Who, Mrs Pitt-Holyoake? Who was it?"

She told me.

"And do you know, and this is the funny thing, he still is! Yes! Though I expect he's forgotten it himself by now. You see, when poor Godfrey . . . Passed On, they never made him Registrar in his place — well, naturally, they only agreed to him being Assistant in the first place for Godfrey's sake, really — they appointed Mr Bullock instead. But they never appointed a new Assistant, that I know for a fact. Just imagine!"

"Yes indeed," I replied. "Imagine."

I negotiated the purchase of a digital clock paperweight in the likeness of the Pictish Stone of Craigfieth as a birthday present for my brother-in-law Nigel, the investment consultant, and took my leave some twenty minutes later, leaving Mrs Pitt-Holyoake to silence, and her Coos.

It does not pay to be hasty, even when one is not being paid by the hour. I returned home to digest my news, and found a message on my answering machine from my friend in Kew. I dialled her number.

"Goodness!" she said. "You *are* eager, aren't you!"

"It was a very tempting message," I said.

"Poor MacIain! Reduced to digging up the dirt for divorces already, are you? A squalid end to a once-promising legal career, I call it!"

"It isn't, and I'm not — not as such, anyway. It's just a — well, a little ploy of my own to help a client in distress. I'm being very public-spirited actually, did you but know it. You'd approve, honestly."

"I doubt it," she said. "Anyway, mine not to reason why, mere woman that I am, though I must say I find it all very depressing. When are you going to stop piddling your life away up there and do something worthwhile?"

"When are you going to leave your husband?"

"When he gives me good reason to. Don't nag, MacIain, you'll spoil it. Now then, do you want me to tell you what I found out, or don't you?"

"I can't go on like this, you know," I said.

"I do know. Exciting, isn't it? Now then: first of all, the answer to your question is no. I drew a blank."

"Damn!"

"Well really, dear, you can't expect people to leave their shady pasts conveniently lying around just because you want them to, you know."

"I know — it's just that it runs counter to my estimation of the man, that's all," I explained.

"Ah, not so fast! You may find your estimations didn't go far enough."

"Meaning?"

"Meaning I dug a little deeper, my dear!"

"Oh?"

"That's what I like about you, MacIain, your spontaneous gushes of gratitude. Fair bowl a girl over, they do."

"Sorry," I muttered. "Consider it gushed. What are you talking about?"

"I'm talking about Deed Polls, that's what. Subject did not always answer to his present name, you see."

"You're a genius! What —"

"Bull," she said. "Cedric Bull. Not very imaginative, is he?"

"Perhaps he felt years younger after he'd done it. Are you going to tell me he did what I hope he did?"

"Yup! In 1938, to a Miss Daphne Dullis, Spinster of the Parish of Deptford. Sounds awful, doesn't it?"

"Awful? It's wonderful! And you're sure there's no annulment?"

"Nope. He upped and left, the dirty devil. And before you ask, yes, she's still alive, somewhere, only you must promise me one thing."

"Go on."

"Promise you won't screw her life up — I mean, if she's got married again without bothering with the formalities, you won't land her in the shit, will you?"

"Cross my heart, no I won't. Honestly. Anne, how can I thank you?"

"Not over the phone. Look, I must dash — it's all in the post, I photocopied it. I just hope it's in a *really* good cause, okay?"

"It is," I assured her, but she had gone.

There followed three days of frustration, resulting from Mr Crawford Senior's decision to favour me with the paperwork necessary to enable one of Scotland's minor feudal barons to make his workforce redundant and convert their leases to Shorthold Tenancies as part of the preparation required for the realisation of his assets. Although the promised material duly arrived in Thursday afternoon's post, it was not until Saturday morning that I was able to do anything about it. Lawyers do not normally labour at weekends, of course, but I had little else to do of any consequence and Miss Wemyss' condition argued haste, lest she be obliged to celebrate her swelling nuptials furth of the burgh.

I called first at the home of the unexpected Depute Registrar who, contrary to Mrs Pitt-Holyoake's prediction, was perfectly aware of his office and keen, once I had explained to him all the ramifications of my little scheme, to go along with my somewhat unorthodox plan for the acquittal of it.

I decided, on grounds of conspicuity, against his offer of transport. I parked my car some distance from the ordered fecundity of the Jerusalem House garden and left him in it.

Mrs Elspeth Bullock answered the door.

"Good morning," I said. "I should like to speak to the Registrar, please. Is he in?"

"Have you an appointment?" she snapped.

I admitted I had not. "I didn't expect to need one," I explained. "Is this a busy time of year for Registrars?"

"Mr Bullock is busy just now at his sacred affairs. If you give me your name and address and state the nature of your business I will arrange an appointment for you. In the Registrar's office."

Her mouth slammed shut and she prepared with one beefy arm to do the same thing to the door.

"My name doesn't matter at this stage," I said. "Perhaps you could just give him this instead. I think he will find it merits urgency."

The informal curriculum of the Law School of Edinburgh University included lessons in the coarser aspects of the craft from a retired bailiff who used to haunt the howffs of the city in search of undergraduate prey. I handed Mrs Bullock a sealed brown envelope in such a way as to preclude her refusal to accept it. ("The victim," our mentor taught us, leering over a glass of Trawler rum, "can never resist the temptation of a sealed brown envelope.") She left the front door wedged on my foot in forced compromise between slamming it in my face and inviting me to wait inside.

Barely a minute passed before it was opened again by Mr Bullock himself, his redeemed countenance betraying little of the depredations doubtless being wrought by the maggots of uncertainty within. Mrs Bullock stood at the end of the passage, whose sombre walls were hung with texts of complacent admonition and framed certificates from various Bible schools and religious publishing houses, her arms folded grimly below the subjugate swell of her girdled bosom.

"So sorry to have kept you," purred the Evangelist. "Perhaps you'd care to step into my study?"

He showed me into a poky ground-floor room at the rear of the house. The floor was lined with the sort of parquet-imitating linoleum usually favoured by students' landlords and the set designers for Harold Pinter plays on television.

There was a small Victorian iron safe in one corner, a desk complete with inkstand and blotter bearing inverted evidence of Mr Bullock's conscientious copperplate, and a swivel chair of the type once reserved for Secondary School headteachers. A trestle table against the far wall supported a spirit duplicator, the progenitor of *Craigfieth Gospel News*, an occasional publication that is, in its way, as unrelenting in its pursuit of doctrinal rigour as *Militant* and as unheedful of the niceties of defamation as *Private Eye*, though without the humour of either. Above this, on the wall, was a large signed photograph proclaiming fraternal expressions of solidarity from the Falwell Mission of America (International) Inc.

Mr Bullock shut the door firmly behind us and crossed the floor to face me, his burnished brogues hard and heavy on the pounded lino.

"Now then sonny," he hissed. "Just who do you think you are?" He drew my envelope from the inside pocket of his jacket. "And what do you call this?"

"I am Iain MacIain of Crawford, Crawford and Potts," I replied. "And I'd call that a copy of a Certificate of Marriage, Mr Bullock."

"*You!* I thought I'd dealt with you the other day. Well, *Mister* MacIain, and what do you think this proves, eh? Coming here on a Saturday morning, disturbing my wife at her domestic work, what's your little game? You'll find me a formidable adversary, MacIain, I'm warning you. You're just a child. I'm well used to cutting your sort down to size."

I essayed a smile. "I don't think this need come to adversarial dealings, Mr Bullock. I am merely attempting to act in the best interests of my clients, Mr Ganglion and

Miss Wemyss, who are, I understand, experiencing some apparently unaccountable difficulties with regard to their intended marriage."

Mr Bullock's face darkened. "That's nothing to do with—"

"As to the document you are holding, Mr Bullock, of course by itself it means nothing until it is viewed in the light of this Deed of Poll which, together with the certificate, appears upon investigation to be the sole documentation of your status prior to your present union."

I passed him Anne's other photocopy.

Craigfieth's lay pastor scanned the document recording his nominal death as Bull and resurrection as Bullock, while his transatlantic brother in Christ looked sternly on.

"I take it Mrs Bull was not in the habit of reading the *Daily Telegraph*," I ventured. "One could always ask her, of course. Did you know she was still alive?"

His mouth opened and closed, once, twice, wordlessly. The temptation to embroider in a good cause proved irresistible.

"Oh yes! She had a hard time of it, naturally, after your army pay stopped coming in but she managed somehow, and never tried to track you down. Apparently she is still under the impression that it was all her fault, in some way, and that one day you will forgive her and come back. I find that very touching, don't you Mr Bullock?"

He flung the papers at me, then strode across to the safe.

"All right, MacIain, how much do you want?"

"I beg your pardon?"

"*How much?* To keep this quiet and leave me alone? Come on, I know your sort, you needn't look so surprised."

It was my turn to blush.

"Myself, I want nothing, Mr Bullock. My clients, however, for reasons I must say I find quite incomprehensible, wish you to perform the secular ceremony of marriage for them in their own town. That is all."

He froze, his hand still on the combination lock.

"You bastard," he said. "Honest-to-goodness blackmail's too good for you, isn't it?"

I shrugged. "Take it or leave it, Mr Bullock. I'm not in a position to alter the terms."

He straightened, slowly.

"My position in this town . . ."

"Won't be worth much if this gets out, will it? Of course I realise unmarried partners get a pretty bad press in Deuteronomy, along with ox-rustlers and so forth, but even the ancient Hebrews had a form of words for divorce, didn't they?"

"I see the Devil knows his Scripture," muttered Mr Bullock.

"Can you blame him? There's so much in it that's right up his street, after all. Now look, Mr Bullock: I can't promise anything, you must realise that, but there is just a chance —"

"Yes?"

"— and it *is* only a chance, I must stress that — that my clients might be prepared to settle for a compromise."

"Wh-what compromise?"

"Should you be prepared to nominate your Assistant to perform the ceremony in your unavoidable absence — through illness, say, or —"

"Yes! Anything, even that! I'll phone him up now, I'll —"

"No, Mr Bullock, don't do that. That would be premature. You will have to leave it to me. In the meantime I take it you would be willing to do so yourself should there be, let us say, no alternative? Having made the necessary apologies first, of course, for the distress you have caused."

Mr Bullock closed his eyes.

"Yes," he breathed.

"Well?" asked the Assistant Registrar for the District of Craigfieth.

"Success!" I said. "Now for the final fence. I'd like you to stay in the car, but keep your eye on the window in case I need you. Okay?"

"You're the boss," he replied.

We drove to the Scottish Produce Centre and Herb Garden (formerly Smellie's) where, it being by now the sacred hour of the commercial day observed even by the entrepreneurial Cllr Haq, the would-be happy couple were resting from their labours over bowls of Granny Ratter's Home-Made Scotch Broth With Noodles, mopped up with ScotBake baps, fresh from the microwave.

I apologised for my intrusion, declined Grace's kind offer to open another sachet, accepted a can of Export from Hamish, and sat down.

"I thought you might like to know what's happened," I told them. "Bullock's agreed to do it."

"Oh!" exclaimed Grace. "Oh, Mr MacIain, that's . . . how can we —? Oh, thank you! Thank you!"

"Yeah!" added Hamish, "Great — thanks pal!"

"Ooh, Hamish — we can go ahead and book the hotel now, can't we?"

"You bet!" said Hamish.

"Is this for the honeymoon?" I asked.

"Yes," Grace gushed. "Of course we can't be away for long, with the shops to run and everything, but we promised ourselves a night in the Bridal Suite at the Hydropathic, didn't we, Hamish?"

"Yeah," her swain confirmed.

"The Hydropathic? My word!"

"It's where all the personalities go," explained Grace. "When they're in Perthshire, that is."

"We saw it on *Russell Harty*," added Hamish.

"Hamish was very taken with the daycore, weren't you Hamish?"

"Yeah!" Hamish confirmed. "Mirrors." They gazed adoringly at each other.

"Well," I coughed. "There's just one thing I should add."

"Yes?"

"Oh, nothing bad, don't worry. It's just that Mr Bullock has agreed to nominate his depute, should you prefer. I thought it only right to offer you the choice."

Grace looked puzzled. "But why, Mr MacIain? Why should we want that?"

"Well —" I began. "It's probably better if I introduce you, really — I hope you don't mind, but I've got him in the car outside, if you'll just hang on a minute . . ."

I went to the window and signalled my patient accomplice.

"He's just coming," I said.

"Erm," began Hamish. "Like, is this what solicitors normally do?"

I grinned back. "Dunno," I said. "Ask a normal solicitor."

The door opened.

"Wotcher cocks!" said the Assistant Registrar. "Lickle bird tells me young Amishere's gorrour Gracie up the stick at larst. Cworr! tookyerlongennuf, dinnit? Nah then, wossorl this abahtcher gerrin-itched?"

Some time later I drove old Ganglion back to his little pinkwashed cottage in the Lummocks.

"So," he said. "Plan B it is, then. Serpity, innerway, innit?"

"In a way, I suppose," I replied. "Not that our Gospeller friend won't still be sweating a bit, but it might have been nice to see him sweat a bit harder."

"Nah then! Fort yew lot weren't serposed ter gerr-involved, never mind vindictive!"

"Ha! Yes, you're right of course. One thing puzzles me though — how did the old bugger get away with it?"

"Wot?"

"What?"

"Wot pertickler piecer thuggery-buggery woz yew halludinter?"

"Oh, I see: I was thinking about his marriage — the one here, I mean."

"Ho well! Yew can stop wunnerinabaht that. Arst yores trewly!"

"You?" My car threatened momentarily to make a dent in Lord Margoyle's beech hedge. "You mean it was —"

"Yup! Me wunnanonly discharger duty, up tiw nah. See, e'd jus become Registrar hisself, annie, an e sez ter me, Mr Ganglion, e sez, I should be obliged if yew'd do the onners fer me an Miss Calderwood, onnercounter I carn ardly dew it fer meself, nah canni? So I did, dinni?"

"I see . . . but the papers. I mean — Birth Certificates, you know —"

"Orl loss inner Blitz, *ee* sez, every friggin wun, orful trajerdy. Annercorst, I never bovvered sendinorf fer dooplicates, not my styw, narmean? Far as I'm concerned, fercuppuw wonnerget married, lerrem get married, snunnermy bizniss if they've bin a bit norty foreand, ass their lookaht an good luckter them. Corse, ole Bollocks ad that wew sussed, dinne?"

He cackled suddenly.

"Mine jew — goin backter wotjew woz sayin urlier — e wiw be sweatinnerbit, wenne finks abahtit. I mean, sposin — perish the thort, ercorse — yew an me woz ter see the light, narmean? Come over orl born agen an blab the trewf ter save our immortal wossnames? Eh? Eh!"

And he cackled again, all the way home.

The Ganglion Wedding passed off smoothly and, I have no doubt, to the great satisfaction of all concerned. In itself it was a quiet enough affair. Mr and Mrs Wemyss were there, of course, looking apprehensive and not a little suspicious, as if getting used to the couple living together had exhausted their stocks of psychological adjustment; on the groom's side were Mungo 'Slim' Beauly, ace reporter and the *Perthshire Gazette*'s resident Contemporary Music Critic, and, I am flattered to record, myself. Even this small gathering made quite a crowd in the cramped surroundings of Craigfieth Registry Office. Ganglion Senior did them proud, his morning suit (ex-Army Civvy Stores c. 1946) lending a welcome air of pageantry to the otherwise spartan ritual of the civil ceremony. The reception was held in the Rear Function Suite of the Ben Almond Hotel which Mr Wemyss, as a senior Stag, obtained at a discount. Mungo read the telegrams, some of which were phrased with just the degree of prudent ribaldry appropriate to the occasion and the place, Mr Wemyss wished his daughter well and hoped Hamish would always remember that hard work and diligence were the key to happiness, and Ganglion, evidently determined to make the most of his unique opportunity (he had not been invited to the Bullock reception) said he was blowed if he could understand what a splendid girl like Grace there could possibly see in his Amish and concluded that, whatever it was, he must have got from his mum — a remark which caused much excited speculation among the lieges, as no doubt it was intended to. Then — another surprise item — some of the bride's old comrades from her halcyon days as an O'Rourke Girl gave an animated if somewhat massive performance of Sir Peter Maxwell Davies' arrangement of 'Step We Gaily', accompanied by the Misses Urquhart on the pianoforte. Finally, the estimable banquet having been disposed of, the happy couple took to the Slippereen'd floor to lead the company in a Wedding Reel to the strains of Hector Howieson and His Harlequin Harmony Band.

At last it was all over, and Mr and Mrs Hamish Ganglion were whisked away, courtesy of Oswald Ochilree and Lady Lazarus, to the sybaritic proprieties of the Strathlummock Hydropathic Hotel. They were both back in harness on Monday morning, no doubt strengthened in their union by having secured society's blessing on it.

There are two sequels to be chronicled before this tale, and this collection of tales, is done.

Some three weeks after her honeymoon, Grace Ganglion (how she loved the reassuring alliteration of her new name!) once again presented herself in the surgery of Dr Thaddeus Ghouleagh.

"Ah! Grace my dear girl, it's yourself again already, and how's married life suitin' yer? — no! don't answer for I'm sure I can see the evidence writ large on yer smilin' handsome features! And now you'll just be slippin' yer things off for the good doctor, won't you me dear?"

"No, Dr Ghouleagh," Grace replied.

"No? Tut tut, that's not a pretty word to be using now. Whyever not?"

Grace told him whyever not.

The physician flung his arms ceilingwards.

"Well! If that isn't what I call a regular miracle, if not strictly speakin' a wholly Catholic one! Still, let's leave the

Holy Father out of this, shall we, as the nun said to the nuncio. And to be strictly scientific we'd have to say it was those naughty little Mammogynons that were playin' tricks wid yer cycle, wouldn't we, and tick the boyos in the lab off for their little mistake wid yer wee-wee. So, I suppose you'll be wanting me to put you back on yer Misogynons again, shall we say three months?"

"Oh no, Doctor!" exclaimed Grace.

"Er — no, did you say? Dear oh me, what a day this is for those noes!"

"Yes — I mean no, Doctor, I don't, I mean we . . . well, I'm married now, aren't I?"

"Indeed you are, my dear girl! And hooray for you, say I! Hooray for my wee Gracie!"

Grace blushed very prettily. "Thank you, Doctor," she murmured.

"Bless you my child! Now then, was there something else?"

"Oh no, I just came to tell you I'd . . . wasn't."

"Well, run along then my dear, back to your goodman and mind, there's to be no slip-ups this time! I'll be waitin' here for you when you've rung the bell."

"Thank you, Dr Ghouleagh," said Grace, and departed to take up her matronly vocation.

A little over three months after that I was at last able to forward to the Ganglions a letter from Register House, Edinburgh, regretting the unfortunate misunderstanding which had apparently arisen with regard to my clients' arrangements and expressing the confident belief that, this being the first time such a misunderstanding had come to their notice, it would not occur again. My clients were good enough to reply to this with a picture postcard of sunset over Ben Gunn, on the back of which was written the following message:

Thanks for yrs of the 18th we had all
most forgotten about it actually, it
seem's along time ago and we have
Something Else to think about now!!!!!
     Kind Wishes, G.Ganglion (Mrs)

And that — if, forebearing reader, you have won through with me to the end of these strange eventful histories — seems as good a point as any at which to lay them down, mindful — as who could not be? — one day to heed the polite request so tastefully expressed at these crossroads of Central Perthshire: Haste Ye Back!

The world's greatest novelists now available in
paperback from Grafton Books

Jack Kerouac

Big Sur	£2.50	☐
Visions of Cody	£2.50	☐
Doctor Sax	£1.95	☐
Lonesome Traveller	£2.50	☐
Desolation Angels	£2.95	☐
The Dharma Bums	£2.50	☐
The Subterraneans and Pic	£1.50	☐
Maggie Cassidy	£1.50	☐
Vanity of Duluoz	£1.95	☐

Norman Mailer

Cannibals and Christians (non-fiction)	£1.50	☐
The Presidential Papers	£1.50	☐
Advertisements for Myself	£2.95	☐
The Naked and The Dead	£2.95	☐
The Deer Park	£2.95	☐

Henry Miller

Black Spring	£2.95	☐
Tropic of Cancer	£2.95	☐
Tropic of Capricorn	£2.95	☐
Nexus	£3.50	☐
Sexus	£3.50	☐
Plexus	£2.95	☐
The Air-Conditioned Nightmare	£2.50	☐

Luke Rhinehart

The Dice Man	£2.95	☐
The Long Voyage Back	£1.95	☐

To order direct from the publisher just tick the titles you want
and fill in the order form.

GF281

The world's greatest novelists now available in paperback from Grafton Books

Kurt Vonnegut

Breakfast of Champions	£2.50	☐
Mother Night	£1.95	☐
Slaughterhouse 5	£2.50	☐
Player Piano	£2.95	☐
Welcome to the Monkey House	£1.95	☐
God Bless You, Mr Rosewater	£2.50	☐
Happy Birthday, Wanda June	£1.95	☐
Slapstick	£2.50	☐
Wampeters Foma & Granfalloons (non-fiction)	£2.50	☐
Between Time and Timbuktu (illustrated)	£3.95	☐
Jailbird	£1.95	☐
Palm Sunday	£1.95	☐
Deadeye Dick	£1.95	☐

John Barth

The Sot-Weed Factor	£3.95	☐
Giles Goat-Boy	£2.95	☐
The Floating Opera	£2.50	☐
Letters	£3.95	☐
Sabbatical	£2.50	☐

Tim O'Brien

If I Die in a Combat Zone	£1.95	☐

To order direct from the publisher just tick the titles you want
and fill in the order form.

The world's greatest novelists now available in paperback from Grafton Books

Angus Wilson

Such Darling Dodos	£1.50	☐
Late Call	£1.95	☐
The Wrong Set	£1.95	☐
For Whom the Cloche Tolls	£2.95	☐
A Bit Off the Map	£1.50	☐
As If By Magic	£2.50	☐
Hemlock and After	£1.50	☐
No Laughing Matter	£1.95	☐
The Old Men at the Zoo	£1.95	☐
The Middle Age of Mrs Eliot	£1.95	☐
Setting the World on Fire	£1.95	☐
Anglo-Saxon Attitudes	£2.95	☐
The Strange Ride of Rudyard Kipling (non-fiction)	£1.95	☐
The World of Charles Dickens (non-fiction)	£3.95	☐

John Fowles

The Ebony Tower	£2.50	☐
The Collector	£1.95	☐
The French Lieutenant's Woman	£2.50	☐
The Magus	£2.95	☐
Daniel Martin	£3.95	☐
Mantissa	£2.50	☐
The Aristos (non-fiction)	£2.50	☐

Brian Moore

The Lonely Passion of Judith Hearne	£2.50	☐
I am Mary Dunne	£1.50	☐
Catholics	£2.50	☐
Fergus	£2.50	☐
The Temptation of Eileen Hughes	£1.50	☐
The Feast of Lupercal	£1.50	☐
Cold Heaven	£2.50	☐

To order direct from the publisher just tick the titles you want and fill in the order form.

Outstanding fiction in paperback from Grafton Books

The world's greatest thriller writers now available in paperback from Grafton Books

Anthony Price

Soldier No More	£2.50	☐
The Old Vengeful	£2.50	☐
Gunner Kelly	£1.95	☐
Sion Crossing	£2.50	☐
Here Be Monsters	£2.50	☐

Julian Rathbone

A Spy of the Old School	£1.95	☐
Nasty, Very	£2.50	☐

Matthew Heald Cooper

To Ride A Tiger	£2.50	☐
When Fish Begin to Smell	£1.95	☐

Donald Seaman

The Wilderness of Mirrors	£2.50	☐

Dan Sherman

The Prince of Berlin	£1.95	☐

To order direct from the publisher just tick the titles you want and fill in the order form.

The world's greatest novelists now available in paperback from Grafton Books

Gore Vidal
The American Quartet

Lincoln	£3.95	☐
Washington DC	£2.50	☐
Burr	£2.95	☐
1876	£2.95	☐

Other Titles

A Thirsty Evil	£1.50	☐
The Judgement of Paris	£2.50	☐
Two Sisters	£1.25	☐
Myron	£1.95	☐
Myra Breckinridge	£2.50	☐
Messiah	£2.50	☐
Williwaw	£2.50	☐
Kalki	£2.50	☐
A Search for the King	£1.25	☐
Dark Green, Bright Red	£1.25	☐
In A Yellow Wood	£1.25	☐
On Our Own Now (Collected Essays 1952–1972)	£1.50	☐
Matters of Fact and of Fiction (Essays 1973–1976)	£1.50	☐
Pink Triangle & Yellow Star	£1.95	☐
Creation	£2.95	☐
Duluth	£1.95	☐

To order direct from the publisher just tick the titles you want and fill in the order form.

The world's greatest thriller writers now available in paperback from Grafton Books

Len Deighton

Twinkle, Twinkle, Little Spy	£2.50	☐
Yesterday's Spy	£1.95	☐
Spy Story	£2.50	☐
Horse Under Water	£2.50	☐
Billion Dollar Brain	£2.50	☐
The Ipcress File	£2.50	☐
An Expensive Place to Die	£2.50	☐
Declarations of War	£2.50	☐
SS-GB	£2.50	☐
XPD	£2.95	☐
Bomber	£2.95	☐
Fighter (non-fiction)	£2.95	☐
Blitzkrieg (non-fiction)	£2.50	☐
Funeral in Berlin	£2.50	☐
Goodbye Mickey Mouse	£2.95	☐

'Game, Set and Match' Series

Berlin Game	£2.95	☐
Mexico Set	£2.95	☐
London Match	£2.95	☐

Jack Higgins

A Game for Heroes	£1.95	☐
The Wrath of God	£1.95	☐
The Khufra Run	£1.95	☐
Bloody Passage	£1.95	☐

Trevanian

The Loo Sanction	£2.50	☐
The Eiger Sanction	£2.50	☐
Shibumi	£2.50	☐
The Summer of Katya	£1.95	☐

To order direct from the publisher just tick the titles you want and fill in the order form.

GF1681

Outstanding American fiction in paperback from Grafton Books

Outstanding fiction in paperback from Grafton Books

Muriel Spark

The Abbess of Crewe	£1.95	☐
The Only Problem	£2.50	☐
Territorial Rights	£1.25	☐
Not To Disturb	£1.25	☐
Loitering with Intent	£1.25	☐
Bang-Bang You're Dead	£1.25	☐
The Hothouse by the East River	£1.25	☐
Going up to Sotheby's	£1.25	☐
The Takeover	£1.95	☐

Toni Morrison

Song of Solomon	£2.50	☐
The Bluest Eye	£2.50	☐
Sula	£2.50	☐
Tar Baby	£1.95	☐

Erica Jong

Parachutes and Kisses	£2.95	☐
Fear of Flying	£2.95	☐
How to Save Your Own Life	£2.50	☐
Fanny	£2.95	☐
Selected Poems II	£1.25	☐
At the Edge of the Body	£1.25	☐

Anita Brookner

Family and Friends	£2.50	☐
A Start in Life	£2.50	☐
Providence	£2.50	☐
Look at Me	£2.50	☐
Hotel du Lac	£2.50	☐

To order direct from the publisher just tick the titles you want
and fill in the order form.

GF1381

All these books are available at your local bookshop or newsagent, or can be ordered direct from the publisher.

To order direct from the publishers just tick the titles you want and fill in the form below.

Name _____

Address _____

_____

Send to:
Grafton Cash Sales
PO Box 11, Falmouth, Cornwall TR10 9EN.

Please enclose remittance to the value of the cover price plus:

UK 60p for the first book, 25p for the second book plus 15p per copy for each additional book ordered to a maximum charge of £1.90.

BFPO 60p for the first book, 25p for the second book plus 15p per copy for the next 7 books, thereafter 9p per book.

Overseas including Eire £1.25 for the first book, 75p for second book and 28p for each additional book.

Grafton Books reserve the right to show new retail prices on covers, which may differ from those previously advertised in the text or elsewhere.